SPECIFIC PERFORMANCE

D. R. Frohlich

To Cheryl, Danielle, Christopher, Paul & Margaret

ACKNOWLEDGMENTS

Were it not for my wife's loving encouragement, editing, proofreading, patience, laughter at appropriate places while reading my works and not laughing at my foolish grammatical mistakes, I would not be writing novels. So, you can either thank or blame her for this and my first two novels. Personally, I am deeply grateful to Cheryl for giving me the freedom and support it takes to write.

Don't believe everything you read, especially in this novel. It is a work of fiction after all. The main characters are the product of the author's imagination, and to the extent you think otherwise, they are the product of yours. Also, while some historical events did take place, as related herein they have been fictionalized to make a good story.

CHAPTER 1

A Lucky Break

February 18, 1933

Clyde already knew who was pounding on the front door. Besides being forewarned, the visit was inevitable under the circumstances.

"I'll get it, Momma," he called out over his right shoulder as he reached for the doorknob.

Two Denver police officers, one a young medium-build, plainclothes detective complete with moustache and fedora and the other a much older and stouter, uniformed cop with rhinophyma were standing on the stoop of the North Denver, brick home in Little Italy. Clyde knew both of them, not only because of his numerous run-ins with the law, but because such knowledge was necessary to the success of his business.

"Good Evening, Clyde," said Terrence Murphy.

"Detective Murphy—Officer Ricci. What brings youse out to my folks' home?"

Detective Murphy gave Clyde an as-if-you-don't-know look and said, "May we come in?"

"Why, of course. Where are my manners? Please, come in, officers," replied Clyde, who was known as the gregarious Smaldone, capable of charming even honest cops. Detective Murphy still was one. Officer Ricci was not. In fact, it was Vincent Ricci who had called Clyde earlier in the evening to warn him that he and Detective Murphy were on their way to see him and his brother, Eugene, generally known as Checkers because of his love of the board game by the same name. Clyde's sobriquet was Flip Flop, a moniker that no one dared use to his face. Checkers and Flip Flop had been decorating Officer Ricci's mahogany for some time and knew they could rely upon him. Decorating the mahogany was mob lexicon for bribery.

As Murphy and Ricci crowded into the small foyer and removed their overcoats, Ricci briefly locked eyes with Clyde in a knowing, cordial way. Murphy turned just in time to see the unspoken, friendly exchange, but pretended he didn't.

"Quite a ruckus back there," observed Murphy, referring to the happy chatter of voices coming from the interior of the house. "Celebrating something?"

"Naw...just a normal family evenin' together. We're a close-knit, happy family, Detective Murphy. Ya shou' know that by now."

"Yeah, well, some sorta family."

Clyde ignored the pejorative jab at his family and its business and instead said, "How did ya know I was here?"

"Stopped by your house and when neither you or Mildred answered, just figured you'd be over here with your 'close-knit,

2

happy family.'"

"Well, again, how can I be a service to Denver's finest?" Clyde pulled a fresh cigar from his shirt pocket and inhaled its rich aroma as he ran it under his prominent Roman nose before placing it in his mouth and igniting its end.

"Your brother, Eugene, here? He's part of my topic of conversation too, so I'd like to have him present."

"So happens he is. He's in the kitchen with Momma. Did youse know she an' our pop are thinkin' 'bout openin' a Italian restaurant? Right now, she's cookin' up some of her can't-be-beat Bolognese she wants ta offer the public. Why don't youse two come in an' make yourselves comfortable in the livin' room. I'll get Gene. Hey, youse want some wine or whiskey?" Clyde waited for their reaction.

While Ricci wished he weren't with Detective Murphy so he could have a drink, Murphy refused, saying, "Clyde, I'm on duty and here on official business, and in case you—"

"Oh, yeah, yeah, the Prohibition thing is still on," interrupted Clyde, enjoying Murphy's gullibile response to his joke. "I'm jus' messin' with youse. I wouldn't keep none a that demon drink aroun' here."

Actually, he would, and did, and no law could prevent him from keeping it, drinking it or for that matter selling it. It was his business' major product. And, the fact that Murphy was a cop on duty wouldn't stop him from providing Murphy with a drink, either, if Clyde thought he could get by with it. In fact, when Franklin Delano Roosevelt's campaign train stopped in Denver on September 15, 1932, Clyde managed to sneak three cases of whiskey—one each of Chicken Cock, Four Aces and Quaker— onto the train and to spend an hour with the future president. Nor did he discriminate against one political party in favor of the other in his cavalier flaunting of his lawlessness. When President Herbert Hoover came to Denver, Clyde met him in the president's Brown Place hotel room at the invitation of one of Clyde's close judge buddies and told the president right out that he was a bootlegger. Hoover admired his honesty and laughed. For Clyde, it was an opportunity to rub shoulders with the rich and powerful and to brag about it later. Not only did he rub shoulders with them, but he owned several, including politicians, judges and law enforcement officers. Mahogany decorating—it was just a cost of doing business. Quite an achievement for someone who started out clearing fifteen to twenty cents a day selling newspapers on the streets of Denver, until he learned that crime paid better.

As Murphy and Ricci were finishing settling into a couple of comfortable chairs in the living room, Clyde strolled in with his brother and crime partner, Checkers, in tow. While Eugene Smaldone was also known for his gentlemanly manners, he was less affable than Clyde, and it was rumored that he was the muscle in the family. He certainly did not look the part. He looked more like a medium-build, well-groomed, bespectacled school teacher. It was the perfect mask for his ruthlessness.

"Detective Murphy, Officer Ricci," said Eugene in greeting. Then he and Clyde also took seats opposite the two officers and waited.

"So, gentlemen, where were you around three this afternoon?" asked Murphy.

"Come on, Detective Murphy, ya gotta' tell us what's this 'bout before launchin' into a bunch a questions. We've been real nice here an' invited youse in an' youse made yourselves comfortable in our folks' home. Don't ya think ya should give us a little respect in return?" said Clyde.

4

Ricci had said nothing during this whole encounter and just sat listening. It really wasn't his place to ask questions or make comments since he wasn't the investigating officer. He was there as a witness and in case an arrest had to be made, which he dearly hoped there wouldn't have to be. Murphy didn't like or trust the guy and doubted that he would support Murphy in case there was a dispute about what was said, but Ricci was probably no worse than any of the other cops Murphy had to choose from for this evening's meeting.

"OK, sure," replied Murphy. "Giuseppe Roma was murdered today around that time—in his home—in his favorite lounge chair, in fact."

"Oh my gosh, that's terrible," said Eugene, as both he and Clyde crossed themselves and then said in unison, "May God have mercy on his soul."

Murphy smiled slightly, barely moved his head from one side to the other and thought, *You fucking goombahs are really precious. Nice act.* Outwardly, he said, "Yeah, I'm sure God will be real nice to him, especially since he just murdered his rivals, the Carlino brothers, not very long ago. Guess his rise to be top dog didn't last very long."

"I heard that wasn't real clear, jus' a suspicion," observed Eugene.

It was true that no suspects had been arrested for the murder of Sam Carlino on May 8, 1931, and his brother, Pete, on September 10 of the same year, but word on the street pegged both crimes on Joe Roma, commonly referred to as Little Caesar because of his one hundred twenty pounds packed into his five-foot-two frame.

"Since that's not why I'm here, let's get back to my question."

"Well, that's easy. We wasn't anywhere near Little Caesar's house at that time."

"Really? What if I told you we had a witness? Would that change your mind?"

Murphy barely finished his sentence when Officer Ricci blurted out, "Yeah, Roma's wife said she saw you, Eugene, along with Jim Spinelli, Louis Brindisi and a fourth guy she couldn't see—"

He was cut off by a severe stare from Murphy. Ricci's sudden outburst was his way of warning his friends and benefactors not to fall into the trap that Murphy was laying out in front of them and to let them know who the witness was.

"So, Nettie said she seen me today aroun' the time Joe was shot?" asked Eugene.

"Shot? Who said anything about being shot? I didn't." Looking over at Officer Ricci, Murphy said, "Not even my partner (he said 'partner' with a sneer in his voice) here said Roma was shot."

"So, how'd he die?" asked Clyde.

"Injection," said Detective Murphy watching for their reaction. Before Ricci could coach the Smaldones again, Murphy added, "Lead injection from what looks like a .38. Either of you own one of those?"

"No, sir," answered Eugene. "That wouldn't be legal. Ya know, I think Nettie is a little confused 'bout who an' what she seen."

"Well, now that we're on that topic—Mrs. Roma said she saw you, Brindisi and Spinelli clearly through a crack in the parlor door as she was leaving to go to her mother's to help her with making some sauce. She left around two, and when she came back around two hours later, Joe was slumped over in his favorite chair with his head mostly gone and a pool of blood around him on the floor. Took us a hell of a time to even figure out how many bullet holes he had in him. At first, we thought fourteen, but it turned out to be seven with six of them in his head. Reason we thought it was fourteen is that each bullet made an entrance and exist hole. For what she had just experienced, Mrs. Roma seemed very clearheaded and certain of who she saw where."

"Well, she's wrong. I wasn't there, an' I can vouch for the other three 'cause they was with me," said Clyde. Part of that was true. "We was all at the movies; Gene, James, Slippers—I mean Louis—an' me. All of us—at the movies this afternoon. It was a matinee."

"Boys' afternoon out, eh? Do that often? What movie?"

"It was that new gangsta movie with Barbara Stanwyck. She's great, don't ya think?" answered Clyde.

"Yeah, great movie—ah, 'Ladies They Talk 'bout.' That's the name. Look, I still got my ticket stub," said Eugene as he rummaged in his pocket for the stub he had previously planted there. "See, here it is. Says right on it, 'Matinee' under today's date. Clyde, ya still got your ticket?"

"Yeah, think I do. Whew, here it is. Good thing, huh, officers? I hope James an' Louis still got their stubs."

"I'll just bet they do," said Detective Murphy. "But, I'll be sure to check with them. I'm surprised they're not here celebrating too. Well, you two are pretty lucky today. Not only was your erstwhile boss and only competition in town eliminated today, but you have convenient alibis. I'll bet the theater management will

7

back you up too, huh?"

"Huh, that's a good idea. They should since they seen us there. Hard to miss the four of us – right, Detective Murphy?" offered Clyde.

"You mean like Mrs. Roma seeing you just before her husband was murdered?"

Clyde raised his left eyebrow slightly as if in salute of Detective Murphy's quick wit and then smirked and said, "Told ya, I wasn't there, an' Gene was with me. We showed ya the proof. Nettie's all shook up—poor woman. Ya know how emotional an' confused women can get."

"All right, Ricci, we're getting nowhere here. Let's go."

"Sure hope you catch the killer or killers, Detective," teased Clyde as Murphy and Ricci put on their overcoats and showed themselves out.

Outside, Murphy grabbed Ricci's right arm, spun him around and chided, "So how long you been on the take, Ricci?"

Yanking his arm out of Murphy's grip, Ricci said, "That's damned insulting, Murphy."

"Only if it weren't true. From now on, stay out of my path."

After the two police officers left the house, Flip Flop turned to Checkers and said, "Why don't ya take Fat Paulie over ta Nettie's an' offer our sincere condonlenses. Bring her somethin' nice, maybe some flowers, some of Momma's Bolognese an' some cash—say…a thousand dollas. An', while you're there, ask how sure she is 'bout what she told Murphy she thinks she seen."

CHAPTER 2

Homeless Cats and Mobsters

Before the Civil War, it was a campaign for voluntary abstinence. Afterwards, it became a culture war fueled by bigotry. The rapid industrialization of the country brought with it increased urbanization of the nation's population which attracted tens of millions of immigrants who were desperate to escape their calamitous lives for something hopeful, if not better. At the same time, crime, poverty and disease were also on a rapid incline, and what better place to lay the blame than on the overburdened shoulders of the new arrivals. It was easy. It was convenient. It was arrogant, insensitive and parsimonious.

These new arrivals were different from those who had the good fortune to have ancestors who had arrived a generation or more earlier. These alien interlopers were spawned in Eastern and Southern Europe—and worse yet, they were mostly Catholic and Jewish. On the other hand, the established trespassers on Indian territory were descendants of mostly northern Europe, lived in small towns and rural areas—and they were Protestant.

Conveniently, alcohol in its various incarnations was central to the cultures of these newcomers, and alcohol was the menace responsible for all that was going wrong in the country, according to many increasingly influential, right-thinking patriots. These good people formed various temperance groups bent on ridding the nation of alcohol and its consequent evils.

One of the most influential of these groups was the Anti-Saloon League, which worked in, and closely with, Protestant churches. It unabashedly used abuse, half-truths and whole lies in its aggressive campaign, but since its members were bringing about the "Lord's will," there was no foul or sin committed. In the leadup to World War I, it became easy pickins' and even patriotic to attack the German immigrants, who, according to one of the League's leaders, Purley Baker, "eat like gluttons and drink like swine." William Hamilton Anderson, who was in charge of drying out both the city and state of New York, also attacked German immigrants, but reserved his vilest attacks for Catholics, especially Italian and Irish Catholics. According to Anderson, the Ku Klux Klan's resurgence in the twentieth century was a welcome, natural response to Catholic opposition to prohibition. Anderson was later caught with his hand in the till and sent to Sing Sing maximum security prison for extortion, embezzling from the League and forgery, which was a welcome, natural response to his crimes. He wasn't the only League leader blinded to their hypocrisy by their hubris. Wayne B. Wheeler ghostwrote self-aggrandizing articles about his fictitious achievements and made false accusations against his rivals and then bragged about his prevarications. William E. Johnson, known as Pussyfoot and who often had the appearance of a bespectacled, exophthalmic, bald deer caught in headlights, publicly bragged that he told so many lies for the cause that it would make Ananias ashamed of himself. The Bible records that Ananias suddenly died after lying to Peter about the sales price of his land, a portion of which Ananias held back from his allegedly voluntary gift to the early church. But the crème de la crème, or more accurately—pire du pire, was Bishop James Cannon, Jr. of the Methodist church. The good Bishop hated Catholicism and immigrants, referring to them as that "kind of dirty people," and especially Italians whom he separated into the general category of Italians and the special soiled category of Sicilians. When Albert E. Smith, a Catholic, ran for president of the United States against Herbert Hoover, Bishop Cannon launched a vicious campaign founded on lies and innuendo against Smith. Later, the pious Bishop lost his luster when it was discovered that he used church funds to support political candidates, hoarded flour during World War I and then sold it for a substantial profit, and embezzled a fortune from the church. The topping on his turpitude was his illicit affair with his secretary while his wife was terminally ill, which was clearly evident from publicized letters between the two paramours. Throughout the mounting discoveries about his misdeeds, the Bishop took the aggressive stance of denying it all, which paid off in the end. Twice the bishops of the Methodist church voted not to convict him and after a series of trials and appeals Bishop Cannon was found not guilty of the criminal charges. With his immense ego fully intact, but his reputation shattered, he was sent packing by the Methodist church to a parish in California where he lived his final years in ignominy.

Another equally powerful temperance organization with questionable leaders was the Woman's Christian Temperance Union. The use of "Woman's" rather than Women's in the title was a deliberate, if syntactically questionable, attempt to emphasize that the required membership, temperance pledge was taken by each woman individually. As one would expect, the WCTU accepted only women into membership, but not just any woman. It did not accept Catholic, Jewish, or African-American women, or any woman who had not been born in North America, for, like so many other temperance organizations, it blamed the nation's woes on the "undesirable" "immigrant hordes," as one leader labeled the newly arriving "huddled masses yearning to breathe free." After many decades, the WCTU finally agreed to accept African-American women, but set up separate, though not equal, chapters for them. While some of its missions, like women's (not woman's) suffrage were admirable, they all were borne by a stubborn perception of superiority – white-woman, anti-immigrant superiority. Two of its most famous members brought the hatchet into the nation's limelight—Lizzie Borden and Carrie Nation. While Borden was accused of chopping up her father and stepmother, Nation stuck to inanimate objects associated with alcohol. Nation had a large ego, a large frame and a large divine mission to campaign for the abolition of alcohol. She also heard voices, or at least one voice that she assumed was God's, telling her to, as she put it after an early-morning conversation with the incorporeal voice on June 5, 1900, "Take something in your hands, and throw at these places in Kiowa and smash them." So, she did, and when there was a tornado follow-up in eastern Kansas to her destruction of two saloons there, she knew that God approved of her actions. Later, the "something" in her hands became her trademark hatchet. She called her attacks "hatchetations." While destroying other peoples' property, she could be heard shouting, "Glory to God, peace on earth and goodwill to men," which could only make sense to someone with Nation's mental condition. Although her birth certificate listed her name as Carrie Amelia Nation, she later changed her first name to the way her father had written it in the family Bible—Carry. That was a lot catchier, in her opinion. In sync with her inflated ego, she would proclaim that her name meant Carry A Nation for Prohibition. The WCTU that Nation was a member of, not only was against alcohol, but it favored women's right to vote, Protestantism, the protection of domesticity and eugenics—that pseudoscience for the improvement of human beings through controlled breeding and sterilization to increase perceived desirable, heritable characteristics.

Another organization in the fight against alcohol shared these same callings. It was an old, Southern-venerated organization that was seeing a resurgence across the nation during the temperance movement in the early twentieth century. It strongly opposed alcohol and immigrants, and it supported, and worked hand-in-hand with, the Anti-Saloon League and the WCTU, and even contributed large sums to each organization. The new and improved Ku Klux Klan had a more anti-Catholic and anti-Jewish mission than its seminal design and was embraced by a broader base that exceeded four million in the mid-1920s. In fact, there were more KKK members outside the former Confederate states than in them. In order to attract more members and advance its anti-alcohol campaign, it supported women's suffrage, since women were more likely to support prohibition than men, and established the Women of the KKK, or WKKK, where like-minded, white women could froth and fume and feed each other's hate. The WKKK and WCTU shared several prominent members. Lulu Markwell was honored to be the first national leader of the WKKK and also served as leader of the Arkansas chapter of the WCTU for twenty years. Lillian Sedwick was the state head and a county director of the young women's branch of the WCTU and later an influential member of the WKKK. Myrtle Cook of the Iowa WCTU and WKKK was martyred with a bullet to the heart after documenting names of bootleggers. Lillian Rouse, another young woman in the WCTU, joined Lillian Sedwick in the WKKK. And, perhaps most noteworthy, was Daisy Douglas Barr, a prominent WCTU champion for temperance, a Quaker minister in two eminent churches, the Imperial Empress of approximately 250,000 WKKK members in eight states and an Indianapolis board of education member who successfully promoted racial segregation. The WCTU was well aware of, never protested, and, therefore, was complicit in, the unorthodox, brutal and illegal vigilante methods used by the KKK to bring about and later enforce prohibition laws.

Although the KKK was largest in numbers in Indiana and Ohio, it had a very strong following in Colorado, where the Smaldone family would ultimately benefit from its and the other temperance organizations' success in criminalizing alcohol. Arguably, the KKK had its strongest hold in Colorado, where the focus for its hate was on Roman Catholic immigrants, especially Italians. Fermented grapes were at the center of their filthy culture, and they sent their children to parochial schools, thus evidencing their refusal to assimilate into American culture. They were a menace to America that the Klan promised to control, if not exterminate. So effective was the Klan's infection of Colorado that in the mid-20s it took over Colorado's Republican party and even the government on state and local levels. In the 1924 elections, Klansman Clarence J. Morley, a bigoted Denver judge, became the twenty-fourth governor of Colorado. Klansman Rice Means became a U.S. senator. Multimillionaire Lawrence Phipps contributed heavily to the Klan in exchange for votes in his bid for reelection to the U. S. Senate. Klansman Benjamin Stapleton became mayor of Denver. Klan members were lieutenant governor, auditor, attorney general, secretary of state, several judges, a supreme court justice, state legislators, city attorneys, chiefs of police, and city and county council members. They were insinuated into city and county governments throughout the state with one exception—Colorado Springs. When prohibition came into effect, most of the two hundred prohibition agents in Colorado were Klan members, and they abused their authority with impunity and particular gusto against Italians. R. N. Mason led many raiding parties on random searches for bootleg liquor. Mason was the Exalted Cyclops of the Trinidad KKK.

Trinidad was a hotspot for the KKK, bigotry in general and fear—fear of immigrants—the very immigrants who had been welcomed, and ferried in, to bolster the local economy and keep the wheels of industry turning and the ultrarich rich. The Colorado Fuel and Iron Company was the largest coal mining company in Colorado in amount of coal produced—approximately forty percent of Colorado coal; in number of miners employed—three times more than the second largest company; and, of course, in profits. When CF&I needed capital in 1902, John D. Rockefeller, Jr. from New York was quick to come to the rescue and eventually become the majority shareholder. Other coal companies in Colorado took their lead from CF&I and the man behind its veil, Rockefeller.

Life in the mines was abysmal and not much better outside. Every aspect of the miners' lives and of their families was regulated under the arbitrary authority of the mine owners. Miners and their families were required to live in company towns; to shop in company stores for company goods at inflated prices using otherwise worthless company scrip; to go to company doctors for medical treatment; and to send their children to company schools. Any work that did not produce coal, like building proper shoring for safer mine shafts, was dead work for which the miners received no pay. Shortly after Rockefeller's investment in CF&I, the United Mine Workers called a strike in 1903 requesting better and safer working conditions, higher wages and more autonomy. CF&I's and the other mine owners' response was swift and ruthless. Company armed guards terrorized the miners and their families. Strikers were herded up by Colorado's military authority and deported from the state. Then, non-union strike breakers were recruited from eastern coal-mining towns and transported to the mines in Colorado. These strike breakers were the same recent immigrants from Europe whose cultures included imbibing in some form of alcohol. The strike of 1903 died like every strike before, with nothing accomplished for the benefit of the miners. And, strikes there were—every ten years beginning in 1883.

By 1913, the former strike-breaking, immigrant scabs were ready for their own strike for the same reasons at the center of the 1903 strike. Among their seven demands were a couple that should not have required any additional bargaining—enforcement of existing Colorado mining laws and an eight-hour workday, which was part and parcel of the former since it was already the law in Colorado. In addition, the miners demanded simple basic freedoms that most people in the US take for granted, like the right to shop at any store they chose; the right to choose their own living places; the right to choose their own doctors; and payment for their dead work. In addition, they demanded a raise in wages and union recognition. Rockefeller's personal representative and hand-picked manager of CF&I, Lamont M. Bowers, was unmoved and thought the demands unreasonable and a plot by socialists, anarchists, and political demagogues. It was nothing short of an attempt to steal the mines from the rightful owners.

CF&I kept Pinkerton and Baldwin-Felts detectives, a/k/a gunslingers, on the payroll to pacify the miners. In August 1913 Gerald Lippiatt, a thirty-eight-year-old union organizer, was in Trinidad for a week preparing for a Federation of Labor convention. He had been hounded and baited by CF&I's private detectives the whole time he had been in Trinidad, especially by two who had been imported from the West Virginia strikes, George Belcher and Walter Belk, chief of detectives. On the evening of August 16, 1913, Lippiatt was headed to his hotel down North Commercial Street, when his passage was blocked by Belcher and Belk. Other detective-gunslingers attended them in the background, lazily smoking cigarettes while leaning against buildings and taunting Lippiatt. In a deadly lapse of logic, Lippiatt broke, shouting, "All right, you rat, let's have it out." That's just what the gunmen were hoping for as they drew down on Lippiatt and delivered seven bullets to his body. As he was going down, Lippiatt managed to squeeze off one shot to Belcher's thigh. Belk was later acquitted of murder, but not by a jury of his peers—by a biased judge who took the case from the jury by ruling the killing a case of self-defense. Belcher received a closer approximation of justice. On the evening of November 20, Belcher was shot in the head with a soft-nosed .38 bullet on almost the very spot where he had murdered Lippiatt. The shooter had been forewarned that a shot to Belcher's torso would do little damage since he wore steel plates under his clothing. The assassin was a miner by the name of Louis Zancanelli, one of those wine-drinking Italian immigrants.

On September 23, 1913, around nine thousand miners went on strike in southern Colorado. Almost immediately, the mining companies led by CF&I responded by forcefully evicting the miners and their families from their homes, since, after all, that was the right of the mine owners when a work stoppage occurred. The miners had little choice but to set up a tent colony near the town of Ludlow. CF&I sent out advertisements for more thugs with guns and had a plethora of responses from several states. Guerilla warfare ensued between mine goons and miners. The state stepped in to help the mine owners and eventually sent in the Colorado National Guard on October 28. It was all done at the expense of the taxpayers of Colorado because both the National Guard and the private goons were paid with state funds. The state was paying the Guardsmen directly, and CF&I was paying its militiamen on certificates of indebtedness bearing interest and collectable from the state. As time wore on without resolution, many of the Guardsmen who were businessmen and salaried employees asked to be relieved from duty. Most were replaced with mine guards. By the Spring of 1914, the cost was bankrupting the state, so Governor Ammons recalled most of the

National Guard, leaving only troops comprised of the mine guards. Striking miners' civil rights went from darn few to none. They were beaten, arrested without charge, denied the right to legal counsel, refused visits from friends and family and kept incommunicado.

On April 20, 1914, the skirmishes were escalated into a full-out massacre—the Ludlow Massacre. The National Guard and other CF&I thugs surrounded the miners' Ludlow tent colony and opened fire with machine guns. Mothers and their children hid in shallow pits dug below the tents' floors for protection from bullets, but the pits provided no protection from the fires set by the troops. Twenty-four died that day, including two women and eleven children who suffocated to death from smoke inhalation while hiding in a bunker that had been used by the miners as a maternity ward. Within two days, the miners responded in kind and launched attacks on one mine after another, killing mine guards, militia and employees and immolating buildings. Ten days after the Ludlow Massacre, federal troops arrived under order of President Woodrow Wilson with orders to disarm everyone— militia, company guards and strikers. Although this restored peace, the strike dragged on until December 1914, ending with the defeat of the strikers and the United Mine Workers of America. Union miners were once again replaced with non-union workers, and the violence was blamed on the immigrant miners and was used to the advantage of the temperance movement.

The Colorado Coalfield War, as it is sometimes called, was concrete proof that the new immigrants could be, and were, dangerous, even without alcohol in them. They'd be even worse if they were all liquored up and descended on Godfearin', native, Protestant white folk. Though fear of drunk immigrants bent on death and destruction was not the primary reason for Colorado voting in favor of going dry, it was a factor in the whole mix. In

November 1914 the temperance-bigoted groups won in Colorado when Coloradans voted for state prohibition. The law went into effect at midnight on December 31, 1915, a full four years and seventeen days before the Volstead Act implemented the enforcement of the Eighteenth Amendment, ratified in January 1919. Like the Eighteenth Amendment and Volstead Act, the law in Colorado ushered in a new era of winners and losers. What once was legal was suddenly illegal. Since there were some exceptions to the law for sacramental and medicinal purposes, there was a spiked increase in medicinal-alcohol prescriptions written by doctors. One church was so pious that its members consumed four hundred gallons of sacramental wine in a month. Crime increased almost immediately. The Volstead Act went into effect at midnight January 17, 1920. At 12:59 a.m. six armed men stole $100,000 worth of "medicinal whiskey" from two freight-train cars in Chicago. In Colorado, mobsters, like the Smaldones, were also winners. They just got an earlier start than mobsters in most of the rest of the country. Among the losers, cats were some of the biggest, at least those that were kept in saloons to keep the rat population in check. When Colorado went dry, these cats were kicked out into the streets to fend for themselves.

CHAPTER 3

Largesse and Smaldones

August 27, 1926

"Governor, there are a couple of gentlemen here to see you," said Gladys.

After looking at his calendar, Governor Morley replied, "I don't have anyone on my schedule, Gladys, and I thought I told you I didn't want to be disturbed."

"It's Mr. Smaldone, Mr. Clyde Smaldone, and another young...gentleman."

"Well, why didn't you say that from the start? Jeez, Gladys, show them in, show them in."

"Yes, sir—sorry. Both of them?" squeaked out Gladys, who like her boss was a dutiful KKK member first and a servant of the people—white, American-born people—second and usually never of Italians like the two waiting in her anteroom.

"Of course, both of them."

Clyde, who was just outside the door to the governor's inner sanctum, heard the whole exchange and smiled to himself, while thinking, *My twentieth birthday, and I get to talk to the governor without callin' ahead a time—and his secretary's callin' me gentleman and sir. That's jus' too good. Pretty good birthday present.*

Gladys turned from the governor's office door and said, "Gentlemen, please come in."

Clyde raised his left eyebrow, smiled at Gladys and said, "Thanks, ma'am," as he swept into the office with the other male in close pursuit. Both were dressed in very expensive suits.

"Clyde, what an unexpected pleasure. Please, please, come in."

"Good to see ya too, Governor,"

"And, who is this with you?"

"This here is a young man I want ya to meet—Leonard Petroni." Leonard, or Leo or Professor among the Smaldones, was not even a year younger than Clyde, so the reference to him as a "young man" was not a reference to chronology, but to relative social status.

To the casual observer, the friendship between Clarence Morley and Clyde Smaldone would have seemed incongruous and, perhaps, attributable to Clyde's ability to charm the most uncharmable. Morley campaigned on a law-and-order platform and hated criminals, other than Klansman, of course. Clyde already had a long rap sheet starting from when he was thirteen, but his criminal behavior started well before that. Morley hated Catholics, especially Italian Catholics. Clyde was both. Morley was bitterly opposed to alcohol. Clyde was a bootlegger. It took more than Clyde's endearing personality to overcome all that baggage. It took something Morley valued above his lip-serviced, allegedly higher ideals. Morley loved money. As far as Morley was concerned, money had the same look, feel and value regardless of its source. Clyde had it, and he had contributed substantially to Morley's campaign after it was evident Morley was going to win the governorship of Colorado. After Morley's election as governor, Clyde still made special contributions and gifts to Morley—mahogany decorating, as Clyde would say.

Morley could rationalize his graft by telling himself that Clyde and his brother, Eugene, weren't like the dirty new arrivals from Italy. Their father, Raffaele, had arrived from Potenza, Italy in 1884 when he was two. He married Mamie Figliolino when he was nineteen and immediately got busy siring eleven children, nine of whom lived to maturity. He was a good family man and demonstrated good American entrepreneurial spirit by working his way up from being a railroad laborer for the Denver and Rio Grande Western Railroad to foreman, then scraping enough together to buy a horse and cart to sell fruit and vegetables door-to-door throughout Denver—and, yes, finally, a bootlegging business for which Clyde and Eugene were runners starting when they were preteens. Raffaele preferred to be called Ralph. Mamie and Ralph raised their children speaking English around the home. Clyde even left parochial school to attend a real American public school after a sister tried to beat some of God's mercy into his hand with a ruler. In other words, they were Americanized, just like the KKK and so many other bigoted organizations preached that the newcomers were not. Clyde was also very generous, and one product of his generosity was standing in Governor Morley's office with Clyde.

Governor Morley stuck out his hand and shook Leonard's while saying, "It's a pleasure to meet you, Leonard."

Leonard was miffed that Morley didn't address him as Mr. Petroni, but he smiled anyway and shook the Kluxer's hand, while fantasizing about separating it from the rest of his body. "And, it's a great honor to meet you, sir," said Leo in his most obsequious voice.

"Let's go over here and sit down." Morley motioned them over to an area set off to the side of his office that resembled a living room more than a government office. He pointed to two comfortable-looking, overstuffed chairs next to a coffee table for Leo and Clyde to perch on. Morley took his place in a larger overstuffed chair across the table from them.

Once they were all in place, Clyde opened the conversation, "The reason I wanted ya to meet Leo is that I'd like ya to consider him for a position in the goverment."

Morley betrayed no surprise, and just sat quietly while displaying his most expectant countenance left over from his days as a district court judge.

After reading the other man's face, Clyde went on, "Ya see, Leo here is one of them really smart people—a prodiggidy."

By now, Morley was very accustomed to Clyde's unique ways of slaughtering the English language and knew better than to correct him.

"He's so smart, he's skipped a couple a years a school and is in law school already. He's goin' to the Denver law school. I've actually given him a bit of a shot in the arm."

"What Mr. Smaldone means is that he financially supported my college education and now is doing the same for law school. He's a very charitable man," said Leonard.

"That is true—very true," observed the governor.

Clyde gave Leonard a I'll-do-the-talking look and continued, "That's what people do for each other. Ya see a need, and ya do somethin'. Leo has brains and talent, but he and his family ain't got no money to help him make somethin' of himself. Anyways, I thought it would be good for him to get some practicals while he's in law school, and you'd benefit from his help."

"Well, Clyde, I don't think having Leonard work in my office shuffling papers around and answering the phones like some common secretary is going to do him much good," said Morley.

"Well, that's not really what I was thinkin'. I was thinkin' he could work in the attorney general's office." Clyde watched Morley's face and saw the brief hardening and then softening as Morley thought about the past money received and future money that would be sacrificed if he refused.

After his quick cost-benefit analysis, Morley looked at Leonard and said, "I'd need to see your college and law school transcripts and *résumé*."

Leonard reached into his suitcoat inner pocket and came out with a clump of neatly folded papers and handed them to Governor Morley, "Here they are, sir."

Morley chuckled, took the papers, unfolded them and whistled once while reading them. "Very impressive, Leonard. If you want to work in the attorney general's office, I can talk to Boatwright." Attorney General William Boatwright was not a Klansman, but he was a member of, and former attorney for, the Anti-Saloon League which had close ties with the Klan. Morley felt confident he could get the job for Leonard.

"I do, sir," came Leonard's reply.

"Then, I'll make sure you're hired."

"That'd be great—real great. Thanks, Governor," interjected Clyde.

"Please, Clyde, just call me Clarence, and I'm always happy to help out such a good friend as yourself."

"All right…Clarence, but I jus' thought it'd be better to be more formal in this office."

Leonard, who knew better than to assume the same offer of familiarity was also being extended to him, said, "Thank you, Governor Morley. I really appreciate this."

"Say, today's your birthday, isn't it, Clyde?"

"Sure is, Clarence. I'm surprised you remembered."

"Well, Happy Birthday, Clyde."

"Thanks, thanks a lot."

"Any special plans for celebrating?"

"Nothin' special—just dinner with the family at my folks' home later this evenin'."

Actually, Clyde did have something special planned before the gathering at his parents' home. He and Checkers were low on product. Demand was high and even with their stills in the mountains, sources in Mexico and his new connection with his Chicago friend, Al Capone, he was having trouble meeting it. He had a big order that had just come in, and he needed to fill it by tomorrow. He didn't have the bonded whiskey on hand that was ordered, and he had insufficient time to drive to Mexico or to Burlington, Iowa, which was the pick-up location for product coming from Capone. However, Checkers had followed another bootlegger, Googie the Goose, to Aurora and saw him stash some bonded Quaker and Chicken Cock whiskey in a garage there. Nothing but bonded whiskey would do for Clyde's customer. Bonded whiskey was aged and bottled according to certain legal standards, now no longer legal in the US but still demanded by Clyde's rich customers. Bonded booze had to be distilled at a single distillery by one distiller in one distillation season. The Smaldones did not deal in cheap moonshine—stuff laced with embalming fluid, paint thinner or lead from the lead pipes on some rusty old still. It was one reason for their success. The amount that Goose had stashed was enough to fill Clyde's current order plus a little to spare. Clyde would use his hopped-up Ford with overload springs for the heist. As Checkers and Clyde saw it, Goose had no business working in their territory anyway, so it really wasn't theft—just establishing their territorial rights and market dominance. But even before the trip to Aurora, Clyde had a few deliveries to make of food and clothes to some neighbors in need in Little Italy. He was a very generous man quick to look out for those less fortunate, but a man who jealously protected his business interests.

"Well, you have a great time with your family, Clyde."

"Thanks, Clarence. Come on, Leo, let's let this busy man do what he needs to to serve the citizens of this fine state."

They all got up, shook hands and said their goodbyes.

After exiting the capitol building, Clyde said to Leonard, "Got time for a cup a coffee?"

"Absolutely, Clyde."

Clyde drove back to Little Italy where they entered Fabio's and took a booth in the back. Everyone noticed their arrival, but feigned otherwise. Fabio himself came over to serve them. Like

26

so many others in Little Italy, Fabio had been a beneficiary of the Smaldones' philanthropy. When Fabio's little restaurant fell on hard times, Clyde had heard and gave him a loan, when banks wouldn't—not the usurious type of loan that the Smaldones would later become infamous for, but an honest-to-goodness loan at an interest rate better than any offered by the banks.

"Great to see you, Mr. Smaldone...hello, Leonard." Fabio did not like Leonard. In fact, very few in Little Italy did. He was known as an arrogant, mean punk—but smart, real smart. He was as mean as Checkers Smaldone, but a lot smarter. "What can I get you?"

"Two coffees is all. Ah, no, wait...an' a couple a cannoli."

"Comin' right up, Mr. Smaldone."

"So, Professor, whaddya think?"

"About what, Clyde?"

They fell silent as Fabio came over with their coffees and cannoli.

When Fabio left their table, Clyde said, "'bout what happened back there with Morley."

"I think you just got me a job in the attorney general's office. And, thanks for that."

"OK, lemme explain somethin' to ya. Ya just got a foot in a door. That's what happened. Ya just got job security. That's what happened. Ya know, that Attorney General Boatwright, he had ta get elected ta get his job. Ya didn't have ta do that. And, once ya get your law degree, ya can become one of them assistant attorney generals. And, as long as ya do a great job and do a little kiss-up to the guy who has to get elected, which ya will, you'll stay in that office and watch governors come and go and attorney generals come and go—and you'll still be there."

Leonard looked impressed with Clyde's insights, but said, "Yeah, but I won't have as much power as the attorney general."

Clyde looked at Leonard like maybe he wasn't as smart as he made out to be. "Look, you've been wantin' to be part of our business—right?"

"Yeah."

"And, I keep tellin' ya, your talents would be wasted jus' doin' what we do. I've got bigger plans for ya. See, I can use somebody smart like ya, 'specially with a law license, workin' in the attorney general office and givin' me a heads up once in awhile 'bout stuff that might not be so good for business. Ya could even deflect..." Clyde paused for a bit to savor his use of the word deflect, then continued, "...yeah, deflect, some heat comin' my way."

Leonard liked what Clyde was saying, but he also wanted to do some of the things Checkers did too. He wanted to rough people up, maybe even kill a few. "OK, Clyde, I'll do what you want me to. You've been good to me and my family. There's no way I could have gone to college and law school without your help. I owe you."

That was music to Clyde's ears. Charity was good, but charity with personal return was better. Clyde smiled and bit off a big mouthful of cannoli.

April 23 to May 27, 1933

It was 9:36 p.m. on April 23, 1933. Clyde and his wife, Mildred, were just returning from a charity drive at Our Lady of Mount Carmel where they had contributed the very significant amount of $3,000 to feed and clothe the poor in Denver and miners and their families in southern Colorado. They were still basking in the glow of appreciation expressed by the parish priest and other parishioners as Clyde opened the side door to their home and heard a phone in his private office ringing. Clyde had two phones in his office—one for general business and one a direct line to Assistant Attorney General Leonard Petroni. By the tone of the ring, Clyde could tell it was the second that was ringing. *Why the hell is the Professor callin' me this late on a Sunday night?* he wondered as he casually strode to his office. The phone was still ringing when he got to his office and picked up the receiver.

"Hello? Leo?"

"Finally," said Leo in a highly agitated voice. "Where the hell were you? I've been trying to call you and Gene and your folks all evening."

"Gene and Frances and my folks were with me and Mildred at a money drive at our church. We gave away a bunch a money and had a pretty good time doin' it, 'cept for Frances' hackin' fits." Frances was Eugene's wife who had only one lung which failed to inhibit her chain smoking but did enhance her smoker's cough. "So, what's so important?"

"The feds are going to bust your parents tonight—and are probably waiting for them at their house right now."

"On a Sunday night? Those bastards. Why am I only hearin'

'bout this now, Leo?"

"I don't know. I don't know."

"Leo, I mean, why didn't ya know 'bout this before and tell me?"

"I just found out about it tonight by accident when a secretary I know from the detective's division told me over dinner." He left out the part of getting her drunk and raping her at his apartment and then threatening her if she complained about it. That's really when he discovered the planned bust, not over dinner. He told the secretary he'd pick her up next Friday for another "date."

"The city?"

"Yeah."

"How does the city cops know 'bout a feds' bust, and ya don't?"

"Maybe it's because of that wet dream you fucked up in January."

Leonard was referring to a botched heist of booze by Clyde and Checkers. They had heard that there was an eight-hundred-gallon bootlegging operation in the little mountain town of Florissant that was easy pickings. The Great Depression had hit the Smaldones just like it hit everyone, and as a result, competition for market share of the bootlegging business was fierce, resulting in several unsolved murders—murders that were never pinned on the Smaldones, but that always benefitted them. It also was the mother of inspiration for thefts of alcohol among bootleggers, like the one Clyde and Checkers attempted in January. They and four of their men sped into the Florissant still with two large trucks led by Clyde and Checkers in Clyde's hopped-up blue roadster. The plan was to intimidate the small crew they thought would be watching the booze. Instead of being met by cowering flunkies, they were greeted with a withering crossfire of bullets. Their blind return fire managed to gain them an exit, but not without a price. Their only cargo back to Denver was one dead man and another wounded. Leo had helped them clean up the subsequent inquiry by the state by allowing some evidence to go missing.

"Be careful, Leo. Remember who you're talkin' to. And, just what do ya mean?"

"Sorry, Clyde, but I'm pretty nervous right now. I mean, that while I don't think I was ever suspected of helping you, the feds probably know someone in the AG's office destroyed the evidence from the investigation into the January caper. Or, at least they suspect someone did, and they're not taking any chances with this bust. What're you going to do?"

"Callin's not gonna do no good, so I'm goin' over to my folks' house."

"Clyde, that might be just what the feds want. You might be playing right into their hands."

"Can't help it. They're my folks, an' I'm not gonna let 'em face the cops alone. Can't do it. See ya, Leo."

Leo managed to squeeze in a "Good Luck" before Clyde slammed the receiver down and ran out the door.

When he arrived at his parents' house eight minutes later, there were three black sedans and a Ford Model A pickup in the street and driveway and two guys in suits guarding the front door. One had a Thompson submachine gun. Clyde parked his car under a streetlight directly in front of his parents' home and slowly got out with his hands in clear view so as not to spook the feds. As soon as they saw his car roll up, the two guards at the door stiffened and became visibly more alert.

As he approached with his hands held out to his side, Clyde said, "My name's Clyde Smaldone, and this here is my folks' home. I'm goin' in there to see 'em."

"I don't think so, Mr. Smaldone. No one's allowed inside."

Just then, the front door opened and inside stood Detective Terrence Murphy. The irony of their reversal of positions from their February 18 encounter on the very same stoop was not lost on either of them.

"Detective Murphy…may I come in?"

"Of course—where are my manners? Please, come in, Clyde."

"So, what's this all about?"

"Prohibition law violation, Clyde. You should know that. We're finding a lot of liquor in this house."

"Prohibition is almost dead and gone, Detective."

"Almost isn't already," replied Murphy.

Both of them were correct. Prohibition had lost its luster and was coming to a rapid end in 1933, but in April it was still the law.

"And who's the 'we' you're talkin' 'bout?"

"Federal agents—come in and get acquainted."

"What're ya doin' here then? You're no fed."

"Special invitation."

"Where're my folks?"

"Told you to come in. They're in the dining room."

Several cases of bonded whiskey were stacked on the floor and on the dining table. Three agents in suits were rushing in and out of the dining room to ransack other parts of the house. A fourth was standing guard over his parents who were seated on straight-back dining chairs in the corner of the room. Clyde went over to them and gave them reassuring squeezes on their shoulders while shaking his head indicating that they should stay silent. He turned at hearing someone enter the room and saw Eugene being escorted in by the front-door guard without the submachine gun.

The two brothers looked at each other, and Clyde gave Eugene the same twist of the head he had given their parents indicating that Checkers should keep quiet and let him do the talking. Clyde could tell that Checkers was about to blow. His face was red and a vein in his neck was engorged and pulsing.

The three agents who had been rummaging the house came in together and the one who was obviously in charge said, "You two the Smaldone boys?"

Clyde said, "We're two of the six. Who're you?"

When all he got in reply was a steely glare, Clyde said, "I'm Clyde Smaldone, and this here is my brother, Eugene. Now, your turn. Who're ya, and what're ya doin' destroyin' my folks' home late on a Sunday night?"

"I'm Agent Darryl Smith of the Alcohol Beverage Unit of the US Bureau of Investigation, and I'm here bustin' up a bootlegging operation."

"That's still a thing? Booze is practically legal. Prohibition was a bad idea, an' it's bein' eliminated. Why go through all this fuss now?"

"Because it's still the law, and this is a hell of a lot of alcohol, and furthermore, I don't have to explain anything. Come on, boys, let's get this hooch loaded in the pickup and the prisoners secured."

The other agents in the room started to carry cases of liquor out to the pickup while Agent Smith had Ralph and Mamie stand up and turn around so he could cuff them.

"Jeez, is that really necessary?" asked Clyde. The sight of his parents, especially his mom, getting handcuffed and taken off to jail was torture for him.

"Standard procedure—you, of all people, should know that," said Smith, as he snapped the cuffs shut on Mamie's wrists.

In all their past brushes with the law, the two Smaldone brothers had always been polite, if not deferential, to the police, but going after their parents crossed a line. Checkers made a move towards Agent Smith, and Clyde grabbed his arm.

"Wanna add assault on a federal agent to the charges, tough guy? This is a crime scene, so you two need to vacate—now."

"We're not gonna let you go to jail, Momma...Pops," said Clyde as he and Eugene left while their parents were escorted to the back seats of two separate black sedans.

Clyde and Eugene had strong family values, in spite of the way they earned a living. As they saw it, their business supplied a market demand for something that really didn't hurt anyone, except the competitors who got in their way, and it was something that had once been legal—not like drugs and prostitution, which they were very much opposed to. It was obvious even to Checkers that this latest ploy by the feds was a transparent way of getting to the two Smaldone brothers through their parents, whom they loved dearly.

As the federal agents were finishing up and getting ready to leave, Detective Murphy came over to Clyde and Checkers on the sidewalk and said, "If I were in your situation, first thing tomorrow morning, I'd go down to the US attorney's office and see if the prosecutor would be open to a deal."

"This is a frameup. Our folks don't know nothin' about no Prohibition laws," alleged Clyde.

"Oh, come on, Clyde. Word is your dad is partners in a speakeasy down by the tracks."

"Ain't never been proved— 'sides, what can we offer?"

Murphy came up close to Clyde and just poked him in the chest with his right index finger. Then he left.

Over the next three days, Clyde and Eugene negotiated a deal with the federal prosecutors whereby they would plead guilty to violating federal liquor laws in return for the release of their parents. At the end of the three days, Clyde and Eugene were taken into custody, and Ralph and Mamie were released. Later in May, Eugene and Clyde were sentenced to eighteen months each by Federal Judge J. Foster Symes, a quirky judge whose wife was a stripper, both before and during their marriage, at the Moonlight Ranch, a speakeasy far out of the city. On May 27, Clyde and Eugene Smaldone became inmates 43540 and 43539 at Leavenworth Federal Prison. By then, Leo Petroni was helping Ralph and Mamie with, and himself to, their illicit income. He also was still "dating" the shy, frightened Irish girl from the city police department, as well as several other young women, all of whom were terrified of him—for good reason.

December 8, 1936–December 24, 1942

Around seven in the evening, Leo Barnes and his wife, Pernee, walked to their '35 Ford sedan parked along Grant Street in downtown Denver. They were in a romantic mood after a pleasant early evening dinner and set a brisk pace in anticipation of the adult activities soon to come. When they arrived at the car, Leo positioned himself behind the wheel while Pernee got into the passenger's seat. As Pernee closed the door, Leo touched the starter on the floor and their world erupted with a deafening explosion. Car parts were launched a hundred feet in all directions with much of the windshield coming to rest fifteen feet up a nearby maple tree. Pernee was thrown twenty feet out the side door, but, miraculously, had only minor cuts and bruises. Most of Leo was launched through the roof while his left buttocks remained in the car, adding irony to Clyde's reference to him as a half-assed punk. He, too, managed to live through the blast, although with a different measure to his gait.

Prohibition was repealed in December 1933 while Clyde and Eugene were still in federal prison. When they were released in 1934, they needed to find a substitute for booze running in order to make a living. Since drugs, prostitution and legal ways of making money were not options, gambling made perfect sense. It was another victimless crime, if one ignored the fact that they rigged the various games and slot machines they ran. There was a learning curve, however. For that they had an experienced mentor from Colorado Springs—Ova Elijah Stephens, also known as Smiling Charlie. Smiling Charlie never smiled. Smiling Charlie had operated several first-rate restaurant-casinos in Colorado Springs since 1926, always catering to the rich who felt the need to share their wealth with him by gaming it away. In 1933, before Clyde and Eugene were released from prison, Smiling Charlie had crept north, opening one of his upscale nightclubs that advertised the restaurant and showroom, but not the roulette, craps and slot machines that mainly held his customers' interest. It was called Blakeland Inn and featured dancing girls and big-name acts, like Donald O'Connor and Judy Garland when she was one of the traveling Gumm Sisters. Sometimes, there even were female impersonators on stage. Clyde and Eugene wanted to be Smiling Charlie's partners, which he gladly agreed to even though he already had a partner, Leo Barnes. Barnes was a smalltime Denver gambler—smalltime in fame, fortune and stature. Barnes and the Smaldones operated the Blakeland for Charlie until it was closed by Douglas County authorities. Then, Barnes and Charlie had some arguments over, of all things, money and turf, and who could do what where with Smiling Charlie telling Barnes that if he ever opened another casino in the area, he'd better include Charlie or Barnes wouldn't live a week. So, Barnes, of course, opened another gambling operation in the area without including the nonsmiling one. Shortly after doing so, his car went boom.

Whether the Smaldones were responsible for the explosion on December 8 or not was not even a question for the police. They had an eyewitness. Mrs. Jack Gilmore was in her car parked behind Barnes' car when two men drove up and double parked beside it. One got out and commenced to work on something on the inside of the car. There also was a delivery truck for Daniels and Fisher department store that was stalled on the street. The driver told the police he had to push his truck around the double-parked car. After the two impromptu car mechanics left, Mrs. Gilmore started her car and drove away to conduct some errands. When she came back minutes later, there were little pieces of car all over, and just a car chassis where the Barnes' car had been. Mrs. Gilmore was positive that the man she saw working on Leo's car was Checkers Smaldone. She had not gotten a good look at the man with him. Clyde had been seen by a cop coming out of a telephone booth three blocks away around fifty minutes earlier. Earlier in the day still, the Smaldone brothers had been seen meeting Smiling Charlie at Ralph and Mamie's restaurant, the Tejon Bar and Café. It was all perfectly explainable, according to Clyde. The meeting and the phone call were all about buying a fifty-dollar ice box for the restaurant from Smiling Charlie. Detective Murphy was there again for the arrest, and after hearing Clyde's story, said, "Come with me. I'll show you a walk-in cooler you can have for nothin'."

"Whaddya mean, ya 'can't help?' That's the kind of gratitude I get for puttin' ya through college and law school? Not satisfied with the decoration on your mahogany?" said Clyde, during his telephone call allowed by the police.

"I think I've been very grateful and have shown it with the services I've performed on your behalf," replied the Professor.

"Yeah, not all of it asked for, either."

"I don't know what you're talking about."

"Think I don't know 'bout you and Gene hangin' out together?"

"No law against that. You're the convicted felon, not me."

"Keep hangin' out with my brother an' that might change."

"Look, Clyde, there was a witness that saw Eugene at the scene of the crime moments before the explosion. There's no way I can possibly overcome that, and if I try, my cover will be blown for good."

"Well, I wasn't there, an' nobody seen me there…cuz they couldn't."

Leo decided to play along and said, "Any news on his accomplice, Clyde?"

"Naw, cops won't tell me or Morrissey nothin', 'cept the other guy was drivin' an' in the shadows with a hat pulled low coverin' his face." Thomas Morrissey was Clyde's long-time criminal-defense attorney who had made quite a comfortable living defending Clyde and Eugene over the years.

"Well, that's a relief."

"Relief? Is that what ya think I'm feelin' sittin' in jail right now?"

"What I meant was that no one saw you."

"Since I wasn't there, that would be a hell of a trick, if they did. Maybe it'd been better if they seen the driver."

"OK, look, Clyde, I'll see what I can do without exposing myself."

"Yeah, ya do that," said Clyde before hanging up.

After finishing his telephone call with Clyde, Leo turned and looked at the naked, drunk girl lying behind him on the bed where he was sitting, and decided to have another go at her before she woke up.

––––––––––––

At his trial in the Denver district court, one of Clyde's decorated-mahogany detectives testified that Clyde had been with him the whole day of the bombing, but Judge Henry A. Hicks intervened and told the jury that the cop was lying for Clyde and that Clyde had something to do with the bombing. Clyde could only wonder why they were bothering with a trial at all, if the jury wasn't allowed to make its own decisions about the facts. After being found guilty of assault and conspiracy to commit murder, Clyde, Checkers and Smiling Charlie were each sentenced to seven to ten years in the state penitentiary at Cañon City.

Clyde decided to bow to the sentence and just go to prison while the other two appealed, ultimately all the way to the Colorado Supreme Court. Clyde was welcomed to the penitentiary in July 1938 by Warden Roy Best. The two men already knew each other. Clyde had decorated Best's mahogany when Best was a highway patrolman. Also, Best had had several meals at Tejon Bar and Café owned by Clyde's parents. When Clyde saw Best in Cañon City, he had said, "Hello, Roy." In reply, Best said, "That's warden to you, inmate." Besides being ungrateful for Clyde's past generosity, Best was mean, pompous and dishonest. He would strut through the prison yard in his Stetson with his whip tied to his belt and Chris and Ike at his side. Chris and Ike were Best's two nasty Dobermans. Every day Best beat at least one prisoner with his whip and for special infractions, like attempted escape, had prisoners tied up bent over a sawhorse and flogged with a leather strap. He called that the "Old Grey Mare." In recognition of their past friendship, Best had Clyde and another prisoner handcuffed to a wheelbarrow they had to fill with dirt and haul away from a construction site for a new cellblock. Best also had a lot of confusion about what were his personal finances and what were those for the penitentiary. When Clyde's father died in 1938, Best refused to give Clyde a pass to go to the funeral. Clyde took it all in stride and worked on bettering himself by earning correspondence certificates in diverse subjects, including philosophy and metaphysics, and by taking up painting, which he showed a bit of talent for.

Clyde's philosophical attitude about his predicament worked to his advantage. Checkers and Smiling Charlie eventually lost the appeals of their convictions and came to join Clyde in Cañon City in March 1939. Coincidentally, on January 10, Smiling Charlie's trial lawyer, Ralph Lawrence Carr, had taken office as the governor of Colorado. Carr was a fiscally conservative Republican with a steady moral compass whose father was a Scotch-Irish miner. Carr's early life in mining towns gave him insight into the lives of, and compassion for, those of modest means. He also had the courage to stand up for them. Ten days after President Franklin Delano Rossevelt issued Executive Order 9066 authorizing the forced evacuation of men, women and children of Japanese descent from the West Coast, Governor Carr publicly declared that Colorado was willing to provide temporary quarters for them and that "they are as loyal to American institutions as you and I."

His compassion and understanding also extended to Clyde with a little reminder from Leo Petroni, who once again had stepped in to help Clyde's parents in his absence, and when Ralph died, he became particularly solicitous of Mamie and her money. Governor Carr had put out a request to the attorney general for some research on prisoners who could be paroled under governor's order. Leo was quick to volunteer for the task and returned with a list of recommendations that included Clyde close to, but not at, the very top. His model-prisoner performance was highlighted in the report, which enhanced Carr's belief that Clyde had been treated poorly by Judge Hicks. Thus, under order of the governor, Clyde was paroled on December 24, 1942.

January 1, 1943–November 30, 1962

After trying to do his patriotic duty by enlisting in the army to fight for the Allies and being rejected because of his criminal record, Clyde went to work for his momma in the Tejon Bar and Café, which was having serious economic problems due to the war and the Professor's prior skimming. Creative as ever, Clyde devised a way to enhance the restaurant's profits with the help of a federal agent in charge of government rationing in seven states. In short order, Clyde and, after his parole on January 11, Eugene, were making a killing selling rationed goods and ration coupons on the black market. Even Clyde's wife, Mildred, helped out with the unwitting aide of their twelve-year-old son, Eugene. Mildred, with her son at her side, would drive from Colorado to California to deliver black-market gasoline coupons for Hollywood movie moguls and stars, like Ronald Reagan and Frank Sinatra, to cheat the war effort by grabbing more than their fair share. It was a great cover—a mother taking her son on a road trip to California— much better than a man driving alone, or worse, with a buddy or two. Misogyny would get in the way of cops profiling a woman and kid as black-market runners.

It was just a short move from running black-market enterprises to getting back into gambling and loansharking, but never drugs or prostitution. If a gambler ran out of cash—no problem. The Smaldones were there to loan him more money…with interest, of course—very high interest that compounded rapidly. Interest could be as much as 150 percent. And, if the borrower couldn't, or worse for him, wouldn't, repay the loan, Checkers would provide the physical incentive for changing his mind.

By 1946, the Smaldones had gambling locations throughout

the state, including drugstores, bars and clubs. They offered slot machines, poker, roulette, craps, football parley cards, bookmaking and barbooth, also known as barbuit, barbotte or barbudi, an Italian dice game. The Smaldone dice came with a special enhancement—for the benefit of the Smaldones. The dice could be manipulated magnetically by the flip of switch in a control room. Money was flowing into the Smaldone coffers.

But, not just illicit business was booming for the Smaldone family. Mamie's café was also very popular and profitable—so much so, that Clyde decided to buy a drugstore and meat market on the corner of West Thirty-eighth Avenue and Tejon in order to open an Italian restaurant. It was only a block away from the Tejon Bar and Café, but it was a step or two up in class. Clyde named the new restaurant Gaetano's after his paternal grandfather. It was a success, some would joke a "mob hit," from the day it opened. For years after, Mamie did most of the cooking in the kitchen, patrons ate out front in the restaurant, and Clyde and Checkers conducted their nefarious businesses on the second floor and games of chance in the basement that drew even some celebrities, like Frank Sinatra and Sammy Davis, Jr. Clyde added some features usually not found in a restaurant, like bulletproof glass in the windows, reinforced doors to withstand bomb attacks and a hidden door in the men's restroom that led to the second-floor offices. A highlight for the two brothers was schmoozing with the customers. They would separate and work the tables, asking patrons how their dinners were, what brought them to Gaetano's, where they were from and other small-talk.

Also, in 1947, Clyde sweet-talked his way into a sweetheart deal with local government officials in the mountain town of Central City. For twelve weeks in June, July and August, Clyde would run slots, roulette and craps out of a small casino called Monte Carlo—a grandiose name that promised more than it could deliver. In return, Clyde funded improvements to the crumbling infrastructure of the town. It had no sewer system. Raw sewage flowed into the creek and right through the middle of town. Drinking water wasn't safe. Streets were dirt and the sidewalks were board planks, neither of which had been improved since the gold-rush days. Homes had inadequate insulation, and children lacked proper clothing and nourishment. Clyde helped change all that, and he was delighted to do so. Homes got insulation and upgrades. The town got new sewer and water systems. Streets and sidewalks were upgraded. Needy children were fed and clothed. The town leaders were delighted and looked the other way while Clyde conducted his business. State officials were not so obliging. On occasion, raids were organized in Denver, but the drive to Central City was a long and slow one, and with enough forewarning, the Smaldones could camouflage the Monte Carlo to look like an abandoned storefront. Forewarning often came from the Professor, but if he failed, there was a lookout in El Rancho just outside Denver who would sound the alarm. There was never a successful bust of the Central City operation. However, with the arrival of the new justice of the peace, Lowell Griffith, things changed. Griffith's vow to clean up the town was greeted warmly by the town citizens—in the form of Griffith's effigy and those of two of his followers being strung up and ignited over Eureka Street. The people liked the Smaldones and especially the money they brought into the community, so much so that they were willing to riot in their support and against the law. Griffith fought back with the help of Clement R. Hackethal, the district attorney for the area. A new road between Denver and Central City also meant the town wasn't as isolated as it once was. In response, Clyde chose discretion over valor and moved out of Central City in 1949.

During these golden years, Leonard Petroni cozied up even closer to Clyde and Checkers and their money. He made himself invaluable with his financial advice and protective warnings. And, while Clyde and Checkers had their families, church and other charities and mahogany to decorate, Petroni had none of these obligations. He was quite frugal with the enormous sums he was gaining from the Smaldone enterprises and started to invest his savings, something the Smaldones never did—outside of family business, that is. However, Leo didn't risk his fortune on the stock market which had proved too untrustworthy during the crash that started on October 24, 1929. The Professor chose real estate as his investment of preference. In order to do so without attracting attention to himself, he formed shell corporations and fictitious partnerships to buy strip malls, small office buildings and even residences. He also separated himself from the daily care of the properties by hiring real estate firms to manage the properties. This, not only buffered him from public recognition of his ownership, but gave him more time to refine his seduction, grooming and rape of young women.

In September 1951, Governor Dan Thornton named a recent deputy attorney general, Max D. Melville, to the Colorado Crime Commission. In October 1951, President Harry Truman appointed Charles S. Vigil, a Hispanic from Trinidad, as the US district attorney for Colorado. These two formed an informal partnership that turned the heat up on the Smaldone brothers while chilling their relationship with the Professor. With Melville in the same office as him, Leo realized that any friendly connection between him and Clyde and Checkers would be viewed with suspicion and end poorly. For anyone who could read it, the handwriting was on the proverbial wall. Leo had no trouble understanding the message. It was time to get out of the country before things really heated up and he was dragged into an investigation on behalf of the state against his friends. He asked for, and due to his past excellent public service was granted, an extended sabbatical. As fast as he could, he got on a plane for

Colombia. It was a country he had wanted to explore for some time, anyway. But, as-fast-as-he-could was slowed down by La Violencia in Colombia, a violent civil war among the Colombian liberal, conservative and Communist parties. When power was seized, and amnesty declared, by General Gustavo Rojas Pinilla on June 13, 1953, there was an abrupt and significant decline in violence and an opportunity for Leo to execute his travel plans.

Melville and Vigil launched an all-out campaign against Clyde and Eugene. The Smaldones and their associates were hit on all sides by federal, state and local law enforcement. They were brought in for questioning about illegal gambling, rigged gaming, bribery of political officials and police and for testimony in grand jury investigations into income-tax evasion by members of their organization. Raids were conducted that busted up many of their gaming establishments. Clyde's nerves started to give in to the pressure. Even so, the most that Melville and Vigil could stick them with was a one-hundred-dollar fine for gambling, until Checkers was charged with failure to pay $5,000 in income taxes. Clyde begged Checkers to just pay it, but Checkers was the pigheaded, less intelligent brother. He refused to pay. His trial before the hard-drinking, hard-nosed, controversial Federal Judge Willis W. Ritter from Utah began on June 2, 1953. It ended with a hung jury, but soon spawned grand jury charges against Checkers and Clyde for jury tampering. After a brief detour in front of another judge, both brothers this time ended up before the infamous Judge Ritter who had managed to rack up an impressive appellate-reversal record of fifty-eight-percent civil and forty-percent criminal cases. At the end of the trial, Clyde and Checkers were found guilty of conspiracy, offering bribes to jurors and obstructing justice. Initially, Judge Ritter sentenced Clyde to 370 years in prison. Then, he cut it to 170 years. Finally, he made up his mind on sixty years each for Clyde and Checkers. The whole experience created a lasting rift between the two brothers.

Clyde blamed Checkers for causing the whole problem by stubbornly refusing to pay the taxes against Clyde's better advice. Clyde also had loaned Checkers a sizeable sum for his defense, which Checkers never repaid. After the United States Supreme Court reversed Judge Ritter's sentence and remanded their case for a new trial before a different judge, the Smaldones each received three, four-year sentences to be served consecutively for a total of twelve. They had thought they were agreeing to concurrent sentences totaling only four years. They felt double-crossed.

During his second time in Leavenworth, Clyde helped bring about improvements, not the least of which was removal of the cockroach infestation. Corruption had been rampant. Funds that were meant for food for the prisoners were siphoned off by prison officials, leaving little food, that often was spoiled, for the prisoners. Prisoners ate at filthy tables while sitting on equally filthy, backless benches. Prisoners were on the verge of rioting. Then a new culinary steward was employed, and he enlisted Clyde's help to improve the food and dining area. New tables and chairs were brought in to replace the filthy tables and benches. Clyde and Eugene worked in the kitchen, cleaned it up and even introduced pizza to the menu. Clyde was awarded certificates in culinary sanitation and baking. He also continued his education and painting with a focus on religious art. Even Eugene, who dropped out of school after the eighth grade, took classes in psychology and anthropology.

On a snowy day in November 1962, Clyde and Eugene returned to Denver. The previous May their momma had died of cancer. Clyde was ready to retire from mob life. It wasn't so much that he had been completely rehabilitated, as that he saw the end was in sight for the gambling and loansharking business. With prescient clarity, he warned other family members that when the government realized how much money could be made in gambling, it would get into the business itself. Also, there was increased pressure with wiretaps and surveillance from law enforcement. While he had been away, his youngest brother, Clarence, known as Chauncey, and his nephew, Paul Villano, or Fat Paulie, had operated the business. They would continue to do so with Checkers' participation. There would be more arrests, more murders, but less drama for Clyde who became a born-again Christian.

CHAPTER 4

Devil's Breath from Angel's Trumpet

August 1953 to December 1954

Leo entered the room and looked down on the young woman lying on the bed. She seemed to be resting peacefully after a very fitful night. Even so, she had performed his every direction and demand without question. He doubted that she had ever done, or much less imagined, some of the things he had gotten her to do. He was almost completely satisfied with her sexual prowess in spite of her obvious youth. She looked even younger than the eighteen years she had given him as her age last night. In the early morning light that now crept over her face through the slit between the shabby curtains of the bedroom window, she looked very young—fifteen maybe. He wasn't very good with determining ages. Anyway, that was a moot issue now, and no use brooding over. It was time to get ready and go.

Her name was Vicky—or, Becky—maybe, Micki. Like her age, it really didn't matter, since this would be the last time he dated her. Their meeting had been quite serendipitous. He was returning from a long day of botanizing in the jungle and saw her in his headlights along the side of the road trying to hitch a ride. He rolled to a stop. She came over to his open passenger window and looked in. He had said, "You know, it's really not safe to be out here, especially for a young woman. There are all kinds of creeps and criminals starting to come out this time of the evening." She had assured him that she was capable of handling herself, but in a voice that betrayed vulnerability, and then quickly jumped into the cab of his pickup for a ride to Nicho, the only pueblo within miles. He stopped at a small café that was along the way and bought Vicky, Becky, Micki dinner of chicken enchiladas and beer. That's when she gave him her age as being eighteen—when he asked if she was old enough to drink alcohol. Towards the end of dinner, he had run his hand all the way up her thigh, and she moaned in response. As she seemed to be very cooperative, he suggested that they go to the house he rented outside Nicho, and she could stay there for the night. It proved to be an evening of wild sexual abandon that he enjoyed thoroughly. She had also told him practically her whole life story. She was a runaway who had managed to get herself all the way to Colombia from Lohrville, Iowa, where her father had beaten and otherwise abused her. Until yesterday, she had been traveling with four friends she met in Panama. After an argument over travel expenses, her traveling companions had abandoned her several miles from where Leo had seen her, by which time she was horribly lost—his good fortune and her misfortune.

"Time to go, young lady," said Leo as he gently picked her up since she was in no condition to walk on her own. After getting her into his pickup, he drove in the opposite direction from Nicho and took her into the jungle and dumped her body along with her backpack into the hole he had dug much earlier. After throwing dirt on top of her and tamping it down, Leo said, "Sorry for the miscalculation, kid," and headed into town for breakfast.

He chose a different café from the one he had been at with the girl from Iowa, not only because he did not want to raise any questions among the owners about the absence of little-miss-no-name, but because it had some of the best arepas de huevo he had come across in Colombia. Like all arepas de huevo, they were egg-filled corn cakes, but the ones at Comedor de Maria had chunks of chorizo and cheese mixed in with the eggs. *Arepas to die for—a rapist to die for, huh,* he mused, as he drove up onto the rutted, rocky ground that served as a parking lot.

When Maria saw him enter and sit down at his favorite table in a corner facing the door, she came over with a cup of coffee and took his order of arepas with a side of plantains—an order she could have guessed as soon as she saw him. Maria, as well as other members of the small pueblo, actually seemed to like Leo, a reaction he failed to elicit back in Little Italy. Leo attributed this to the quality of his Spanish and his efforts to charm—a lesson he had taken from the playbook of Clyde Smaldone. "Youse can trap more flies with honey than somethin' they don't like," he used to say in typical Clyde fashion. The thought of his time with the Smaldones brought a smile to Leo's face.

While he waited for breakfast, Leo pulled a small vial with a cork stopper from his pocket and stared at the white powder inside, wondering, *So, what went wrong last night?* Although he had no remorse, Leo had not had the intention of killing the Iowa girl—just raping her without her knowledge. It was a standard MO he had used in Bogotá. None of his previous subjects had died. There had been, of course, side effects of wild hallucinations, disturbed perception, rapid heartrate, extreme dry mouth and headaches to the sought-after effects of amnesia and hypnotic suggestibility, but never death.

He concealed the vial in his jacket pocket as Maria came over to deliver his breakfast. Leo was famished after the morning's labors. He poured honey over his plantains and dug into his arepas with gusto. After finishing the last bit of honey-covered plantain on his plate, he brought the vial out again, sipped his refill of coffee and reviewed the possible causes of death while turning the vial over in his hand. The girl had shown no signs of allergic reaction. The dosage had been the same as in the past. The method of production had been the same. The only difference was the source—a different variety of *Brugmansia vulcanicola*, a species of Angel's Trumpet—the rarest in fact. Angel's Trumpets were small trees or bushes that produced beautiful, large, pendulous flowers shaped like trumpets. They were native to Colombia, and the reason for Leo's sudden visit there, after being incentivized by law enforcement's crackdown on the Smaldone family.

Leo's botanical avocation started in 1938 when Clyde Smaldone was an inmate at the Cañon City state penitentiary. Leo's then-boss, Attorney General Byron Rogers, was interested in an experiment being conducted by Roy Best, the corporal-punishment warden with a penchant for harassing Clyde. By promising more lenient work assignments, Best was enlisting prisoner volunteers to test a truth serum, that really wasn't a serum, called scopolamine. Scopolamine was derived from the seeds of certain plants from the Solanaceae family of plants, one of which was *Brugmansia vulcanicola*. Paradoxically, some Solanaceaes are edible, like tomatoes, potatoes, eggplants and Capsicum peppers. When Leo heard of Attorney General Rogers' interest, he volunteered to investigate Best's experiments in the hope of getting closer to Clyde in order to help him through his incarceration in any way he could. While his hope was not fulfilled, Leo did gain a great deal of information about, and a burning interest in, scopolamine, commonly known as Devil's Breath.

While scopolamine, also known as hyoscine, was first isolated from plants in 1880 by Albert Ladenburg, a German-Jewish scientist, and was used in obstetric anesthesiology in Germany beginning in 1902, it did not gain any notoriety in the United States until 1922. Doctor Robert House, a Dallas obstetrician, had been using scopolamine on women during childbirth to induce what the Germans had coined as Dämmerschlaf—twilight sleep. Dr. House noticed that during twilight sleep his patients answered questions truthfully and even volunteered embarrassingly candid information. Afterwards they had no memory of doing so or of giving birth or even of much of what had happened before the administration of the drug. House theorized that scopolamine could prove invaluable in interrogating criminal suspects, so he arranged to act upon his epiphany by interviewing two prisoners in the Dallas County jail whose convictions seemed imminent. Under the influence of scopolamine, the suspects denied their guilt and provided information that later led to a finding of not guilty at their trials. Dr. House was emboldened to continue his research and to write several articles about the new truth-enabling drug. Somewhere along the way, some reporter who didn't know the difference between a serum and a syringe, labeled the drug a "truth serum" and Dr. House as the "father of truth serum." After at first resisting the unscientific labeling and claims, House himself became swept up in the glory and promoted the drug and himself to levels of which neither were worthy. In the meantime, with little fanfare or public scrutiny, law enforcement agencies and officers used scopolamine in criminal interrogations—with Roy Best being among them.

It was during his observations of Best's experiments that Leo had his own epiphany about the possible usefulness of scopolamine in his favorite hobby—raping young women. Being the consummate student that he was, Leo soon became an unknown expert in scopolamine—its various plant sources, how to extract it from plants and how to administer it, though the latter needed some modifications as evidenced by the recent death of the Iowa girl who was little more than a glimmer in his consciousness and none on his conscience—since he had none. When it was time to take his leave of Denver until the heat died down, Colombia was the obvious choice for his temporary home since many of the plants that contain the alkaloid scopolamine were found there.

While he was in Bogotá, Leo met, and became friends with, an obviously intelligent German who brazenly bragged that he not only knew, but had worked with, the Angel of Death, Dr. Josef Mengele. The name of this fugitive Nazi was Urs Schlosser. Urs claimed that among the various experiments Mengele had performed were some that included the use of scopolamine. Mengele's interest in scopolamine was not as creative as Herr Schlosser thought it could be. Mostly, Mengele had used scopolamine in interrogations of prisoners and in combination with morphine to kill children. While observing its effects on subjects, Schlosser thought it had many more beneficial secrets to be unlocked. Thus, as it turned out, both Schlosser and Leo were on the same mission to find various plants from which scopolamine could be extracted and to harvest the seeds and cultivate them. Schlosser wanted his for medical research while Leo wanted his for law-enforcement purposes—at least, that's what he told Schlosser. Schlosser was the one who had pointed Leo in the direction of Nicho as a potential source of some excellent specimens of Angel's Trumpets. Nicho was a small pueblo in the Andes about a six-hour drive north-northwest from Bogotá—six hours due to road conditions, rather than distance. Its remoteness was the reason it had avoided La Violencia. Schlosser had suggested that the two of them go on the expedition together. It was a suggestion that Leo pretended to embrace, but had wished he could avoid since he preferred to work alone. His wish was granted when Urs had failed to make a scheduled meeting and a few days later the police had found his battered body hanging upside down in a warehouse in the seediest part of Bogotá with a bullet hole where his right eye had been. Leo had no idea who had beaten and killed the Nazi, but just in case Leo was a target by association, he decided to head to Nicho earlier than he had planned.

After four weeks of using Nicho as home base for his forays in quest of Angel's Trumpets and other Solanaceaes containing scopolamine, Leo had an impressive collection of seeds to take home for propagation and experimentation. However, judging by the previous night's experience, his latest discovery seemed to be the most potent—and lethal. To be sure and to gauge proper dosages, he needed to test the new product on some more subjects before he could return to Colorado. He drained his coffee cup, bid "Hasta luego" to Maria and then got into his pickup to do just that.

Six to ten young women should be sufficient, but Nicho and the surrounding country was not the place to conduct his experiment. Leo had gotten lucky with the Iowa girl—a young runaway no one would miss. But, runaways were few and far between in this rural part of Colombia where families were tight, Catholic and protective of their daughters. It would be too much work and take too long to get close to any desirable targets out here in the sticks. No—the best place to ensnare prey would be near a university—actually, bars near a university—and the best place for universities was Bogotá.

Carlita was the happiest she had been since her parents and two younger sisters were killed. It was July 9, 1950—a Sunday. *A Sunday! Why would God do such a thing on a Sunday, and to some of His most devout followers?* she thought. She knew it was God who killed them because they died in an earthquake that hit her hometown of Arboledas where her father was a respected doctor. Who else could be responsible? No man could create such an earthquake. Her parents had been the most compassionate people she knew. Besides being a wise and loving man, her father had provided his professional services to those less fortunate without any compensation, and her mother volunteered at the local school and parish. And, her sisters, her dear sweet sisters, were her best friends and.... Carlita pushed back her sadness and anger with God, and told herself, *I will not be sad or angry tonight. I will honor my parents and hermanitas dulces by getting my medical license and serving my village as my parents did. And, I will be happy tonight and celebrate my accomplishment with my friends and in honor of my family.* Carlita had just been accepted to medical school and was celebrating with two of her girlfriends at La Biblioteca—The Library. La Biblioteca was a favorite hangout of college students, and its name was a running joke that never got old. If asked where she was going to spend an evening, a student could honestly reply "to the library," which usually got a snicker and a response like, "Yeah, and you're studying an Aguila label." Aguila was Colombia's most popular beer.

When her two friends said they wanted to dance and invited her to the dancefloor, Carlita declined and said she'd stay at the table and watch their drinks. She drank from her bottle of Aguila and swayed with the music as her girlfriends moved to the music as best they could on the crowded dancefloor. After a brief time, someone came over with three new bottles of beer and placed them on the table.

Carlita looked up, gave a quizzical look that faded into suspicion and said, "Who are you?"

"I'm your waiter."

"What happened to the other guy?"

"He was at the end of his shift. I'm on now."

"Well, we didn't order any more beers. So, what are you doing putting these on the table?"

"You looked like you were ready for another order. I'm sorry. I can take them back."

Carlita looked at the beer bottles and saw that they had not been opened and decided they were safe, and she was ready for another beer—but two would be her limit. She then said, "No, you can leave them, but leave the opener. I'll open them."

"You're the customer. Here you go," said the obviously non-Hispanic waiter as he put a bottle opener on the table and left.

Was he wearing surgical gloves? she wondered and then quickly dismissed the idea as a misperception.

When her friends returned, Carlita explained why the fresh beers were on the table. They drained what remained of their first order and opened the new bottles. Within a few minutes they were all woozy. At first, they thought they were intoxicated, but that made no sense since none of them had had more than two beers. As they quickly became more disoriented and their mouths dryer, they realized they had been drugged, but even that thought slipped away from them as they entered a twilight state.

Carlita was the first to wake up. She was in an embrace with Gabriela, and she was naked—they were both naked. She pushed herself away, raised herself and tried to focus while looking around her. Everything was blurry, but she was able to make out the bedroom, her bedroom, in the apartment she shared with Salome. She looked down at herself. *Oh, my God, I've been raped.* She was awash with fear, anger and embarrassment. She shook Gabriela awake, who looked back with unfocused eyes.

"Salome, Salome," she screamed. "Salome, are you here?"

As Carlita began to get up, a hand appeared at the foot of the bed followed by Salome's face masked in bewilderment. She too was completely naked—and violated. The clock on the nightstand indicated 4:12. Carlita went to the window and looked outside. The sun indicated it was afternoon. *Afternoon? What afternoon?*

They all were suffering from severe headaches and shame—a feeling they did not deserve, but couldn't shake. They each grabbed a sheet or blanket to cover their nakedness and took turns showering and cleaning up. There was no discussion of going to the police because all three of them knew it would do no good and only compound the guilt they felt with the lack of sympathy and leers of male cops. They wanted to suppress what happened and try to live their lives as normally as they could. Other than knowing they had been raped, they had no idea of when, how or by whom—or even by how many. But, at least, they had each other and agreed to support each other in their struggles to overcome their degradation.

Two weeks after their rape, the three friends were having coffee together at an outdoor table of a café they regularly used for their little support group. While they were talking, sipping their coffees and eating postres, a man sat down at a table next to theirs.

"Lovely afternoon, isn't it, ladies?" said Leo while smiling.

They looked over at him and murmured that it was and then went back to their conversation.

Leo knocked over his carafe of coffee and jumped up, exclaiming, "Oh, no. I'm so clumsy. I am so, so sorry. Did I get any on you?"

They looked at their dresses and at him, and Carlita said, "No, no, we're fine."

"Are you sure—you're fine?" asked Leo, making sure they all got a good look at him.

They each assured him they were.

After finishing his second carafe of coffee, Leo stood and went over to the three women and said, "Once again, I'm sorry for the mess I made. Have a good afternoon, ladies." Then he left feeling smug and very reassured. The three friends watched him leave, and Salome commented, "We have to keep reminding ourselves that some men are kind—like that gentleman."

Leo had returned to Colorado with new knowledge and carefully-labeled, paper packets of Solanaceae seeds and vials of scopolamine that a bribed Colombian agriculture official had sealed and certified as scientific specimens and a customs officer had let pass after some mahogany decorating negotiated through inuendo. Leo's field investigations, lab research and product experimentation with young women in Colombia, whom he thought of as "subjects," had confirmed some rumors he had heard and read about the effects of scopolamine and had yielded some crucial knowledge about administration methods and proper dosages. He had been quick to learn from his mistakes, especially his biggest, and never had a repeat of the Iowa-girl incident. Disposing of bodies was not what he wanted to do. Besides being a lot of work, it exposed him to discovery which would be more of a risk back in the States. Fortunately, the Iowa girl had died in a remote part of Colombia where the earth was soft and prying eyes were few.

Scopolamine had proved to be the perfect aide to his sexual violations and perversions. Under its influence, his subjects willingly performed the most-deviant sex acts upon his demand and would beg for more if he ordered them to. Afterwards, none of them had any memory of what they had done—or of him. It was a perfect combo—hypnotic-trance suggestibility and amnesia. As often as not, the amnesia extended to several minutes or even hours prior to administration of the drug. And, administration was versatile and so very easy. Since scopolamine had no odor or taste, it was undetectable until it was too late. Leo also had established that it was equally as effective if ingested, inhaled or absorbed through the skin. Absorption was the method he had used on Carlita and her two friends. He had rubbed a solution of scopolamine on the outside of the three beer bottles he had delivered to Carlita under the guise of her waiter. Surgical gloves had protected him from succumbing to the drug's effects. As soon as Carlita and her friends had touched the bottles of beer, they were doomed to be his sex zombies. It had been an empowering night of debauchery and sexual release for him. Domination and denigration of his victims were his aphrodisiacs. Even the thought of his past abusive conquests aroused him. Scopolamine was a godsend to him, and while his method of, and reason for, using it were not legal, its production and possession were.

There was only one desirable quality of the drug that he

had not been able to test, but he had a reliable source as to its veracity. According to Urs Schlosser, the dead Nazi, scopolamine dissipated quickly within the body. Depending on the metabolic rate of the individual, it could be detected in a victim within one to five days after administration before there was no trace at all. Schlosser and Mengele had conducted several tests after interrogations of prisoners of various sizes and in different physical conditions. The larger, healthier prisoners had no detectable scopolamine in their blood, or livers, twenty-four hours after they were given the drug, while less healthy and smaller victims of their sadism lost all trace after the fifth day. With his seeds, Leo now had the ability to make his own virtually undetectable wonder drug from plants that he wanted to start propagating in his own greenhouse; however, before he could do so, he had some groundwork to lay.

First on his agenda was getting back to his old position as an assistant attorney general. That proved to be no problem since before departing for Colombia, Leo had negotiated an extended sabbatical with his boss, Attorney General Duke Dunbar. Dunbar was still Colorado Attorney General when Leo returned to Denver, and Dunbar was delighted to welcome Leo back. But, he could no longer act as a spy for Clyde and Eugene. It was too risky given all the attention law enforcement was giving the two Smaldone brothers. Leo needed to distance himself from the Smaldones. Since they were still very busy fighting the jury tampering charges against them, that also proved easier than it would have been otherwise. By making no attempt to contact anyone in the Smaldone family, much less Clyde and Eugene, Leo could go about the business of being an assistant attorney general. It also freed him up to pursue his pastime, and in order to facilitate that, he negotiated his way into the Public Utilities Commission Unit of the Attorney General's Office. In this position, Leo would have more travel associated with his office and, thus, more opportunities to meet young women around the state.

Once his position at the Attorney General's office was secured, Leo focused his attention on finding a suitable home within driving distance of work, removed from nosey neighbors and with enough land to build a greenhouse sufficiently large to house his exotic plants. He selected a five-bedroom house on two acres in Wheat Ridge in a subdivision called Indian Paintbrush Estates. Construction on his greenhouse started six weeks after he closed on the purchase of his new home. There remained just one more thing that he needed to do.

Leo wanted to conceal his Mr. Hyde persona with an impenetrable cloak of respectability and domesticity. He needed a wife—a churchgoing, garden-club, dutiful wife and mother of his children. To his surprise, she arrived at his boss' Christmas party.

"Leo, come over here. I want you to meet my daughter—Clara," said Dunbar.

Clara was plain, of modest intelligence, ten years younger than him and somewhat shy. She'd do nicely.

CHAPTER 5

Bear Essentials

Katmai National Park and Preserve

Summer 1985

"Wake up, sleepy head," said Elliot as he gently nudged Rita.

Rita groaned and rolled over away from him and the nightstand lamp he had turned on.

"I have coffee," he lilted. "It's bear coffee."

Rita abruptly turned over again to face him, but with her eyes still closed. Then, parting them to slits said, "What? What kind of coffee?"

"Bear coffee."

"What the hell is bear coffee?"

"It's coffee that's bruin," he replied.

"Phft—you're a nutball," she said with a giggle in appreciation of his corny joke. "What time is it?"

"Little before three."

"I sincerely hope you mean p.m."

"Nope—come on now, we've got a big day."

"Does that bear coffee come with breakfast?"

"Sure does—an all-Alaskan one—salmon, eggs and hash browns all fried and swimmin' in bear grease with an extra side of bear fat for those whose arteries can pump it."

"Are you always this annoyingly perky at this time of night? And, did you say salmon eggs?"

"Yes, although I don't think of this as night, and no, not salmon eggs—now, it really is time to get up."

"OKaaay," she whined, as she rolled out of bed to head to the bath for her morning ablutions.

When she arrived in the cozy kitchen of the cozy cabin, Rita was greeted with a set table, the aroma of coffee and an amalgam of other odors that seduced an involuntary response from her salivary glands. "Smells delicious—I'm famished."

"Ah, perfect timing," replied Elliot. "I'm not surprised that you're hungry after last night's adult athletics. Have a seat. How do you like your eggs?"

"Over easy," replied Rita as she pulled out a chair from the solid-pine table and sat down.

"Me too, four over easy comin' up. Would you like some smoked salmon along with those?"

"Sounds yummy, yes please."

Elliot gently and expertly flipped the eggs without breaking a single yoke and then slid two each to separate plates, added some salmon and set the plates along with a basket of warm baking-powder biscuits on the table. Once he had delivered two cups of coffee, he sat down and pushed a small Mason jar over to Rita.

"That doesn't look like the bear fat you promised."

"Sorry, I lied about the bear fat and grease. That is a jar of my very own blueberry preserves using berries picked by these very hands. I also caught and smoked the salmon."

"Well, aren't you the little homemaker."

"Just two of many survival talents I've picked up living out here as a park ranger."

"I don't know if blueberry preserves are necessary for survival in the wild, but it does enhance the experience," observed Rita. "Mmm, it's delicious—as are the eggs, and salmon and biscuits. Aren't you afraid you'll be teased for being a sissy by the other park rangers?"

"We're park rangers, not wildlife troopers." Elliot's pejorative reference was to Alaska Wildlife Troopers who were Alaska law enforcement officers charged with enforcing Alaska's laws on fishing, hunting, trapping, guiding and boating—laws that often came into direct conflict with the national parks' mission to protect and conserve wildlife and the environment. As a result, the relationship between federal park rangers and state wildlife troopers was often strained, if not contentious.

"Aren't we meeting one today?" queried Rita.

"Rusty's more tolerable than a lot of his buddy Alaska

Wildlife Troopers."

"And, why again, do we need to have a wildlife trooper with us? I thought we were still going to be within the park."

"OK, so there are two parts to Katmai National Park and Preserve. There's the park, and then, there's the preserve. No hunting is allowed in the park, but it is in the preserve part. The reason for that was—well, political battles in Washington starting back in 1971 with passage of the Alaska Native Claims Settlement Act which directed the Secretary of the Interior to draw up a list of eighty million acres of federal land to be withdrawn from development for conservation purposes. In 1972, Interior Secretary Rogers Morton did just that with what became known as the Morton Proposal and included land to expand Katmai park. The native claims act had a sunset clause that required the interior secretary to make the designation within nine months of passage of the act. Morton met his deadline, and in 1973 separate bills were introduced in both the House and the Senate to implement the Morton Proposal. But, over time, things got skewed in Congress by special interests with the aid of their hip-pocketed politicians. One of those was Senator Mike Gravel from Alaska who had a national tantrum and refused to support the compromise bill because it didn't leave enough federal land for development. He even threatened to filibuster to prevent passage of a bill that would have done nothing more than extend another sunset deadline for only a year so that the politicians could work out the kinks in the current proposal. It was a very complicated mess. I mean, Democrats and Republicans were supporting stuff you might not expect based upon their party affiliations. For instance, Morton was a Republican and Gravel was a Democrat. But one thing is for sure in Alaska, extraction industries rule, and don't kid yourself, hunting can be just as extractive as mining and oil drilling."

"So, how did Katmai get split?"

"I was just getting there. So, as I said, time was running out. December 18, 1978 was the deadline—the sunset—under the native claims act for Congress to implement the Morton Proposal. If no law was put in place by that date, then all those lands listed in the Morton Proposal would be opened to development. That, of course, would just make the mining and oil barons giddy in their greed. My group, the National Park Service, got into gear and in July 1978 began drafting national monument proclamations for protection of various areas. President Carter then used the Antiquities Act to protect several million acres by executive order. He did that on December 1, 1978. And then all hell broke loose. Many Alaskans abandoned their bullshit image of rugged individualism for concentrated tribal rage. Carter's effigy was burned in Fairbanks. People from Eagle and Glennallen declared open anarchy by adopting official proclamations that they would not support National Park Service authorities or regulations and that they would harbor anyone who defied them. Residents of Cantwell went into Denali park and fired their guns, lit campfires and generally broke as many park regulations as they could. It was called the Great Denali Trespass."

"Yeah, I heard about that."

"Yeah, well, to make a very long story just long, Carter's executive order worked to get politicians more reasonable until when Reagan beat Carter and the Republicans took control of the Senate in early November 1980. Conservationists and other people with common sense realized that a bill protecting some lands was better than no law at all. So, they worked lickety-split to pass that law in late November 1980. And that law is the Alaska National Interests Land Conservation Act, and it added the preserve land to Katmai and, as a concession, allows hunting in that preserve— hunting that is all governed by Alaska hunting laws. And, that, my dear, is why we need a wildlife trooper to go in there and meet the people who think they are great-white hunters. Also, those people are more—let's say, open—with Rusty than me."

"You don't like hunters, do you?"

"I don't like certain types of hunters. The people you were with for a month before you came back yesterday are just fine with me. It's the lazy, braggart assholes you're going to meet now that I have no respect for. They don't need the meat to survive like the Yup'ik Eskimos."

"Russian Mission," Rita said thoughtfully. "That was an interesting and rewarding experience. I got some great photos and interviews from those folks. I think Nat Geo will be pleased."

"The Yup'ik at Russian Mission are just the type of people the subsistence hunting and fishing laws were meant for. Generally, they don't intentionally hunt bears in their dens unless times are tough and the village needs the meat. Sometimes, they do stumble upon a den when they're poking around in the snow to find a trap on their trapline, and if the bear wakes up cranky and comes for the trapper, they'll kill it in self-defense. Our urban hunters and some of our misanthropic hermits will intentionally kill bears in their dens, and they don't discriminate against any sex or age bear when they do. They think that's sport and that they're real brave. Those guys also bait bears, which I find cowardly and disgusting, but Alaska law allows it, which means you're goin' to see some bait stations when we're out there in the wild."

"Well, it's all part of the assignment from National Geographic, so I have to see it, photograph it and talk to the hunters who do it."

"Did anyone at Russian Mission tell you how their hunters kill a bear, or as Alaska and hunting enthusiasts like to say, 'harvest a bear?' And, that's a good example of what I was saying about hunting being an extractive industry. We harvest the forest. We harvest the animals. No, we kill the trees. We kill the animals. That's it. They're dead, and there's no replacing them. It's like removing minerals or oil from the ground. And, what's left behind? Just ugliness and death. Anyway, back to my question."

"Sure, they prefer black bears because the meat is better—they say. Most brown bear kills—harvests—were done in self-defense. But, they would hunt the grizzlies if they were short of food in the village. Most of the time the hunters would see a likely bear den while berry picking or hunting moose and make a mental note for the future. I like the fact that they respect the bear as a powerful being. They don't worship the animal, but once they kill one, they have a bit of a ceremonial way of dressing it. Weird isn't it, that we call skinning and gutting an animal dressing it? So, the hunter lays the bear out with the head facing east or toward the mountains, which is generally east there. Also, out of respect for the bear, the skull is buried or at least left at the kill site. They don't want dogs carrying it around in the village or kids sitting on it, or otherwise showing no respect."

"Well, excellent, sounds like you got the straight story. Look, we have to go. We have a plane to catch. Let's get this cleaned up and the cabin locked down. Our new accommodations won't be as upscale as this, but I think you'll like them. Rusty and I got the camp set up while you were in Russian Mission, and I have a Sugpiaq friend watching over it. His name is Natak, but his friends call him Nate."

After they had cleaned up the breakfast dishes, Rita went to get her bags which she had packed before her tussle under the sheets with Elliot the previous evening. She paid particular attention to her cameras, lenses and film. They all looked in order and ready to go on her next three-week adventure into the wild.

As she and Elliot emerged from the Brooks Falls ranger cabin, the sky was brightening even though it was only a little after four. While Rita placed her bags in the carriage on the ATV, Elliot locked the cabin and then threw his bags on top of Rita's and took his place in the driver's seat. The airport was little more than a mile away and nothing more than Lake Brooks. Another man was waiting for them and helped them load their gear into the plane.

"Why don't you sit in the copilot's seat," said Elliot. Then he crawled into the pilot's seat.

"Wait—what are you doing? Isn't the pilot supposed to sit there?" asked Rita.

"Well, of course—with all your bush flying, you know that."

"You're the pilot?'

"Yup—got a problem with that?"

"Not as long as you've done this before."

"Nope—first time," he answered with a twinkle in his eye. "Well, today, anyway. Yes, I've done this more times than I can remember."

"Well, who's that guy?"

"A young ranger who's here to help shove us off. Ready?"

"As I'll ever be."

"Put the headphones on, check your seatbelt and please keep your feet off the rudder pedals. Oh—the used-breakfast bags are in the pocket to your right."

In response to her quizzical look, he said, "In case you get motion sick." Then, with a thumbs up to the other ranger, they were pushed off, and Elliot started the engine, taxied out into the lake, did a runup check and away they went. "Beautiful day for a little flying, don't you think?"

"Spectacular," she replied, before they each slipped into their own thoughts—his on flying and hers on the beauty below her which drifted into a reverie of her good fortune in meeting Elliot. He was a many-talented and passionate man, and not just in bed. His passion extended to protection of the environment, Alaska's wild animals and the aboriginal cultures that struggled to survive in Alaska's wildlands. He could cook, fish, make delicious blueberry preserves and fly an airplane. She could only wonder about what other talents he had. He had a kind, handsome face punctuated by intelligent, mirthful blue eyes and a mouth with a ready smile. His shoulders were broad and his frame was tall and muscular. As part of her National Geographic assignment to cover the hunting of bears in Alaska, Rita had flown to Brooks Lodge in Katmai National Park to do a photo shoot of brown bears, commonly referred to as grizzlies, before heading out to Russian Mission to live with the Yup'ik Eskimos and learn about, and photograph, their bear-hunting practices. That's when she first met Ranger Elliot Mercer. Elliot had been assigned to escort her to the best bear-viewing areas around Brooks Falls. He got her to vantage points that tourists never see. Elliot and Rita didn't have sex during that first meeting, but it wasn't because of lack of desire on her part. In fact, they never kissed or had expressed any romantic desires to each other. However, when Rita returned early yesterday, she made sure their relationship sped forward past courting and kissing and right into the bedroom. Rita loved men, especially men as gorgeous as Elliot, which her fiancé was not.

Elliot broke Rita's daydream with, "That's Nonvianuk Lake directly in front of us. Once we land, I'll taxi to our campsite along the south shore. You can barely make it out if you squint and use your imagination."

"Either I'm not squinting correctly or my imagination sucks cuz I don't see it."

Elliot pointed to a small clearing near the shore and said, "There—see it? I'll drop down and make a pass so you can get some good shots."

"Oh, yeah, yeah—I see it," she said, as she readied her camera.

After making two passes of the camp and tipping the wings in salute to Nate who was waving at them from the ground, Elliot set the plane down on the water and taxied toward camp.

"That was the smoothest landing I have ever experienced—on water or land. I guess you have done this before. Really, I couldn't tell when we were finally down," exclaimed Rita.

Nate was in water nearly to the top of his waders waiting for them as Elliot cut the engine and let the plane drift toward him. Nate caught the front of the left pontoon, grabbed the towline and pulled the plane toward two large tree trunks that extended into the lake. Elliot climbed out of the cabin and onto the pontoon and jumped to the trunks when he was within five feet. After securing the plane, Rita handed her camera-equipment bags to Elliot and Nate, before they all pitched in to unload the rest of their gear through a relay line with Elliot getting bags out of the cargo hold and handing them to Rita who passed them on to Nate.

Once the plane was unloaded and all the duffels and containers of supplies were stored, Nate stuck out his right hand and said, "Welcome to Camp Taquka'asinaq. My name's Natak Kakee-Harris. You may call me Nate."

Rita reacted with mild surprise and extended her hand in

greeting. "Pleased to meet you. I'm Rita Draper."

Elliot laughed and said, "I saw that—so did Nate. Yes, he speaks fluent English, Russian, a bit of Spanish and German, and, of course, Sugpiaq. Guess I forgot to tell you that and that Nate is our resident expert on pretty much anything Alaskan, but he holds a master's degree in wildlife biology with a focus on bears."

"I'm sorry for my reaction. It was culturally insensitive, but I just came back from a month in Russian Mission, and none of the Yup'ik there were nearly as articulate as you. When you spoke, it took me off guard."

"Those folks weren't lucky enough to have the opportunities or parents I did. No offense taken. In fact, it's a little game that Elliot and I play on people the first time I meet them. Count it as a life lesson we could all benefit from—don't judge a brain by the color of its head."

"I'll try to remember that."

"My father was a cultural anthropologist, and my mother lived in a village where he was living and conducting his studies. They fell in love, and I'm the result."

"Fascinating—I hope to hear more about that later. I didn't quite catch the name you said for this camp."

"Camp Taquka'asinaq—which means Camp Large Brown Bear in Sugpiaq. Elliot and I thought we needed a camp name, and we're in brown bear country, and the brown bears are large here, so…"

"The Yup'ik have a different name for brown bears, ungungssiq and another I can't remember, but I have it written down in my notes."

"Well, that's very good. You're absolutely right. Ungungsiiq means nothing more than land mammal or quadruped—not very descriptive, in my opinion. Their other name is carayak, which is the same term for monster or ghost in lower Yukon communities. Ghost would apply maybe, but I don't care for any names that conjure up negative reactions from humans. I now prefer Ursus arctos, their scientific name."

"So, maybe you should have named the camp Camp Ursus Arctos," joked Rita.

"Got me there," said Nate after laughing. "Elliot tells me you're a professional photographer with National Geographic, but he really didn't go into much detail after that. Tell me more about yourself."

"I'm not really employed by Nat Geo. That's not how it works. I'm a professional photographer, but I'm independent. In other words, I don't have a steady job where I get a payroll check from Nat Geo. They asked me to do this job as an independent contractor. It's a one-piece assignment with a mission to photograph and report on Alaskan bears, primarily brown bears, bear-viewing guides who depend on there being live bears to view and hunters from aboriginal people and subsistence hunters to people who like their taste to trophy hunters. As part of that, I need to get information about the bears and about the laws, both federal and state, that protect them and allow them to be hunted. That's where you, Elliot and Rusty Bowen come in. By the way, where is he? I thought he was going to meet us here."

"He was here, but he took off to see if he could find some of those hunters you want to photograph. He should be back soon," answered Nate.

"Rita is being a bit modest, Nate," interjected Elliot. "The info I got from National Geographic before she showed up included a short biography. She's a nationally, if not internationally, known photographer. And, she told me that she intends to include her work here on bears in a book about various animals around the world."

"Really? Tell me more," said Nate.

"Well, I've got some great photos collected from around the world of various animals that are endangered or getting there. I have photos of jaguars, leopards, elephants, rhinos, gorillas, tigers, sea turtles and many more—both while they're alive and after they've been hunted and killed. I also have photos of the people who kill them for food, sport and the black-market. It's a big undertaking, but the Alaskan bears will be my last group of photos. So, the idea is to show the animals, hunters and poachers and talk about conservation, including whether legal hunting is a conservation tool or one that helps exterminate the animals through weakening their populations."

"Killing for conservation," added Elliot.

"That is huge. How long has this taken?" asked Nate.

"Over six years—I travel a lot."

"Sounds like an understatement," observed Nate.

"And that sounds like a plane coming this way," observed Elliot.

The far-off buzz of an airplane motor was soon followed by the plane itself that flew over, then along the distant ridgeline until it swooped down toward the lake turning into the wind. It, too, made a graceful landing, but Rita could tell it was not quite as graceful as the one Elliot had previously executed. As the plane taxied toward them, Elliot slipped on his waders before heading into the water after Nate. Like the plane Elliot had piloted, the approaching plane had an official emblem on its sides. Instead of a National Park Service emblem, this one was near the tail of the plane, rather than on the door like Elliot's, and said Alaska Wildlife Troopers in large blue letters under an image of an official-looking, gold shield with a bear at the top and Alaska State Wildlife Troopers written on four separate ribbon designs starting with the word Alaska under the bear and ending with Troopers at the bottom.

As Nate and Elliot pulled the plane to the opposite side of the tree trunks from Elliot's plane, a blue-uniformed man with bright red hair got out and onto the left plane float. As he came ashore, he put on an official Alaska Wildlife Troopers baseball cap and then greeted Elliot and Nate with a broad smile and a hearty handshake.

Upon seeing Rita, the man in blue came directly toward her with the same open smile and extended hand he had used with Nate and Elliot and said, "Howdy, my name is Rusty Bowen, and you must be Rita Draper. Pleasure to meet you, ma'am."

Rita couldn't resist glancing at the fringe of bright red hair sticking out under his cap before shaking his hand and saying, "Pleasure to meet you too."

"That's right, Rita, his real name isn't Rusty. It's Lester," said Elliot.

"What're you talkin' about? Rusty's a real name—just as real as Lester," corrected Rusty.

"Rusty sounds like metal that's lost its luster, or would that be mental that's lost its Lester in this case," said Elliot.

"Funny guy, isn't he?" said Rusty to Rita.

"Don't pull me into this, but it was kinda creative," answered Rita.

"I have to agree, but let's get out of these waders and talk about what we're going to be doing here," said Nate once he finished laughing.

Rusty went with Rita to a plank table in the middle of camp and laid out a map while Elliot and Nate removed their waders and hung them on a tree branch to dry. They then joined Rita and Rusty as Rusty was marking locations on the map.

"So, these are places I saw from the air of locations of hunter camps and probable bait stations," said Rusty.

"Bear-baiting stations—right?" interjected Rita.

"Right," answered Rusty.

"Damn—that many," exclaimed Elliot.

"As far as I can tell from the air, and I really don't need to hear your lecture about how bear baiting isn't sport, Elliot. I know how you feel, but it's legal under Alaska law, even in the preserve, so that's what I deal with. OK?"

Elliot just grumbled in reply.

"My suggestion is that we go up in your plane this afternoon, Elliot, and take a closer look at some of these that we can visit tomorrow. We'll take my plane tomorrow, since I'll be the one making contact and checking licenses and permits." Rusty pointed to circled locations on the map and said, "We should take some of the easier ones, like here and here, to give Rita an easy introduction to the hunting process and how we inspect it. These have small lakes close by that I can land on."

"Sounds good to me. What do you two think?" asked Elliot looking at Rita and Nate.

"Sure, looks great to me," said Rita.

"Yeah, me too, but what about this circle? Is that a bear-baiting station or hunters' camp?" asked Nate pointing to a circle on Rusty's map inland from the southern shore of Kukaklek Lake to the north of them.

"Well, I think so, but we need to get on the ground to make sure."

"Looks pretty close to native lands. Sure it's not—on—native lands?" said Nate. Nate moved his finger from Rusty's circle to a large area along the western shore of Kukaklek Lake marked Native Village Corporation Lands.

"No, can't say for sure, and I can't be certain that whoever has that bait station, if it is a bait station, isn't straying over to native lands. I'll have to get on the ground for that, but let's save that for a couple of days from now."

"All right, let's have some lunch and then get up in the air. Rita, that's your tent over there, and ours are over here," said Elliot.

Rita noticed that Elliot's tent was positioned a little closer to hers and that since they both had entrances at both ends, either of them could sneak out in the middle of the night to join the other. She also noticed a bright orange and yellow wire around the outside of the camp.

Elliot followed her line of sight and said, "Yeah, that—don't go near it. It's an electric fence to keep our bear friends at a safe distance."

"Does that actually work?" she asked.

"Oh, yeah. I actually think some bears can sense the electricity from several feet away. I've seen them head toward a fence and abruptly turn away ten or fifteen feet out. Others aren't so sensitive and have to stick their noses on it. That happens only once. Electric fences have been used by Alaskans to protect their food caches since the 1930s. It's powered by an auto battery and pushes out a little over five thousand volts through a step-up transformer. That'll land you on your rump, but won't do any serious damage, other than a bruised butt," said Elliot, trying not to imagine Rita's butt.

After a lunch of cheese-and-lunchmeat sandwiches with a side of potato chips, they got in Elliot's National Park Service float plane and surveyed the areas Rusty had circled on his map and identified some large enough bodies of water to land on. They paid particular attention to the one that Nate expressed concern over being on native lands. Whatever the area was, it appeared to be uninhabited when they flew over.

That evening after a dinner of fresh-caught salmon, which still was a treat for Rita, but she felt would lose its appeal at the end of her time in the wild, they sat around a campfire and got to know each other better—at least Rusty, Nate and Rita did. Rita and Elliot had a head start on the other two.

At one point, Rita turned to Nate and said, "I've lived with the Yup'ik in Russian Mission and have seen how and why they hunt bears, but I really did not get to know much about the bears themselves—scientifically. What can you tell me?"

"Much—I mean, that's a broad question, and bears are amazingly complex and interesting animals. I think they are the most amazing animals there are, but my parents and their backgrounds helped with that view, as did their encouragement to pursue my education. Mostly what we see here in Katmai are Ursus arctos gyas or coastal brown bear with the rare sighting of Ursus arctos horribilis or grizzly which is a bit smaller usually than Ursus arctos gyas but with a nastier disposition. That's not to say you can go up to a coastal brown and pet it on the nose and keep your fingers or life. They can get just as large as Ursus arctos middendorfii—Kodiaks. All three of these are subspecies of Ursus arctos and most people have a hard time distinguishing who's who, and all come from the same genetic pool. You can call them all grizzlies and get by with it in most groups, except the ones I travel in. The distinction between them is based upon where they are and what they eat. Grizzly refers to the coat of horribilis and not to the fact that is horrible, although it tends to be because of its diet which is less plentiful than the diet of coastal browns, gyas. Grizzlies tend to have gray coloring on their shoulders and hump and live on interior mountain slopes, tundra plains and forests. Coastal browns live in lush grasslands and around lakes and streams rich in salmon, like here. Besides salmon, coastal browns eat clams and grasses and sedges. First time I saw browns eating grass, I couldn't believe it. They were out in a meadow eating grass and sedges like cows. Their dung even looked like cow dung. Given their diet, coastal brown's will put on an amazing amount of weight before hibernating. Males average nine hundred to a thousand pounds with the largest one on record being one shot near Cold Bay in 1948—one thousand seven hundred pounds. Oh, here's a riddle for you. Females will mate with several males from mid-May to early July, and copulation is—well, enthusiastic—and can last over twenty minutes."

Rita looked over at Elliot, who didn't notice, while Nate did.

"Now, listen carefully," continued Nate, "the gestation

period is fifty days, but the cubs, which are only around one pound, are born in January or February while the mother is hibernating. How do you think that happens?"

Rita gave an I-don't-know shrug and shake of her head.

"It's a survival technique provided by nature. The fertilized egg floats around and becomes an embryo in the mother's uterus until her body indicates that she has enough stored fat to survive the winter. If she does, the embryo implants in the wall of her uterus and becomes a cub. If not, the embryo is sloughed off. Cool, huh? Now, here's another mystery for you. During hibernation, bears develop muscle. They don't lose it."

"How is that possible?" asked Rita.

"Thought you'd never ask. We don't know for sure, but some current research with urea injections into some hibernating black bears indicates that they are able to convert the urea into amino acids and protein and then into muscle."

"Now, that's the kind of exercise program I want, except for gaining all that weight and sleeping all winter," said Rita.

"OK, Mr. Wizard, I think it's time we turn in—at least it is for me—early and big day tomorrow," said Elliot.

And, some middle-of-the-night wrestling in the sleeping bag, thought Nate, but he said, "Yeah, you're right. Glad I don't have to work out tonight. I'll try to put on some muscle while I sleep. Be careful of that fence when you go out to—commune with nature." Then he smiled and said, "Nite, all."

Five Days Later

Over the previous four days, the team had dropped in to talk to seven different groups of hunters. They would land on a large-enough body of water and then hike to hunters they had seen from the air. Sometimes they would take both planes out to cover more territory and identify locations for later inspection. Elliot and Rusty would interview the hunters and inspect their hunting licenses, permits and remnants of what once were magnificent animals. Nate performed his own measurements and scientific tests on hides and skulls, and if the debased, skinned corpse was close by, he would analyze the health of the bear—which obviously wasn't good after it had been killed. Rita had been able to talk to each of these groups and to photograph them while hunting, shooting and field dressing their "harvests." There was a father and son from Texas who had stalked their bear with the aid of a guide. There was a group of five hunters from Anchorage, three of whom had killed bears. A different group of five was from Homer. All of them had slaughtered and butchered bears. Four other hunters were safely sitting on their butts on platforms in trees waiting for unsuspecting bears to sample bait on the ground as their last meal. The preferred bait was cooking grease and doughnuts mixed together. Bears loved it. These hunters' rationalization for baiting bears was that it was easier than stalking them, and it was legal. Rita pointed out to them that the bears within the borders of the preserve usually had previously come in close contact with humans who had no guns and were on bear-viewing tours, so really the bears were easy to walk up to. They had no fear of, and no previous reason to fear, humans. It would be like the bears being placid and nonthreatening to human viewers until one day a rogue without that prior experience came on the scene and mauled a human to death. That just got an indignant stare with one guy taking another pull on his beer before walking away. Every one of the hunters that the team interviewed had the requisite licenses and permits. And, each one stated that they were conservationists and that hunters did the most of anyone to promote conservation primarily through the fees they paid and in the case of bears, keeping the number of predators in check so that their prey was not depleted by the bears' overhunting. The prey the hunters were referring to were other animals the hunters liked to kill, like deer, caribou, elk and moose, which were not the primary food sources for bears. The real irony of their statement, and one that escaped them, was that they were the predators who were depleting the number of bears—and not just any bears, but the strongest, most virile bears, leaving the weakest to continue the species. Rita had resisted the urge to point this out and ask whether there should be a license to hunt them too. None of these hunters took the meat. It was left for scavengers or to rot in the field. By Alaska law, hunters were required to take only the skull and hide with its genitalia and claws attached, and that was all they wanted—that, and a photo of them next to the bloody sacrifice to their bogus bravery. However, Rita did recognize that it was true that the money from their hunting fees was used in part for conservation, but it wasn't something that the hunters had to break a sweat for. Clearly, these hunters were the entitled and very different from the Yup'ik she had lived with for a month.

In each of their forays to find hunters and bears, the team had made a pass over the area that was a possible hunting site near native lands, and in each of those passes they could see no trace of a human—until the sixth day. Their airplane fuel reserves were running low, so after breakfast, Rusty decided to fly to the spreading metropolis of Igiugig to replenish them. Igiugig was a Yup'ik village with a population of thirty-three. Airplane fuel was precious out there, and the Yup'ik of Igiugig didn't share theirs with just anyone. Nate used the excuse that he might be needed to smooth negotiations for the fuel, but he really wanted to see some old friends. Since the Yup'ik and other native people had a close relationship with Alaska and federal authorities in the joint protection of wild lands and wildlife, there would be no trouble in securing the needed fuel without Nate. Rusty didn't bother to argue the point and instead let his friend slide into the copilot's seat. Elliot elected to stay behind to provide more weight capacity on Rusty's Cessna 185 Skywagon, but Rita didn't want to miss any potential for more photos and adventures so she crawled into the seat behind Nate. Their flight path took them to the southwest of the mystery site and right over the native land nearby, and as luck would have it, they saw someone on the ground and not just any ground—it was native lands. Also, the person on the ground had a rifle and something on his back that looked suspiciously like a rolled-up brown bear hide. They didn't have sufficient fuel to get lower to inspect, much less land on the nearby lake and take off again, so they made a mental note of the location and heading of the hunter on the ground with the intent of getting a closer look on their return trip.

Loading the needed fuel on the plane took time, but catching up, and having lunch, with old friends took even longer, so their departure was delayed until late afternoon. By the time they passed over the place where they had seen the hunter, he was long gone, and there was no sign of him or of a plane or any other means of transportation. When they arrived at camp, they related their sighting to Elliot, who suggested the obvious—fly up to Kukaklek Lake and take another, closer look.

Rita had fallen asleep after her romp with Elliot in his tent and barely woke up in time to make it over to her tent before Nate emerged from his. It really wouldn't have mattered if Nate or Rusty had seen her furtive retreat. By this time, even Rusty knew what they were up to. Only Elliot and Rita were being fooled about the secrecy of their tryst. Rusty and Nate actually wished they would come out in the open about it. It would save a lot of skulking about by Elliot and Rita and conscious avoidance of stumbling in on them by Rusty and Nate. But, it had become a camp game of stealth and avoidance they played every night and morning.

Rita loved salmon, or at least she used to. It was delicious, nutritious and now, monotonous. Once again, they were having salmon and eggs for breakfast—or was it eggs and salmon this time? One thing was for sure, it was plentiful and fresh.

On this morning, however, Nate did the cooking and the salmon was much different from prior days. It was neither fresh nor boring. The eggs were different too. Rita noticed soon after she made her clamorous, public appearance from her tent as if to say, "See, I really stayed here all night."

Nate was bent over the camp cookstove with his back to Rita as she approached. When she was within six feet of him, Nate said, "Mornin', Rita. Sleep well?"

"Good Morning—how did you know it was me?" she asked.

"We Indians have our ways," replied Nate.

"What is that you're cooking? Doesn't smell like the usual."

"Sit down. I'll serve you some. Your timing couldn't have been better."

While she took a seat at the table, Nate did some assembly

of her breakfast, and Rusty and Elliot came out of their tents. As he set the plate in front of her, Nate said, "Hope you like eggs Benedict with smoked salmon."

Rita gave him a surprised, blank look, and he said, "Go ahead, try it, unless you don't like eggs Benedict."

Rita cut some off, put it in her mouth and savored the rich medley of smoky salmon, perfectly poached egg, English muffin, buttery Hollandaise sauce, and caper and dill garnish.

"This is incredibly delicious," she exclaimed after swallowing. "Why haven't you been cooking all this time?"

"Because I didn't want to be cooking ALL the time," came his reply.

"Where did you learn this recipe?" asked Rita.

"From my Sugpiaq mother," said Nate with a wry smile.

"Really?" she asked with a look of suspicion.

"What? You don't think my Sugpiaq mom could read a Julia Child cookbook?"

By this time, Rusty and Elliot had joined them, and they all laughed at Nate's little joke with Rita.

"I got the smoked salmon yesterday in Igiugig, and I brought the other ingredients from Anchorage via King Salmon."

"So, do we get any of that deliciousness?" asked Rusty.

"Comin' right up, boss."

Breakfast was something to celebrate slowly and deliberately, but they did not have that kind of time, especially since cleanup would take a bit longer than usual. Once the last morsel was finished, they moved into action with each person performing a necessary task without being asked or instructed on how to do it.

Soon they were in Rusty's Alaska Wildlife Troopers plane taxiing for takeoff. When they were over their target, Rusty said into his mic, "Looks like we missed him again."

"I'm not so sure of that," said Nate. "I think I saw a glint off something shiny over there about eleven o'clock."

"Yeah, I saw that too," confirmed Elliot. "I think we ought to land this time and hike over there."

"That's a good three miles in. It will be the only ground work we do today," declared Rusty.

"Worth it, since you saw somebody hiking on native land toward that area," said Nate.

"All right, here we go," said Rusty as he brought the plane around and into the wind to land.

As they touched down on the lake, Elliot said, "I'll be damned. Look over there under those trees."

Everybody looked in the direction Elliot had indicated, and Rita said, "Look at what?"

"I think there's a plane over there—under camo netting."

As Rusty taxied closer toward the object, it became clear that Elliot was right. There, under camouflage netting, tucked up against the shore and as far under some trees as it could get was a float plane.

Rusty cut the engine and floated next to the other plane and up onto the shallow lake bottom within a short hop of the beach. They all crawled out and started toward the camo-netted plane after surveying the land for its owner.

"Bobby Buttoff—shoulda known," said Elliot.

"Yeah, Buttoff," confirmed Nate and Rusty almost in unison.

"Who's Bobby Buttoff?" asked Rita.

"Oh, just one of Alaska's biggest assholes, is all—and that's sayin' a lot, because we have some mighty big ones," said Elliot.

"Why? What's he done to deserve that label?" she asked.

"Well, to begin with, he's an avid gun nut and self-professed survivalist and white supremacist. The fuc.... Sorry, he's proud of it too. But, he's a licensed guide and has a much-coveted, float-plane slip at Lake Hood in Anchorage. That's the float plane portion of Ted Stevens Airport that you flew out of to get to Brooks Falls."

"Yeah, yeah, I know," said Rita. "What else?"

"He hunts game all the ways I find to be inhumane and unsportsmanlike. For instance, he baits bears, only there are rumors that he poisons some of his traps. Maybe we'll find one today. Also, he'll kill bears—males, females, cubs, no matter—while they're hibernating in their dens using intense lights so the bears wake up confused before they're executed."

"It's mostly legal, Elliot, and the part that isn't is all rumor," noted Rusty.

"Don't I know, but it's not moral, and it's not

sportsmanlike. You don't hunt that way, do you Rusty? Why's that?"

After allowing Rusty a few minutes to answer, Elliot went on, "I'll tell you why—because it's a cowardly way to—hell, I can't even say the word 'hunt,' because it isn't. It's just slaughter for the sake of slaughter. He also runs down elk and caribou with a jet boat and shoots them while they're swimming. I know, I know, Trooper Bowen, it's legal, but I'll tell you what isn't—shooting them from shore and then going out with a boat to hitch them up and drag them to shore."

"Now, he's never been caught doin' any of the illegal things," added Rusty.

"No—and while I think he's as dumb as wolf piss, he's cunning, and has been able to evade the law. For one thing, there just aren't enough of us rangers and troopers to patrol all of Alaska. It's a big state, in case no one noticed. But, I have my information from some reliable sources—just none who want to come forward and testify against Buttoff. They're afraid that while the legal system plugs along, they'll get plugged by Bobby. Some have been threatened by him."

"Well, I have to admit that I have no love for Bobby Buttoff, but so far, I haven't seen him do anything illegal," rationalized Rusty.

"And we won't today, if we don't get going. If he is doing something illegal out there, he's destroying evidence and covering his tracks right now because he couldn't miss seeing us circling and landing, and I'm sure he knows we're the law coming his way," said Elliot.

"Agreed—let's get going," said Rusty.

They all grabbed their packs, and Rita checked her cameras and had two at the ready before they left. Two-and-a-half hours later they arrived at a small clearing that had a required-by-law notice that there was a bear-baiting area just ahead. After that they saw a large, circular, metal container that on closer inspection was revealed to be a fifty-gallon drum cut in half and dug part way into the ground. Inside the metal rim of the metal drum was a greasy glop that had doughnuts swimming in it. A few short yards away was a tree with a platform about twelve feet up covered in camo netting like the plane and a wooden ladder leading to the ground on which a stout, barrel-chested man dressed in camouflage was descending. Once on the ground, the camo-man turned and walked toward the four friends. Under a soiled cap was a weathered, puffy, acne-scarred face with an out-of-place pug nose. At first Rita thought his face had another deformity since his right cheek was puffed out, but when he spit a stream of brown saliva, she realized it was caused by a massive wad of chewing tobacco between his cheek and teeth.

"Mornin' Ranger Mercer, Trooper Bowen...chief," said Bobby.

Nate ignored the cultural slur and looked at Bobby as if he were a yapping cur.

Then Bobby leered at Rita, exposed his blackened teeth in an attempted smile, and said to her, "And, who is this?"

Rita said, "'This' is Rita Draper." She was thankful that Bobby did not extend his hand for shaking. She tried to block out any images of where that hand had been and what it had done.

"Rita's here on a National Geographic assignment to photograph and interview you, Bobby," said Elliot, as if Rita had travelled three thousand miles just to meet Bobby Buttoff.

"Well, ain't that sweet," said Bobby, playing along.

"Do you have your hunting license and bear-baiting permit, Bobby?" asked Rusty.

"Sure do, right here's my license and the permit is over there under the platform just like it should be."

After reviewing the documents, Rusty said as much to Elliot as to Bobby, "Looks in order. So, why are you out hunting instead of guiding?"

"Just don't have any clients today. It's not because I wouldn't rather be guidin'.'"

"So, you haven't taken your bear, yet, Bobby?" asked Elliot.

"No sir, Ranger Mercer," said Bobby in mock deference to Elliot's authority.

"You wouldn't go onto native land to take a bear, would you, Bobby? Cuz, yesterday, Rusty flew over there and saw someone who looks a lot like you carrying something that looked suspiciously like a brown-bear hide."

"Somebody who looks like me? You mean somebody in camo and with two legs and two arms? That could be anybody— except me. Nope, it wasn't me, officer."

You forgot to say a squat little turd in camo, thought Elliot.

Rita said, "Mind if I take some photos?"

"Actually, I do," said Bobby with a cold, threatening stare that made Rita shiver.

Rita walked away so she could take some surreptitious

photos with a miniature camera she kept for such purposes.

Elliot pointed to the camo netting and said, "Why the camo over your platform and your plane, Bobby? Concerned that flying bears might see you?" That was an allusion to flying troopers and rangers who were often referred to as bears or smokies.

"No law against it, is there?" was his only answer.

"There is if something illegal is going on under them. Takes some effort to put those up. Most people don't go to a lot of trouble to hide nothing," said Elliot.

In reply, Bobby shot out another jet of brown sludge from his lower lip that arched and fell with a splat on the ground around eight feet from him.

You do have a way with words, thought Elliot.

Rusty noticed the building fire in Elliot's eyes and said, "All right, Bobby, you're good to go. Hope you get your bear. Let's go, Elliot." Then he called out to Rita and Nate. After a few seconds, Nate emerged from the bushes.

Rita decided to use her charm on Bobby in the hope of getting an interview with him.

"Pleasure meeting you, Mr. Buttoff," she lied. "I really would like to come back and talk to you. I think you probably have some interesting stories and opinions that should be shared with the world. I can do that through the article I'm writing for National Geographic."

After looking her up and down and stripping her with his eyes, Bobby said, "Sure, as long as you don't bring these three with you."

Elliot was ready to pounce on him before Rita answered, "Well, I can't fly a plane."

That actually placated Bobby who usually was avoided by women who saw him for what he was—repulsive and abusive. Rita's response was friendlier than the angry rejections he was used to.

"Yeah, all right, stop in again, and we'll see."

"I'll make a point of it."

"See you soon, Bobby," said Rusty as Nate and Elliot turned their backs to Bobby as if he didn't exist and headed back to their plane.

Once they were far enough away so that Bobby couldn't hear them, Elliot said to Nate, "So, what did you find out while you were sniffing around in the bushes?"

"Not a lot, but I did see some traces of what looked like blood on some rocks and some trails heading toward native lands. Whoever made those trails was taking a different way to go in the same direction. Some of them led toward, if not to, Bobby's baiting station and some loop around and probably go there. I didn't have enough time to find out for sure. But, I have a theory."

"Which is?" asked Elliot.

"I think Buttoff.... Don't you love that name? It fits his personality so well. Anyway, I think he has that legal bait station in that location so that he can easily sneak onto native lands and poach bears. We wouldn't know unless we saw him from the air, and even then, like he pointed out, he just looks like any guy in camo. And, if it looks like he's been spotted by the law, then he can always ditch the evidence and say he has a legal station, and unless we catch him on native land with bear parts, we have nothing to pin on him. And, catching him is next to impossible, since the native lands he'd be on have no convenient large enough bodies of water for us to land on and get to him in time to catch him red-handed. I also wouldn't be surprised if when he does take a bear, he takes the whole hide with genitalia and claws in place on the hide as required. That way, if he's caught on this side of native land, he can show it as his legal bear and walk away."

"Why would he want to poach bears?" asked Rita.

Elliot gave Nate a raised-eyebrows-and-twist-of-the-head gesture, as if to say, "You tell her."

"Asian black market," replied Nate. "Bear paw soup is considered a delicacy in many Asian countries, and gallbladders are even more prized. They can fetch a thousand dollars or more. Bear bile contains ursodeoxycholic acid which has been used in traditional Chinese medicines for over three thousand years to treat fever, gallstones, heart disease, eye irritations and liver issues. And, that's not just in China, or Korea. Remember, we have a long history of Chinese in Alaska. They originally were brought in to work in the seafood industry in the late 1800s. They still hold onto their traditional medicines, and bear parts are part of that."

"So, is that a reason the claws and genitalia are required to be attached to the hides?" asked Rita.

"Yeah, one, and, of course, it's illegal to possess gallbladders, detached claws, penises—any detached bear parts, except heads and hides that have been properly sealed."

"Why not bust the merchants who sell them?" asked Rita.

"Believe me, we've tried," answered Rusty. "The Asian communities are tight. Everybody knows everybody, and the merchants who deal in these parts won't sell to anyone they don't know. Also, they don't keep the parts in their stores. They're kept offsite and sold offsite. Catching them is more difficult than catching poachers like Bobby, assuming that's what he's doing."

"Wow, you guys really have your work cut out for you," she observed. "I'd really like to get an interview with the merchants trafficking in bear parts."

"You can forget that, although if Bobby is poaching, he must have a connection—surprising, since he's such a bigot," said Elliot.

"Money trumps all else," said Nate.

The days following their first encounter with Bobby Buttoff included several stops to check on him. Although Elliot and Rusty were not able to find anything illegal in his operation, Rita had charmed her way into several interviews with, and photographs of, Bobby. It was a repugnant task, but it was in the line of duty to National Geographic, and her eventual book deal. She even gained enough of his confidence for him to open up about poaching while out of the presence of Rusty, Elliot and Nate. Bobby gave the information all as being hypothetical and what he had heard through the grapevine, but his hearsay information was obviously the product of firsthand experience. Although she tried, she had never been able to get him to divulge any contacts in the Chinese community who trafficked in bear parts, until her last visit with him the day before her departure back to Brooks Falls with Elliot.

That last visit was inspired not only by their usual desire to catch Buttoff in the act of poaching, but also to warn him that some Yup'ik hunters on the nearby native land, but outside the preserve, had spotted an aggressive, rogue, inland grizzly. When they arrived at his bear-bait station, Bobby was waiting expectantly as he had in the past.

During this visit, Bobby was more talkative with Rita than he had been in past interviews. He told her that he had gotten some information for her that she had wanted.

"What information is that?" she asked.

"I got a couple of names of Chinamen who deal in bear parts, and they might be willing to talk to you, as long as you keep it confidential and don't use their names in your article."

"That's fantastic. Why would they do that?"

"Let's just say, they owe me," said Bobby who was anxious to brag about his connections and ability to get information that law enforcement, like Elliot and Rusty, couldn't. "Here's their contact info. They know you'll be contacting them and that it's safe to talk to you."

While Rita was in her private conversation with Buttoff, Elliot, Rusty and Nate were doing their usual separate searches of the area. Nate inspected the bait-station area, including Buttoff's pack and other hunting equipment, before heading into the woods. Elliot was the first to return and interrupted the clandestine conversation between Buttoff and Rita.

"Hate to interrupt, but we need to wrap this up and get back to camp; but before doing so, I wanted to give you a warning, Bobby," said Elliot.

"I ain't done nothin' illegal, so keep your fuckin' warnings to yourself, Mercer."

"Well, aren't you the feisty one today, Bobby? What

happened to Ranger Mercer? Save it, Buttoff, I don't care, but you should care about my warning. It has nothing to do with your illegal activities."

"You mean alleged illegal activities, don't you?" said Bobby.

"I said what I meant. Now, shut up and listen. I got a radio call from some Yup'ik hunters that there is a rogue, inland grizzly over on native land, so you'd be wise not to go over there."

"You don't have to try to scare me with imaginary grizzly stories. Told you, I haven't been over there, and don't intend to go."

"Make sure you don't. I heard this imaginary bear looks real hungry and mean."

"Yeah, whatever—I think I can handle myself out here...Ranger Mercer," said Bobby in a mocking tone of voice.

"Up to you." Then to the other three members of his team, Elliot said, "Let's get out of here."

Three hours later when he heard their plane take off, Bobby Buttoff cinched on his pistol belt, strapped on his pack, grabbed his rifle, and headed toward native territory.

He was three miles into native land when he stopped to rest. As he was putting his rifle down, he heard a huffing sound behind him that he had heard many times before. He quickly turned while simultaneously raising his rifle to his shoulder, and was greeted by the sight of a large inland grizzly very close to him. *What the hell are you doin' so far south?* he thought as he smiled and took aim, being careful not to hit the head which would bring its own high price on the black market. *You are a beauty. So long, big fella.* Then, click—click, click. His gun misfired. He pulled on the bolt as hard as he could, but it wouldn't budge. His rifle was hopelessly jammed. The bear sensed his distress and started toward him. Bobby pulled his Smith & Wesson .357 magnum from his holster and took aim and—click. It, too, misfired. The bear came to within six feet of him, went into a crouch, and then extended its head at him and roared with so much intensity Bobby could feel its hot breath and smell the fetid odor of rotting flesh caught in its teeth. Bobby relieved his Bowie knife from its sheath and his bowels into his pants at the same time. The bear raised up on its hind legs to an imposing height of over seven feet. Bobby steadied himself with his knife at the ready. The bear took a couple of steps toward him and swiped at him with its massive left paw bristling with fearsome claws. Bobby managed to avoid that swing and delivered a wound to the inside of the bear's foreleg. The bear seemed not to notice and with amazing alacrity swung with the other paw catching Bobby on his left shoulder, breaking it in several places and sending him into a nearby boulder. Before Bobby had stopped rolling after sliding off the boulder, the bear was on top of him with its mouth covering his whole head. Bobby screamed and pleaded to no one in particular to save him. The crack of his skull as the bear bit down echoed off the surrounding cliffs. Somehow, Bobby kept screaming for almost two minutes after his head had been split.

The bear released Bobby's head after it was convinced that he was dead and rolled the body over and tore at the backpack. When the pack was open, the bear pulled out the salmon skin and roe from the pack and devoured them. After that it rolled Bobby over and opened his stomach and ate its contents in the same fashion it had with the pack and its contents. The rest of Bobby was mostly eaten by the bear with the scraps being cleaned up by some fortunate wolves, ravens, a wolverine, ants and bacteria. It was without question the greatest contribution Bobby had ever made to the world.

It was over a week later that anyone paid any attention to the fact that Bobby's plane was missing from its slip at Lake Hood in Anchorage, and another week after that before anyone decided to report it. By then, Elliot was back at work at Brooks Falls trying to get over being dumped by Rita. Nate was back at the University of Alaska Anchorage working on his field notes and a paper about the health and depletion of bears in Katmai National Park and Preserve. Rusty was helping with the investigation of several mutilated caribou carcasses near Denali National Park. And, having finished her investigation of Chinese black-market, medicinal use of bear parts, Rita was on a plane headed back to her fiancé in Colorado with photos and notes for her National Geographic bear story and her book on the degradation of wild animals for the pleasure and profit of humans.

CHAPTER 6

Open House

Wheat Ridge, Colorado

January–February 1986

Seventeen years with no end in sight. That's not to say that there had been no prior almost-conclusions. Over those seventeen years, there had been several near-completions, but nothing that warranted a pronouncement of done, complete, finished, or bravo from the master planner, architect and builder. Such a decree would have meant the attainment of perfection, and perfection was not possible—never was, never would be. Nevertheless, perfection was his Holy Grail, his White Whale—the tease and tormentor he lusted after, but could never possess. However, perfection would never come without order, and he had none right now. All was chaos. His chaos—caused by his own hands. Order had been so close. Perfection had been within his grasp.

No, no, no—had to destroy it—had to start over. The door— the master-bath door was wrong—the wrong place. The wrong size. That meant the whole bath was arranged all wrong. The whole house was wrong. And all because I started from the living room. Stupid! Stupid!

Beat sat on the floor of what had been the master bathroom until he had destroyed it along with much of the rest of the interior of the house he had been building for seventeen years. He sat with his knees bent up close to his chest and rubbed each side of his head just above the temples with the base of each thumb. Then he slid his hands down along the sides of his face until they came to rest with the heels of the palms under his jaw, fingers curled with the tip of each pinky stuck into a corner of his mouth. He repeated his error over and over in his mind while muttering his self-loathing and rocking forward and back.

After several minutes of rocking and loathing, Beat blinked and began to see with his eyes that had been open in a glassy stare the whole time of his obsessive downward spiral. Looking up, he saw wires hanging from the wall where he had ripped out light fixtures, that if not perfect had been perfectly adequate. Slowly, he rolled to his side onto his hands and knees and got up. Walking from room to room, he took stock and mental notes of the situation. Knocked-down walls and other construction rubble lay about, while still-standing walls and the ceiling had yards of electrical wires hanging in serpentine tangles. Although the chaotic mess disturbed him, the mental challenge of creating a new house design soothed his nerves and focused his runaway mind on the creation of a house that would meet his needs and desires—his perfect home.

He didn't need pen and paper to record his findings. If not a genius, Beat was highly intelligent. However, his obsession with perfection made him ineffectual, unemployable and unwedable. He could never complete a task, because it would never be perfect. Since he could not complete any task, no one would hire him.

And, if that weren't enough to drive away any potential bride, his penchant for perfection eliminated every woman on Earth as a potential mate. It also meant that no one would work for him, so he had to be his own master planner, architect and builder of his home. He preferred it that way—no employers, no employees and no wife.

Fortunately for Beat, he had had a rich father—a divorced, rich man who had set up a trust for Beat before his early death and who had given Beat the land he now endlessly sawed boards and hammered nails on. Beat's father was Nigel Nicholson, the developer of the subdivision where Beat's lot was located. Beat's lot was one of only two large, prime lots tucked away on a private cul-de-sac. The other lot was fully developed with an expansive home built by Nigel in 1954 as part of his development of the subdivision. Both lots had magnificent views of the Front Range and a large yard that sloped away from the houses to a wooded ravine. That's where the similarities ended. While the one lot was occupied by a beautiful home and outbuilding added by the owner that were surrounded by a high fence and lush, well-groomed landscaping, Beat's was bare dirt with a large hole in the backyard excavated years ago for a swimming pool and a house in progress that had one section open to the sky.

Nigel's gift of the lot to Beat was given on his twenty-first birthday in 1962. Having experienced the Great Depression as a child, Nigel was all too familiar with the volatility of the stock market and the relative stability of real estate. There was no better investment in his opinion. So, he had kept five prime lots from sale to the general public for himself, his wife and two sons. When his wife left him, Nigel checked her off the list of beneficiaries. Beat and his brother, Lawrence, each received a lot when they turned twenty-one. Lawrence sold his to start what became a thriving, popular, upscale art gallery in Santa Fe. When Nigel's forty-eight-year-old life was cut short by a heart attack in 1968, he left a mountain of debt that required the liquidation of all of his assets, including the three lots that were still in his name. Fortunately, the trusts for his sons and the lot previously given to Beat survived.

Beat was devastated by his father's death. Nigel had been Beat's protector—his shield against a treacherous world and a turbulent brain. Although Lawrence had neither the time nor the desire nor the ability to replace Nigel and his compassionate concern for Beat, he did love his brother, from a distance. When Beat floundered after Nigel's death, Lawrence advised him to get out of his head by getting into a project that required the use of his hands. Since Beat had hung around his dad and his business and knew how to use construction and drafting tools, building a house on the lot he owned was the only logical choice.

With Lawrence's help, Beat easily convinced the bank that was the trustee of his dad's trust to provide him with the funds necessary for his construction project—funds both in the form of distributions from the trust and of a loan for construction that was secured with the trust and not the house. It was good business— more money for the bank in the form of loan fees and interest. The longer the project dragged on, the more to suck into the bank's bottom line. Wheat Ridge had the same attitude as the bank, but a smaller return. As long as no one in Beat's neighborhood complained about his never-ending construction project, Wheat Ridge was happy to collect his building permit, water and sewer tap, site preparation, renewal, and other construction-related fees. Neighbors didn't complain out of respect for Nigel, a rarity in his business, and because Beat's eyesore was out of their eyesight, except for the elderly couple next door.

Before Beat started construction on his house, the Petronis had enjoyed fourteen years of quietude on their secluded cul-de-sac.

Beat's next-door lot had acted as a greenbelt essentially adding another two acres to the two they owned without the added purchase, tax and insurance costs that went along with ownership. At first, when Beat moved a small camping trailer onto his lot and started construction, Leo was upset and considered ways to legally harass him into stopping the work. But, before launching into a legal battle with his neighbor, Leo remembered the words of Clyde Smaldone, "Youse can trap more flies with honey than somethin' they don't like." The thought of Clyde's quaint and clumsy use of the English language had made him smile. Even though he never went to see his old friend, mentor and benefactor, Leo still had warm feelings towards him. So, Leo had decided that his first approach should be the extension of a warm welcome to the neighborhood with a segue into exploring the possible purchase of Beat's lot. However, after a lengthy visit with Beat, Leo realized that he was a better neighbor than possible alternatives, so Leo abandoned his plan for acquisition or aggression and adjusted his attitude to one of tolerance. Leo realized that Beat's construction noise was offset by some benefits. Beat's twenty-four-hour, watchful presence was like having a free security guard at the entrance to the cul-de-sac. Furthermore, Beat was completely focused on the construction of his house to the exclusion of any human interaction. He had no interest in socializing or in his next-door-neighbor's affairs. That was ideal for Leo and, by extension, Clara, who lived in her husband's umbra and had no opinions independent of his. It was a default arrangement of convenience. One that came to an end on February 6, 1986.

───────────

Five days later, Officer Danny Tercel was driving his Wheat Ridge patrol car solo for the first time. His partner, Sergeant Tom Urban, was out sick with the flu, as was just about half of the Wheat Ridge Police Department, along with a large part of the general public. The whole country was experiencing the largest flu epidemic since the 1968-1969 season, and February was the peak month. Even though he was still a rookie, Danny got the solo assignment because the department was seriously understaffed. Fortunately, crime was low. The weather had not gotten above freezing since February 5 and currently was seventeen degrees with a windchill of five. It was miserable weather to be out in for everybody, but cops had no choice while crooks did, and they preferred warm, comfortable weather to conduct their nefarious deeds.

God, it's cold. I hate this weather, but I hate crooks more, so I hope it holds at least until I get Tom back. Just then, his radio sprang to life.

"Car 28." It was the voice of Dispatch Officer Mary Sturgis. She was a good cop with way more seniority than Danny, but she got stuck on dispatch because she was a woman. Danny knew it wasn't fair, but he was just a rookie and had to keep his mouth shut if he ever wanted to be anything other than a rookie.

"Car 28, Officer Tercel here."

"Got a 10-57 in Indian Paintbrush Estates for you, Danny."

"Hell of weather to go missing. What's the address?"

"10209 Wild Rose Circle."

"I'm about five away, Mary. Who's the 57?"

"Beat Nicholson, Caucasian male, five-six, ragged-around-the-ears, brown hair, graying at the temples, blue eyes. His brother called it in. He lives in Santa Fe and hasn't heard from Beat in over six days. Says that's not normal."

"On my way, dispatch."

Most missing-person reports turned out to be false alarms turned in by an overly protective mother, or a suspicious spouse or some other overwrought, overreactive relative or lover. But each one had to be taken seriously and checked out. Officer Tercel was hoping for the norm, while thinking he was ready for the exception. He wasn't ready for the scene that greeted him at the address given by Mary Sturgis.

"Dispatch, this is Officer Tercel. I'm at 10209 Wild Rose Circle in Indian Paintbrush Estates. You sure about that address, Mary?"

"Sure as I can be. What's up, Danny?"

"There's a house here, but it doesn't look habitable or inhabited. The lot is brown dirt and dirty snow with construction materials piled around, a large dumpster, and a small camping trailer. There's no construction crew—no sign of anyone, actually. Looks abandoned."

"Yup, it's 10209 Wild Rose Circle. The brother was very clear about it being Wild Rose Circle and not street."

"All right, I'll pull my earflaps down and check it out, dispatch," came Officer Danny's reply.

"Stay warm."

"Very funny—don't sound so gleeful. If I'm not back in twenty, send out the Saint Bernards."

Officer Tercel pulled his coat zipper up, his earflaps down and his gloves on. Then he stepped out of his patrol car and into the arctic air. After a brief involuntary shiver to his core, Tercel headed to the small camper, knocked on its door, and called out to no one inside.

The door was unlocked. He opened it while announcing, "Wheat Ridge police. Mr. Nicholson?" The camper was empty, so he turned to the house next.

The front door was partially open. He pushed it all the way in and got a nose full of putrescence that his brain registered as a mixture of rotten eggs, dirty diapers and strawberry cotton candy. Tercel pulled out his handkerchief to cover his mouth and nose against the stench of death and entered cautiously. The place looked like something out of a horror movie, a frozen horror movie.

"Rats."

He exhaled the word in a whispered hiss, not only as an expression of disappointment, but of disgust. Five of the vermin scurried away from a body on the floor. One had been so absorbed in its feast that for a few seconds it failed to sense a live human's presence. When it did, it backed out of the body in a rush and was so bewildered it came at Tercel weaving from side to side in a confused rush to nowhere. Tercel kicked at it, but missed. Having gained its bearings, the naked-tailed rodent ran with focused purpose in the direction its relatives had gone.

Before he took another step, Tercel surveyed the scene. He was in a three-story foyer. A long stepladder was leaning against one wall with the top partially embedded in the drywall. The body was lying on its right side facing away from him next to a space heater that was still on. It looked as if the person had fallen from the ladder while working on something near the ceiling, maybe the wires that were dangling from a hole up there. Since the body was lying next to the space heater, it was probable that death had not been immediate. Also, it probably was not frozen solid since rats were gnawing on the remains.

Tercel pressed his handkerchief harder against his face and walked over to the body to check for life—a silly action, but required SOP. When he got to the other side of the body and bent down to look at the face, he puked in his mouth and then ran outside to puke on the ground. This was only his second dead body. The first was a lot fresher and neater with just three bullet holes in its chest. This one had no eyes and little face left—ruin caused by the rats—and it stank to high heaven. After relieving himself of his breakfast, he rushed to his patrol car.

"Dispatch, Officer Tercel here. I have a code 55-K—need the ME and forensics." A code 55-K meant that there was a dead body that probably was not a homicide, but still required investigation and pronouncement of cause by the medical examiner.

"Is it the 10-57?" came Mary's reply.

"Hard to tell."

"Hard to tell? Why's that?"

"Sure you want to know? No eyes or face on the corpse. Rats. Stinks too."

"All right, I'll get the assist you requested," said Mary after swallowing hard in order to avoid the reaction Officer Tercel had just had.

Leo Petroni had been tending his plants in his greenhouse when Officer Danny Tercel rolled onto the Nicholson property. Leo's greenhouse sat on a rise with an excellent view of Beat Nicholson's property and the mountains to the west. It was an expansive, domed beauty with five separate, climate-controlled rooms that on its own would have been the envy of any botanist, if Leo had ever opened it to any for display, which he didn't. Its contents were even more impressive. Over the years since his visit to Colombia in the fifties, Leo had collected and cultivated a wide variety of plants, including some of the rarest orchids in the world and, of course, various scopolamine-producing specimens. He had several species, subspecies and varieties of the genera *Atropa*, *Datura*, and *Brugmansia*—all in the Solanaceae family and all good sources of scopolamine. However, he had never found a source of scopolamine that rivaled the *Brugmansia vulcanicola* he had found in 1953 near Nicho, Colombia. The scopolamine he was able to refine from it was the most versatile, potent and fast acting of any he had been able to produce from other plants. Privately, since he did not want to draw attention to himself and his leisure activity of raping young women, he named it *Brugmansia vulcanicola petronis*. Over the years since his first visit, he had returned two times to the area in Colombia where he first discovered his prized Angel's Trumpet, but he could find no trace of it, or, for that matter, of any other wild *Brugmansia*. It was very possible that the plants in his greenhouse were the only ones in the world. During his visits to Colombia, he had also looked for the grave of the teenage runaway he had buried in the jungle, but that too was gone. He had done so only out of curiosity as to whether the grave had been discovered, and not because of any remorse or desire to pay his respects to the young girl who had had the misfortune of crossing his path.

Although his eightieth birthday was less than a year away, Leo was in excellent health and physical condition, which he attributed to being a vegetarian, practicing yoga on a daily basis and having sex with young women. The latter he practiced whenever he could, which wasn't enough in his opinion. Leo preferred women in their late teens and twenties. They were generally more voluptuous and easier to ensnare than older women. He noticed that the older he got, the less threatened young women felt by him, as if the older a person got, the nicer they became. Just the opposite was true of him. Although he was retired from the attorney general's office, he traveled a lot around the country as a public-utilities legal consultant, political lobbyist for power and coal companies and as a Republican Party utilities adviser. This gave him access to a bevy of young women who were easy to impress with his power and wealth. Sometimes, he would mentor and groom them into his snare. Some of his victims suspected that he had raped them, but they could never be sure since the scopolamine wiped out their memories. For the rare few who were bold enough to confront him with his transgression, he threatened to ruin their careers and reputations and correctly pointed out that no one would accept their word over his. Since his name was quite prominent in the Denver area, as added protection against discovery, he stopped practicing his dark art in the Denver area years ago and never brought any of his prey to his home. To do so would have risked discovery by neighbors, his wife and his two daughters when they had been living at home. He was a wily and cautious predator.

On February 11, Leo had gone to his greenhouse to make sure the climate controls were properly set to protect his plants against the cold. After he had assured himself that all was good, he decided to process some scopolamine for an upcoming trip to California since his supply was running low. As he unlocked the cabinet where he kept his processing equipment and supply of processed scopolamine, he glanced over at the Nicholson property and noticed a police squad car parked near the camping trailer. An involuntary shiver ran over his body at the sight of police so close while he has preparing for future felonies. It was a brief, illogical reaction soon overcome by logic and curiosity. Within a few seconds, he saw a cop come running out the front door and bend over near the side of the house. *Is he puking?* It was hard to tell from his vantage point, but it looked like the officer was throwing up. Leo decided to continue with his work while periodically looking up to monitor the Nicholson property. Within fifteen minutes, a white van and another police car arrived. Both had their lights flashing. Leo picked up a pair of binoculars he kept on his workbench and scanned the vehicles. The van had Wheat Ridge Medical Examiner written along its side. Two uniformed people got out of the van while a cop got out of the patrol car. They briefly huddled with the cop who had puked before rubbing something from a jar under their noses and entering the property. Leo finished his work, locked up his equipment and scopolamine, grabbed his coat and gloves, and headed for the Nicholson property.

After he slipped and slid his way with one ignominious butt plant, Leo arrived at the Nicholson property, walked past the police vehicles and arrived at the front door. Since it wasn't taped off as a crime scene, there seemed no harm in opening it. He did so slowly and immediately experienced the heady aroma of death. There were two cops and two others he assumed were the medical examiner and his female assistant, an attractive woman of about thirty. They had all been engaged in deep conversation in a circle around the corpse on the floor, but turned when he entered.

The woman came towards him and commanded, "Sir, don't come any farther."

Leo stopped in his tracks and saw on her jacket that she was the medical examiner in charge. *Guess the times are changin' and not for the best,* he thought. Out loud he said, "What happened?"

"That's what I'm here to find out," said the woman. "I'm Doctor Mercedes Planter, medical examiner. Who are you?"

"Leonard Petroni—I'm a neighbor. I live next door. So, what happened?" he inquired again as deferentially as he could.

"As I said, that's what I'm here to find out. You any relation to the Petroni whose name is on the strip malls and office buildings around town?"

"That's me," said Leo. Since he had disengaged himself from the Smaldones three decades ago, there was no longer the original danger of being discovered as their government spy. Thus, it was safe to rebrand the properties he had bought with laundered mob-related funds. Having his name on the properties was a bit like a wild animal marking its territory to establish its dominance. It bolstered his already enlarged ego and enhanced his confidence in entrapping young women and in bullying any who later stood up to him.

By this time, the other two police officers were standing next to them, making Leo a tad uncomfortable. Only Officer Tercel registered anything close to being impressed at Leo's announcement.

"How well did you know Beat Nicholson?" asked Dr. Planter.

"Not well—he kept to himself and just focused on working on his house. Is that him?" asked Leo while pointing at the corpse. Leo was almost certain it was, since the corpse had the same clothes on that Beat usually wore.

"When was the last time you talked to him?" she asked, ignoring his question.

"Oh, I don't know—weeks ago."

"And, the last time you were on this property?"

"The last time I talked to him," said Leo, trying very hard not to sound snarky.

Officer Tercel looked at Dr. Planter who signaled with a sideways glance that she was done, so he said, "All right, Mr. Petroni, if we need anything more from you, one of us will be in contact with you. Come outside with me so I can get your contact information."

Leo was eager to get way from the stench. Although he doubted that the odor-masking salve under the others' noses did much to disguise the smell of decay, it was more than he had to suppress his gag reflex. After giving his contact information to Officer Tercel, Leo headed back to his house but kept a close eye on the Nicholson property from then on.

Over the ensuing days, Leo not only kept his eye, but put his feet, on the Nicholson property. During his years of preying upon young women, he had gained some skills of a thief—lock picking being one. Compared to many he had encountered, Beat's lock was child's play.

At first, he was drawn by base curiosity about what he might find. Other than some construction materials, tools and debris and a lingering scent of decomposition, there really wasn't much of value in the way of personal items in the house, or outside it. However, the house and the lot were another matter. Leo knew value when he saw it, especially when it came to real estate. He already knew that the lot by itself was very valuable. He had witnessed the sales prices of even standard lots in Indian Paintbrush Estates skyrocket after the recession in the early eighties, and the Nicholson lot was way better than standard. It was one of only two in this desirable, secluded cul-de-sac. However, he was surprised with the house. It appeared to be very well made with a well-thought-out floor plan. Leo believed that entrances, whether of people or in houses, should be impressive, and this one was. It was three-stories high with glass extending from the entrance all the way to the pinnacled cornice that provided magnificent views of the Rocky Mountains from the spiral staircase and second- and third-floor bridges. It gave a sense of arrival and established the wealth and primacy of the homeowner. There were fireplaces with beautiful rockwork in the living room, kitchen and all the bedrooms. The floors had hot-water pipes running under them, and there were outlets in the walls leading to a central vacuum system. There also were electrical wires dangling from the ceilings and walls; knocked-out walls; an open-to-the-sky section covered with plastic; a large hole in the backyard; and the miasma of death. There was a lot of potential, but also a lot of work to be done and redone.

Nine days after his conversation with Dr. Planter and Officer Tercel, Leo was once again in his greenhouse when he noticed activity at Beat Nicholson's property. This time there was a pickup, a U-Haul van and a blue sedan in the yard. He grabbed his coat and dashed out the door. Since the temperature was in the forties, this time there should not be any near-disastrous falls caused by ice. There was mud, however. In his rush, he carelessly stepped on a mat of soggy, muddy leaves that lubricated the sole of his left shoe sending his foot out in front of him and his body soundly into the muddy ditch next to the street. In order to extricate himself, he had to roll over and lift himself with his hands and knees, thus getting himself filthier. *Dammit, what a fucking mess,* he thought. There didn't seem to be anything more damaged than his ego, so he got up and proceeded to the Nicholson property with a more regulated pace. As he approached the house, he decided to use his muddied condition to his advantage

When he arrived at the front door, Leo knocked once and then again more loudly. When the door opened, Leo was momentarily caught off guard and exclaimed, "What the..." Except for a neater haircut and less-shabby clothes, the man before him was either Beat Nicholson raised from the dead or an exact copy. Since he wasn't sitting in Hell, he knew the Second Coming had not occurred; therefore, it must be the latter. Until then, Leo had not known that Beat's brother was a twin.

The man's face also registered surprise and then concern. Leo looked like a pathetic old man in need of help and not the villainous scoundrel he really was.

Having recovered from his initial shock, Leo collected his thoughts and said, "I'm Beat's next-door neighbor, Leonard Petroni. You must be Beat's twin brother, Lawrence, from Santa Fe. I am so sorry for your loss. And, I'm really sorry to bother you, but I was taking a walk, and I slipped and fell."

Lawrence said, "Are you all right?"

"I fell into some mud—obviously. I'm a little shaken and a bit dizzy." Leo was an expert at playing the sympathy card.

"Let's get you over to Beat's trailer and have a cup of tea— if you can walk OK."

"I'm a little wobbly, but I think I can make it with some help."

Lawrence held Leonard's right arm to steady the old man. As they walked towards the camper trailer, a couple of Hispanic men carried some tools and chairs past them and loaded them into the pickup.

When they got inside the trailer, Lawrence brought Leo some old towels. "Here, you can use these to get some of that mud off. Then have a seat at the table. Unfortunately, the water to the house is shut off and the pump in the trailer froze, so the only water I have is the drinking water I brought in that five-gallon container and most of that is gone. But, I have enough for the tea I promised."

Lawrence brought some water to a boil on the small gas stove as Leo toweled the mud off as best he could and wondered how Beat had managed to live for so many years in the close confines of this aluminum can. When the tea was ready, Lawrence poured a cup for Leo. Leo took a sip and wished he hadn't. It tasted like it had been brewed during the Ming Dynasty.

After repressing the urge to spew it in Lawrence's direction, Leo said, "Oh, this is good, very good. Thank you."

Lawrence looked at Leo like he was nuts, and said, "It's all I have to offer right now. I'm afraid my brother didn't leave much in the way of supplies—or estate."

"Really, this is great," lied Leo. "When did you arrive in Colorado?"

"Night before last."

"Do you have a place to stay?" asked Leo in a voice that suggested he might be willing to offer Lawrence a room in his house, which he wasn't. Since Lawrence had arrived two nights ago and had stayed somewhere else those two nights, it was a safe gambit while appearing to be generous.

"Yeah, I have a room at the Radisson. I'd just as soon stay there and not too close to this."

"So, did the rest of your family come with you or stay in Santa Fe?"

"You're looking at the rest of my family—just me. I was married several years ago, but we both agreed it wasn't working. Fortunately, we didn't have any kids."

"So, are you taking care of all this yourself? Don't you have any other family—brothers, sisters, whoever—to help?"

"No, just me. I'm the dead end of the Nicholson line. Anyway, I have everything pretty much under control. I'm giving away most of Beat's worldly goods to the guys who are moving things out to the U-Haul and pickup, so unless you can make this house disappear, I don't see how you can help." Lawrence was independently wealthy and did not need or want the house or any proceeds from its sale. It was nothing more than a huge burden that he needed to dump as quickly as possible in order to get back and run his highly profitable art gallery. However, given the condition and smell of the property, he knew it would be a challenge to do that.

Like the predatory animal he was, Leo sensed vulnerability and an opportunity to profit off that vulnerability. Leo feigned thoughtful contemplation even though he had already formulated a plan. After a count of ten, he said, "You know, I'm an attorney, and there just might be something I can do for you. Would you give me a ride up to my house? We can discuss it up there. I'm still a bit unstable and could use the help. Bring your water container, and you can fill it at my house."

"Yeah, sure—happy to help. Not much I can do here right now, anyway."

Leo maintained the ruse of a frail old man. In response, Lawrence responded with kindness and assisted the old faker to his car and then from his car into Leo's house. There, Leo led the way to his kitchen where he offered something a little stronger to drink than tea—liquor, the elixir for bad deals. Lawrence accepted a scotch, and Leo waited for its warming effects to settle in while making small talk. After pouring a second for Lawrence and taking a sip of his first, Leo moved in on his target.

"So, like I said back at Beat's, I may have a way of helping you. Let's explore that together and see what you think," purred Leo.

"OK," replied Lawrence before taking another drink of his scotch.

"That house appears to be an unwanted problem for you, and I don't blame you. It would be for me too. I mean, it's in a state of...well, I'm not even sure how to characterize it. It's a mess—a mess that's going to take a lot of work to correct. I'm not even sure it can be corrected. The whole house might have to come down, and that's going to be expensive. And, that.... I don't know any delicate way of saying this, so please excuse how this may sound. I mean no disrespect to your brother or to your loss. The smell of death is everywhere in the house. That's a hard smell to get rid of. There aren't many, if any, potential buyers who are going to want to buy a house, their future home, with that. That in itself really drives the value down."

"Yeah, I know. It's been weighing on my mind."

Good, good—just what I wanted to hear you say.

Out loud, Leo continued with, "Now, like I said, this would be difficult for me or anyone who owned it, but I'm the only person who lives next door to Beat's house, so it would be easier— not easy, mind you—just less onerous for me to deal with everything, and out of respect for Beat, I'd be willing to take it on. I really liked Beat. We were pretty close, you know."

"Really? Beat never mentioned you."

"Well, I'm not surprised, I guess. That sounds just like Beat, doesn't it?"

"Yeah, I suppose it does. Always focused on his house—that was Beat."

Nice, very nice, now let me reel you in, thought Leo.

"So, what's your proposal?"

"Well, have you ever heard of a quitclaim deed?"

"No, can't say that I have," answered Lawrence.

"A quitclaim deed kinda does what its name implies. The person who signs it agrees to quit any claim they have or may have to a piece of real estate and to transfer that claim to the person being granted that claim. You could sign a quitclaim granting me any rights you might have to Beat's house and land."

"Don't I have to go through the courts first? I think it's called probate."

"That's what it's called, and no you don't. See, that's the beauty of a quitclaim deed. You don't have to own the property to quitclaim it. You're just sayin' that if you do own any interest in the property, whether you do or not, that you're giving up that interest to the person you're granting it to—me in this case. Hell, I could quitclaim any interest I might have in the Empire State Building, and it would be totally legal, and I wouldn't have any liability for doing it. In fact, you'd be getting out from under any liability and handing it over to me."

Lawrence blinked while absorbing what he had just been told. He drained the last of his second scotch, and Leo refilled his glass. After taking another drink, Lawrence said, "And, after signing one of these quitclaim deeds, I can just drive away from here and not have to think about this property again?"

"That's right," said Leo with repressed excitement.

"All right, then, let's do it. How long till you can get a quitclaim deed drawn up."

"Ten minutes sound good to you? I have a quitclaim-deed form about thirty feet away. It's a one-page, fill-in-the-blank form. I know the legal description already. It's just a lot and block description that is one lot lower than mine. Just need a notary to notarize your signature. We could go to my bank about ten minutes max from here."

"What are we waiting for?" responded Lawrence enthusiastically.

Within an hour, Leo was back in his home with a signed and notarized quitclaim deed to his deceased neighbor's property signed by the owner's only surviving heir. Other than some paper, ink and scotch, it had cost him nothing. Of course, he would have to record the document with the Jefferson County Clerk and Recorder, so there would be some cost there, and he would have to clear title through a court action, which would cost a little. But, essentially he paid nothing for the title to a very valuable piece of property.

The next day he walked, careful not to slip, down to his new acquisition and posted a handmade sign in front of it and another at the entrance to the cul-de-sac, advertising "OPEN HOUSE" over "HOME FOR SALE" with his name, address and telephone number underneath.

CHAPTER 7

Lodging Complaint

March 1986–August 1988

Blair Barker and Rita Draper were perfect for each other. They depended upon each other; empowered each other—enabled each other.

Rita had trust issues—of others and in herself—while also craving approval. One way she fed that craving was through public recognition of her excellent photography. Another was through indiscriminate sex with multiple partners—male and female. She also feared rejection and abandonment. In order to prevent that, she tried always to be the first to reject and abandon. Her affair in Alaska with Ranger Elliot Mercer was just one example among many of how she dealt with her foibles. But her list of weaknesses did not stop with trust, approval and sex. Rita found decision-making, truth-telling and anger-managing to be challenging at times. However, her relationship with Blair Barker was different while being born out of the same flaws.

Blair could be inordinately optimistic and joyful or just as pessimistic and sorrowful. Sometimes he was filled with uncontrollable energy making grandiose plans for the future, and at others he moped about expressing inner thoughts of suicide. He could be warm and friendly or bristly and hostile. None of his broad mood swings came with a schedule. Blair was bipolar. He needed someone to care for him—someone he could depend upon. Because of his disorder, there was no possibility that he would reject or abandon the person providing that care, as long as that person was willing to devote, if not martyr, herself to his care and as long as his mood swings could be moderated. Blair needed someone to rescue him, and Rita needed someone to rescue. Blair was a safe haven from men like Elliot Mercer who was too handsome, too intelligent, too kind and too desirable by other women to be trusted. Rita would rather be one of those other women than the wife who feared them. Although she thought she loved Blair, Rita's true core emotion for him was pity, and that pity cemented her return to him after each of her escapades with other lovers.

For mood moderation there were drugs—specifically, lithium-based drugs. As is the case with mood-moderating drugs, lithium came with side effects—some worse than others. Those experienced by Blair included persistent thirst and the need to pee; loss of hair and gain in weight; and muscle weakness. Lithium was difficult to modulate. Taking a nonsteroidal anti-inflammatory drug, like ibuprofen, could increase the levels of lithium in his body. Too little salt in his diet could do the same thing, but too much increased his blood pressure, and his blood pressure was already a little too high. Mostly, he was fine with his manic highs. It was the people around him who suffered. But the depressive lows were very difficult on him. While lithium didn't completely or always bring him within a normal range of highs and lows, it did tamp both ends of the emotional spectrum together so that most people didn't notice his affliction. He was tolerable, for the most part, when taking the medication. He needed the drug, but it couldn't be used like a fire hose to put out a fire. He had to take it, not only during a manic or depressive episode, but between episodes as maintenance therapy. Unfortunately, long-term use could cause permanent kidney damage. He felt like he was a damned test tube in a child's chemistry set—filled with a random mixture of chemicals while always at risk of being broken at any reckless moment. He needed Rita to give him balance in his life, and she needed him to need her.

They met a little over two years ago at a party of a mutual acquaintance. Blair was off his lithium and on one of his manic highs pontificating on anything and everything to a rapt group of four females, since he was an authority on anything and everything when having a manic episode. One of the females was Rita. Upon seeing Blair hold forth from across the room, Rita's date came over to hear the conversation and, after listening to some it, told Rita that Blair was full of crap. When she said she wanted to hear more, her date grabbed her arm and pulled her away. Blair jumped to her rescue and delivered a Sunday punch to Rita's date with such force it sent him into a table of hors d'oeuvres and Blair into a barred cell for three months followed by three more of probation. As a result, Blair lost his lucrative job as a construction subforeman on a long-term residential construction project and his apartment lease. Prior to the party, Rita had been in the final stages of her relationship with the man covered in hors d'oeuvres on the floor, and rather than ministering to his injuries, she used the incident as an excuse to finish it for good. She then started to visit Blair in jail and fell in pity of him. During those visits, she witnessed his depressive lows—the hardest being the day before his release from incarceration when his mother died. Upon Blair's release, they got permission from his probation officer to go to California for his mother's funeral and to mop up her estate which mostly consisted of a small retirement fund and a house in Los Angeles. While in California, Blair became more and more dependent upon Rita while Rita enabled his dependence by mothering him. Toward the end of their time in Los Angeles, Blair proposed to Rita, and she accepted with the intent of stretching the engagement out as long as possible. During the whole time of their relationship, Rita would impulsively have sex with other partners anywhere and anytime the mood struck her. Blair either didn't notice, or if he did, he didn't seem to care. When they returned to Denver, Rita helped him get his personal belongings out of storage where his landlord had sent them, and then Blair moved into Rita's cramped apartment. It was obvious that Rita's apartment was too small for the two of them, especially with her makeshift photographic darkroom, cameras, developing equipment and photos taking up a majority of the living space. However, her assignment to Alaska got in the way of doing anything about it. After her return from Alaska, Rita found it impossible to work on her book in the close confines of her apartment and was barely able to finish the National Geographic piece. It was time to look for somewhere else to live, and she now had the time.

They soon rejected renting anything in downtown Denver. It was too busy for their liking and too expensive for their wallets. After more searching, they decided that renting anything anywhere was not a desirable option. Rita wanted some place where Blair could build a darkroom to her specifications, and they could never do that in a rental. They also wanted some place close to the foothills with beautiful views. Wheat Ridge was the obvious choice, so they focused their search there. Since Rita was wealthier and had a better-established credit history than Blair, free of a police record, they agreed that title to their new home would be in her name only.

March 8, 1986

Blair awoke full of energy. His mind was flooded with creative ideas about where he and Rita should look for a home; how they should purchase one; a new construction business he would start to develop residential subdivisions; taking up flying so he could visit his projects across the state and then the nation; and so many things, he couldn't hold any one in his mind long enough to realize its flaws. He was euphoric. He was horny. It was two fifteen in the morning. He nudged Rita. She woke up and grunted.

Blair said in a rush of words that collided with each other as he said them, "Oh good, you're awake. Let's have sex."

She looked over at the clock radio on the nightstand and then back at him, "It's two in the morning."

"Actually, it's two fifteen—nope, two sixteen. I feel like Superman," said Blair as he tugged at Rita's nightgown.

"Faster than a speeding bullet?" asked Rita, immediately regretting her comment. Such a comment could bring on a violent fit, but this time it did not. She knew what that meant. It meant that Blair was having one of his lesser-manic episodes. His therapist called it hypomania—not as pronounced, or dangerous, as a full-on manic episode, but still filled with its own challenges. Until Blair came down off it, he would be hyperenergetic, talkative, grandiosely creative, distractible and driven by hypersexuality. The last one she liked even though his technique could use some refinement.

"Oh, come on," he whined while pulling her gown over her head.

After their third coupling, Blair sat up in bed and said, "I think we should look for a house in some place different today."

"You mean, not in Wheat Ridge?"

"No, no, still in Wheat Ridge—just a different place in Wheat Ridge—a different subdivision."

"You obviously have something in mind. Where?"

"Listen to this, OK, so listen, you're gonna love it—Indian Paintbrush Estates. Doesn't that sound great? The places there are high end—much better investments than some tract housing or the mid-range stuff we've been looking at. Whaddayathink, huh?"

Rita pretended to be considering the idea before breaking the obvious to Blair. "Well, Blair, the houses out there are very nice—"

"Yeah, aren't they? I think we deserve something that nice."

"Well...sure...but they're very expensive. I don't think my credit would do it, Blair."

"Don't worry about that. I'll figure something out. I feel real good about this. Doesn't hurt to look, does it?"

"No, I suppose not," Rita conceded.

"All right, so, let's have breakfast and get an early start," said Blair ignoring reality.

"I'd like a little more sleep, hon, so I'm fresh when we go. Besides, no one with a house for sale is going to be up at this time. Why don't you come back to bed and snuggle and then get some more sleep too?"

"Can't sleep. I have too many ideas I want to think about. Wouldn't be able to sleep anyway. I'll just make some coffee and do some work on them. But, try to get up pretty soon so we can go and scope out some properties before anybody else beats us to it. OK?"

"Sure," muttered Rita as she rolled over and fell asleep.

An hour and a half later she couldn't sleep because of the noise created by Blair scurrying about the apartment and in and out of the bedroom while muttering great insights. *Fine, you win, Blair. I'll get up.* She rolled out of bed and shuffled toward the shower where she lingered in order to energize and avoid Blair's bustle. When she ran out of warm water to waste, she came out, dried off, put clothes on and ventured forth to minister to Blair's elevated ego.

She came over to Blair, careful to approach from his front, and said, "How you doin', sweetie?"

"I feel great—better than great. You shouldn't have to ask after this morning's start," he said referring to their earlier sexual frolic and expecting a compliment.

"That was fantastic. You were fantastic," she replied, giving him what he expected and needed and getting none of the same in return.

"Wanna go out to breakfast? We could stop at the Chicken Or Egg. It's on the way to Wheat Ridge," offered Blair.

Rita knew he would suggest the Chicken Or Egg. Not only was it open twenty-four hours a day, but it was Blair's favorite restaurant, mainly because of its open-at-all-hours schedule and not its excellent cuisine, which was absent from its menu and kitchen.

"Sounds like a plan," she said. "Why don't you get our coats?"

When he turned to get their coats, she picked up his bottle of medication, opened it and quickly counted the tablets inside. There were two more than there should have been.

When he returned, she said, "Thanks, I have your meds, so you can take your next dose at the restaurant."

Blair gave her a guilty look and said, "I don't think I need them. You know I feel awful when I take them." He did not want his current sharp edge blunted.

She stroked his arm and said, "I know, sweetie, but we're going out in public, so we need to be on our best behavior."

"Oh, all right—let's go," he said in a pouty voice, and then quickly elevated to his earlier euphoria. "I'm going to have their scrambled eggs, cheese and ham over waffles with coconut syrup."

The Chicken Or Egg advertised "delicious meals served so fast, you won't know which came first—your meal or your order." *They should say, "your meal or your check,"* thought Rita since the check was always laid on the table when the meal was delivered. The clumsy parody of the chicken-or-egg paradox was not what Rita wanted, so she asked the waitress to have the cook take his time. That turned out to mean that instead of taking ten minutes to slap together their meals, it took twenty. Slowdown came through Blair's fast-paced monologue about his current brainstorms, Rita gently nagging him to eat and take his lithium, and repeated refills of coffee.

The sun was just coming up as they left the parking lot. It was a beautiful sunrise, and the weather was pleasant. Already the temperature was in the sixties and was forecasted to get up to seventy-two. It was a good day to shop for a home.

A large expensive-looking sign with a garden around its base brimming with blooming pansies confirmed their arrival at Indian Paintbrush Estates. During their drive through the subdivision, they were able to find five homes with for-sale signs out front. Each of the signs was from the same real estate agent, and each of the homes looked expensive. Regardless, Rita and Blair took notes about each house and the agent's contact information.

At the fifth, Blair made a smacking noise out the side of his mouth.

Rita asked, "So, what did you mean by that?"

"Each of the houses for sale is listed by the same real estate agent," he announced as if that were an answer.

"Right—so what?"

"Well," he began as if lecturing a class of first-graders, "that means that he won't be as willing to take a cut in his commission as he would if he was in competition with other agents in the same neighborhood. That takes away some of my leverage in negotiating."

"Do you really think that he would, or could, cut his commission enough anyway for us to afford any of these houses?"

"Oh, that would only be part of my negotiations. I'm an excellent negotiator."

Blair started the car, drove down the street and around the next corner and stopped suddenly.

They were both staring at Leo's crude, handmade sign.

"Well, that's interesting," said Blair.

"And weird," replied Rita.

Blair drove into the cul-de-sac and turned into the driveway of Beat Nicholson's former construction project. For a moment, they just sat in the car processing the sight before them.

"Let's take a closer look," said Blair.

After walking around the property and peering in windows, Blair turned to Rita and said, "This has promise."

"This is a mess."

"Yeah but, I could fix it up—and to our liking, and it should be less expensive than all those other places. Worth an inquiry, right? Let's drive up to this Leo Petroni's house and find out."

"Sure, nothing to lose, I guess," said Rita, having never met Leo.

A couple minutes later, they were standing in front of the Petronis' front door. Blair rang the doorbell twice in rapid succession and started to a third time, but Rita grabbed his hand and said, "Give the first two some time."

The door opened to reveal an elderly, diminutive, weary-looking woman. "Yes?" was all she said.

"Hi, my name's Blair Barker, and this is my fiancée, Rita Draper. We saw the for-sale sign on the next-door property and were interested in learning more about it."

The old woman turned without responding to him and called, "Leo, someone's here about the Nicholson property."

Within a few minutes an elderly, but fit, man with a charming smile came to the door, and the old woman left without a word more.

"Hello, my name's Leonard Petroni. How can I help you?"

Blair extended his hand and shook Leo's. "I'm Blair Barker and this is my fiancée, Rita Draper. We saw your signs about the next-door house, and we're interested enough to learn more about it."

"I'll get the keys so you can see the inside," said Leo, who took note of Blair's rushed speech pattern.

Leo left Rita and Blair at the door as he went for the house keys. He came back in less than a minute and said, "It's such a beautiful day, let's walk over."

Blair and Leo walked side by side while Rita trailed a few steps behind them. Blair prattled the whole way about his expertise with home construction and real estate ownership; his and Rita's cramped living situation; and Rita's business as a professional photographer and need for a larger space than their current apartment to practice it. Blair even disclosed where they had been looking for houses and the price range of the houses they had inspected. Leo could tell there was something more than slightly askew with Blair.

Leo opened the front door for Rita and Blair to enter, and as they did, they noted a strong, slightly sweet and earthy smell with an undercurrent of something less pleasant.

Blair turned to Leo and asked, "What's that smell?"

Rita answered with her own question, "Patchouli? Smells like an old-dirty-hippie love-in."

Leo laughed and said without answering Blair or the 'why' in Rita's statement, "No, I doubt there was any love-in by anyone, much less hippies—clean or dirty." He then escorted them through the rest of the house and, later, took them for a walk around the perimeter. During the walkaround, Leo volunteered nothing while monitoring Rita's and Blair's facial and body language the whole time. Rita expressed much with hers but held her tongue. The only one who made any sound was Blair who overplayed the skeptical potential buyer by murmuring, grunting and umming for dramatic effect.

When they came to the end of the tour, Leo locked the doors, turned to Rita and Blair and said, "Want to come up and talk more?"

That won't be hard, since we've done damned little talking so far, thought Rita.

"Sounds good," said Blair thinking he sounded less excited than he did.

On the way back to his home, Leo expounded upon what a delightful neighborhood Indian Paintbrush Estates was and how quiet and friendly the neighbors were while respecting each other's privacy. Blair bit on the bait and related how he and Rita fit that profile perfectly, especially Rita who was a professional photographer focused on her photography and not gossip about others.

Upon entering his home, Leo led his quarry to his kitchen, as he had with Lawrence Nicholson, but given the early hour of the day, offered coffee and tea rather than anything intoxicating. He had a strong feeling that booze would not be required this time to get what he wanted.

"Thanks, I've already had enough coffee to launch a battleship. I'll just take a glass of water and directions to your bathroom," said Rita.

"Same for me, thanks," said Blair.

Upon their return, Rita opened with, "What was that smell? There was something besides patchouli. Something less pleasant. Smelled like a big dead rat."

"Oh, yeah, we had rats," answered Leo, neither lying nor telling the truth. "I'm getting those exterminated though." Leo had no intention of following through with that promise.

"Just a rat?"

Thinking better of carrying the lie of omission further, Leo said, "The previous owner died in the house while building it and wasn't found for a few days. The smell will go away with time. It's one of the main reasons I'm willing to sell the place so cheap. The other is that the house is only partly finished. It would be perfect for someone like you two, especially you, Blair, since you obviously have a lot of construction experience and talent." There was nothing obvious about Blair's construction skills or talent, but Leo was playing to Blair's ego which was obvious. With Rita's and Blair's arrival, Leo now thought he might have a way for cleaning up the property and completing construction on the house that would benefit him with little cost or risk on his part.

Flattery and talk of a cheap price were all it took for Blair to abandon his grand scheme for finessed negotiations, which had already been abandoned through his incessant prattle. "So, what's your cheap price?" he blundered in.

Based upon Blair's previously volunteered disclosures about the types and prices of houses he and Rita had looked at, Leo had a pretty good idea of what they could afford. "How about somewhere around two hundred thousand dollars."

Blair practically exploded with surprise and delight. Even in its current condition, Blair guessed that the property was worth four, maybe five times, that price. Using all his willpower, he managed to keep most of his enthusiasm inside, and said, "Well, that wouldn't be too bad if it didn't have that smell and need so much work to complete the house, and then there'd be grading and landscaping."

"You drive a hard bargain, Mr. Barker. You know, I'd like to get this off my back, and I'm kinda picky about the people I want for neighbors. If I didn't live next door to that property, I'd just sell to the highest bidder. But the highest bidder is probably going to be somebody who buys the place as an investment, sticks a bunch of money into it and then sells it in one or two years for a huge profit. You two don't impress me that way. You seem like folks who want a home and would stay in it even though the value goes up like they have been here in Indian Paintbrush Estates. I don't know if you know this, but the values here have been increasing way faster than anything else in Wheat Ridge."

"That's true," said Rita. "We intend to make this our long-term, permanent home."

"Well, all right, tell you what," continued Leo. "Let's see how we can make this happen. How about we make the purchase price two hundred thousand and you put down—oh—say, five thousand? The rest would be in the form of a promissory note payable at the closing when you get some financing together for the purchase." After a pause for effect, Leo said, "You know what? I'd even be willing to make the promissory note interest free, and you could move into the house and start repairs and remodeling before the closing. Of course, I'd want to check some credit references, like your bank, first."

At that announcement, Rita stepped into the negotiations with, "Well, that would be my credit rating since title would be taken in my name only."

"Hmm," was all Leo said, before adding, "Well, I'd want some references for your past construction work, Blair. That wouldn't be a problem, would it?"

Blair glanced at Rita before answering. "Well, I don't have a job right now. And, I lost my last job after I…"

"After you what?" asked Leo.

"Well, I, ah. I was in prison for a couple a months and lost my job as a construction subforeman. Let me explain."

This was good. Leo had thought he was in the weakened bargaining position because he didn't own the property he was selling, but with this announcement, Blair just became the crippled negotiator. "Please do," said Leo.

"A couple of years ago, I was talking to Rita at a party—that's where we met—and some guy came up to her and harassed her, so I hit him and got arrested. I got three months jail time for that, lost my job and haven't been able to get another since."

Leo suspected that Blair wasn't giving the whole story to him, but he didn't care. Since Blair had been a construction subforeman, he must have some construction skills, and since he couldn't get a permanent job now, he would be totally dedicated to working on the Nicholson property if Leo could lure him into living there. "Sounds like you did the chivalrous thing to me. After all, you did get the girl. The justice system can be so unfair sometimes. Do you think your former employer would still give you a good rating on the quality of the work you did?"

"Oh yeah, I think he would. I did the best work of anyone out there."

I doubt that, but if you did halfway-decent work, you'll suit my needs. "Good, then assuming that all checks out, I'm willing to enter into a contract to sell the property to you. What do you say, Rita?"

"Yeah, I guess, sounds good," she replied. "I can call my bank and let them know you'll be calling them."

"Blair, you should do the same with your old employer," said Leo. "Assuming that all checks out, I can prepare a contract for the sale. I'll make it as simple as possible by using a preprinted, standard, buy-and-sell real estate form—printed by Bradford publishing."

"Oh, I know those. I can do it," offered Blair.

Leo was tempted to let Blair fill in the blanks on the form since there was a legal rule that any ambiguity in a contract should be interpreted against the person who drafted it. However, to ensure that the contract had an escape clause for him to get possession of the property back after he had gotten what he wanted from Blair and Rita, he needed to take control of that task. "I'm sure you can, Blair. You're a very talented man, but I am an attorney. Why not let me do this?"

"It's OK, hon," said Rita. "Let Leo prepare the contract."

"Oh, OK."

"Let's get together again on Tuesday. That should give me enough time to call your bank rep, Rita, and your former boss, Blair, and to prepare the contract. Meet here at ten in the morning?"

"OK, ten on Tuesday the eleventh," said Rita, and Blair shook his head in agreement.

Rita and Blair left after providing their telephone numbers and the contact information for Blair's former employer and Rita's bank officer. As they neared Rita's car, Blair said, "Did you see how I handled that? Boy, did I get you a great deal or what?"

"Yes, you did, dear."

March 11, 1986

On Tuesday, Rita and Blair were back in Leo's kitchen drinking coffee. Blair had been taking his medication and was in a good mood, neither hyper-elevated nor hopelessly depressed.

"Both your bank and former employer checked out, so here is the contract I put together. It's pretty straight forward like I said it would be. The promissory note is underneath," said Leo.

Rita took the contract and Blair took the note. When she got to the part about the closing date, Rita asked, "There's no closing date filled in. Why not?"

"As you know, we can't know what that is until I get title. See, there, under paragraphs 12 and 19(e), it says that I need to get title to the property before transferring to you."

Rita and Blair gave each other blank stares.

Leo said, "I told you that. Remember?"

Blair was tongue-tied. Rita said, "No—no, you didn't."

"Are you sure?" asked Leo with a feigned-worry look.

"Yes, I'm sure. How could you even put a for-sale sign on the property if you didn't own it?" continued Rita.

"I don't know how I could have forgotten to say that. Sometimes I worry that I might be losing my mind. I am almost eighty, you know." Leo was mentally sharper than most men in their twenties. "In a way, I already have title. I just have to get a court to declare that I do. See, after the owner died in the house, his brother and sole-surviving heir relinquished all of his rights to the property to me by what's called a quitclaim deed. All I need to do is go through something called a quiet title action to get legal title."

"I'm sure I would have remembered if you had said anything like that, Leo."

Finally, Blair awoke from his trance and asked, "How long will that take?"

"That's a really a good question, Blair. It all depends," answered Leo.

"Depends on what?" asked Rita.

On how much work I can squeeze out of the two of you before you give up, he thought, but said, "How long it takes my lawyer to do it." *Which will be as long as I tell him to take.* "See, notices have to be published in the paper a certain number of times and some record searches have to be made to see if there are any other potential heirs, creditors or whoever that might think they have a claim to the property. Then, there has to be a hearing. I'd say we'll be done with all that in six months max—more likely three. In the meantime, you live in it like it's your own, because it will be." *Until I take it back.*

"Well, let's write something in the blank for the closing date to reflect that," said Rita.

"OK, that's a good idea," said Leo, and he got out his pen and wrote, *once Seller gets legal title,* in the blank. "There, how's that?"

Blair was so hungry for the property that he blurted out, "That does it," before Rita could speak.

After a little more attempted review of the contract while their attention was riveted on the verbal bomb just delivered by Leo,

Rita signed the contract, promissory note and a check for $5,000 made out to Leo.

Leo then signed the contract and said, "Let me make a copy of this for you."

"When can we pick that up?" asked Rita.

"In just ten minutes. I have a new Savin copier in my office. You can relax here with another cup of coffee. I'll be right back."

Leo went to his office and started his copy machine. While it warmed up, he took out his pen and made a note on the third page of the contract before making a copy. Leo felt smug and empowered, as he always did when he got what he wanted, whether from a business transaction or the young women he raped.

May 8, 1986

After leaving Leo on March 11 with a copy of their newly signed contract in hand, Rita and Blair immediately got busy with making their new home habitable enough for them to move in. That meant winterizing a bedroom and small living area and making the kitchen functional. Glamorization would have to come later. With both of them working together, they were able to move out of Rita's monthly rented apartment and into their work-in-progress on April 1. The irony of their date of possession was not lost on Leo. Next came constructing a darkroom and getting it set up so that Rita could work on her book and photo projects that came along while Blair continued to work on the rest of the house. That took more effort and time since the final product had to be a first-rate, professional-photographer's work area. By sacrificing all of their time and social life, they were able to get it done just before Rita left for a photo assignment at the Exploratorium in San Francisco. She had been called in by Andrew Edison, a staff writer and photographer with the Associated Press, to help him with a piece on the museum and its founder, Frank Oppenheimer, who had just died in 1985. Oppenheimer had a long and colorful history, including working on the Manhattan Project, being blacklisted by the House Un-American Activities Committee, then operating a cattle ranch in Colorado before getting back into academia at the University of Colorado and starting the Exploratorium. It was an exciting piece that would help pay the bills while she and Blair were trying to stabilize their living situation. It also gave her some respite from the construction and Blair and a chance to work under Andy Edison with whom she had collaborated professionally and sexually in the past.

Since the contract signing, Leo had kept his distance from the two. He wanted them to work undisturbed and get fully committed to the house before revealing his next move. Although he did not see Rita leave for San Francisco on May 5, he did notice her absence, and by May 8 it was evident that she would be gone for several days. It was time for that move.

Leo walked in on Blair while he was bent over some old plans left by Beat Nicholson. Blair had his back to the door that Leo came through and didn't notice him until Leo said, "How's it goin', neighbor?"

Blair jumped knocking over a cup of coffee on the table he was hovered over.

"Oh, no, I'm sorry. Did I scare you?"

Blair turned to see Leo standing within ten feet of him with some papers in his right hand. "No, no, just a little surprised. Wasn't expecting anyone to come in—least of all you."

"Yeah, I've been keeping my distance so you could work without any distractions. Place looks like it's coming along pretty good, Blair."

"You think so?"

"Oh, yeah, it looks great. I'm impressed," said Leo trying to honey-trap a fly.

"Let me show you what I've done."

Blair led Leo on a tour of the portions of the house he and Rita had worked on with special emphasis on the darkroom while taking all the credit himself. When they ended at the place they began, Leo said, "Very impressive, Blair. Guess I'd better get out of your hair. Keep up the good work." After he turned to leave, he suddenly turned back and said, "Darn, I almost forgot why I came over. Gotta watch out for those senior moments."

"It wasn't to take a look at the house?"

"Well, of course," he said while thinking, *but I wouldn't deliver these if I had seen little progress.* "But, I realized I had forgotten to bring these over before." He handed the papers in his hand to Blair and watched for his reaction.

As he looked at the papers, Blair said, "I don't understand. Why are you giving me these—now?" The papers in his hand were invoices for property taxes, homeowner association dues and insurance premiums on the house he was working on.

"Well, you know, those are your responsibility—well, I guess Rita's really."

"I don't think so," said Blair.

"Sure, they are, Blair. Do you have your copy of the contract here? I'll show you."

"Yeah," said Blair in a daze from the shock of Leo's announcement, as he left to get Rita's copy of the contract.

When he returned, they went over to the makeshift table Blair had been leaning over when Leo first came in. Leo took the contract and opened it to page three and said, "See, right there."

Blair couldn't believe he had missed what he was reading, but Leo was correct. Right there on page three were the words in Leo's handwriting: *Buyer shall pay when due all costs associated with the property, including, but not limited to, taxes, HOA dues and insurance premiums.* Blair was dumbstruck.

"We talked about that. Don't you remember?" lied Leo.

"No," was all Blair could force between his lips, as he headed downward into depression.

"Well, I'm pretty sure we did. Look, tell Rita she has to pay those before they incur a bunch of late fees and interest. She doesn't want that to happen. Not only would it be expensive, but it would be a breach of the contract, and I'd hate to have that happen."

Blair had tears welling up in his eyes.

"You going to be OK, Blair?"

"Yeah, I'll have to talk to Rita."

"OK, good—great job on the house, Blair. Keep it up," said Leo as he made his exit.

———————

Just before six, the telephone rang. Even though he knew it would keep ringing until he answered it, Blair let it go on for a full twenty rings before picking up. It was Rita's checkup call before she went out to dinner and into bed with Andy Edison.

As soon as he picked up the receiver and said "Hello," Rita knew something was wrong.

"Hi, hon," she ventured cautiously. "You OK?"

"Uh-huh—how are you? Having a good time?"

I was until you answered, she thought, but said, "Yeah, Andy and I are doing some great work together. The article is going to be very interesting. Look, sweetie, you sound a little down. Did you take your lithium like you're supposed to?"

"I might have missed this evening's dose."

"Hon, will you take that right now, please?"

"Sure," he said and put the receiver down. When he picked it up again, he said, "OK, all taken."

"Did something go wrong today, sweetie?" asked Rita.

"Oh, no, got a lot done on the house. Leo did come over, and I gave him a tour of the work."

"Leo? Haven't seen him for a couple of months. What did he want?"

"Oh, nothin' too important. I can handle it."

Rita could tell that whatever happened with Leo was too important and Blair could not handle it.

"OK, hon—just wanted to check in. You have a good night. Love ya."

"Uh-huh," was all he said.

After hanging up, Rita gave her regrets to Andy and caught a redeye flight to Denver.

May 9, 1986

As Rita drove into the driveway, she noticed that one of the large windows next to the entry was broken and covered with a clear-plastic sheet. She got out of her Jeep and walked toward the door trying to avoid the broken glass on the ground. She approached guardedly. If Blair was off his lithium, he could be dangerous—even to her. She knocked on the front door and waited. The door opened revealing a wide-eyed, disheveled Blair. Upon seeing her, he was both relieved and worried, but remained agitated.

"May I come in?" she asked.

"Oh, my, of course—it's your house, after all. I wasn't expecting you. The place is a bit of a mess."

That was an understatement she discovered upon entering the foyer. It was apparent that Blair had had one of his uncontrolled lashing-out episodes. She was glad she had missed it, but then again, probably could have prevented it if she had been present.

Rita gave Blair a hug and said, "You sounded like you needed a hug when we talked."

"You didn't need to come home. Everything is fine."

"I could use some coffee and breakfast. How about you?" asked Rita.

"Yeah, me too," said Blair while following Rita.

As she walked to the kitchen, Rita took note of other damage wrought by Blair and was relieved to find that most of his violence had been concentrated in the foyer. She then prepared a simple breakfast of fried eggs, bacon, toast, jam and coffee.

Talk was limited to banal banter about work to be done on the house until Rita felt that Blair's blood sugar was stabilized enough for her to delve into the topic of her concern. "So, what happened yesterday to upset you? And, don't say nothing. The evidence of something is out there in the entryway."

Blair exhaled a big sigh and said, "Leo came by yesterday, and I gave him a tour of the house to show him all the work we've done already."

"That should have impressed and pleased him."

"Yeah, it did, but before he left, he handed me these." Blair opened a drawer in the kitchen and took out the invoices Leo had delivered.

Rita looked at the invoices and then looked at Blair with a questioning look and said, "So, he was just showing you how much these expenses are?"

"No, not just that—he wanted me to have you pay them."

"Well, I'm sure he would, but that's his responsibility."

"That's what I thought, but then he showed me this." Blair pulled out the contract for sale of the house and pointed to Leo's handwritten statement on page three.

Rita read the offensive words out loud, "'Buyer shall pay when due all costs associated with the property, including, but not limited to, taxes, HOA dues and insurance premiums.' How can that be? I never saw this in the contract."

"It must have been there. This is a copy of what you signed."

"I guess I was pretty shocked by Leo's announcement that he didn't own the property. I suppose that could have distracted me from paying attention to the rest of the contract. I know I had a hard time concentrating after he said that." After some more thought, she added, "There's another possibility. Leo could have added those words before he made our copy."

"Maybe, if he were someone other than Leonard Petroni, but he's got a good reputation, and he's powerful. Even if he did, we wouldn't stand a chance accusing him of something dishonest like that. Nobody would believe us over him."

Rita thought some more before she spoke again. "Maybe this isn't so bad after all. I mean, sure, we didn't anticipate these extra costs, but on the other hand, I'm not paying rent anymore for that expensive Denver apartment. And, I'm not paying rent for this big house, and, besides that, when Leo gets the title all squared away, then I'll own the property. So, I'm not going to sweat it. There, see—there's really nothing to get all upset about."

Blair was relieved. Rita wasn't angry with him, and he could still feel exaggerated pride about the deal he negotiated with Leo. "Yeah, that's right," he agreed.

"So, tell you what—let's get this breakage cleaned up. I'll pay these bills. Then, you can get back to work on the house, and I can get back to San Francisco." *And, the strong arms of Andy Edison.*

November 14, 1987

"I don't want to spend any more money on this place—well, the remodeling. I know I'm on the hook for the taxes, dues and insurance, but I don't want to put any more money into the house itself," screamed Rita. "Leo has been stringing us along and getting us to do all this work to improve the place, and what has he done on his end? Nothing, as far as I can tell." She was angry, and she was showing it by yelling. After more than a year and a half, Rita had had enough. She wished she had never met Leo Petroni or seen his for-sale signs.

"He says his lawyer has been having trouble searching for other possible heirs of the previous owner. All he got from the brother was a quitclaim deed. He didn't even get that from other people who may be heirs," offered Blair.

"Yeah, that's the bullshit line he's been feeding us. I know."

"It makes sense. Doesn't it?"

"Of course, it makes sense. He's a wily old goat—a crafty, fucking old goat. He's going to make up anything that sounds halfway sensible and say it in a way like he's your closest friend. Well, I'm tired of being used, and I'm sure as hell tired of spending winters in this icebox. One was enough. Not one more, I tell you."

"What do you want to do?"

"I want to make sure this place is winterized, lock it up and go live in your mom's old house in Los Angeles. I'll tell Leo that we're leaving and that once he gets title to the property, he should call me, and I'll return and finish the closing."

"What about your darkroom? What about your book? And your agent…"

"Molly. Her name's Molly Richards. I haven't been able to focus on my book for months because of this damned house. Molly will have to understand."

"It will be warmer in California," said Blair, stating the obvious.

"And far away from this pain in the ass."

"We can talk to Leo next Monday."

"No, we can talk to Leo right now. Come on."

Within a few minutes they were ringing the Petronis' doorbell. Uncharacteristically, Leo was the one to answer the door and not Clara.

"Where's Clara?" asked Blair in typical Blair fashion.

Having long ago adjusted to Blair's unusual way of interacting socially, Leo answered as if he were speaking to a child, "She's visiting our daughter, Larinda, in Seattle, Blair. What brings the two of you to my doorstep?"

"May we come in?" asked Rita.

"Of course, come in. Want some coffee?"

146

"Yes—" replied Blair before being cut off by Rita.

"No. We came by to tell you that we're leaving the house until you get legal title. We're going to live in Los Angeles in Blair's mother's former house. I've written down the address and telephone number out there so you can let us know when that happens."

"Really...what about the work you've been doing on the place?" asked Leo.

"Well, the work we've been doing is done, and the work we have planned will have to wait until we get legal title from you, Leo."

"Don't you need that nice darkroom Blair built for your work?"

"I can rent one from a friend in LA. It's not your concern anyway, Leo. Your concern is getting legal title straightened out. How is that going?"

"About the same. My lawyer's still trying to sort out whether there are any heirs or other people with potential claims."

"Your lawyer should go to Salt Lake City and go to the Mormon church," interjected Blair with great authority.

Leo gave a brief snort through his nose and said, "I don't think he wants any salvation offered by the Mormons, Blair."

"That's not what I'm saying," said Blair defiantly, rightly thinking he and his suggestion were being dismissed as childish and irrelevant. "They have the most extensive family records in the world. Your lawyer should do his research for heirs there."

"Sure, Blair. I'll pass that on to my lawyer," said Leo patronizingly.

Rita intervened by handing a piece of paper to Leo and saying, "Here's my address and telephone number in Los Angeles."

Leo took the paper without making any promises.

As Blair and Rita walked down Leo's driveway, a black sedan pulled away from the curb at the entrance to the cul-de-sac. Blair's rant about Leo's disrespectful dismissal of his invaluable advice distracted both of them from noticing.

January 1988

Leo waited until well into the new year before calling his real estate lawyer. He had several reasons for waiting. One was that he wanted to make sure that Blair and Rita were not going to return. That became certain enough when the temperature became frigid. Another was the Christmas holiday season. His two daughters and their families visited from Seattle and Pittsburgh, and he wanted to spend relaxing family time with them and his three granddaughters without the intrusion of business. The third reason was that just after the first of the new year he had a conference to attend at Georgia Tech in Atlanta. The conference was on the adverse climate effects of producing and burning coal, oil and gas, and he was sent on behalf of the Colorado Mining Association and Colorado Petroleum Association. The CMA and CPA wanted Leo to find out what the enemies of coal and gas were up to, and he wanted to rape one or two more young women with all expenses paid. In just the six days he was in Atlanta, he got lucky twice with coeds from Georgia Tech. Both were snagged in loud, busy bars where no one noticed. He was proud of his attacks. Eighty-one—and he was as virile as a twenty-year-old, or at least a thirty-year-old.

On January 28, 1988, Leo called his real estate lawyer, Michael Wesley.

Michael took the phone call his secretary had announced. "Hello, Leo. How are you?"

"Fine, Michael. Michael, remember that quiet title action I told you I probably wanted to start some day?"

"Yes, of course, Leo,"

"Today is that day. I want you to get that going as soon as you can."

"I'm pretty much ready to go, Leo. I'll get right on it."

While he was on the phone with Wesley, Leo looked out his upstairs office window and saw a black car in the driveway next-door.

"Good—keep me posted."

"Sure thing, Leo," said Wesley to a busy tone.

Leo saw a man come out of the Nicholson house, so he went downstairs to investigate and shoo the intruder away. By the time he got out the front door, the car was gone. *I wonder if Rita has somebody looking after the property?*

April 20, 1988

Leo woke up before daybreak even though he had gotten to bed late. Clara was off again. This time she was visiting their daughter, Sophia, and her family in Pittsburgh. She did that more now since she was over seventy—not that many more years before she fell off the end of life's conveyor belt. She needed to make the most of every breath she took. For her, that meant seeing her daughters and granddaughters more—and Leo less. Her life with Leo had been loveless. At least she had her girls to show for it. Leo didn't miss her either. From his vantage point, marriage had been nothing more than a convenient veil of respectability to camouflage his evil deeds. Those he enjoyed. The deeds themselves were thrilling and empowering, but so was the aftermath of evading law enforcement and punishment for his crimes. He felt invincible, especially today. He had just returned last night from another mission for fossil fuels and satisfaction of his lascivious cravings—this time in Santa Fe.

After his morning yoga exercises in his sunroom, he headed to the kitchen for a frothy, mango-and-banana green smoothie. As he passed the large windows in the living room, he glanced over at the Nicholson property and then stopped to focus on something at the far front edge of the house. It looked like it could be a small portion of the hood of a car parked on the side of the house out of view from his house. He rushed off to get some binoculars that he failed to find, even after trying to summon them with various curses directed at Clara. She must have taken them for one of her "birding adventures" and then put them in a place they didn't belong—at least a place he didn't expect them to be. When he finally got back to the window to look again, the black image he had seen was gone. He decided to keep an eye on the place from his greenhouse after drinking his smoothie and taking a shower. The greenhouse was closer and provided a better view than his house.

As he walked from his house to the greenhouse later in the morning, he surveyed the grounds and made mental notes of plants and hardscaping that needed the attention of his gardener, who came once a week. A gardener was needed for the outside landscaping, but no one, other than him, had rights of entry to his prized conservatory. Arriving at the entrance, he straightened the security keypad and made another mental note to get that fixed. Better yet, he decided to replace the whole antiquated system, but not with anything that tied into the police or an outside security company. When he opened the door, he closed his eyes and took in a long, deep breath savoring the warm, earthy-sweet scent of humus and floral perfumes. After a prolonged exhalation, he opened his eyes and said, "Good Morning, my pretties." He then closed the door, inspected his climate and automatic-watering controls and equipment, fertilized plants and deadheaded spent flowers. That took close to three hours. Once his chores were done, he headed to his favorite cabinet, unlocked it and removed his scopolamine-production equipment. He pulled on black coveralls and surgical boot covers, gloves and mask and set about making some new product for future assaults. He had started these safety precautions six years ago after he broke a test tube containing scopolamine and had to evacuate his work area until the dust had settled. After producing a batch of scopolamine, he went to his cabinet and removed a rack of vials. As he set it down on his work counter, he thought he noticed something that gave him goosebumps. There was an empty slot where an empty vial had been. Then he imagined that two other vials containing scopolamine had less in them than the last time he looked at them before he went to Santa Fe. After a careful inspection of the cabinet, its lock, the entrance door and the general interior, his nerves settled, and he dismissed his fears as flawed memory, which he dearly hoped was not an indication of early-onset dementia. *Nonsense, I'm as sharp as ever. Everybody has moments of lapsed memory.*

By the time he returned all of his equipment, protective clothing and newly created scopolamine to the locked cabinet, it was lunchtime, so he walked up to his house and prepared a spinach salad garnished with toasted, sliced almonds and fresh raspberries and lightly seasoned with raspberry-vinaigrette dressing. As he sucked a raspberry from his fork and savored its sweet, slightly tart flavor, he thought of the young Navajo woman he had raped in Santa Fe. After relishing thoughts of his latest conquest and the rest of his lunch, Leo sat and focused upon the property next door. Time was wasting away. Warm weather was here, and he needed to acquire title and get on with completing construction so that he could sell the house before Rita Draper returned. *What the hell is Wesley doing?*

August 28, 1988

Leo had nothing to worry about. The quiet title action was a cakewalk for Michael Wesley, since no one contested Leo's claim. And, Wesley was a capable, if run-of-the-mill, real estate lawyer. However, there were certain procedures to follow, timelines to honor, and that's what Wesley did. He also had other clients than Leo, and Leo had been only a once-in-a-blue-moon, and pretty small-potatoes, client in the past. Wesley had written a few standard leases and handled a few penny ante evictions and collections for Leo, but mostly, Leo handled his own legal issues the old-fashioned mob way—with bully and bluster. It was a technique he had learned from Checkers Smaldone, and it worked ninety-five percent of the time and was a lot cheaper than hiring a lawyer. So, to the extent there was any slowdown in finishing Leo's quiet title action, it was due to the legal hoops Wesley had to jump through and his attention to more profitable clients and issues. If Leo wanted better legal service, he should have been a better client, according to Michael Wesley's way of thinking.

Regardless, time clicked by, legal hoops were jumped through, and on July 29 Leo got his wish when the district court for Jefferson County granted his quiet title action. He was now the official, legal owner of Beat Nicholson's former erection disaster. However, thanks to Rita Draper and Blair Barker, it was not the disaster it once was. The open section now had a roof, the walls were winterized, the kitchen was useable, bathrooms were close to complete, and the stench of death was gone. Essentially, Leo had stolen a valuable piece of property with the blessing of the legal system and had gotten two dupes to spend their money and time improving it. He was very proud of himself.

After gaining title, Leo got to work by hiring a cleaning service and a small construction business to remove Rita's signature marks of possession—her darkroom and her art. Darkroom equipment and supplies were moved into the garage and marked for sale after moving her '71 Jeep Wagoneer into the street. It too got a for-sale sign stuck on it. Her negatives and photos were hauled out of the house and unceremoniously tossed into the hole for the never-to-be-installed swimming pool. Deconstruction of her darkroom was then begun. And, Leo posted a handwritten, four-by-four-foot sign at the entrance to the driveway.

On Sunday, August 28, Rita and Blair stood in stark horror staring at the sign that read: "Rita Draper and Blair Barker are not permitted to enter and will be subject to legal action if they do." Next to it was a professional for-sale sign of the same real estate agent who had the listing for all the other properties in Indian Paintbrush Estates.

Without a word, they turned and got into Rita's car and drove up to Leo's house. Once at Leo's entrance, Blair repeatedly pushed the doorbell while Rita pounded on the door, and they both yelled for Leo to come out.

Clara, who had heard the racket from the backyard patio, put down the novel she was reading and headed through the house toward the front door. Leo was on the same mission when their paths crossed.

"I'll handle this. Go back to your book," he ordered. She dutifully obeyed and was relieved to do so.

Before he opened the door, he checked the peephole to confirm what he already suspected. *So, you finally came back. All right, let's get this going.* He set his face to intimidation and opened the door.

As soon as the door started to open, Rita stopped banging on it, but Blair kept on pushing the doorbell button. Rita grabbed his hand and yelled, "What the hell do you think you're doing with my property, Leo? What's the meaning of this?"

"I know exactly what I'm doing, and the meaning is quite clear."

Blair started in with a rambling assertion of legal rights based upon his imagined knowledge of the law. "We have a legally binding contract. What you're doing is a serious breach, and you'd better cease and desist immediately. Our right of possession is paramount. We'll sue you for everything you have. We'll sue you for...for...for breach of contract, mental anguish...and...fraud...and...and...defamation. And, punitive damages and—"

"Oh, shut up, Blair. You're not even a party to this. Keep spouting off about things you know nothing about, and I'll report you for practicing law on her behalf without a license."

Blair stopped to think about that, and Rita took the opportunity to intervene.

"Well, I am a party. I have a contract that you signed."

"An unenforceable contract that you abandoned," countered Leo.

"What do you mean unenforceable?"

"A real estate contract is required to have a date for closing," said Leo.

"And, as I recall, you left that blank, and I got you to add a closing date after you got legal title. So, did you—get legal title?"

"I did," came Leo's reply. He was enjoying his little sparring match with Rita.

"Well then, this is after you got legal title."

"So is ten years from now, or twenty, or one hundred," countered Leo with a smug sneer.

Rita looked baffled.

"See what I mean? There's no identifiable closing date. Now, get off my property and stay off. And, that goes for the property next door."

"But..." started Rita with nothing to follow.

Blair finally regained his voice and said, "You won't get away with this, Leo."

"Looks to me like I am. Now, I'm going to count to five, and if you two are still on my property when I finish, I'm going to call the police, and we'll see who has what legal authority to do what. One...two...three—

"We're leaving, but we're not going away," said Rita.

Rita and Blair headed back to her car, and she drove to the other property and parked along the curb. Rita grabbed a camera and started out the door.

Blair said, "What are you doing? Leo said he'd call the police if we went on the property."

"I have property in there. Hell, my professional life is in there. I have every right to check on it."

She went to the front door. It was locked—her key failed to unlock it. The same was true of the garage doors, sides doors and back door. While she was turning away from the back door, she saw bits and pieces of photographic film on the ground leading to the swimming-pool pit. At first, the meaning of those bits of film failed to register with her. Who would do what she thought she was seeing? Who could do it? She picked up a few of the pieces and ran to the edge of the hole and stood transfixed by the nightmare before her. She slumped to the ground and began to wail. Blair sat down next to her with tears running down his cheeks.

After running out of tears, Rita got up, climbed down into the hole, surveyed the damage, snapped a few photos and then extended her hand for Blair to pull her up.

"Let's get what we can salvage, and put it in the car," she said.

"Then what?" asked Blair.

"Then I get a lawyer—a good real estate lawyer."

"Do you have any in mind? I don't," said Blair who was slipping into a depressive mode.

"No, but I know someone who might. I sold some photos some time ago to this real estate agent in Boulder. He wanted them for his office and his mansion. His name is Buddy Dunse."

CHAPTER 8

An Ernest Enjoining

August 29–September 1, 1988

Buddy Dunse was as dumb as a stick—a very dumb stick. He was known for some classic, self-perceived-witty sayings—Dunseisms, as they were generally known among the Boulder real estate community. Besides selling commercial and residential real estate, Dunse also sold minority limited-partner interests in partnerships that owned office and retail property, while he kept for himself a whopping fifty-five-percent interest for doing nothing more than hauling in investors. Invariably, at some point in Dunse's sales hype, his trusting targets would question Dunse's taking controlling interest in exchange for nothing and them paying a lot for very little. Then would come one of his favorite Dunseisms: "I'd rather have one percent of a hundred percent than a hundred percent of nothing." And that was supposed to mean something. Evidently it did because Dunse was very successful at what he did. To further his desired prestige among his clients, many of whom were very intelligent, he liked to brag about his IQ of 94. Most people who knew him thought he got his numbers transposed. In addition to his other many character flaws, he was a misogynistic, womanizer who often displayed all the social grace of horse apples on fine china. But, if there was anything that Buddy knew, it was quality—quality in property and quality in people. Thus, when Rita Draper called him for a referral to a good real estate attorney, Buddy had no hesitation in responding, "Ernest Schreiber."

Since Ernest had at one time rented an office from Buddy and since then had developed a reputation as an excellent real estate attorney and since Buddy was an integral part of the real estate scene in Boulder, they both had a wealth of knowledge about each other. Dunse tried to implement his knowledge by hiring Ernest while Ernest did his best to avoid The Dunse—one of Buddy's many pejorative sobriquets used behind his back. Once, however, Dunse had managed to, in a sense, ooze in the back door of Ernest's legal practice. A local businessman who owned a small office-supply store had hired Ernest to represent him in order to enforce an option to purchase the property he rented from another local businessman. The option was a short one-sentence statement handwritten into the lease that left a lot to interpretation. Ernest's client had claimed that he orally exercised the option while the landlord claimed the opposite. It looked like a hopeless case for the tenant, and a slam dunk for the landlord. After hearing the tenant's story, Ernest was convinced that he was telling the truth and that the landlord was breaching his agreement and lying about it. At Cornell Law School one of Ernest's favorite professors had said that if a wrong has been committed, a good attorney will find a remedy to right it. Ernest had taken that proclamation to heart and adopted it as his credo. With his professor's words echoing in his brain, Ernest came up with something he called a nexus-of-events argument that pieced together a chronology of actions and words by the two parties that he claimed evidenced their intent regarding the option. The nexus-of-events argument was so esoteric that it was hardly known by other lawyers and, even if known, understood even less. When the opposing attorney saw Ernest's complaint putting forth the argument, he called it bizarre and laughable at best and filed a motion to dismiss claiming that there was no such thing and that Ernest's complaint on behalf of his client should be dismissed. After the back-and-forth of paper on that motion was over, the judge called a hearing. It was an all-or-nothing hearing for Ernest and his client. Ernest had prepared extensively, analyzing all the potential arguments by his opponent and questions by the judge, and prepared a hand-drawn chart connecting his events to show that their sum total amounted to a proper exercise of the option to purchase. When he turned to sit back down after presenting his argument to the judge, Ernest saw Buddy Dunse in the gallery. After the hearing, Dunse came up and complimented Ernest on a job well done, even though there was no way Buddy had understood anything Ernest had said. It was then that his client told Ernest that Buddy Dunse was actually going to purchase the property with one of his limited partnerships if Ernest's client was successful in the lawsuit. In a sense, Ernest had been working for Dunse the whole time, and he hadn't known it. When the judge agreed with Ernest and denied the motion to dismiss, the landlord caved and settled the lawsuit by selling the property to Dunse's limited partnership. After that, Ernest was a legal wizard in the eyes of Dunse who tried to get Ernest to represent him in other matters while Ernest claimed he was too busy. That was a big step for Dunse because he had blamed Ernest for stealing his secretary, Tracey Trent. In reality, Ernest had merely provided Tracey with an opportunity to do what she was longing to do anyway because of Dunse's coarsely veiled sexual overtures and uninvited physical contact, especially between his hands and her derriere.

At nine in the morning on August 29, Tracey buzzed Ernest on his intercom line and said, "Ernest, I have a new client wannabe on the line for you. Her name's Rita Draper, and catch this—she was referred by The Dunse."

"Thanks, Tracey, but tell her there are other attorneys in Boulder."

"I think she knows that. I, of all people, should know how you feel about our Buddy, but she sounds desperate. She says somebody is destroying her property, and she can't stop them."

"All right, I'll talk to her, but not because Dunse referred her."

Tracey rang the call through and Ernest answered, "This is Ernest Schreiber."

"Oh, Mr. Schreiber, thank you so much for taking my call. You come very highly recommended by Mr. Buddy Dunse. I'm so glad to be talking with you."

Mention Dunse one more time and you won't be. "My secretary tells me that someone is destroying your property. What do you mean by that?"

"Well, I have a contract to buy a house—my new home—and the seller is refusing to close the sale. And, Mr. Petroni—that's the seller—let me and my fiancé move in before the closing and make improvements to the house, which we did. One major improvement was a darkroom for my business. I'm a professional photographer. We left for a while and when we came back, there were signs saying we were not allowed on the property; that he'd sue us if we did go on it; and the worst is…" Her voice broke and trailed off as she began to sob.

"Just take a moment and catch your breath." Ernest was a sucker for a good sob story. Once she seemed to have settled down, he continued, "Are you ready to go on?"

"Uh-huh—the worst thing is that he's destroyed some of my photos—my negatives," said Rita before she began to cry again.

"You said the seller's name is Petroni."

"That's right."

"Any relation to Leonard Petroni—the Leonard Petroni with his name on a bunch of commercial buildings and who used to be an attorney with the Public Utilities Commission?"

"That's him—same guy."

Ernest breathed out a heavy sigh. It was obvious that there was a lot to this story that couldn't be covered over the phone. *If anybody other than Buddy Dunse was the referral source I'd jump on this—but, Buddy Dunse. Crap!* "Ms. Draper, can you come in this Thursday to talk about this. I'm not agreeing to represent you, but I am willing to hear more to see what, if any, case you have."

"That's wonderful, but—is there any chance we could meet sooner? I'm very afraid that Mr. Petroni is destroying more of my property, maybe more photos, or even selling it. He had my jeep parked along the curb with a for-sale sign on it. My fiancé and I got that out of there, but he's got my life's work locked up. I was putting together a book of photos of endangered wild animals, and some of those were thrown into the pit in the backyard. Maybe all of them. I tried to save some photos, I mean negatives, but I really don't know what has been destroyed already. I haven't had a chance to do a full inventory yet."

"Pit in the backyard?"

"There was a hole in the backyard dug by the previous owner for a swimming pool that never got built."

After releasing another heavy sigh and thinking, *well, there goes another short lunch break,* Ernest said, "All right, how about noon tomorrow? Do you have my address?"

"Yes, Mr. Dunse said you're in a cute little redwood building on the corner of Eighth and Walnut."

"That's it. See you tomorrow and bring the contract and anything else you think is relevant."

"Oh, thank you so much, Mr. Schreiber."

August 30, 1988

At 11:45 a.m., Ernest looked out his street-side bay window and saw a couple coming up the walkway to the front porch of his redwood office building. Several years ago, Carl Manthey and he had purchased and remodeled the little house that now served as their offices. Carl and Ernest shared the building, but not a law practice. Their practices were very different. Carl focused on criminal defense and Ernest on real estate. The man and woman approaching the porch were engaged in conversation. The woman seemed to be giving instructions to the man who was shaking his head in agreement.

Blair was properly medicated and in stable condition this morning. Rita had made certain of it. She needed legal help, and this attorney came highly recommended. She didn't want her chances with him blown by Blair spouting legal advice to a legal expert.

Ernest answered his intercom, and Tracey announced, "Your lunch appointment is here. Oh, that's right, you don't get lunch today." She said it for the benefit of Rita and Blair so they would know that Ernest was sacrificing his lunch in order to meet with them. Tracey was very protective of Ernest.

"Thanks, T. I'll be right out."

Ernest came out of his office and saw an attractive, thirtyish woman with short, light-brown hair showing some strands of gray and a short, balding, pudgy man of probably the same age but looking mid-forties. Ernest extended his hand to the woman and said, "Hi, my name is Ernest Schreiber."

Rita was momentarily struck by Ernest's good looks. She shook his hand and said, "I'm Rita Draper, and this is my fiancé, Blair Barker."

After shaking Rita's hand, Ernest went for Blair's. Blair gave a quick glance to Rita, as if to ask permission before shaking hands. Ernest briefly wondered what that was about, but quickly moved on to the reason for their visit. "Come into my office and let's get started. I have a very tight schedule today." *Today, tomorrow, every day,* thought Ernest as he directed Rita and Blair to seats across from his desk. "Why don't you tell me about what happened starting with the contract you mentioned yesterday."

Rita handed Ernest her copy of the contract. Then, for the next fifty minutes she related the story of how she and Blair found the Nicholson property and Leo Petroni; Leo's informing them that he didn't own the property at the time they were signing the contract; Leo's addition of language for closing after he got title; their moving in and improving the house; Leo's revelation that she was obligated to pay all the expenses of the house; their leaving for California; and their recent return to find they were locked out of the house and Rita's photographs had been dumped into a pit. It was an incredible story. It was a compelling story—especially for someone like Ernest. Ernest had an inquiring mind and a sense of justice that drove him to right wrongs committed against underdogs. With Leonard Petroni as the antagonist, it was clear who the underdog was in this legal drama. Before speaking, Ernest read the contract.

"Well, I see what Petroni is saying about there being no closing date, but I think that can be overcome."

Blair started to puff up as if he were going to say something, but he deflated as soon as Rita touched his right knee.

"Did you want to say something, Blair?"

"Nope—no," he answered while shaking his head "no" for added emphasis.

"What do you think I should do? What can I do? What could you do?" asked Rita.

"If—and I want to emphasis the 'if' in that—I were to take this case, I would start by putting together a complaint just to get it on file, and, at the same time, I would petition the court for a temporary restraining order and permanent injunction. You have to stop whatever Petroni is still doing to the property, your property, and get possession while the lawsuit goes forward. That's what the restraining order would do. Once you got possession, you could take inventory of the damage he's done and add that to the original complaint by an amendment."

"You could do that?"

"I believe so, but the law that governs the issuing of a restraining order requires the person who is requesting it to put up some security to protect the person against whom it's issued from possible damages if the restraining order is later found to have been issued wrongfully."

"How is that determined?"

Usually, by hyperbole and guesswork, thought Ernest, but he said, "In this case, Petroni would make some claim that he's losing his right of possession and that computes to lost rent, or maybe he'd say he's losing profit from a potential sale. I would counter that he already has a promissory note for one hundred ninety-five thousand dollars, so that would more than cover any damages he might suffer from a wrongfully issued injunction."

"That sounds good. You said restraining order, but you also said injunction. Is that the same thing?"

"Yes, in its effect, but no, in how it is achieved. A temporary restraining order is temporary as its name implies. It's also issued on an emergency basis. Something bad is happening, and it will continue to happen causing a lot of damage before the injured party can get into court to remedy it. There's also a section in the rule governing a temporary restraining order that covers your situation—a person who has been denied or kept out of possession of their property by fraud or by threats, words or actions that naturally excite fear or apprehension of danger. I'd say you have that here. A more detailed hearing would come soon after the temporary restraining order in order to convert it into a preliminary injunction that would last until a trial. So, a restraining order in your case would not only stop Petroni from doing what he is doing, but when made a preliminary injunction, would give you possession until the final trial. A petition for a temporary restraining order can be issued without notice to the other party, but I wouldn't recommend that. I'd try to give Petroni notice at least by phone. So, a temporary order, if issued without notice, terminates automatically ten days after it is issued. That means having the preliminary injunction hearing within those ten days in order to preserve the rights gained under the temporary restraining order. But, the ten days can be extended under certain circumstances. In any event, the process is, or can be, complicated. Look, courts are busy, and judges hate to have their daily schedules *(for a few, their doughnut breaks)* interrupted by emergency hearings, so what you can expect is a hearing on the petition for temporary restraining order that will deal with the basics under the rule—that's Rule 65 of the Colorado Rules of Civil Procedure. Those basics are that you are suffering immediate and irreparable injury or loss of a continuing nature that the court can stop right now. Once you get a temporary order, I would hope for a hearing on a preliminary injunction where the facts are presented in more detail to set the order of the TRO—sorry, temporary restraining order—in place until the final trial. The reason I would want that is because the evidence presented at the hearing on the preliminary injunction will be part of the record and won't have to be repeated at trial. It also might give me an opportunity to get Petroni's testimony on the record without having to go through a later deposition of him."

"He'll lie," said Rita.

"Fine—but I want him to be locked into one lie, if he does. I don't care what Petroni's lie is. I just don't want him to change it over time. Once I get his sworn testimony on the record, that's the lie he'll be stuck with. The sooner I get that lie on the record, the better it will be—no going back and changing it."

"Sounds like a lot of work just to get my own property back. What about the house? Can I get that? I put a lot of money into it, and I lost a lot of time working on it."

"Glad you recognize that there's a lot of legal work involved—and a good deal of it comes fast and early. As far as the injustice of having to go through so much just to get what you already own is concerned—all I can offer is that the law doesn't deal in magic. It can't undo any damage that's been suffered by a victim of some injustice. But, in your case it can come closer than in most. Let me explain."

"Please do," said Rita.

"In most cases where someone has breached a contract, as Petroni has with you, the victim at most can get damages, or their own property back, or both. That's the way it has been since way back in early English law. However, there were courts created back then to do more than that in special cases because it was recognized that sometimes damages alone weren't enough to make the victim whole. Those courts were called courts of equity, and one of the remedies they created was something called specific performance. That remedy and the reasoning behind it have been handed down through the ages and is available in the United States—and specifically Colorado. Specific performance allows a court to order the breaching party to do what he or she promised to do under the contract. However, the contract has to deal with something unique, and without going into all the details about what that could mean, let me just say that real estate qualifies. Every piece of real estate is different from every other. Realize that in a real estate contract the only person in the contract who can lose that unique property if the other party breaches the contract is the buyer. Since the only thing the seller loses if the buyer defaults is money, money damages for a breach will make the seller whole. Thus, a real estate buyer will have a claim to specific performance, but a seller won't. There is an exception for that, but not under your contract with Petroni. That was a long way of saying you have a claim for damages for loss and destruction of your property and to get title to the house—specific performance in other words."

"Does all that mean you're going to take my case?" asked Rita. It was obvious to everyone that Ernest was drawn to the case.

As much to himself as to Rita, or much less Blair, Ernest said, "I have a lot of work right now, but I suppose I could push some of it aside for a while to get this put together. It's going to take some late-night work. And, I wouldn't be able to take any new cases or clients until I got your case stabilized and well on its way, and even then, we'll have depositions of Petroni and his wife and workers. We'll need an expert to talk about the value of your photos that were destroyed." After a heavy sigh, he said, "Yes, I'll take the case, but I'll expect to be paid on a monthly basis. I'll charge by the hour at one hundred ten dollars an hour plus expenses which I'll bill against your retainer of—five thousand dollars."

Rita looked shocked. Blair started to protest, but Rita tapped his knee again and said, "I...That would be a little stressful right now. But, I have some commissions due for some photo assignments in a couple of months. Would you be willing to take two thousand now?"

In the back of Ernest's mind lurked a concern of whether this foretold a pattern of behavior to expect through the course of the case, but the truth was he felt sorry for Rita and angered by what Petroni had done. His wife, Claire, said he had a Sir Galahad complex that often got in the way of protecting his own best interests. When he saw someone abuse their wealth or power to take advantage of someone less powerful, he'd leap on his charger and enter the fray at full tilt heedless of the personal danger. He was both flattered and annoyed by her characterization of him, but couldn't deny its element of truth. His Galahad came forth and said, "I can do that. Let me get a fee agreement prepared. I'll be right back." Ernest left Rita and Blair in his office while he went out to talk to Tracey and fill in the blanks on a standard fee agreement he had drafted some time ago.

When they were alone, Blair turned to Rita and said, "I have some ideas about how he should do this. I think you should let me work with him."

"Blair, we talked about this. Remember? Let the attorney do his work. You can get involved later if it looks like he's floundering. OK, sweetie?"

"I guess, but my ideas are really good. I just don't want him messing up your case."

"He has a very good reputation. Let's just—" Rita's comment was cut off by Ernest's return.

As he handed a copy of the fee agreement to Rita, Ernest said, "OK, I have a fee agreement for you to review. It's one page and essentially says I'll charge you at one hundred ten dollars per hour plus costs, which I can, and will, draw from the retainer of two thousand. When the retainer, which I'll keep in my trust account, gets down to five hundred, you'll put in another two thousand. It also says that I will represent you through the trial, but I have no obligation to represent you in an appeal, either that you want to bring or that Petroni brings. Go ahead and read through it and ask questions, if you have any."

"Don't I get a copy?" asked Blair.

"Only if Rita wants you to. She'll be my client and not you."

"Do you have another copy?" asked Rita.

"I do."

"Please, it's OK to give him a copy. I trust him with everything we do."

Ernest did as she instructed and waited while the two of them read.

"Why won't you agree to do the appeal? That should be part of the case too," said Blair.

"Not really—first of all, there is no appeal right now. We're dealing with a civil trial on the merits of your claim. An appeal is a separate matter that I don't want to commit to until that comes up, if it does."

"That's fine with me," said Rita trying to break off any further discussion of something that wasn't relevant to getting the house and damages for her losses.

"This second to last paragraph says that interest will be charged on any of your fees and costs not paid when due. It also says that you can sue Rita if she doesn't pay you and that you can get your attorney fees if you do."

"That's correct. Not going to be a problem is it?" asked Ernest.

"Not at all," said Rita hoping to shut Blair up before Ernest changed his mind. "This is fine with me." She grabbed a pen off Ernest's desk and signed two copies of the fee agreement while Blair slumped back a tad sullen for being shut down.

After Ernest signed both copies and handed one back to Rita, he said, "All right, let's get some more facts that I can put into the complaint and TRO petition. We can work on this until my two o'clock appointment. Then, you two can leave. I'll free up the rest of my afternoon by pushing some less urgent matters into the future." He pushed the com button for Tracey and said, "Got any plans for this evening?"

"You're taking her case, aren't you?"

"That is correct."

"Oh, Ernest—Buddy Dunse? OK, whatever, no, the only plans I have are to be here helping you."

"Great. Thanks, Tracey."

Turning back to his new client and Blair, Ernest asked Blair, "From what Rita has told me so far, you did almost all of the construction work when the two of you moved into the property after Rita signed the contract with Petroni—correct?"

"Yeah—Rita helped me at first, but it was all under my direction as the contractor in charge."

"Really? So, you got paid for your work, even though the two of you are engaged?"

"Uh-huh."

Strange, but maybe helpful, thought Ernest. "Then, you gave her invoices for all your labor and materials, and she paid you off those invoices. Is that right?"

"Not exactly." Blair was starting to flush and feel threatened.

"How 'not exactly' do you mean?" asked Ernest.

"Well, when I needed money for the work, I would tell Rita, and she would give me a check, and I would then deposit that in my checking account and draw from it for materials and my labor. When I needed more to continue my work, I'd ask her for more money."

Well, that sucks. "Did you give her invoices for the work you had done after you made payments to yourself and for the materials you bought?" *Please say, yes.*

"No. Why is that important, anyway?" asked the self-professed legal expert.

"Well, if we lose on the specific performance part of our case, I would at least like to get a judgment for Rita's damages, and part of those damages would be the cost of improvements she had you do on the house. Also, if any of those improvements have been damaged in some way by Petroni, we'll want those as damages, even if we get specific performance."

"Oh."

"Did you at least keep track of the hours you spent working on the house?"

Seeing redemption for his previous transgression, Blair eagerly said, "Oh, yes—yes, absolutely. I keep excellent time records."

"I'll want copies of those and all your invoices for materials. You'll have to testify to those at trial to demonstrate what was paid for your labor and the materials from the funds Rita gave you. Since you never gave her invoices for your labor and materials, that's not within her personal knowledge. All she can say is that she gave you lump sums of money, but she has no idea what you did with it afterwards."

"Oh, I can do that. Don't worry about me." That made Ernest worry.

The rest of their time together was spent firming up the facts that Ernest needed in order to draft the complaint and petition for temporary restraining order and preliminary injunction. That evening, Ernest called Claire to tell her he wouldn't be home to spend dinner with her and their two lovely children. Then, he and Tracey worked until eleven drafting and typing the complaint, petition and related documents for Rita's lawsuit against Leo Petroni. They were exhausted when they finished.

August 31, 1988

Tracey and Ernest spent the early morning preparing for a meeting with Rita by sprucing up the documents they had worked on the previous night. At ten Rita arrived without Blair. Rita felt obligated to explain his absence as being due to not feeling well. Ernest didn't care and didn't miss him.

Ernest brought Rita into his office and immediately started to explain the documents he and Tracey had prepared. The principle documents were the complaint and the TRO petition which Ernest drafted in the form of a motion. Both went into extensive detail about the facts from the execution of the real estate contract with Leo Petroni through Rita's recent discovery of Petroni's retaking of possession of the house and exclusion of Rita from the premises. Both also required Rita to sign a sworn, notarized verification that the allegations in each were true. After some minor adjustments to the wording were made at Rita's request, she signed the papers, and Tracey notarized them.

Ernest then called the Jefferson County District Court to schedule a hearing on the TRO motion. It took several minutes before he was connected with the clerk of the one judge who was available to hear the motion. Then it took even longer for Ernest to explain the situation, the reason for an emergency hearing and the documents supporting it. The clerk asked him to fax the complaint and TRO motion, so Ernest requested Tracey to do that while he stayed on the phone with the clerk. Rita watched the whole process with admiration for the skill and efficiency of Ernest and Tracey.

After the clerk had read the faxed documents, she asked, "Have you served these on Mr. Petroni, yet?"

"No, I wanted to run them by you and get an emergency hearing time for the TRO first. After getting that, I plan on calling him and telling about the hearing. I also will try to have him served by my process server."

"And, you haven't filed these with the court, either?"

"That is correct—same reason."

"OK, let me see what I can do. Hold on while I talk to the judge."

He was put on hold to be serenaded by Barry Manilow. While Barry crooned on, Ernest asked Tracey to call his process server to find out if he was available later to drive the twenty miles to the Jefferson courthouse to file the original documents.

Several minutes later, the clerk returned and said, "Mr. Schreiber, Judge Gentilini said that you can have an hour tomorrow morning starting at eight sharp to present your motion."

For a heartbeat, Ernest was taken aback. Although he had never appeared before Judge Saralee Gentilini, he had heard about her. And, what he had heard wasn't good. She had a reputation for violent outbursts often seasoned with profanity. A Boulder county court judge he knew well once told him that Gentilini had a scholar's mind and a sailor's mouth. Rumor was that she didn't like men. And, if she wasn't a misandrist, the perception among the male members of the bar was that she was harder on them than their fellow female jurists. Rita noticed his momentary hesitation and gave him a narrow-eyed, quizzical look.

After his momentary pause, Ernest continued his conversation with Judge Gentilini's clerk, "Great—thank you. I'll call Mr. Petroni after I hang up with you to tell him about the hearing and then have the documents filed. Thanks again for your help."

"See you tomorrow morning, Mr. Schreiber. Don't be late. The judge is very punctual."

When he hung up, Rita said, "You looked like there was something wrong with something you heard."

"Oh, nothing, really—it was just that I've heard that the judge we'll be in front of tomorrow, Judge Gentilini, can be rather rough on attorneys (*of a certain gender*) and has a reputation for colorful language. Don't worry. It has nothing to do with her fairness (*I hope*)."

"You going to be OK?"

"Oh yeah. I've been yelled at before by judges and opposing counsel."

He picked up the phone and dialed the number Rita had given him. The phone on the other end rang several times before being answered. When it was, a male voice answered, "Hello."

"My name is Ernest Schreiber. I'd like to speak with Leonard Petroni."

"So, speak," came the gruff reply.

"Are you Leonard Petroni?"

"Didn't I just say that?"

Not really. This is starting off well. "Mr. Petroni, I'm an attorney in Boulder—"

"Never heard of ya," said Leo.

"Mr. Petroni, I represent Rita Draper, and I'm going to file a complaint against you this afternoon along with a motion for temporary restraining order and preliminary injunction to stop you from damaging her personal property and allowing her to have possession of the property at 10209 Wild Rose Circle—"

"Who the fuck do you think you are telling me what you're going to do to me? Do you know who I am? Do you know who I am?" yelled Leo.

Ernest couldn't resist the urge to goad his opponent. "The guy who's taking unfair advantage of my client and exercising unlawful control over her property? How am I doin'?"

"Why you smart-mouthed piece of shit."

"Look, Mr. Petroni, there's no need for such flowery language. I just want to let you know that I have a hearing set for tomorrow morning at eight in Judge Gentilini's court on the TRO motion. You can be there or not, but I will be regardless, and I'll be presenting my case for the TRO."

The announcement of a hearing so soon brought Leo up short and squelched his mouth but not his rage. After a brief pause, he said with less volume than before, "You can talk to my attorney, Michael Wesley—"

It was Ernest's turn to interrupt. "I know Mr. Wesley. I have his contact information."

"You're going to regret ever tangling with me, Schreiber," threatened Leo before abruptly hanging up.

Rita said, "That didn't sound like it went well. I could hear Leo yelling from over here."

"He was a bit agitated," came Ernest's understated reply as he looked through the Rolodex on his desk for the number of Michael Wesley. Ernest knew Wesley only from a real estate closing several months before where Wesley represented the buyer and Ernest the seller. As he dialed the number he had found, Ernest said, "I must have caught him at a bad time." That got a laugh from Rita.

Wesley's receptionist answered, and after Ernest explained who he was and that he wanted to talk to her boss, she said he was on another call. Ernest said he'd hold. It turned out to be a fifteen-minute hold. Ernest wondered if Wesley was on the phone with Petroni. After Wesley answered, he didn't have to wonder. The phone call with Wesley was considerably more civil than the one with his client, but no more productive. Ernest explained the complaint and motion and requested Wesley's telefax number so he could transmit copies to Wesley after their conversation. The conversations with Petroni and Wesley and the fax transmissions were adequate to get Ernest before the judge for the TRO motion, but they were not legally sufficient for service of the complaint. In the hope of satisfying that legal hurdle, Ernest asked Wesley if he would accept service on behalf of his client. It was then that Ernest learned that Wesley's other phone call was indeed with Leo Petroni. Wesley said that his client had already instructed him "in emphatic terms" not to accept service. Petroni wasn't going to make things easy for Ernest.

After he hung up from the conversation with Michael Wesley, Ernest dictated to Tracey a simple affidavit describing his conversations with Petroni and his attorney. While Tracey typed the affidavit for Ernest's signature, Ernest faxed the complaint and TRO documents to Michael Wesley. At Ernest's prior instruction, Tracey had called Ernest's process server and private investigator, Manfred Dickerson, an imposing figure of a man and master of Jeet Kune Do, the method of street fighting developed by Bruce Lee. Although he would never start a fight, Dickerson finished several. Once, three guys had jumped him in a dark Denver alley and beat him severely. After recovering, he spent over a year tracking each one down in different states and giving them extended hospital stays. It was a story he shared only with his closest friends. When Ernest came out of his office and headed through his waiting room to the telefax machine, Dickerson was there waiting for instructions from Ernest.

"Hang on, Manny. Not much longer and I'll be ready for you. Thanks for coming so fast."

"Not a problem, Ernest. Take your time. You know me—patience of Job." Though opposites in many ways, the two men really liked each other.

After all the faxing, affidavit signing and document copying was complete, Ernest handed the original set and a couple of copies to Manny Dickerson.

"I want you to go to the Jefferson courts first and file these documents. After that, get service on Leonard Petroni. He's in his early eighties, fit, with gray hair parted on the right, dark eyes, and about five eight and one hundred eighty pounds—distinguished looking. And, feisty."

"Ya wan' I should fix his feisty, boss?" asked Manny in mock-mob lingo.

"Very funny. No, but he's probably going to try to duck service, so use your cunning. Doubtful that you'll be able to get him outside his estate." Ducking service was a childish game that only delayed the inevitable, but Ernest sensed that delay would be part of Petroni's strategy.

"Well, I'll try to get him at the courthouse tomorrow. If that doesn't work, I'll get more creative."

September 1, 1988

At 7:30 a.m. Ernest, Rita, Blair and Manny Dickerson were all gathered outside the doors to Judge Gentilini's courtroom. They marched in together and once inside split up to take separate positions. Manny was the first to peel off from the group. He took a seat on a bench in the back close to the doors so he could snag Petroni on his way into the courtroom. Blair stopped at the gate of the bar and sat on a bench. On the other side of the bar, Rita and Ernest sat down in front of Blair at the plaintiff's table with Ernest next to the podium. Ernest intended to call Rita as his only witness. For a TRO hearing, he just needed to establish that there had been irretrievable damage, that damage probably would

177

continue without a TRO from the court and that there was a probability of success of the lawsuit on the merits. In lawyer talk, it was called a prima facie, literally first face, showing of the presumptive accuracy of his facts. He could do all that through Rita. Besides—his lawyer senses tingled around Blair. There was something he had not identified that he didn't trust about Blair—just a feeling. However, Ernest's feelings were usually spot on. His officemate, Carl, often marveled and remarked on Ernest's intuitive insight into facts and arcane laws that later proved correct.

Michael Wesley arrived five minutes before eight—without Petroni. Ernest looked back and gave an eye signal to Manny. Manny nodded and left the courtroom.

A minute before eight, the court reporter came out from behind the wooden partition that screened the judge's bench from the door leading to the judge's chambers. She then sat in the chair by the steno machine in front of the bench. Before the reporter was fully adjusted in her seat, in came the court clerk who called, "All rise. This session of the First Judicial District of the State of Colorado is now in session." As the last words were leaving the clerk's lips, in swooped the judge with her robe almost fluttering behind her. She was a stern-looking blond with dark glasses perched on a Roman nose in front of penetrating blue eyes.

"Case number eighty-eight CV three zero one eight—enter your appearances, counsel," ordered Gentilini.

Both Ernest and Wesley shot out of their seats as if their pants just caught fire. First Ernest and then Wesley stated their names, their clients' names and their Colorado attorney license numbers. Wesley further stated that since there had not been proper service on his client, he was making a special appearance solely for the purpose of defending against the TRO motion and that neither he nor his client were admitting to the jurisdiction of the court over Petroni for any other purpose.

Then Gentilini glared at Ernest and growled, "Well, Mr. Schreiber, I don't have all day. State your case."

Ernest hopped to and outlined the motion for temporary restraining order, being as precise and time efficient as he could. Then he called Rita to the stand and questioned her about the contract for her purchase of the house at 10209 Wild Rose Circle; her taking of possession of it; the work she had done to it; her decision to leave for California since Petroni had not gained title; her photos and experience as a professional photographer; and the discovery of the destruction of some of her photos, her Jeep being up for sale and the probable ongoing sale and destruction of her other property still in the house. For evidence, he offered the contract and promissory note. Both were received into evidence without objection from Wesley. The whole time Gentilini moved her intense gaze back and forth between him and Rita with an occasional diversion to Michael Wesley. She reminded Ernest of a predatory bird waiting for a mouse to make a fatal mistake.

When he had finished, Ernest sat down to leave his client open to cross-examination. Wesley had none. Ernest was starting to understand his opponent's game plan. That was the end of Ernest's presentation, so he rested and waited to hear what Wesley had to say.

Wesley got up and said, "Your Honor, may it please the Court." Gentilini didn't looked pleased. "My client, Leonard Petroni, is unable to be here today. As you probably know, Mr. Petroni is a very important and busy man. He is a highly sought-after expert on energy related matters due to his extensive history with the Public Utilities Commission and the Attorney General's Office. This hearing came on us quite suddenly, just yesterday, and Mr. Petroni had already made plans to attend one of his many—"

"Cut the bullshit, counsel, and get to your point," ordered Gentilini.

Well, at least she dispenses her contempt equally, thought Ernest. *Or, maybe, that's just equally for men, like her reputation would indicate.*

"Yes, Your Honor," acquiesced Wesley in his most servile voice. "Before leaving for his meeting out of state, we were able to put together Mr. Petroni's sworn affidavit showing that the contract that you have a copy of in evidence had no closing date and therefore was not enforceable. Furthermore, not even Ms. Draper believed it was enforceable because she left for several months without giving Mr. Petroni any way of contacting her. Thus, she abandoned any rights she may have had under that document. I offer into evidence Mr. Petroni's affidavit as Defendant's Exhibit A."

Yup, I saw that coming. Not bad. Then, he said, "Your Honor, I object—"

"Overruled, Defendant's Exhibit A is accepted into evidence," interjected Gentilini, cutting Ernest off.

Maybe if you heard my reason, you'd agree with me.

"Anything else, Mr. Wesley?" asked the judge. When Wesley said he was done, Gentilini looked at Ernest, who called Rita back to the stand to refute Petroni's allegations that she had abandoned the contract and house and that she had failed to give him her contact information in California while she was gone. Then, the two attorneys gave their arguments for and against the granting of the temporary restraining order. Wesley pressed hard for a deposit by Rita into the court registry of $100,000 to cover damages to Petroni in the event the judge granted the TRO. As Ernest had predicted, Wesley's supporting argument for such a large sum was that Petroni would suffer that much in damages for lost rent or a lost sale or both. In the end, Judge Gentilini didn't buy any of Wesley's arguments. She granted the TRO, including most importantly Rita's right to have immediate possession of the property at 10209 Wild Rose Court at least until the preliminary injunction hearing. She also ordered that the $5,000 Rita already paid and her promissory note were adequate security for any damages Petroni might suffer if later the TRO was found to be wrongfully entered. She ordered Ernest to prepare the order and to get it to her for her signature by the next day. Finally, she ordered a hearing on Ernest's preliminary injunction to be held at 9:00 a.m. on October 3, the only date the judge and two attorneys could agree to.

Outside the courtroom, Rita was very happy with the results and with Ernest's performance in the courtroom. Blair looked less impressed but kept his mouth shut.

"That judge is somethin'," said Rita. "But you were great. That was pretty stupid of Leo not to show, that is, assuming he could."

"No, that was pretty smart," said Ernest. Both Rita and Blair looked puzzled at that. "By sending his attorney in to make a special appearance with an affidavit, Petroni got his testimony in and didn't have to risk getting served with the complaint. We still don't have personal service on him. He probably realized that there was a reasonable chance that he'd lose the hearing, but there was just as good a chance that he would succeed. Best way of avoiding getting served and still getting a shot at beating the TRO was just what he did."

That evening Leo sat in his living room feeling very self-satisfied even though his attorney had lost the TRO hearing. The longer he could delay the ultimate trial, the more money Rita Draper would have to pay in attorney fees and the more likely it would be that she would finally cave and abandon her lawsuit, which still had not been served on him. Also, he had plans for how he would win the trial if and when it finally came. It was late, around nine, when he headed to bed. As he passed the living room windows, he looked over at his greenhouse as he always did before retiring. A red light was flashing from the greenhouse. That could mean only one thing. There was a failure in the climate controls. *Shit, why does this sort of thing have to happen just when I'm going to bed.*

He grabbed a flashlight and headed out the front door toward the greenhouse. When he arrived at its entrance, he noticed that the flashing light had stopped. *Better check it while I'm here. Won't get any sleep if I don't.*

As he entered the code, he heard something rustle behind him. He turned and jumped at the sight of a tough-looking man standing before him with a large flashlight covered in a red-plastic bag in his left hand.

"Leonard Petroni?"

"Yeah?"

"You've just been served," said Manny.

When Leo made no move to take the papers in Manny's outstretched right hand, Manny threw them bouncing them off Leo's chest. Manny smiled and then turned and left.

CHAPTER 9

Truckload of Assholes

September 1, 1988

With one fluid movement, the white line disappeared. Sandy stretched her eyes open and sniffed while savoring the delicious drip down her throat. Some thought the drip was disgusting—not Sandy. To Sandy it was haute cuisine. She took a momentary break to pick up the cigarette from the ashtray on her desk. After flicking some ash into the tray, she took a long pull of nicotine-laced smoke to enhance her high. Placing the Marlboro back in its cradle in the ashtray, she bent forward while holding one end of the 14k-gold nasal straw next to her other nostril and made another smooth swipe, this time over the remaining line of white powder on the mirror in front of her. This snort sent an even more intense rush rocketing to the top of her head and another drip of blended cocaine and mucus down the back of her throat. She pinched her nose between the index finger and thumb of her left hand and rubbed her nose with the back of her hand while going for her smoke with the other. After another extended inhalation of toxic fumes, she wiped the nasal discharge off her left hand with a tissue and returned her drug paraphernalia to its engraved, silver box. As anticipated, numbness spread through her nostrils, throat and mouth, but the rest of her was awash with euphoria and razor-sharp focus. She snuffed out her cigarette, locked her stash in the credenza behind her desk, grabbed her briefcase, and headed to court.

Sandra Stephanie Pitt, also known among some jurists as The Pitt Viper, graduated in the top fifteen percent of her class from the Sturm College of Law at the University of Denver in 1980. After three years at the prestigious law firm of Holland and Hart, she left taking with her (some senior partners said "stealing") as many wealthy clients as she could. She had a reputation for cold-blooded ruthlessness in and out of the courtroom. That appealed to the clients she took and those who gravitated to her after she set up her own one-woman law firm. She fast became a successful trial lawyer, taking both criminal and civil cases. She owed a great deal of her success to her willingness to do anything to win. No sewer was too filthy for her to swim through in order to reach her goal. She honed that skillset at law school, where she would often hide critical research materials for assignments in order to gain an advantage over her classmates. It worked. In addition to her other talents, she was a masterful liar. In her opinion, the truth was for chumps and could always be improved with a lie. Consequently, she often suborned perjury from her clients and witnesses. Most lawyers who knew her hated and feared her, but none respected her. She was an expert at reading and manipulating juries and was adequately respectful of judges. She could be charming when the occasion called for it. At bar gatherings, she made a point of sidling up next to judges to schmooze and compliment without being oleaginous. However, under her faux ingratiating exterior, Sandra Pitt had a general contempt for others, unless they were wealthy. It was an entitlement bestowed upon her by her rich, doting father and warned against by her mother. Her father had received his fortune from the coal-mining business by hard work—of miners—and shrewd investments—by his father. Unlike her father, Sandra needed to work—not for money, but for winning and savoring the defeat of her opponents. She relished the beaten looks of her vanquished adversaries. The money was a fringe benefit.

When Sandra was within ten feet of the entrance to the courtroom where her morning hearing was to be held, the doors opened and out came Ernest, Rita and Blair. At first, Ernest hardly noticed her, but when they were within five feet of each other he was struck by the sickening sweet scent of some fruity-floral perfume and cigarette smoke. Ernest could barely tolerate cigarette smoke by itself, whether in the air, on a smoker's breath or entrapped in the threads of clothing. But the combination of this woman's perfume and the odor coming off her clothing and probably oozing from her skin was enough to make him gasp and look at her. The woman he saw was thin to the point of skeletal; medium height; with dark, well-coifed, mid-length hair and dark eyes behind black-framed glasses. She was dressed in a form-fitting, dark-blue business suit and white blouse with a deep-burgundy floppy bowtie. He thought the skirt was too tight and too short to be professional. But what struck him most was a sense of hardness about her in spite of the cheerless smile she gave him. In a matter of seconds, the encounter was over and forgotten by both of them.

Today was the last day of the criminal trial of one of Sandra Pitt's repeat clients—a drug dealer by the name of Stanley Turner. Mr. Turner had been arrested in the alley of a house where he and his girlfriend, Gelda, had been attending a party. Sergeant Curtis Ortega and his partner responded to a complaint by a neighbor about the loud noise and specifically about what sounded like a fight in the alley. Sergeant Ortega left his partner inside the house dealing with the revelers while he went to the back of the house to investigate the possible fight. When Ortega came into the alley, Turner was kicking the stuffing out of a man on the ground while Gelda watched from the backyard fence. When Gelda saw Ortega, she tried to get Turner's attention but he was too focused on pummeling his victim to notice. The altercation between Turner and the man with footprints on his body was over a past drug deal. The man on the ground claimed that Turner shortchanged him on a past coke sale and wanted Turner to make it up to him by providing some snow—gratis. Turner expressed his disagreement with his fists and feet. Sergeant Ortega had to pull Turner off his target and slammed him against the brick wall of the car garage next to the alley. That, and the resulting shiner and cut over his left eye, gave Turner and Sandra Pitt part of their later defense. After cuffing Turner, Sergeant Ortega found a zip of coke in Turner's sport-coat pocket. That was twenty-eight grams of coke that he could have ditched if he had paid more attention to Gelda, or, better yet, been able to keep by not being such a hothead. But like most dealers, Stanley Turner was more emotional than rational. At the trial, Sandra Pitt had Gelda take the stand in defense of poor, police-brutalized Stanley, who still sported a bandage over his left eye even though it wasn't necessary, except for eliciting sympathy, and a hint of discoloration where he once had his black eye. Gelda had been extensively prepared and suborned prior to her testimony. On direct examination by Ms. Pitt, Gelda testified that her Stanley had no cocaine on him, that the cocaine the prosecution entered into evidence was planted by Officer Ortega, that Ortega beat Stanley severely, and that Stanley was defending her honor by beating the other man who had groped and tried to rape her. The incensed district attorney did his best to counter the lies, but the torpedo to his case had been delivered well and Gelda held firm under his intense cross-examination. The jury was obviously impressed by Gelda's testimony as they were with the evident difference in treatment of the two attorneys dispensed by Judge Gentilini. The only thing left in the trial now was the closing arguments of the two attorneys.

After the district attorney finished with his carefully prepared and professionally delivered closing argument, Judge Gentilini called upon Sandra to give hers. Rather than popping right up, Sandy scanned the jury and then turned slowly in her chair to give a view above her hemline to the male jurors in the front row before rising dramatically, almost solemnly. She began with a brief explanation of the evidentiary standard of beyond a reasonable doubt and how that differed from the lower civil standard of preponderance of the evidence. Then, she went into specifics of the case, especially the testimony of Gelda, realizing that many, if not most, jurors had a hard time refining the concept of any doubt into reasonable doubt. If she could create any doubt in the minds of the jurors, then they would do the rest and convert that into reasonable doubt. After all, who among us doesn't think our doubt is reasonable? Then, she crossed a line. She attacked Sergeant Curtis Ortega.

"I don't know how many of you are familiar with recent scientific studies that show there is a connection between eye movement and lying, but I'd be willing to bet that most of you have heard of it. After all, you're a smart, informed group of jurors. That's why I agreed to you being on this jury. The scientific name for this behavior is neuro-linguistic patterns or programming. If a person's eyes go up to the right, regardless of how long they do, it's an indication that the person is lying. I hope you noticed that when I asked Sergeant Ortega, while he was under oath, whether he planted that packet of cocaine on Mr. Turner—"

"All right, that's enough. I object, Your Honor," said the assistant district attorney. "I know this is closing argument where there's a lot of leeway given to counsel to present what they think they have proven, but this is nothing short of defense counsel testifying as a witness, and not just any witness—an expert witness. None of what she has said is in the record—"

"Overruled—I'm going to allow it. Please continue, Ms. Pitt. And, you better keep your mouth shut." Gentilini made the last comment while staring angrily at the prosecutor. Again, the jury noticed.

With impunity for her bad behavior being granted by the judge, The Pitt Viper slithered in to strike again and again. She hammered at what she labeled as "the obvious veracity" of Gelda's well-crafted testimony and the lack of it in Sergeant Ortega's. Repeatedly, she referred to his eye movements up and to the right, none of which were observed by any of the jurors because they didn't happen, but a lie repeated enough times will become the truth. That's what happened, and later in the jury room, all it took was for four of the jurors to remember the eye flicks for the rest to fall in line. By three that afternoon, the jurors came in with their verdict of not guilty of drug possession or felony assault and guilty of one count of third-degree misdemeanor assault, a minor offense that would get Stanley Turner back on the streets that day for time served to sell cocaine to his needy clientele. It was another grand success for Sandra Pitt that she was anxious to celebrate with some of Stanley Turner's highest-grade cocaine and a bottle of scotch.

September 2, 1988

At 7:57 a.m., Michael Wesley received a call from Leo Petroni. "Morning, Leo. How's Miami?"

"Far as I know, it's doin' just fine," came Leo's response.

"As far as you know? I thought you had an important oil and gas meeting of some sort down there that you had to leave for two nights ago."

"Something came up, and I had to cancel."

Michael wasn't sure he believed that, but he kept his doubts to himself. "So, where are you now?"

"I'm at home, Michael. Same place I was when I got served last night with that Draper lawsuit."

"Well, that was fast."

"Thanks for pointing out the obvious, Michael."

What a jerk. Why do I keep taking his abuse? "All right, bring the papers in this afternoon so I can get to work on your response."

"I can bring them in, but I don't want you to rush to get an answer out."

"Well, we do have until the twentieth to respond."

"Yeah, yeah, I know, but I want to delay even more than that."

"Why? Seems like you'd like to get this to trial as fast as possible."

"'Why?' Because I said so, that's why. And, don't assume you know what I want."

"All right, Leo, but I do have the time to work on the answer, and I don't want to lie to the court about some contrived reason why I don't." *Like I apparently did about you being in another state.*

"Huh," was all Leo said.

"So far, you haven't asked me about how the hearing went yesterday."

"Well, how did it go, then? I assume you lost."

Why, oh why, do I stay with this guy? "We lost, Leo, and probably not just because you failed to show up in person."

"What's that supposed to mean? You lost because I wasn't in the courtroom?"

"No judge, not even Gentilini, would risk not ordering a TRO when told, convincingly, that there was on-going damage to a contested piece of property that could be stopped right then, so the facts could be sorted out later. Besides, the other attorney did a fine job."

"Whatever. So, you're not going to stall for me?"

"I'm not going to lie for you."

"Maybe you're forgetting who the client is here."

"Oh please, Leo, I know who and what the client is."

"Gentilini—she has a rep for hating men. You believe it?"

"Hate is a strong word, Leo. Yes, she has a reputation for being harder on men than women lawyers. So, do I believe it?" Heavy sigh, then he continued, "Unfortunately, yes."

"How about I make this easy for you? I hire another attorney to replace you, and while I'm making a diligent search, you file a motion for extension of time until I can find an attorney and for him to get up to speed."

Wesley saw his opportunity to be rid of Leo Petroni for good, so he took it. "That's a good idea, Leo, except for the last part. To make it even more convincing, maybe you should take all of your business to another attorney. Since I made a special appearance yesterday solely for the purpose of that hearing, I'm not on record as your attorney in the case, so you can go to any attorney you want." *And, while you're at it, go to hell too.* Wesley hung up without saying goodbye or promising to file for an extension of time for Leo to answer the Draper complaint.

At first, Leo was furious with Wesley. Then the words of Clyde Smaldone came back to him, "Youse can trap more flies with honey than somethin' they don't like." Even at his current stage of life with all the power and wealth he had amassed, those words were relevant. Clyde would have handled the conversation with Wesley differently, with finesse. He blamed his crankiness on his long dry spell without any gratification from "enjoying" young women. Fortunately, that would soon be remedied with an actual trip to Miami. Young women were easy to come by there. In the meantime, he needed a quick substitute for Michael Wesley.

He chose someone randomly from the yellow pages—a throwaway attorney—one that would follow orders.

September 16, 1988

"Ernest, you have a call from an attorney by the name of Bernard P. Cunningham the third," announced Tracey over the intercom line.

"The third, eh? Sounds important," said Ernest sarcastically.

"He seems to think so. Says he represents Leonard Petroni."

"Really? He's calling at four thirty on a Friday afternoon just before an answer is due on our complaint. Sure, put him through, Tracey, but I can guess what he wants."

"Ernest Schreiber here," said Ernest after he was connected by Tracey.

"Mr. Schreiber, my name is Bernard P. Cunningham the third. I am an attorney in Wheat Ridge, and I represent Mr. Leonard Petroni, Esquire in the civil action filed by you in the Jefferson district court on behalf of Rita Draper." Bernard P. Cunningham III made that statement as if he were announcing the arrival of a royal couple at a formal ball. Then he paused for dramatic effect. When he realized that Ernest wasn't going to say anything, he continued. "I have to tell you that you haven't stated much a case, Mr. Schreiber. In my opinion, it is defective on its face. Nonetheless, since I have just begun this case, I am going to need more time to research the facts and law before I file a proper answer to your complaint, weak though it is. Consequently, I will be filing a motion for an extension of time to respond. I'd like to have your agreement to the extension." More dead air between the two before Bernard P. Cunningham III decided to fill it, "Well, will you agree to an extension of time or not?"

"Oh, you want an answer from me. I thought you were just expressing one of your heart's desires. You didn't tell me how long you want."

"I'd like twenty more days—until October 10."

"I'm sure you would. October 10 is Columbus Day, a legal court holiday."

"Very well, October 11."

"No."

"No, you won't agree to twenty days?"

"Seems like way too much time to respond to a defective complaint, especially for someone of your obvious self-importance."

Did he just say self-importance or importance? wondered Cunningham. "Well then, how much time will you agree to?"

"None."

"None?"

"We seem to be getting an echo on the line."

"So, you intend to contest my motion for extension of time?"

"Didn't say that either, counselor."

"Well, just what—"

"Oh, stop struggling. Look, you have never met me and on our first conversation you open up with your phony, nasal, affected snobbery to insult me and then ask me for a favor. I don't know what law school you went to, but they obviously taught you nothing that stuck about effective negotiating skills."

"How insulting—"

"Glad you agree. Now, listen to me. I listened quietly while you bloviated. You called me around four thirty on a Friday afternoon to tell me you were going to ask the judge for an extension of time to file a response that is due on Tuesday. Unless you operate differently from me, you know full well that I'm not going to agree to that without my client's permission. By the time I talk to my client, you will have already filed your motion. And, let's get real—the judge is going to grant your request before I have a chance to object. We both know that's how it works. So, when you file your motion, you have to tell the judge that you talked to me, and you can tell her that I do not agree to your request and that I said it was way too long. Oh, and if you really want to be honest, you should tell her how long you've been sitting on this case before asking her for more time. But we both know that won't happen, don't we?"

In response, Bernard P. Cunningham III gave a few sputtering noises.

"Is there anything else I can help you with this afternoon, Mr. Cunningham?"

"No."

"Good, then you have a nice evening," said Ernest, as he hung up.

What Ernest did not realize is that he had struck an exposed nerve when he questioned Bernard's law school alma mater. Bernard P. Cunningham III had received his Juris Doctor degree from the Thomas M. Cooley Law School in Lansing, Michigan. Every year that it had been ranked after its founding in 1972, the Thomas M. Cooley Law School had been recognized as the number one worst law school in the US, well, that is except for its own internal ranking system which had a different set of standards to meet from those of universally respected ranking systems. Bernard was very sensitive to the point of embarrassment about his law school education and over-compensated for his lack of a respected legal education with vacuous puffery. However, being three-years fresh out of law school, he had not seasoned his effrontery enough to overcome his internal panic when someone like Ernest came close to exposing it. Nonetheless, Bernard's legal training and mind were adequate for the moment for Leo Petroni's purposes. All he needed for a while was a yap dog to do his bidding. Bernard P. Cunningham III was the attorney for the job.

Once he had finished his conversation with Cunningham, Ernest decided to call it a day. He wanted to go home and see Claire, Danielle and Christopher.

When he came out of his office, Tracey was packing up too. She looked up and asked, "So, how was your conversation with Bernard P. Cunningham the third?"

"'Bout like you'd expect. He wanted an extension of time to answer."

"And, of course, you wouldn't do that without talking to Rita Draper."

"See there, you got it right off the bat. He didn't, or acted like he didn't. Hey, Tracey, I thought of another name for Cunningham."

"OK, I'll bite. What is it?"

"Sly Pig." She laughed, and they both said goodnight.

September 20, 1988

The first national preserve in the United States was established on October 11, 1974. It was a novel concept created through the cooperative effort of groups with conflicting interests to preserve what had already been defiled from further destruction by an interloper who had no claim of traditional abuse, as some of them did. The area involved was a freshwater-swamp ecosystem in Southwest Florida and the largest contiguous habitat for panthers in South Florida. The interloper was the Dade County Port Authority and the State of Florida, and the new, proposed abuse was the largest jetport in the world smack dab in the Everglades. Other possible locations for the airport were too close to the rapidly expanding, noise-sensitive human populations of Florida, and in the Everglades only a vast swamp, its animals and flora would be the abused. Of all the groups that had an interest in prohibiting the jetport, the animals and plants had the longest history of traditional use. Fortunately, they had dedicated conservationists and environmentalists to speak for them. Next in line for longevity of use came the Seminole and Miccosukee tribes and then hunters who demanded their right to continue to kill animals in the name of sport. Dade County Port Authority had already purchased the land for the jetport and had begun its construction when these groups came together to stop it. However, there was one influential group that did nothing to protect the fragile environment, but which squealed the loudest about their right to continue what they called their traditional use—big oil companies.

Creation of the Big Cypress National Preserve was the result of the cooperative efforts of the various eclectic groups, but it was a compromise. It did not provide the protections of a national park. The purpose for Big Cypress National Park as stated in the federal law that created it was to:

> "assure the preservation, conservation, and protection of the natural, scenic, hydrologic, floral and faunal, and recreational values of the Big Cypress Watershed in the state of Florida and to provide for the enhancement and public safety thereof."

Those were lofty words for a worthy purpose, but they should have gone on to state:

and to ensure the protection and economic enhancement of, and environmental degradation committed by, big oil companies,

because that is what the law did by allowing what were called traditional uses. The traditional extraction of oil and gas dated back to 1943. However, on April 29, 1988 16 U.S. Code §698m-4 entitled "Oil and gas exploration, development, and production in Big Cypress National Preserve and Addition" opened up the preserve to new exploration, development and production of oil and gas with access on, across and through all lands within the boundaries of the Big Cypress National Preserve. That law was a welcome sign to oil and gas companies and the incentive for Leo Petroni's trip to Miami in September 1988.

Leo had been hired by Wilbur Pitt to attend a meeting with executives of Collier Resources Company. Collier had a long and storied history in Southwest Florida. Between 1911 and 1923, Barron Collier had acquired 1.3 million acres in Southwest Florida becoming the largest land owner in all of Florida. In 1972, Humble Oil and Refining Company discovered oil under part of that land in what was known as the Bear Island Field. In 1976, two years after Big Cypress National Preserve was established, the Collier family transferred 76,790 acres, including the Bear Island Field, to the Big Cypress National Preserve while reserving to themselves all of the mineral and oil and gas rights. This provided a nice tax benefit while keeping the profit center to themselves. It was like selling someone a water melon after cutting out and keeping the sweet center. In 1978, more oil was discovered in Collier reserved mineral rights at the Raccoon Point Field also in Big Cypress National Preserve. After passage of the 1988 law allowing more oil and gas exploration in Big Cypress National Preserve, Collier planned to conduct a 3-D seismic survey of the Raccoon Point Field to see if it would be beneficial to expand the Raccoon Point Field by another gift of land while reserving all the fossil-fuel goodies to themselves. Wilbur had been invited to the trough by a close friend on the Collier board.

Wilbur had received his wealth from coal mining and had no expertise in oil and gas. In fact, since Wilbur had inherited his fortune from his father who had built the coal mining business, Wilbur had no expertise in coal mining either. His sole expertise was in inheriting a fortune and doing all he could to spend it lavishly. At that, he exceled. Although he was not a close friend of Leo's, Wilbur had met him at a few fossil-fuel conventions and fundraising galas and knew his reputation as a sought-after advisor by barons of the energy-extractive industries. When Wilbur contacted Leo about attending the meeting, Leo, of course, saw an opportunity for more adult fun at some young woman's considerable expense.

On the pretense of wanting to spend some free time enjoying the sun in Miami before he had to work, Leo had excused himself from taking the same flight as Wilbur and had arrived in Miami a couple of days early. On the morning of September 20, Leo was in a North Miami Beach motel room for which he had paid cash. There was an inert, beautiful young woman in a naked sprawl on the bed. She was a recent graduate of the University of Miami burdened with student loans that she was trying to pay off with a low-pay job at the Miami Herald and turning tricks whenever she could. She had spotted Leo on a barstool at the end of a bar while trolling for johns in the Fontainebleau Miami Beach. Little did she know that she was about to hook a shark that would turn on her. For the benefit of any security or potential witnesses in the busy bar, Leo had feigned disinterest while instructing her to meet him at his car after continuing to circle the room for half an hour after he left. When she later met him at the appointed location, he immediately blew scopolamine in her face with an atomizer. Instead of receiving her negotiated fee and maybe a generous tip for a job well done as she expected, she was roughly raped without so much as a thank you. As Leo reached for the doorknob to exit, he turned and said, "Was it as good for you as it was for me, honey? Probably not, I guess." He snickered and left to pick up Wilbur Pitt from the airport and bring him back to their official hotel in Coral Gables.

The drive from the airport to the hotel was filled mostly with silence. As a nod to social mores, Leo asked how Wilbur's flight was, not caring one way or the other and not paying any attention to the reply. Wilbur reciprocated by commenting on Leo's obvious exhilaration and how he must have had a pretty good time during his extra days. To which, Leo stated that it was better than he had expected. When they reached the hotel, they split off to their respective rooms and agreed to meet later for dinner. Leo said he would make reservations, mostly because he wanted to be sure the restaurant they went to had plenty of vegetarian selections and wasn't just a high-priced steakhouse.

In the evening, Leo and Wilbur walked the short distance to Anne's of Coral Gables, a vegetarian restaurant with a name that parodied the title of the 1908 novel by Lucy Maud Montgomery. Few got it, and fewer thought it was funny. However, the food was excellent—if you liked vegetarian cuisine. Wilbur did not. When he looked over the menu and saw the absence of any meat of any color, he promised himself not to let Leo pick any more restaurants while they were together.

After two cocktails each and their second glass of wine, the conversation drifted away from business and into Leo's current lawsuit with Rita Draper. After describing the case and the fact that the other attorney, a guy by the name of Ernest Schreiber, had obtained a temporary restraining order against him—him, Leonard Petroni—he said, "I need a down-and-dirty, back-alley fighter. Somebody who can fight dirty and knock an opponent down and then kick them repeatedly to keep them down. Somebody who won't shy away from doing what's necessary just because it might be an ethical problem. Somebody with cojones the size of footballs."

Wilbur laughed and said, "Except for one of those requirements, I have just the person for you."

"What's the one thing?"

"The person I'm thinking of doesn't have testicles."

Leo was slightly drunk and didn't get it. "I sure as hell don't need a eunuch."

Wilbur laughed again. "It's my daughter—Sandra Pitt. I have one of her cards here. You will not be disappointed, Leo—guaranteed."

September 21, 1988

At Leo's request, the next evening Wilbur called his daughter to introduce her to Leo. Sandra was impressed and delighted that her father had brought such a prominent Denver figure to her as a potential client. Leo and Sandra hit it off from the start. After giving the details of the case, Leo explained what he wanted in an attorney.

"I need someone who can make this lawsuit as undesirable as possible for Rita Draper and her attorney and with as little expenditure as possible of my time and money in doing it. She and this Ernest Schreiber crossed a line by challenging me. I want them both to pay."

"Well, I would never intentionally obstruct or obfuscate the judicial process." *Not transparently, anyway.* "However, cases like this can ebb and flow over a long time. This sounds like it could be a very complicated case with a lot of discovery issues to resolve." *Especially if I obstruct and obfuscate.* "I would want to be very thorough and require the other side to provide extensive information. That, of course, will take a lot of this Schreiber's time to accomplish. Also, truth can be a very elusive thing—a very gray matter." *And, it can take gray matter to distort it to your liking.*

Leo loved what he was hearing and knew what it meant. He had an attorney who knew how to convey a message in weaselese. "All right, I like this. Can we meet when I return to get you going? The attorney I have right now is Bernard Cunningham. I'm not impressed, but I needed someone fast after my first attorney dropped out."

Sandra wanted Leo as a client, not just for his current legal skirmish with Rita Draper, but long term, and she didn't want to risk losing him to second thoughts before they had a chance to meet. So, she offered some legal advice, "I think you might want to get the transition going right now. You should call Mr. Cunningham as soon as possible, today or tomorrow, and have him call Mr. Schreiber to concede the preliminary injunction and get that hearing off the docket."

"Why should I do that? That doesn't do what I want."

"You want me to be honest with you, don't you?" *Like that's going to happen.*

"Of course."

"You're going to lose that hearing, and you're going to lose it after more evidence gets into the record. Whatever comes in during that hearing—testimony, documents—will be on the record. That means that evidence will come in and be staring at you during the final trial, and it will come in at a hearing that is coming up in twelve days on the third of October. That gives you damn little time to know what it is, much less to prepare a defense to it." *Or, create a lie to refute it.*

"Yeah, Michael Wesley said something about the evidence at the preliminary hearing being part of the record for the trial. That's why I didn't go to the temporary restraining order hearing," said Leo.

"So, you see, you're not really giving up anything by confessing to the preliminary injunction, but you would be if you went to a hearing on it. Also, when I go into a case, I like to win the first thing to get before the judge, and if not the first matter, the second. It's a psychological tactic—knocks the other side off balance from the start and stays with them through the case. You've already lost the first hearing. And, there's another reason."

"What's that?"

"When you talk to Cunningham about this, try to get him to make this his idea. That way if the case doesn't go to your liking, we have someone to blame for at least part of it." .

"Would that work?"

"I think I could make a strong enough case to survive a frivolous action defense and at least get his malpractice carrier to settle with you. Yeah, it would work."

Leo was impressed with Sandy's insights, confidence and deviousness. "All right, I'll do it."

September 23, 1988

"Ernest, it's Bernard P. Cunningham the third, Esquire, for you," announced Tracey.

"Again on a Friday afternoon—what is it with this guy? Go ahead, T, put him through."

Ernest wanted to prevent Cunningham from announcing his whole moniker, so he said, "Hello, Mr. Cunningham. This is Ernest Schreiber."

"As you know, Mr. Schreiber, there is a hearing scheduled for nine in the morning on the third of October on your client's motion for a preliminary injunction against my client, Leonard Petroni."

Does everything have to be a long-winded announcement? Guess it makes for more billable hours. "Yes, Mr. Cunningham, I know. You didn't call me just to remind me of that, did you?"

"I did not. I called to advise you that Mr. Petroni wishes to confess that matter and have an order for preliminary injunction entered on the same existing terms as the temporary restraining order."

Well, nicely played, Bernard P. Cunningham the third. "All right, I'll go ahead and prepare the stipulated motion for entry of the order along with a draft order for the judge to sign. Of course, the motion will include a request for the judge to vacate the hearing. You going to be around for a while? If so, I can get copies faxed to you this afternoon. If you agree, I'll sign the original motion and send my process server to you on Monday with the original for your signature and a set of copies for you."

"I will await your document transmission."

They both hung up, and Ernest got busy preparing the necessary documents with Tracey. After they finished and had telefaxed the documents to Cunningham for his review, Ernest tried to call Rita to give her the news. No one answered.

September 29, 1988

At 10:00 a.m. Ernest finally got a response to one of his numerous attempts to call Rita. She sounded tired. "Hello."

"My gosh, you do exist. I was starting to wonder whether I had just imagined that you were one of my clients. I've been calling since the week after the TRO hearing."

"I've been around. Had a photo shoot in Leadville for a few days." *And, Blair was hospitalized for several days getting his meds adjusted after a breakdown.*

"Since I didn't hear from you after we got the TRO, I guess you got access to the house."

"Yeah, a couple of days after Leo got served, we went over and found the door unlocked with the key in the door."

"Guess Leo didn't want to chitchat. Look, a lot has happened, but nothing that really moved the case forward. On Friday, September 16, I received a call from an attorney by the name of Bernard P. Cunningham the third. He told me he was replacing Michael Wesley as Leo Petroni's attorney. He also asked me to agree to an extension of time to answer our complaint. He wanted an extra twenty days, until October 11."

"Did you give it to him?"

"No, but the judge did."

"Did you file something with the court to object to it?"

"I did not. I wasn't going to agree or object to it without talking to you first. Anyway, it wouldn't have done any good. Would have been a complete waste of my time and your money. Those types of motions are routinely granted by judges. Besides, as I later discovered, I couldn't get ahold of you for your opinion even if I had tried. You know, you should get an answering machine, so you at least know when I call. I would think you'd want that for your photography business."

Rita had an answering machine that she turned off when it suited her, and over the days since the hearing, it suited her. She had forgotten to turn it back on after getting Blair home. Ernest's comment reminded her to do that.

"I'll be sure to do that. Do you know this Cunningham?"

"Never heard of him. He sounds inexperienced."

"What makes you say that?"

"The way he put on airs to impress, maybe in the hope of intimidating, me. He also made it sound like he was initiating some great legal strategy by requesting an extension of time to answer."

"Anything else happen in the case."

"Matter of fact, yes. Last Friday, I got another call from Mr. Cunningham. He told me that he and his client wanted to confess the preliminary injunction. In other words, he wanted to stipulate to the preliminary injunction on the same terms as the TRO. I tried to call you with that news too."

"Well, that's good, isn't it? You said nothing happened to move the case forward."

"But remember, I told you that I could have gotten some evidence in at that hearing that would not have to be introduced again at the final trial. Also, I was hoping to maybe do some cross-examination, or maybe even some direct, of Petroni. By agreeing to the preliminary injunction, those opportunities were cut down. Besides, I was pretty confident about winning that hearing."

"So, what now?"

"Well, we get our case refined while we wait for Mr. Cunningham's answer to the complaint. What did you learn when you got access to the house? Was any of your property missing, in addition to photos? Did Petroni damage anything?"

"Yes, some of my other property is missing, including some very expensive developing equipment and cameras. Also, he completely ripped out my darkroom and opened one of the walls into the living room. That was a lot of damage. And, he removed my refrigerator and stove. Guess he didn't like the style, or something."

"Wow—how far along are you with getting a list of damages put together?"

"It's going to take a while." Quite a while, since she had not even started making a list.

"Get it to me as soon as you have it. I need that in order to prepare an amendment to our complaint. I need to add a claim for conversion of your personal property."

"Conversion?"

"Yeah, that's essentially the civil action equivalent of criminal theft. Call me when you have the list so we can make an appointment to go over it. Talk soon."

"I will. Thanks again for all your hard work."

October 7, 1988

Ernest came out of his office and saw Tracey slitting open envelopes.

"Mail's late today," said Ernest.

"Yeah, Max didn't deliver it. He's probably taking a long weekend," observed Tracey. "How about you? Got any plans for Columbus Day?"

"It's not a real big holiday around our house, but it is a day off. I'll probably come in here really early for a couple of hours and then head back to spend the day with the family. Maybe later I'll find some Native Americans to abuse in honor of the great man."

"You're terrible," said Tracey appreciatively.

"How about you—any plans?"

"Maybe go for a hike. Oh, here's a new one," she said holding up a thick envelope. "You know a Sandra S. Pitt, attorney at law?"

"Nope," he said as he took the envelope and removed its contents. "Ah, geez, again?"

"What?"

"Leo Petroni is switching attorneys again and this new one, Sandra Pitt, is filing for another extension of time to answer."

As Ernest was saying that, Carl came out of his office, and said, "I overheard part of what you said. Did you say Sandra Pitt is on the opposite side of a case from you?"

"I guess so. I just received a withdraw from Bernard P. Cunningham the third and a substitution of counsel from this Sandra Pitt. Too bad too. I was just getting to really enjoy mocking Bernard. Why? You know Sandra Pitt?" said Ernest.

"I sure do. You don't?"

"No, is there something you want to tell me about her?"

Carl shook his head, gave a wry smile and said, "Let me just put it this way. If you were to order a whole truckload of assholes, and the next morning only Sandy Pitt was standing on your doorstep—you wouldn't be disappointed."

CHAPTER 10

Tall Tales, Shortchange

> "Truth and falsehood are arbitrary terms.... There is nothing in experience to tell us that one is always preferable to the other.... There are lifeless truths and vital lies.... The force of an idea lies in its inspirational value. It matters very little whether it is true or false."

One might think these are the words of Joseph Goebbels, one of the all-time greats in presenting lies as truth and doing it boldly, convincingly and successfully. But they are not. They are the words of an American journalist and commentator—Arthur Bullard. Bullard died before Goebbels came into full power in Nazis Germany, so he was a man ahead of his time. Bullard had been a student of Woodrow Wilson's at Princeton, and he wrote those words in *An Essay on the Beneficence of Fallacious Ideas*. For years, Wilson had proclaimed his commitment to American neutrality in the European war, but in 1917 he found himself in a conundrum—how to backpedal and convince the American people that American intervention in Europe was critical and inevitable. Bullard, along with another journalist at the Denver Post and later the Rocky Mountain News, George Creel, were instrumental in Wilson's propaganda effort through the Committee on Public

Information. CPI, as it was commonly known, was a creator and distributor of hyperbole to bolster the war effort and squelch any opposition to it. Creel was its chairman and Bullard, one of its critical henchmen. At least one historian opined that without Bullard the Committee on Public Information never would have existed. Although Ernest doubted that Sandra Pitt had any familiarity with Bullard or his essay, he soon learned that she could have been a devotee of Bullard's insights into the benefits of lying. Carl had been right in his assessment of her.

Ernest's introduction to Pitt's treacherous nature came on Friday, October 14. Ernest had called Rita on Saturday, October 8, with the news that Petroni had hired yet another substitute attorney to represent him. Although Ernest had explained the cost and probable futility of objecting to Pitt's request for another extension of time to answer the complaint, Rita was adamant that he do so. She specifically said that she did not care about the extra fees and costs of filing the objection. Over the weekend, Ernest prepared the objection which, due to the Columbus Day holiday, could not be filed until Tuesday, October 11. Before filing the objection, Ernest called Sandra Pitt on Tuesday to tell her of his forthcoming objection. The conversation was short and pleasant, not what he expected based upon Carl's description of Pitt. There was absolutely no possibility of confusion about his message. After the call, Ernest had Manfred Dickerson hand-deliver a copy of the objection to Pitt's office and file the original with the court. On Friday, Ernest received Pitt's reply in the mail with her sworn affidavit agreeing that the two of them had the telephone conversation alleged by Ernest in his objection, but asserting that she had initiated the call and that Ernest had agreed to the extension of time. There was nothing to be gained in crying foul to the court, and both Pitt and Ernest knew that. Generally, judges ignore such complaints as just peevish protests that the attorneys should resolve by themselves and not trouble the judge over, even though part of a judge's judicial duty is to ensure the smooth movement of a case to trial under specific rules of procedure that carry stern penalties for their violation—at least in concept. Pitt's willingness to sign a sworn affidavit to the truth of her lies was telling. Under the rules of civil procedure, Sandra Pitt's signature was enough of an assertion to the truth of the facts set forth in her reply, but she chose to up her game by signing a sworn affidavit. By doing that, she had thrown her gauntlet down challenging Ernest to call her a liar to the court. If he picked up the challenge, he would not only lose on his objection, but he would tarnish any credibility he had with the judge, and with Gentilini as the judge, Ernest needed all the credibility he could scrape together for the final trial. So, he let The Pitt Viper win this battle and kept his focus on winning the war.

That was just the beginning of an unpleasant and discordant journey to a trial on the merits. On November 3, Pitt's answer to the complaint arrived in the mail. Service of the answer by mail was entirely appropriate under the rules of civil procedure; however, late service was not. The day for filing the answer with the court and serving Ernest had been extended by Judge Gentilini to October 31. Under the rules, that was the day that Sandra Pitt was required to file her answer with the court and mail a copy to Ernest. As part of her answer, Pitt was required to sign a certification of the day on which she had mailed a copy of the answer. The certification Pitt signed stated she had mailed the answer on October 31, but the postmark on the envelope showed November 1. In addition, the envelope was twenty cents short on postage. Technically, not only was the answer mailed late, but it was not even served on him under the rules. To be valid service by mail, the mailing had to have the correct amount of postage paid on it. In her signed certification of service, Sandra Pitt certified that the mailing to Ernest was addressed to him with "postage prepaid," which in and of itself was true. There was a twenty-five-cent stamp on the envelope, but the weight required forty-five cents. This was more sucker bait for procedural quibbling that Ernest ignored; however, he started to keep a chronological log of Pitt's procedural infractions.

Somewhat surprisingly, the answer that Sandra Pitt filed did not have any contrived counterclaims against Rita Draper. It was something that Ernest had expected and that seemed in character with The Pitt Viper. That's not to say that her answer did not have its share of contrived affirmative defenses, but that was normal even in litigation with opponents who had integrity. Throw a bunch of defenses against the wall in the hope that one of them sticks. However, Pitt got a second chance at what Ernest called the "manure spreader attack."

On November 4, Rita brought her list of missing and damaged property to a meeting with Ernest. She came alone, without Blair. Her list was extensive, but of all the items on it, the photos for her unpublished book upset her the most. Whenever the conversation turned to them, Rita came to tears. All 350 of them were gone or damaged beyond salvage. The damaged and missing property would require amendment of Rita's complaint against Leo Petroni, as Ernest had told Rita it would during their conversation on September 29. However, the basic facts alleged in the original complaint were still valid and would serve equally well as the basis for adding an additional claim for relief—conversion of Rita's personal property. On November 7, Ernest completed the amended complaint and a motion requesting the court to allow the amendment. The motion was necessary because an amendment of a complaint was not something that could be done without court approval. On the same day, he mailed the originals to the court and copies to Sandra Pitt—with correct postage. Pitt had until the day after Thanksgiving, November 25, to object to the proposed amendment. November 28 came without an objection, followed by November 29 and 30, also without an objection. Then, on December 2, Ernest received an envelope from Judge Gentilini's court. Inside was an order by Gentilini dated December 1— granting his motion to amend. Without an objection from Pitt, not even Gentilini could find a reasonable argument for denying his motion. Rita's complaint now included three claims for relief against Leo Petroni—breach of contract, unlawful eviction and conversion.

Pitt had until December 12 in order to answer the amended complaint. None came. Ernest waited until December 15 before filing a notice that he would set up a conference call on December 20 with Pitt and the court clerk in order to set the trial date. On December 20, he called Sandra Pitt first.

"Ms. Pitt, this is Ernest Schreiber. Are you ready for our conference with Gentilini's clerk?"

"Not really. What's the status of the case?"

"What's the status of the case? What do you mean by that?"

"Well, has the court issued an order on your motion to amend the complaint?"

Seriously? You're claiming you didn't get a copy of the order? "Judge Gentilini granted my motion on December 1. Are you saying you didn't receive a copy of the order?"

"There isn't one in my file."

You still didn't deny getting a copy. "All right, look, I'll fax a copy to you after our conversation with the clerk."

"Well, I need to file an answer first."

"No, you don't. First of all, the deadline for filing an answer has passed. Second, the amended complaint just adds a claim of conversion based upon the same facts as the original complaint with a request for damages for loss and destruction of personal property. Not much of an answer is required for that. When I did not receive an answer, I thought, logically, that you were going to rely on your original answer."

"Well, you thought wrong, Mr. Schreiber."

"I flunked mindreading in law school, Ms. Pitt, but I did quite well in civil procedure. How about we come to an understanding in order to keep the case moving forward? When can you get me your answer?"

"I should be able to do that by January 10."

Nice try, lady. "I'll agree to December 30, and that's all."

That was longer than Sandy thought she would get, or knew she deserved. After a pregnant pause and exasperated sigh for effect, she said, "Oh, I suppose so, fine."

"One more thing before we get going with the clerk. The rules require us to discuss settlement. Is Mr. Petroni ready to seriously consider settling?"

"Yes—he's willing to not sue Rita Draper for abuse of process and his attorneys' fees, if she drops her lawsuit, now."

"I guess you didn't hear the 'seriously' part of my statement. I'll get the clerk on the line. Please hold while I do."

Although Ernest was able to get the trial set for three days starting on September 25, 1989, he made a mistake. He failed to follow up his conversation with a letter to Sandra Pitt confirming their agreement that he would allow her to file an answer to his amended complaint by December 30. It was a mistake he would not repeat.

On December 30, Ernest received a bulky envelope from Sandy Pitt. Once again, postage was due. This time it was forty cents. Tracey questioned Ernest as to why he didn't just refuse the envelope and send it back. His response was that he didn't want to lower himself to Pitt's sophomoric level, but he had to admit she was getting under his skin. Pitt's antics would have been bad enough if the Draper-Petroni case were his only case, but he had others, one of which was scheduled for a weeklong trial in Aspen in October, just a couple of weeks after the Draper trial. Inside the envelope from Pitt were thick sets of interrogatories for Rita to answer and requests for admissions and for production of documents, but no answer to the amended complaint. Ernest reciprocated with his own set of interrogatories and requests for admissions and document production, plus a request for a deposition of Petroni. His packet of discovery documents was ready for mailing to Sandra Pitt on January 6, 1989.

Anticipating that Pitt would not respond to his discovery requests in a timely manner, Ernest scheduled the deposition of Leo Petroni for March 8. He felt that should give him plenty of time to get an order from the court to compel the discovery he requested. In the meantime, he worked with Rita to get responses put together to the discovery requests from Sandra Pitt. He also repeatedly requested, to the point of badgering, that Blair provide his itemization of labor and material costs for the construction work he had performed. Not only did he need it for his trial preparation, but it was one of the items requested by Pitt. Finally, the day before his responses to Pitt's discovery requests were due, Blair came in with his itemizations. There was barely enough time for Ernest to get them included in the responses to Pitt's discovery requests and no time to properly review them before doing so. On the day that Pitt's responses were due to Ernest's discovery requests, he received another postage-due envelope with a request to inspect the property, but no responses to his requests. Ernest called Rita to convey the inspection request and his desire for payment of his bill.

Once she answered his call, Ernest said, "Hello, Rita. I just received another discovery request from Sandra Pitt. She wants to enter the property at Wild Rose Circle to inspect it."

"What the hell for?"

"I would imagine to see its condition and to make sure the damage we claim really was done and to get her own appraisal of it."

"I'm not letting that bitch or Leo in the house."

"Rita, her request, for once, is not out of line. I would do the same thing if I were on her side of the case."

"I don't care. It's not happening."

"If you don't allow it, it will put you, and me, in a bad light with the judge, and she'll just order you to do it anyway."

"Fine," she said petulantly. "I'm willing to pay you to stop her."

"Well, speaking of paying me—you haven't."

"I paid your retainer," she replied in a mildly defensive tone.

"Yes, but you haven't paid anything on any of my bills to you since that. The retainer is set aside to pay the expenses of litigation. You do know that if you treat me like a bank, I'm going to charge you interest like a bank. I've turned away at least two potential clients as a result of taking your case."

"I'll send you a check today. But, tell Pitt to pound sand."

"I'll let her know that you intend to prevent her access. However, I'm working in your best interest and won't play childish games like Pitt does and in the process sacrifice your best chances of winning this case just to spite her and Petroni. You hired me because of my legal expertise, so you need to understand that I'm the captain of this legal ship."

"Ernest, I understand that, and I appreciate all you have done so far. I'm just sick and tired of being abused by Leo and this Pitt bitch."

"I understand that, but please hang in there with me."

"OK."

Three days later, Ernest received Rita's check for $150 on the outstanding fees of $3,410. Ernest felt like he was being squeezed in a vice with one side of the vice jaw being Pitt and Petroni and his own client being the other.

After hanging up from his call with Rita Draper, Ernest prepared a motion to compel discovery that asked the court to order Pitt and Petroni to respond to his discovery requests and to pay his attorney fees in having to ask the court's assistance in getting the discovery he was entitled to. In the envelope to Pitt containing her copy of the motion, Ernest included a letter stating that Rita Draper was not going to allow her access to the house.

Ernest had overestimated his ability to get what he had requested before Petroni's deposition. It was obvious that Pitt's intent was to deny him any documents or information that might assist in the deposition. He'd have to get what he needed by a more thorough interrogation during the deposition.

Sandra Pitt's response to his motion to compel came a few days after it was due, but this time it had the correct postage. Ernest figured that Pitt was muddying the waters so that if it came up later, she could feign innocence for her prior failures to pay the correct postage. She could claim it was just an honest mistake that her secretary committed, or maybe it was caused by a faulty postage scale. Essentially, her response was that Ernest's requests were so onerous in their demands that it was taking longer than the allotted time to put together responses and her client was an important and busy man who had been traveling for important and busy reasons. Also in the envelope was Pitt's motion to compel entry to the property.

March 8, 1989

On March 8, Ernest, Rita and Dolly Barber, Ernest's favorite court reporter, waited in Ernest's conference room to take the deposition of Leo Petroni. Sandra Pitt and Petroni showed up forty-five minutes late. It was the first time Ernest and Pitt had seen each other since their chance encounter in the Jefferson County courthouse on September 1. They both recognized each other, but neither admitted to it. Pitt recognized Ernest by his good looks and signature bowtie. Ernest recognized Pitt by her rail-thin physique and distinctive odor—a blend of sickeningly sweet perfume and stale tobacco. Pitt was trailing a collapsible luggage cart loaded with a box of documents that she plunked down on the conference table and announced to be their responses to Ernest's discovery requests. It was a snow job. But, by producing her discovery responses just before the start of the deposition, Pitt could argue to the court that she complied with Ernest's requests as best, and as soon, as she could, and she did it before the scheduled deposition of her client. Ernest swiftly searched through the box. Most of the documents in the box were worthless to the case and most of the answers to interrogatories were objections for bogus evidentiary reasons. Responses to requests for admissions were denials and flimsy reasons for doing so. Ernest quickly separated the wheat from the chaff. There was a lot of the latter and little of the former. Discovery from Leonard Petroni would have to be gleaned through Ernest's examination skills during the deposition. It was going to be a long day—or more.

After being sworn in, Leo Petroni started out belligerent and stayed that way throughout his deposition. Pitt started out noisy and disruptive. Ernest was not distracted or intimidated, and he turned Pitt's gambit of showing up with inadequate discovery responses to her client's detriment. Ernest intended to go through each response and document in detail, but before he could he had to shut down Pitt. After getting Petroni's name, address and background information on the record, Ernest started in on the interrogatories that Petroni had failed to answer completely. Pitt pounced on his first question with an objection for relevance. Ernest looked over at Sandra Pitt and smiled a smile that gave her a chill.

"Is that really how you're going to do this? Unless this is your first ever deposition, you know that you don't waive your objections for relevance if you fail to make them today. You'll still get to make them at the trial," said Ernest.

"Unless the grounds could be obviated or removed today," shot back lawyer Sandy.

"That doesn't apply here, but let's just solve this right now by stipulating that any objections you have as to relevance, materiality or admissibility will be preserved until trial. Agreed?"

Silence.

"Do you agree, Ms. Pitt?" Although she really didn't have to agree for that to be true under the rules of civil procedure, Ernest wanted her to admit to it—as a training exercise for Sandra Pitt to understand he would have no truck with her petty interferences.

Sandy shook her head in the affirmative.

"While I'm sure that the court reporter reflected on the record that you shook your head in agreement, I'd like you to say the words. Do you agree?"

"Yes—I agree."

"Thank you, Ms. Pitt." Ernest then resumed his questioning of Leo Petroni, but within a few minutes, Sandy Pitt started coughing and sniffling and wiping her nose on the backs of her hands. Ernest had a hard time not gagging while watching Pitt wipe her mucus on her hands. Regardless, Ernest did not break stride in his questioning. Instead, he got up in mid-question and went over to a side table, retrieved a box of tissues kept there and set it down in front of Pitt.

As he set the tissues in front of Sandy, Ernest said, "Let the record reflect that opposing counsel has been loudly coughing, sniffling and wiping her nose on the backs of her hands during the examination of Mr. Petroni and that I have delivered a box of tissues to her. I hope that helps with your sudden attack, Ms. Pitt. If not, I can get you some cough drops—or an ambulance."

For a brief moment, Pitt glared at Ernest with such smoldering intensity that Ernest thought she'd burst into flames. It wasn't an unpleasant thought.

Shortly after that, Ernest directed Leo's attention to his responses to Ernest's written interrogatories. "Mr. Petroni, I want you to look at interrogatory number seven and your response to it."

"Yeah."

"Read the interrogatory and your answer, please."

Leo started to read them silently.

"Out loud, Mr. Petroni."

"Why the hell should I do that?" It was clear that Ernest's intense questioning was irritating Leo like sandburs in his underwear.

"Other than the fact that I asked you? You're reading them anyway, might as well do it out loud."

"Interrogatory number seven—your second affirmative defense is 'Rita Draper abandoned the contract, even assuming that there was a valid contract.' On what facts do you rely for your claim that Ms. Draper abandoned the contract? Response— Objection," read Leo. Then he looked up at Ernest.

"Why did you object to that interrogatory?" asked Ernest.

"How should I know? Ask my attorney."

"Your attorney isn't being deposed. You are, and I'm asking you, Mr. Petroni."

At that point Sandy Pitt took her pen, turned it upside down and tapped three times in the upper right corner of her legal pad. Ernest recognized it as a prearranged code between Pitt and

Petroni. Such codes were commonplace between attorneys and their clients during depositions. Leo immediately said, "I need a restroom break."

"All right, there will be a ten-minute break. We'll reconvene at ten forty-five," said Ernest.

A short visit to the restroom and a longer prepping outside by a cigarette-puffing Pitt and Petroni was ready to return to the conference room. After everyone was seated, and they were back on the record, Ernest asked Dolly Barber to read back the last question beginning with Leo's reading of Ernest's interrogatory seven.

Then, Ernest asked, "Do you have a response to that question, Mr. Petroni?"

As it turned out, he did not, but Sandy Pitt did. "I object—attorney-client privilege."

Ernest got a twinkle in his eye and looked over at Pitt and said, "That's an interesting objection. How do you figure, counsel?" Truth was—Ernest thrived on such verbal battles.

"Well, abandonment is a legal theory, obviously advanced by Mr. Petroni's attorney after investigating the facts, and what facts constitute the basis for that theory—that affirmative defense—are facts identified during private conversations between Mr. Petroni and his attorney—me. By asking that question, you're asking Mr. Petroni to divulge those confidential conversations." Then she thought of something else to add, "And, answering that question would also get into my confidential work product." She smiled, obviously very pleased with herself.

I'll give you an A for effort, but F for legal basis, thought Ernest. "All right, we can handle this in a couple of ways. One will take much longer than the other. The longer one is that we present your objection to the judge for her opinion and ruling. That could happen today, or it might take a few days. If we take that course, we'll halt the deposition and resume it once we get the judge's ruling. I'm OK with that. The other is that I ask some additional questions and see how you feel about letting Mr. Petroni answer my question then. I think we should start with the latter. You OK with that?"

"Sure," said Pitt. "It's your deposition."

"Mr. Petroni, you've testified that you're a licensed attorney and have extensive experience with real estate and real estate law. Correct?"

"Yeah," answered Leo.

"Do you understand the legal concept of abandonment of a lease?" Leo started to look at Sandy Pitt. "No need to look at her, Mr. Petroni. I'm over here, and I'm asking the questions."

"Yeah, I understand it."

"Before you retook possession of the property at Wild Rose Circle in Wheat Ridge, is it true that you had reasons for doing that?"

"Well, I sure as hell didn't have them after I took possession."

"And, is it true that those reasons you had were based upon facts that occurred before you took possession?"

"Think I just answered that." Leo was starting to see what was happening. Ernest waited for the answer. "Yeah."

"What were those facts and reasons?"

Sandra Pitt realized she had been outmaneuvered and let the answer come.

Leo thought for a bit before answering. "She just left the place without giving me any notice or way of contacting her. After she had been gone for several months, I went over to see what the place looked like. And, it was a mess." As previously instructed by Ernest, Rita kept her composure in spite of her anger over Petroni's response.

"You went inside?"

"Yes, I went inside. I was concerned about the property—my property."

"Was it your property at that time? I mean, had you received the quiet title judgment at that time?"

Leo tried to puzzle out if it made any difference whether he had entered the house before or after the date of the quiet title judgment, but couldn't find any. In truth, there wasn't. Ernest just wanted to watch Leo's reaction to see if he would struggle with an answer which should have been quick and easy if he were telling the truth, but more difficult if he were constructing a lie. Leo was struggling, but eventually said, "I'm pretty sure it was after."

"Why did you go inside?"

"Asked and answered," interrupted Pitt.

Ignoring Pitt, Ernest said, "Answer the question, Mr. Petroni."

Leo was ready for this one. "I wanted to see if Rita had left any indication of where she went?"

"Did you find anything that would tell you that?"

"No, and it was pretty clear she wasn't coming back. The place was a mess and filthy. There were rat droppings all over, and the refrigerator and oven had spoiled food in them with maggots crawling all over it. It was disgusting."

"Are those the facts that you relied upon in deciding that Rita Draper had abandoned the property?"

"Yes."

"Anything else?"

"No."

"Did you see her darkroom with her developing equipment at that time?"

"Yeah."

"Did you see the Jeep Wagoneer?"

"I did."

"Did any of that give you any doubt about your belief that she abandoned the property?"

"Not at all. They had been gone since November 1987—eight months—without a word. Her boyfriend—Blair Barker—was odd. They both seemed odd to me. For one thing, they claimed to be engaged, but I never saw or heard anything about any wedding date being set. It was like they were perpetually engaged. It was like she and her boyfriend just got frustrated with whatever and left." Sandra Pitt tapped the upper left-hand corner of her legal pad with her pen, a signal to just answer the question and then shut up.

Ernest continued the deposition until lunchtime, getting details of why Petroni thought Blair and Rita were "odd," details that Ernest was finding himself in agreement with. He also got into more detail about some of Petroni's responses to Ernest's discovery documents before the lunch break.

When Ernest called the break for lunch, Sandra Pitt came over to him and said, "Have you heard from the court on your motion to amend your complaint?"

For a moment, Ernest was stunned and just looked at her like another Sandy Pitt was budding out of her forehead. While looking at her, he noticed that there was a hint of clear fluid leaking from her nose to her upper lip. He wondered if she had a cold—or some other problem. He seriously doubted that she could have forgotten their conversation on December 20 about the amended complaint. But who could be so brazen as to deny something like that? "We talked about that during our conversation on December 20. I told you then that the court had granted my motion on December 1. Then I agreed to allow you until December 30 to file an answer to my amended complaint, but you didn't."

"I don't recall that."

Incredible—I've come across a lot of liars in this business, but you take the award for shear chutzpah. "I can't help you with that. Your answer was due a long time ago, and I was gracious enough to give you another opportunity. That ship has sailed."

"Give me until next Monday, March 13, to file an answer. Otherwise, I'll have to petition the court, and you know the judge will allow it."

"It shouldn't take you that long to get the answer prepared. My amended complaint doesn't add any new allegations of fact. It just adds a claim for conversion of the personal property."

"All right, I can get the answer to you tomorrow."

Ernest did not trust her, but he knew she was right about the judge. "OK, I won't object to you filing a late answer, provided you don't assert any new allegations or counterclaims."

"Fine."

Ernest turned and left with Rita for lunch at Lucile's, a small, Creole-cuisine-themed café that was just a half block to the east of his office. After they ordered, Ernest opened the discussion for business.

"What's your reaction to the deposition so far?"

"I think you're doing a great job. Leo is trying to avoid your questions, but you keep pinning him down. And, that Pitt woman is annoying. I loved it when you brought her the box of tissues. I almost laughed out loud."

"That was fun. How about Petroni's claim that when you left, you left trash all over and food in the refrigerator and stove that spoiled?"

"Well, we did leave in a hurry."

"You mean, there could have been trash and spoiled food with maggots?"

"I don't know. I don't think so."

Ernest's eyebrows ticced up at that news. "Do you think Blair might remember?"

"Probably not."

This wasn't good news to Ernest, and the worst part was that he hadn't heard it from his own client. It was something he felt reasonably confident about counteracting, since Rita had left her expensive developing equipment in the house. That was strong evidence of intent to return, rather than abandon of the property. However, what else had she failed to disclose to him?

"Rita, I want to return to the issue of Pitt's request to inspect the house."

"I told you, it's not going to happen."

"Oh, yes, it is. Pitt has filed a motion to compel it, and Judge Gentilini will grant that and order you to pay Petroni's attorney fees to get it done. Is that what you want—having to pay Petroni's attorney fees." *Now, that would really upset me—you paying his fees when you're not paying mine.*

"Of course not."

"Would you at least agree to allow her and her expert, but not Petroni, to inspect the house? Do you understand that Pitt will get to inspect the house and that fighting it is futile? All you'll do is incur more fees—mine and Petroni's—by fighting it."

Rita had on her pouty face. "Yeah, all right, go ahead and do that," she snapped.

Their pleasant lunch arrived in timely intervention of their less-than-pleasant conversation. Ernest was having a light salad in order to avoid post-prandial sluggishness. Rita also had a salad. Sandy Pitt had another way for keeping her edge.

The afternoon session of Petroni's deposition continued with more belligerence from Leo and childish behavior by Sandy Pitt. Before entering the conference room, Sandy had visited the ladies' room to powder her nose with some of Stanley Turner's special powder. Ernest immediately noticed her increased agitation and sniffles. And everyone noticed Leo Petroni's intense hatred for Ernest. Every once in a while, in an attempt to break the stride of Ernest's questioning, Pitt would object to the form of his questions. It was an allowable objection—and completely erroneous each time she made it. After the first half hour of questioning, Sandy picked up a highlighter from the table and started to peel the clear-plastic label and then reseal it to the highlighter tube to start the process again—and again. There was an annoying, abrasive, tacky sound as the adhesive on the label released. However, it did nothing to distract Ernest from his laser focus on questioning Petroni. After the midafternoon break, they all reseated themselves. On the table in front of Sandy Pitt's chair was a container of crayons and a Dr. Seuss coloring book. Before they were on the record, Ernest said, "You looked like you needed something to entertain yourself." Sandy wanted to kill him right then and there with a crayon to his right eye, but she contained her anger—better than Dolly Barber was able to contain her amusement. Dolly tried hard to suppress a smile. She wasn't successful. The rest of the deposition proceeded much smoother than before. It made Ernest wish he had brought the crayons out a lot earlier. At the end of the day, Ernest had gotten what he wanted, including a list of the opposition's witnesses. Leo left to tend to his plants for decompression while Sandy Pitt headed to a bottle of scotch and more coke.

After he sent Rita on her way, Ernest came out of the conference room to say good night to Tracey. On seeing him, Tracey said, "You're going to love this one, Ernest."

"Which one would that be?"

"As your opposing counsel was leaving, she turned to me and said, 'That guy is the biggest asshole.'"

"Huh, guess I did my job. That's a pretty high complement, coming from her. She ought to know. What did you say?"

"Nothing—I just smiled and told her to have a good night."

"Good for you. Goodnight, Tracey."

Before going home, Ernest prepared a response to Pitt's motion to compel inspection of the property, agreeing to the inspection sans Petroni. He also prepared a letter to Sandra Pitt detailing their conversation and agreement allowing for her to file an answer to his amended complaint by tomorrow. He would be glad he did.

Tomorrow came and passed without an answer from Sandra Pitt, even though in the letter he had telefaxed to her the previous evening, Ernest requested Pitt to fax her answer to him the next day. As more days passed, Ernest forgot about Pitt's answer. In the meantime, Ernest informed the court clerk that Pitt had complied with his requests for discovery, but that he wanted to keep the portion of his motion to compel open with respect to his request for attorney's fees because Pitt's response came only after he expended time in preparing and filing his motion. Judge Gentilini's response was quick. She granted Pitt's motion to compel inspection on the terms Ernest had agreed to and denied both of their requests for attorneys' fees.

March 20, 1989

On March 20, Ernest called Larry Spiegel, the real estate agent whose sign was in front of the Wild Rose Circle house on August 28 when Rita and Blair discovered Leo's treachery.

"Mr. Spiegel, thank you for taking my call. I'm Ernest Schreiber, an attorney in Boulder, and I represent Rita Draper in a lawsuit against Leonard Petroni."

"Yes, I know who you are. I have a copy of the injunction you got—stopping the sale of the property in Indian Paintbrush Estates."

"Right—among other things. If you have a few minutes, I'd like to ask you some questions. It won't take more than ten, and probably closer to five, minutes."

"Shoot—I have some time."

"When did Leonard Petroni first contact you to tell you he wanted to sell the property at 10209 Wild Rose Circle—the very first time?"

"Oh, that's easy. It was January 30, 1988, a Saturday."

"Why are you so sure of the date?"

"It was my daughter's tenth birthday, and I was trying to get out of the office to get ready to take her and a group of her friends to Chuck E. Cheese to celebrate. I took the call because it was Leonard Petroni. I mean, he's an important man, and I knew he lived in Indian Paintbrush Estates, and I thought he might want to buy one of the houses I had listed there—you know, as an investment."

"What did he say?"

"He said he wanted to use me to sell a house there and not buy one. And, I asked him why he was selling his house, and he told me he wasn't. Well, I keep a pretty close eye on properties in Indian Paintbrush, and I knew that he had had a for-sale sign in front of that property Beat Nicholson had worked on forever. So, I asked him if that was the property he was talking about, and he said it was. I said that I thought he had a buyer for that, and he said, the deal fell through. So, I—"

This guy's like a bubbling fountain of information. "So, this all took place on January 30, 1988—you're sure?"

"Absolutely, no question. Anyway, like I was sayin'—I said that I could come over on Sunday or Monday and have him sign a listing agreement, but I had to go to my daughter's birthday party right then. And he said that he wasn't ready to list it, yet, because he didn't have the title, but that he was working on that. Well, that took me aback. I said that I sure would like to represent him in the sale, and that he should give me a call when he did have title. And, he did. That was right at the beginning of August. He told me he had a court order awarding him title, and he was ready to sign a listing agreement. I can tell you, I got one of those popped out of our secretarial pool, and I drove over to his house and got him to sign it."

"Did you go into the house at 10209 Wild Rose Circle at that time?"

"Sure did. It was still under construction, but looked in pretty good shape, except for not being completed on the interior. He said he was working on that. And, there were some guys there moving stuff out of the house, throwin' some of it into the pit in the backyard that Beat Nicholson had dug for a swimming pool, so I heard."

"Did you look in the refrigerator or oven?"

"Nope, no reason to. He wanted to do some upgrades to those, and he wanted to tear out the darkroom and spruce that up with an extended living room. But, he did emphasize that he wanted to sell the place as soon as possible and to show it even while he was having work done. So, I put one of my signs in front. I always carry a couple in my car trunk."

"How did the interior look? Was there trash all over?"

"None other than what was created by the guys Mr. Petroni had working."

"Thank you, Mr. Spiegel. I'd like to take your deposition sometime about what we just talked about. When could you do that?"

"Oh wow, this month is crazy busy for me and with tax season and all.... Could we do it after Tax Day, during the week of April 17?"

"Sure, how about Tuesday, April 18, starting at nine in the morning at my office?"

"Yeah, I haven't been to Boulder in a while, and I'd like to check out some properties up there with a friend of mine in the business. You might know him—Buddy Dunce."

"Indeed, I do. Thank you. I'll be in touch." *Oi—Buddy Dunce—hope your integrity is better than your friend's, Mr. Spiegel.*

March 28, 1989

Tracey brought Ernest's mail in to him. "You have an envelope from Pitt."

Ernest looked up at her, squinted his eyes and raised his eyebrows in a questioning look.

"Yup—postage due—forty cents."

"Why does she persist with the games? And to think, I let her color in my coloring book."

Tracey laughed—then dropped the mail on his desk and left.

Ernest picked up Pitt's envelope first and pulled out the document inside and immediately headed into a slow smolder. The document he held was entitled Answer To Amended Complaint And Counterclaim. As he read it, his smolder became hotter and hotter until he had to take a break for fear of having an aneurysm, or spontaneously combusting. After a few deep breathing exercises, he resumed scrutinizing the offensive document. Pitt's answer went beyond just responding to the portions of his amended complaint that actually were additions to his original complaint. Had she stopped at just responding to what he had added, he might have let her trespass slide, even though her answer was excessively late. He might even have overlooked the five new affirmative defenses that she added. An affirmative defense is one that had to be alleged in order to be preserved for the trial and that had to be proved by the defendant at the trial. However, Pitt had added three counterclaims: breach of contract; outrageous conduct; and slander of title with requests for damages for alleged construction Leo had done and that Rita had removed, punitive damages and attorneys' fees. It was the last counterclaim that prompted his call to Rita.

When she answered, he said, "Rita, I just received an answer from Sandra Pitt to my amended complaint."

"I thought you said that the date for her answer had passed a long time ago."

"I did say that, and I was correct when I said it. Listen, I don't want to get into the details of it over the phone. We need to go over this together. In the meantime, I'm going to prepare an objection in the form of a motion to strike her answer as being untimely and in violation of the rules of procedure. When can you come in? And, I want Blair here too."

"I—we—can be there tomorrow."

"How about the day after, March 30? I should have the motion ready by then. I have an opening at ten."

"Yeah, we can make that."

"See you then."

After hanging up, Ernest began drafting his motion to strike, while realizing that this would probably delay the case and that delay was just what Pitt wanted. He was boxed in. He could not let this kind of flagrant abuse go unnoticed by the judge, even though it was likely she would allow the answer, especially given the gender of the attorney filing the answer and of the attorney protesting against it. However, if he didn't protest now, he would probably lose his right to do so later, especially in the event that an appeal would be necessary. He had to give the devil her due—Pitt had maneuvered him into expending precious time and driving up his client's attorney's fees while expending little time on her part. In his motion, Ernest focused on the rules of civil procedure and how his filings complied with the rules while Pitt's did not. The crux of his argument was that Pitt was excessively late in filing her answer and that her answer went far beyond what was allowed for what should have been a simple answer. In essence, Pitt had filed a completely amended answer and counterclaim without getting the court's approval first—something Ernest had done when he filed his amended complaint. Ernest avoided getting into his conversations with Pitt and her claims of not knowing about the court's order allowing Ernest's amendment and his agreements to allow her more time. He was saving those gems for his reply to whatever lies Pitt would present in her response to his motion to strike.

By March 30, his motion to strike was ready when Rita and Blair came in for their meeting. As soon as they were announced by Tracey, Ernest had them ushered into his office. As they were sitting down, he handed each of them a copy of Pitt's answer and counterclaim and a copy of his motion.

Rita finished reading before Blair and said, "Pitt's a bitch. Looks like you handled it, so why did you want both of us to come in?"

"To talk about the reply. I need to prepare our reply to the counterclaims—most importantly, the third one, slander of title. It alleges that you recorded a copy of the contract in the real estate records for Jefferson County. It says you did that on August 31, 1988. That was one day before I got you the TRO—but, more importantly, it was one day after our first meeting when you signed my fee agreement." Ernest stopped to wait for their comments and to watch their reactions. Rita flicked a glance at Blair, who suddenly became intently interested in something outside Ernest's bay window. "It seems that might be something you know about—Blair. Did you record a copy of the contract?"

Blair looked back at Ernest, puffed up and then blew out, "Yeah, I did that."

"Why?" asked Ernest.

"He was just trying to protect my interests," interjected Rita.

"So, you knew he was going to do that before he did it—is that correct?"

"I told her. And, I did it because she needed to make sure that Leo wasn't going to try to do something funny with the title, like borrow against it, or something," explained Blair.

"It was a stupid thing to do—"

"I'm not stupid," interrupted Blair.

"I didn't say you were," said Ernest while thinking *even though I think you are.* "I said it was a stupid thing to do."

"Well, it was not. Leo didn't do anything to damage the title after I did that. There's no proof it was 'stupid.'"

"Au contraire—you did just read Pitt's third counterclaim—didn't you? Also, my TRO—that's MY TRO and injunction—protected the title through trial and final judgment." Ernest realized that he had to back off a bit from his criticism of the little man who wanted to be big. "Blair, look, you have a very important role in this litigation, but it is not as Rita's attorney. I hope you're listening, Rita."

Rita nodded that she was, and she really did not want to lose Ernest as her attorney.

Ernest continued, "I have enough to do in this case just to battle Pitt and her lies. I don't need the distraction of having to look over my shoulder constantly to make sure my own client and her boyfriend aren't sabotaging the case."

Blair started to launch into a protest, but Rita rapped him so hard on his knee that he let out a little yelp.

"How bad is it?" asked Rita.

"Fortunately, I think it is just smoke, but sometimes with some judges smoke like that can win or lose a case. From what I hear about Gentilini, she's not stupid. She may, or may not, be a misandrist—" They both gave him blank looks, so he clarified and continued, "—someone who hates men. But, she is intelligent, and I'm hoping is the kind of smart person who resents it when someone like Pitt blows smoke to cover up a lack of substance. Now, are there any other surprises waiting to pop out of the weeds in this case?"

"No, not from us," said Rita. Blair just shook his head "no."

"All right, let's move on. Blair." At the mention of his name Blair sat more erect. "At the deposition, Petroni claimed that the house was a mess and that he had to have it cleaned out. He said that, besides trash around the interior, there was rat feces and that there was spoiled food in the refrigerator and oven. Do you know if any of that is true? When you and Rita left, did you leave trash strewn about and food in the fridge and oven?"

"No, there was no trash. I mean the house wasn't immaculate, but trash was picked up. For one thing, we didn't want rats to be attracted to the place. I guess I can't say for sure that there was no food in the refrigerator or oven—I'm pretty sure there wasn't."

"Sure enough to swear to it on the stand?"

"Yeah—sure."

"Good, now one more thing, the accounting you gave me of your labor could use a little polish. Did you take back-up notes to support what you gave me? I mean, the list you gave me wasn't a running list, like a diary, was it?"

"No, I recreated that list off pieces of paper that I wrote my hours on."

"Is there a piece of paper for each of the entries that you gave me?"

"Yes."

"I'm going to need those. We'll have to go through some of those at the trial and tie them to what you put on the longer list. In fact, I may have that list typed up and you can sign it. Then after verifying it and some of the numbers at trial, we can enter the whole list into evidence. You good with that?"

"Sure."

"All right, Rita, do you have any questions, changes or comments about the motion to strike?"

"No, as usual, it looks superb. I do have a question about something else, though."

"Shoot."

"Have you heard anything from Sandra Pitt about taking my deposition or Blair's?"

"No, I haven't. I'm starting to think that she won't. Her pattern so far seems to indicate that she's trying to save Petroni attorney's fees. She does things that require a lot of work on our part and not much on hers. Of course, she's pretty mercurial and could do anything."

"Well, that can't be good for her case."

"Don't be so sure of that. Realize, we have the hard side of this case. All she has to do is sling mud and hope some sticks."

After Rita and Blair left, Ernest served and filed his motion to strike.

April 17, 1989

For once, Sandra Pitt served a document on time, but still without sufficient postage—twenty cents this time. Her response to Ernest's motion to strike was packed with so many lies it made Ernest's head spin. She alleged that there was confusion about how and when Ernest's motion to amend the complaint was granted. She alleged that he failed to send her a copy when she requested it and when he did, it came with insufficient postage—a trick that Ernest thought Pitt had cornered the market on, maybe even had a copyright for. But, one of the biggest lies was that she didn't hear about the court's order allowing his amended complaint until March 8, the day of Leonard Petroni's deposition, and when she did, he agreed to allow her to file a completely new answer and counterclaim. It took much of the day for Ernest to draft his reply setting forth in chronological detail the events relevant to disproving Pitt's prevarications, as he called her lies in his reply, but wanted to call bald-faced, deceitful, perjurious effrontery to the court warranting disbarment and disgrace. Ernest was developing a very strong dislike of Sandra Pitt. Some attorneys would resort to name calling and ad hominins in his current situation. It was a practice that Ernest found unprofessional and more demeaning to the detractor than the target of the disparagement. However, Sandra Pitt was deserving of a contemptuous label, but Ernest couldn't think of any that adequately conveyed his scorn or that didn't malign some poor animal. Along with his reply, he prepared his own signed, sworn affidavit and copies of the letter he sent to Pitt on March 8 along with the fax printout verifying its transmission. He and Tracey were able to get the originals and copies in the mail to the court and to Pitt, respectively, before they closed up for the evening.

April 18, 1989

Larry Spiegel arrived right at nine and was ushered into Ernest's conference room by Tracey where Dolly Barber, Rita and Ernest were waiting. Sandy Pitt was not present. After waiting ten minutes, Ernest asked Tracey to call Pitt's office to find out where she was and when he could expect her.

After another ten minutes, Tracey came in and announced, "Pitt's secretary kept me on hold for several minutes and when she came back on, she said Ms. Pitt was in court."

"Court? I cleared this date with her, and she didn't say anything about being in court."

"Yeah, I'm suspicious too, especially since her secretary took so long to get back on the line and tell me that."

"All right, we're starting without her," said Ernest. "I wonder why she's being so cavalier about not showing up to a deposition of one of her witnesses." He didn't have to wonder long.

After Dolly swore Spiegel in, Ernest started the questioning by getting Spiegel's name, address, professional credentials and education on the record.

Then Ernest said, as he did with every deposition he conducted, "Mr. Spiegel, do you understand that you're under oath to tell the truth and that your answers to my questions will be recorded by the court reporter, Ms. Dolly Barber?"

"Mmm-huh," mumbled Spiegel.

"Mr. Spiegel, you need to speak up and answer with a yes or no, so that the court reporter can accurately record your answer."

"Yes."

"All right, that will look a little confusing in the written record, so let me start again. Mr. Spiegel, do you understand that you're under oath to tell the truth and that your answers to my questions will be recorded by the court reporter, Ms. Dolly Barber?"

After several seconds had passed, Spiegel said, "Yes."

"Do you also understand that any false statements by you will be subject to penalty in a court of law for perjury?"

Once again, Larry Spiegel had to think about the question before answering, "Yes."

What's with this guy? Ernest was getting a little concerned and suspicious about Spiegel's hesitancy in answering standard questions about the veracity of his testimony, so he changed his tactic. Instead of leading Spiegel through his history of listings in Indian Paintbrush Estates and how he obtained the listing for 10209 Wild Rose Circle, he went right to their conversation on March 20.

"Mr. Siegel, do you remember having a telephone conversation with me on March 20?"

"I remember you calling me."

"Mr. Spiegel, I asked if you remembered having a telephone conversation with me on that date?"

"Yes."

"Do you remember telling me during that conversation that Leonard Petroni called you on January 30, 1988?"

"No."

"You don't remember telling me that?"

"No."

"Do you remember having a conversation with Leonard Petroni on January 30, 1988?"

"No."

"January 30, 1988 was your daughter's tenth birthday, is that correct?"

"Yes."

"Do you remember telling me that?"

"No."

"Mr. Spiegel, I didn't use a Ouija board to get that information."

"I might have said something about that."

"Why would you do that, Mr. Spiegel?"

"I don't know. I don't remember."

"Is it you don't know, or you don't remember?"

"I guess, I don't remember."

"You guess?"

"OK, I don't remember."

"So, it's possible that at some time in the future, you might remember that and more about our conversation on March 20?"

"Yeah, sure."

"Mr. Spiegel, has Mr. Petroni, or anyone on his behalf, like Ms. Pitt, given, or offered, you anything of value in exchange for your testimony today?"

Spiegel adjusted himself in his chair, before answering, "No, absolutely not."

"When was the last time you talked to Mr. Petroni?"

"That would be at the time he gave me a copy of the temporary restraining order you got—first week of September last year, 1988."

"And Ms. Pitt?"

"Around March 20, same time you called."

"What did she want?"

"I don't know if I can answer that. Isn't that subject to some kind of privilege?"

"Not for you. Go ahead and answer."

"Same thing you did—information about the case. Told her the same as I did you."

"What was that?"

Spiegel then remembered that he had said he didn't remember what he said to Ernest, "I honestly don't remember."

"I hope so. Here's what we're going to do, Mr. Spiegel. This deposition is going to be adjourned until a future date, one where maybe you remember a little better than you are today and maybe Sandra Pitt can join us. You will remain under subpoena, the subpoena I had you served with, and you will remain under oath. This deposition is adjourned."

Spiegel couldn't leave fast enough. When Spiegel was gone, Rita said to Ernest, "What just happened?"

"Perjury."

After Rita and Dolly Barber had left, Ernest went to his office and dialed a number.

"Manny? I could use your services."

CHAPTER 11

Unkind In-kind Offer

May–October 1989

As Ernest had anticipated, but hoped otherwise, Judge Gentilini denied his motion to strike Sandra Pitt's answer and counterclaims to his amended complaint. It was a May-Day gift that he received in the mail on May 2. As part of the order, Gentilini gave him until May 8 to file his reply. *How about—Pitt's a lying cockroach?* he thought as he read the order.

There were certain things that were required of attorneys at certain times during a lawsuit. They were usually tied to the date that a case was at issue, which in the present case would be the date when all parties had been served and all answers or responsive pleadings had been filed. That was no help with the confused mess of pleadings in the Draper-Petroni case, thanks to the efforts to obfuscate by Sandra Pitt. Already, some required actions had been accomplished while others languished. Now, with the acceptance of Pitt's answer and counterclaims and allowance of his reply to them, would the clock be reset to start ticking from the filing of his reply, since that would be the last responsive pleading? Trying to figure that out without Gentilini's intervention was a fool's quest—one Ernest had no intention of engaging in unless, and until, it became relevant. In the meantime, he would focus on preparing his case for trial. Next in that regard, he wanted to fill one critical void in his case—valuation of the lost and damaged photos.

The photos and the damage to the construction formed the largest part of Rita's monetary damages. Blair would have to cover the construction damages, and Rita could adequately testify to the value of the refrigerator, stove and miscellaneous missing personal property. And, while Rita could also testify about the photos that were gone forever, she really did not have the expertise needed for testifying to the anticipated value of those photos in book form. She had never published a book—of any kind. Her book agent, Molly Richards, would be some help, but someone who had actually sold a book something like what Rita was working on would be ideal. He knew it was a long shot, but he had to ask.

May 8, 1989

After getting his reply to Pitt's answer and counterclaims in the mail, Ernest called Rita.

"Hello, Rita. It's Ernest."

"Hello, Ernest. What's up?"

"I just mailed our reply to Pitt's answer and counterclaims to the court and Pitt, and I had some time to think about an issue that has been plaguing me—the photos Petroni destroyed."

She gave a heavy sigh. It was a topic that always brought distress—and for understandable reasons. "I just don't know how he could have been so mean—so vicious. He had to know those were very valuable—priceless."

"Yeah—priceless—that's just what I'm struggling with. How do I convey that message to the judge and also give her a figure she can rely on in order to award damages for their loss?"

"Why is the judge making that decision instead of the jury?"

"Right, I thought I explained that to you. The heart of this case, its major focus, is on getting specific performance of the contract so that you get title to the land and house. The other damages, including the photos, are ancillary to that action. Now, I'm not trying to denigrate your photos or their value. It's just the way the law looks at this. And, specific performance is a type of remedy that doesn't allow for a jury. It's called an equitable remedy. It goes back hundreds of years to old English law. Don't worry about that, just trust me—I've had a lot of experience with equitable remedies and, actually, have made some historic new law for one type of equitable remedy. Now, we could probably ask for an advisory jury as to the value of your damages, but it would only be advisory, so the judge ends up making her own decision anyway, and it would end up costing you more in my fees for the added time spent in selecting and then educating a jury. It's not worth it."

"OK, so I can testify to the value of those photos, since I know how good they were and I have sold photos before."

"Yes, you can, but you can only testify as to their value as individual sales. What's the most you ever received for a photo and what's the highest number of prints you sold of that photo?"

"Well, that's not generally how I get paid—by the photo, that is. I do assignment work. But I have sold some photos. That's how I knew Buddy Dunce. However, I planned to do more of that. So, I guess fifty dollars and five prints."

"That's the max you can expect then for the three hundred fifty photos you lost. At two hundred fifty dollars per photo, that's eighty-seven thousand five hundred dollars. Do you think you would do better than that with your book?"

"Yes—at least my agent thinks so, but she hasn't ever marketed a book like mine."

"There you go. That's my dilemma. I have no one who has done this before to tell me what your damages would be from the sale of your book, plus, of course, what you could get on individual sales of those photos. The only person who knows those photos—what they looked like and how good they were—is you."

"That's not true. Oh, man, I have just the person. He's a respected photojournalist and has sold a couple of books like mine. He's an Associated Press photojournalist. And, best of all, he saw those photos—all three hundred fifty of them."

This sounds almost too good to be true. "That is amazing. Why didn't you tell me this before?"

"You never asked. You were so busy fighting with Pitt bitch over all her lies, we never talked about it."

"Where's this guy live? What's his name?"

"He lives in Aspen, and his name's Andrew Edison."

"Do you think he would be willing to testify as an expert witness?"

"I would be surprised if he wouldn't," said Rita.

"How well do you know him?"

Rita smiled and said, "Very well. Why don't you let me call him and explain what you want? I'd like to talk to him anyway. Then I'll have him give you a call."

They closed off their conversation after Rita gave Andrew Edison's contact information to Ernest.

May 9, 1989

Rita called to tell Ernest that she had talked to Andrew Edison and that he was not only willing to act as her expert witness, but he was quite excited to do so. Also, he was willing to come to Boulder to meet with Ernest within the week, or any other time that Ernest was available. During his conversation, Ernest also confronted the issue of payment of his fees, which Rita had let pile up with minimal payment. After a less than heartfelt apology and even weaker excuse of slow cashflow, she promised to send another payment. So far, she had paid $750 on fees of $15,000. None of her payments had spawned from her own initiation. Ernest had had to ask for payment each time she eventually made one. Ernest found it demeaning to ask, and her nonpayment was insulting of his performance. In truth, Rita had enough funds to pay Ernest, but Blair had advised her not to. His reasoning seemed sound to Rita. Blair had explained that by holding back on payment, Ernest would be more invested in the lawsuit and less inclined to churn fees. For some attorneys, that might have been an accurate assessment, but not for Ernest. Ernest was more concerned about providing excellent legal services for his clients than surreptitiously filling his bank account with inflated billing. Besides, even for fee-churners, Blair's logic was faulty. The fallacy of his argument was that nonpayment of a fee-churner's fees would never stop him from churning, or demanding payment before churning some more.

After his call with Rita, Ernest called Mr. Edison.

"This is Andrew Edison."

"Mr. Edison, this is Ernest Schreiber. I'm Rita Draper's attorney in Boulder, and she told me you were willing to help as an expert witness in her case against Leonard Petroni."

"Ah, Mr. Schreiber, I've been expecting your call. Yes, anything I can do to help. Rita explained the situation. I'm really sorry to hear about her problem. She's such a lovely person. I hate to see her go through this."

"Well, from Rita's description of you and your expertise, you sound like just the person I was hoping to find as an expert—better, actually, since you have seen the photos that I want you to appraise. Do you have time to talk now?"

"Yes, but would it be OK if we met in person? I need to come down to the Front Range anyway. That way we could meet and take as long as it takes."

This was getting better and better. "Sure, that would be fantastic. How soon?"

"The sooner, the better—how about this week—Friday the twelfth?"

"Absolutely, two in the afternoon?"

"I'll see you then, and I'll bring my curriculum vitae."

"I have you on my calendar. See you then, Mr. Edison."

"Looking forward to it." And, indeed he was. Andrew had not snuggled with Rita in a long time—too long.

Later in the day, Ernest received an envelope from his current-least-favorite attorney. The envelope had the correct postage—twenty-five cents—but that was consistent with Pitt's established pattern. She always included some postage on her mailings, usually the twenty-five-cent minimum for the first ounce. Anything over an ounce, and Ernest could count on postage being due. Inside was a motion to vacate the current trial set in September and to reschedule to sometime in 1990. Pitt argued that more time was needed to complete those tasks required of the attorneys by the rules of civil procedure which were now skewed due to Pitt's successful obfuscations—except that wasn't the way she put it in her motion. Her reasoning was that it was Ernest's fault due to his amended answer. While he agreed that deadlines were awash in confusion, he disagreed with Pitt's requested delay until 1990, and he immediately drafted a response stating so. Rather than fight her on delaying the trial to a later date—a fight he was sure to lose—he agreed to reschedule, but to dates still within 1989. In his motion, he pointed out that he had another trial set for October in Aspen, so the new dates should come in November or December. Also, he requested that the trial be set for four days rather than the currently scheduled three because of the counterclaims added by Sandy Pitt. When Ernest finished his response, he had Manny Dickerson rush the original to the court and a copy to Pitt.

May 12, 1989

For once, Judge Gentilini agreed with Ernest. He attributed it to the fact that he had agreed in part with Sandy Pitt. Not waiting for Pitt's reply to Ernest's response, Gentilini issued her order on May 10. It ordered that no later than May 18 the two attorneys should schedule a trial of four days before the end of the year—preferably in November. Early in the afternoon on May 12, Ernest scheduled a conference call among Pitt, the court clerk and himself for May 18 at ten.

A few minutes before two in the afternoon, Andrew Edison arrived. He was a tall, fit, handsome man, who looked intelligent and would prove to be so. Ernest met him in the conference room.

While extending his hand to shake his guest's, Ernest said, "It's a pleasure to meet you, Mr. Edison. Have a seat."

"Pleasure to meet you too."

"Again, I'd like to say how much I appreciate your willingness to help Rita and me with her case."

"Pleasure's all mine." *You have no idea, Mr. Schreiber.* Andy Edison could never resist any excuse to see Rita.

"So, let's get right to it."

Andy handed Ernest a copy of his curriculum vitae, which Ernest reviewed with great satisfaction. This guy had twenty-five years of photojournalistic experience, including some time in Vietnam. He also had published two photographic books that were quite successful. It made Ernest wonder why someone of his caliber was willing to help with Rita's case, and how much he would charge—so he asked.

"Your credentials are—well, quite impressive. Before we go any further, I'd like to know how much your fees will be for acting as our expert?"

"I'll do it for nothing, as a favor to Rita."

"Nothing?" Ernest was shocked. "I don't want to seem ungrateful, but why?"

"I've known Rita for a little over ten years, and she's a good friend and has been a great colleague on several assignments. She's very talented and was right at the cusp of a breakthrough with her proposed book. I know from personal experience how hard it is to break through to that next level of acceptance for your work—by the general public. She was there with those photos that Petroni destroyed. Leonard Petroni committed a terrible, calloused crime not only against Rita, but against the world, by destroying her photos."

Hmph, OK—I'm not going to look in this horse's mouth any more for fear it might run away. "Well, good for you. There aren't many people in your position who would be so generous with their fame and time. Let's talk about the photos. How did you get to see them, and why?"

"As I said, Rita and I had worked together, and I guess I inspired her to do a book. At first, she was not confident that her work was good enough, but she had a burning passion about wild animals and how they were at risk of suffering and extinction because of unchecked hunting, habitat destruction and poaching. Her photos have always been exceptional. She just needed more people to see them, so that the public understood that. In any event, she started taking photos and showing them to me, and I actually picked out some of her best ones for the book. As she collected more photos and experiences, she would share those with me for my opinion. I'm very familiar with those photos and can talk about each one without having to look at them. While she was taking those photos, she also was getting a reputation, nationally and internationally, for her photos with various papers and magazines, like Smithsonian and National Geographic. That reputation would help sell her book on a large scale."

"Well, here's the sixty-four-thousand-dollar question. What's your opinion as to the value of the three hundred fifty photos she lost?"

"It's more like the five-hundred-thousand-dollar question."

"I'm sorry?"

"Each of those photos in the book format would range from one thousand to fifteen hundred dollars each, over the years of its publication. That would be in today's dollars."

"You're kidding." The words just popped out of Ernest's mouth because of his surprise.

"I am not. If the book were as successful as I think it would, or at least could, be that's a very realistic range for their value."

"And, without the book, what's their value?"

"A hundred, maybe one hundred fifty each."

"So, is that number included in the one thousand to fifteen hundred number?"

"No, it's in addition; however, it's possible they could be more."

Ernest whistled. "Would you put together a written appraisal of each of the photos, explaining what you just told me?"

"Absolutely." Andy looked up at the calendar hanging on the wall. "I could have a first draft to you by June 12 at the latest."

"That would fit perfectly with the timing for when I need to disclose my expert to the other side—although, since the trial date has to be rescheduled, I'm not entirely sure when that will be. Thank you, Mr. Edison."

Andy Edison and Ernest spent a little more time together going over the status of the case and the fact that the trial would be rescheduled the following week. When they were done, Ernest walked Andy out of the conference room and to the front door of his office building across from where Tracey was sitting.

As he turned to go back to his office, Tracey said, "I heard you whistle. For a moment, I thought you were calling me." Then she gave a wry smile.

"Cute. I would never do that with you, but I might with Sandy Pitt."

They both laughed. Then Tracey said, "Dolly dropped a package off for you. It's on your desk."

When he entered his office and shut the door, Ernest saw the transcript of Larry Spiegel's deposition lying on his desk. While Spiegel's lies were less damaging to Rita's case than the truth he spoke during their first conversation was to Petroni's side, Ernest still wondered if there was any way he could expose Spiegel for the liar he had become.

May 18, 1989

"Ms. Pitt." *Oh, I hope that didn't sound like I think it sounded,* thought Ernest. Although he did not intend it so, his words sounded a bit like, "Miss Spit."

Sandy Pitt noticed, but said nothing in reply. She just thought that Ernest was finally coming down to her level of law practice. "Yes, I'm here."

"Please hold while I get Judge Gentilini's clerk on the line."

"So, the two of you want to reschedule the Draper-Petroni case for trial—this time for four days," said Beatrice, Gentilini's clerk. "The judge has instructed me to set it before the end of the year, specifically in November, if at all possible. She'll be on holiday in December and wants to clear as much as possible from her calendar before she leaves—this case especially since it was already scheduled once for trial in September. So, are each of you available in November?"

Sandy Pitt really wanted to push the trial into the middle of 1990, but the judge was clear in her order that the new date should be in 1989 and incurring the judge's wrath by quibbling over her preference wasn't worth the risk. "I'm available in November," said Sandy.

Ernest's Aspen trial was scheduled for the week of October 16, so whether this trial was in September or November made little difference to him. Both were equally bad. "Is the week of November 13 available on the judge's docket? That would work best for me since I have a trial in Aspen during the week of October 16, and I'd like some time after that one concludes to prepare for this one."

"It is," said Beatrice. "Ms. Pitt, does that work for you?"

"Yes, absolutely, if that's the judge's preference," said Sandy.

"All right, I'll send out a setting order for a trial of four days before Judge Gentilini beginning on November 13, 1989 at nine in the morning. Have a good day."

Both attorneys thanked Beatrice before they all hung up.

Sandy leaned back in her chair, grabbed her Marlboros, shook one out to grab between her lips and then lit the end with a silver lighter engraved with her initials. She took in a long breath pulling the smoke deep into her lungs, then held it a few seconds before blowing it out into a cloud around her head. As she watched the haze swirl in the sunlight coming through her window, she thought about the Petroni case, wondering what new mischief she could cause to disrupt Ernest Schreiber in the development of his case. Although she was pleased with what she had managed already, especially with tying up the loose end of Larry Spiegel's testimony, she wanted to do more. Frankly, she was running out of options.

Her mind wandered to the chance conversation with Larry Spiegel shortly after he had talked with Ernest Schreiber on March 20. Spiegel had called her to tell her about Schreiber's call. After he told her what was said, she had called Leo Petroni to tell him about Spiegel spilling his guts to Schreiber. Leo was the one who had suggested a possible solution. At Leo's suggestion, Sandy scheduled a meeting with Spiegel and Leo in her office that started with innuendo and ended with an understanding. After hearing Spiegel's account again of his conversation with Ernest Schreiber, Sandy launched into an intense cross-examination laced with suggestions that he might be mistaken in his recollection. At a prearranged moment, Leo interrupted and said that he'd like to change the subject. He had been considering selling some of his commercial properties, a couple of office buildings and a strip mall or two. After hearing the identities of the properties Leo was referring to and making a quick mental calculation of the commissions those sales would generate, Larry Spiegel became less certain of what he remembered in Leo's case with Rita Draper.

The conversation evolved from a fuzzy concept of selling the properties to a handshake deal to do it. But, nothing could be done about the sales, not even talking about them, until after resolution of the Draper case—in Leo's favor. It was a simple and low-risk arrangement. All Spiegel had to do was become forgetful. Since there was no record of their conversation, it was completely deniable by Sandy Pitt and Leo Petroni, should Spiegel later develop ethics that somehow overcame his greed. Sandy loved making deals like that.

Sandy was feeling pretty confident about her case, at least in defending it against Draper's claims for specific performance and damages. She never did expect to win on her counterclaims. Those were added solely to annoy and scare Rita Draper. She had enough of a legal basis to argue that the contract wasn't enforceable because it had no specified closing date. Then there was the question of abandonment. With Larry Spiegel's testimony being neutralized, the case essentially distilled down to Draper's word against the great-and-powerful Leonard Petroni. Well, there was also the word of Draper's boyfriend, Blair Barker, but from Leo's description of Barker, his word wouldn't have much impact. She could easily crack him under cross-examination. But, she'd still like more weight on her side of the scales of justice. She called Leo Petroni to see if he had any ideas that could help her.

"Hello, Mr. Petroni, this is Sandra."

"Hello."

"I called to tell you that the trial has been reset for four days beginning on November 13."

"You couldn't do better than that?"

"Not without pissing off the judge. She was real clear that she wanted this case off her desk before the end of the year and that November was the month when she wanted to do that."

"All right, I'll put it on my calendar. Unfortunately, I don't have anything scheduled then. That it?"

"No—I'm feeling pretty good about the case—"

"'But'—what's the 'but' hidden in that."

"With Spiegel's testimony sidelined, the case comes down to your word against Rita Draper's and her boyfriend's"

"Yeah, well, he's a nothing, so really it comes down to Draper's against mine."

"Right, and that probably is plenty to win the case, but I'd like more. Can you think of anything that might help?"

There was a long pause. "Yeah, maybe, but I'm not sure she'd hold together if she had to testify to some alternative facts—which I'm pretty sure she would, if I asked her."

"She?"

"I didn't mention her before, just because—well, since this is just you and me talking—she doesn't lie well."

"Who is she?"

"Her name is Elva Delgado. She does odd jobs for me. She did some cleaning in the house after I took it over. She's from Peru."

"She didn't have anything to do with Draper's photos, did she?"

"Naw, those guys are gone. I told you—they probably went back to Mexico." It was another lie, but Leo didn't want to divulge the names of the men who destroyed Rita's photos to Schreiber. "Elva was there after all that was done."

"Would she testify to something like rotten food with maggots, maybe?"

"Yeah, I think she would do that for me, but I'm tellin' you, she's intimidated by authority. Gentilini would scare the hell out of her—and the truth."

"You think she could hold up just with Ernest Schreiber and no judge?"

Leo thought awhile, then said, "I don't think so. He's a tough S.O.B."

"Huh—you say she's from Peru. She still have family there?"

"Yes. Why?"

"I think I might have a way of getting her testimony without her being under the intense stare of Gentilini or Schreiber's grilling. Would you call her and prep her, and when you're done call me? I'll get in touch with her and make my own assessment. Then I'll tell you what I have in mind, if I think we should go forward with it."

Leo was going to demand that she tell him what she had planned and then decided that it was better if he didn't know. Conspiracy to suborn perjury was not protected by the attorney-client privilege, and this would be a much clearer case than what they did with Larry Spiegel. Best to let Sandy Pitt take the fall for this if it came to that. "OK, I'll get back to you."

May 26, 1989

As he did every Friday that he could get off work early, Larry Spiegel had his derrière parked on his favorite barstool in the Ship Tavern, a Denver iconic anomaly with a nautical theme complete with a clipper-ship crow's nest. It was opened on August 24, 1934 by Claude "C.K." Boettcher when he owned the Brown Palace with his father, Charles Boettcher Sr., but its seafaring décor came at the suggestion, if not demand, of his wife, Edna. C.K. had collected fifteen, large, model clipper ships during his world travels and tried to bring them home to his mansion. Edna had another idea. She thought they would look better in the Brown Palace, and thus was born the Ship Tavern. Being an establishment in a hotel rich with Denver history and started by a powerful Denver family that was rich, the Ship Tavern was an immediate success. From its inception, it was a hangout for those who wielded Denver's wealth and power and had remained so throughout its long life. It was the primary reason that Larry Spiegel loved to spend time there—that, and its excellent selection of whiskey. Larry had snagged some of his best buyers and sellers in the Ship Tavern. Although it wasn't entirely ethical or legal, he even gave a little finder's fee to one of the bartenders who worked there for any leads that resulted in sales. Up to now, Larry's focus, more by happenstance than design, had been on residential properties, but that was soon to change. He was going to move into the big leagues of commercial property—once, that is, Leonard Petroni was finished with his lawsuit with Rita Draper. He was so excited, he was about to pop. But, Leo and his attorney had sworn him to secrecy until the lawsuit was over. So far, for over two months now, he had kept his silence—well, mostly anyway. That was taxing for a chatterbox like Larry. He signaled his friend, Willy, the bartender, for another scotch and soda.

Willy was Larry's source for some of his most lucrative sales—sales that enriched Willy's life too. Willy also was a man who could keep a secret, so after several Whiskey Sours after the deposition taken by Ernest Schreiber, Larry told Willy about his good fortune with Leonard Petroni. However, before he did so, Larry made Willy swear an oath of secrecy. Bartenders are generally good at keeping secrets. They have to be with all the gossip that slips their way through lubricated lips. But being able to keep a secret and doing it are two different things, especially when money is at stake. Willy saw no harm in breaking his promise once, but only once, and it was for a good reason—

money. The secret just slipped out one evening while Willy was serving and talking to a man who had recently become a regular. The man had made his fortune in mud logging, a tough business run by tough men. Mud loggers recorded and graphed the soil and rock strata pierced by oil drilling rigs. Oil drillers depend upon mud loggers for all kinds of reasons and information gleaned from their microscopic readings of the rock strata—from what speeds of drilling were ideal for safe and speedy descent to the oil, to avoiding untimely explosions from gas buildups. When the topic of real estate came up, it was natural for Willy to explore what kind of real estate the mud logger was interested in. His interest was in all kinds—residential for him and his wife and commercial for investment. When Willy heard that, he saw dollar signs, and was not going to let this catch slip away, so he told him about his friend—a real estate agent, who often came to the Ship Tavern. Later, after the heat of the moment cooled, Willy was concerned that Larry would be upset with his confidentiality breach. He had nothing to worry about. When Larry heard the news, he told Willy he had done the right thing. There was no harm in telling the stranger, especially since this could be some really easy money— once that damned lawsuit was done.

As Willy was delivering the whiskey and soda Larry had flagged him for, a tough-looking man sat down on the barstool next to Larry. The new arrival was wearing jeans, white shirt, an expensive leather jacket, cowboy boots and was topped off with a gray Stetson. Larry glanced over at the man who smiled a broad smile as Willy said, "Oh good—Larry, this is the gentleman I told you about."

The stranger extended his right hand and Larry offered his and said, "Hello, I'm Larry Spiegel."

"Pleasure to meet you, Mr. Spiegel. My name's Manfred Dickerson. You can call me Manny."

August 14, 1989

June and July passed with few petty games played by Sandy Pitt, which was a relief because Ernest had plenty to prepare for the upcoming trials. Ernest chalked up the welcome respite from Pitt's petulance to her being on summer holiday or being distracted by some other prey to torment—or maybe she was running out of pernicious pranks to play, though he doubted the latter was true. There was the house inspection on June 2, which turned out to be ridiculously lame. Ernest had gone to the Wild Rose Circle house and met Pitt and some guy who turned out to be a realtor from the same real estate company as Larry Spiegel. During the inspection, Pitt's treatment of Ernest ranged from aloof to impertinent. Being out of sight of the judge gave her freedom to be contemptuous. The report that her "expert" generated out of that faux inspection opined that work done by Blair and Rita had damaged the previous structure and decreased the value of the house by $40,000. That plus the cost of the work done in destroying Rita's darkroom and extending the living room brought Petroni's fictitious damages up to $60,000. Rita's damages, which were not fictitious, were equal to that on the low end and right at $600,000 on the high side. Ernest spent all of June and much of July working with Andrew Edison reviewing and refining with charts and graphs his estimates of, and final report on, the value of the 350 photos destroyed by Petroni. Ernest thought Edison's report was sure to rock Sandy Pitt back on her heels when she saw it. At the end of July, he sent the final product to Pitt. When she finished reading it, she reached for her stash box. Then on July 31, Manny Dickerson met with Ernest and gave him his report on Larry Spiegel. Ernest immediately called Spiegel to notify him that he was being summoned back in to complete his deposition on August 14 and then sent Manny to Pitt's office with a notice of the new date.

On August 3, Ernest received an envelope from Pitt with correct postage of twenty-five cents. There were just two one-page documents inside, so it was the least she could do. One was a request to postpone the deposition of Larry Spiegel, and the other was a notice of withdrawal as Leonard Petroni's attorney. By now, Ernest was suspicious of everything that came from Pitt, especially words, written or oral. He called the Jefferson County court to confirm a suspicion and then called Sandy Pitt to deliver a message.

When Sandy answered, Ernest said, "Hi, how you doin'?"

"I'm sure you didn't call to check on my health. What do you want?"

"You're good. You saw right through me. I received your request for a postponement of the continuation of Larry Spiegel's deposition. That's not going to happen. The deposition is still on."

"You should also have received my notice to withdraw as Leo Petroni's attorney of record."

"Oh, I did."

"He has the right to have an attorney present for that deposition."

"I'm with you there. Amazing how we can agree on stuff, isn't it?"

"Well, Mr. Schreiber, if Mr. Petroni doesn't have an attorney of record when you take that deposition, it won't be worth much."

"Look at that, I still agree with you."

"All right, what's your point, Schreiber."

"A couple of things—see, you never bothered to file your withdrawal with the court. I know, I just checked with the court."

"Doesn't mean I won't. Just haven't gotten around to it."

"And the other thing is, you can't just drop out of this case, especially at this late date, without having a substitute counsel lined up to take your place—as that attorney of record you're so concerned about. Ergo, you're still the attorney of record and the deposition is still on for August 14. Always a pleasure, Ms. Pitt." *Damn, there it was again—Miss Spit. Why do I do that?*

By August 14, Sandy Pitt was still Petroni's attorney of record when Dolly Barber, Rita and Ernest were waiting for the arrival of Larry Spiegel. Ernest was hoping that Pitt would blow off this deposition too. He wasn't disappointed. Spiegel showed up fifteen minutes late, and Sandy Pitt never did, so Ernest started the deposition at 9:45 a.m.

When Spiegel entered the conference room, Ernest got up and said, "Good Morning, Mr. Spiegel. Please have a seat so we can get started."

Dolly Barber swore Spiegel in even though technically he was still under oath from the first part of his deposition on April 18.

"Mr. Spiegel, thank you for coming in today."

"What choice did I have?"

Little testy this morning, eh? Let's see how that holds up for you. Out loud, Ernest said, "Mr. Spiegel, did you receive a copy of the transcript of your deposition that I took on April 18?"

"Yes."

"Did you read it?"

"I did."

"Do you want to change any of your answers from that day?"

"No."

"Is it your testimony that the answers you gave during that deposition were true then and that they are true now?"

Spiegel flinched slightly and shook his head.

"On the record, please, Mr. Spiegel."

"Yeah, that's my testimony. They were true then and are now."

"On April 18, you testified that you did not remember telling me during a telephone conversation that Leonard Petroni called you on January 30, 1988. Do remember telling me that now?"

"Nope, still don't remember."

"You also testified that you did not remember having a conversation with Leonard Petroni on January 30 of 1988. Do you remember that conversation now?"

"No."

"You testified that the last time you talked to Mr. Petroni was during the first week of September 1988. Have you spoken to Mr. Petroni since then?"

"No."

"Have you spoken with Sandra Pitt since your conversation with her around March 20?"

"Nope."

"On April 18, you testified that neither Ms. Pitt nor Mr. Petroni had given, or offered, you anything of value in exchange for your testimony that day. Is that still your testimony?"

"It is."

"Since then have they, or have they ever, offered you something of value in exchange for you to lie on Mr. Petroni's behalf in Rita Draper's lawsuit against Leonard Petroni?"

What the hell is this about? No way can this guy know about my agreement. He's just fishing. "Absolutely not."

"Not even a promise of maybe some real estate business, like getting listing contracts for the sale of some of Mr. Petroni's commercial real estate?"

Holy crap—that's damned specific. Larry Spiegel decided to take a stronger stance and show some righteous indignation to mask the true reason for his glowing red face. "No, and I find the insinuation that I would do something so obviously illegal and unethical pretty damned insulting."

"I have no intention of insulting you or your ethics, Mr. Spiegel. Let's take a break, and allow the witness to collect himself."

Spiegel made a beeline to the restroom to splash some cold water in his face. When he was out of the room and earshot, Dolly Barber said to Ernest, "I know you, Ernest. You're up to something."

"Oh, now, Dolly. I'm just trying to help our witness remember some important facts."

"'Facts,' as in truth," she said.

Ernest went to his office and left his door open a crack so that he would see Spiegel when he headed back to the conference room. When he saw Spiegel come into view, Ernest called out, "Mr. Spiegel, would you come in please?"

Larry scrunched his eyebrows in a questioning gesture before pushing Ernest's office door open all the way to enter. As the gap in the door widened, a large man who had been hidden to Larry by the door turned in his seat and smiled at him. Larry smiled back and said, "Manny, what are you doing here?" Then a sickening feeling spread over him and his smile evaporated.

"Ah, good, that's one thing you remember. Manny is a private investigator that recently did some work for me," said Ernest. "Have a seat."

Larry Spiegel felt trapped and briefly eyed the door as his avenue to escape.

"You could do that, but let me remind you that you're under subpoena, so I could get a bench warrant for your arrest. Besides, you'd miss out on what I have to say. Please, have a seat. Here read this, and Manny and I will wait until you're finished." Ernest handed Larry Spiegel a spiralbound document entitled on its cover "Investigative Report; Subject: Larry R. Spiegel; Date: July 30, 1989."

Larry took the document and sat to read it. The more he read, the sicker he felt. Inside the report was a detailed, chronological account of his many meetings with Manny and conversations where he revealed that Petroni had agreed to list specific parcels of real estate with him after the lawsuit with Rita Draper was concluded. Manny's report disclosed that as time passed, Larry Spiegel's comfort in discussing the matter increased especially when lubricated with free drinks purchased by Manny. Spiegel had even confided that he had the assurance of Petroni's attorney, Sandra Pitt, that he would get the promised listings. While he never directly admitted to Manny that he had agreed to lie on behalf of Petroni, Larry had confided to Manny that his getting the listings depended upon an outcome to the lawsuit favorable to Petroni. He also had expressed his confidence of that result in order to keep Manny's interest as a potential buyer. It was more than enough to prove Larry Spiegel had lied on April 18 and just a few minutes ago.

Larry's first reaction was, "You can't prove that I lied."

"Never said I could, but I can prove what's in that report and let the judge come to her own conclusions," said Ernest.

Next, Larry threatened, "I'll plead the Fifth."

"And, you can do that, but you'll want to discuss that with your attorney first. From my viewpoint, that won't look good."

Hearing the word 'attorney,' Larry realized he should have started there. "I want an attorney."

"Good idea—you're gonna need one. But before we go back into that room to continue your deposition, let me just say a few things. When we go back on the record, you can plead the Fifth or continue playing stupid or forgetful, but regardless of how this goes, you're burned as a witness in this case. See, you remembered things with Manny that you just can't seem to recall while I question you. And, those future commissions are going to look like quite an incentive to commit perjury."

"Are you threatening to report me to the Real Estate Commission?"

"I am not. I would never do that. I am neither going to report you nor threaten to report you. What you seem to be missing here is that I just want the truth. That's all—the truth. And, you've been denying me the truth. Let me be a little clearer about where you are in this case. One course of action is for you to tell the truth when Sandra Pitt calls you as her witness. If you do that, it's highly likely I'll win the case, then—oops—you lose all those lucrative listings. If you don't tell the truth, then you have me to contend with. I cross-examine you and then have Manny here contradict you. It's quite a quandary for you."

Sweat was beading up on Spiegel's forehead. He looked over at Manny and said, "You broke my trust."

"You broke the law," retorted Manny.

"You lied to me. You said you were a bigtime mud logger."

"You heard what you wanted to hear. I said I had worked in the mud logging business for several years, which is true. My brother owns a mud logging business."

"You said you were interested in buying commercial real estate."

"I said I was interested in commercial real estate you could sell. As you can see from my report, I was very interested in that. You couldn't wait to tell me all about your relationship with the high-and-mighty Leonard Petroni and your access to his real estate holdings. You were like a life-sized Chatty Cathy doll."

"OK, Mr. Spiegel," interjected Ernest. "Enough trying to deflect attention away from your wrongdoing. Let's go back in and continue the deposition."

Larry had no idea what he was going to do when he was back on the record in the deposition. He didn't need to worry. Ernest already had that covered.

Once Dolly Barber announced that they were back on the record, Ernest said, "This deposition is concluded. Thank you for your time, Mr. Spiegel."

Larry Spiegel just sat and blinked his eyes trying to figure out what just happened. He didn't understand why Schreiber had let him off so easy.

After several seconds without Spiegel's movement, Ernest said, "You may leave now, Mr. Spiegel. The deposition is concluded."

Several more seconds passed before Spiegel got up and left. After expressing his thanks to Dolly and finding out when she could have the completed transcript to him, Ernest returned to his office where Manny Dickerson was still getting ready to leave.

Manny said, "That was quick. You must not have asked much more."

"I didn't ask anything more." In response to Manny's questioning look, Ernest continued, "I already have what I need—Spiegel's lies and your contradictions. On the record, it looks like he successfully blocked me from getting anything useful for the trial—and that's true, as far proving my case is concerned. That's all that Sandra Pitt will see when she gets a copy of the transcript. She'll think it's just a junk transcript. However, if she calls Spiegel as a witness, then I can use the transcript and you and your report to discredit him, and I don't have to disclose any of that to Pitt before the trial because it's not part of my case. It may, or may not, become part of my rebuttal of hers, but it's not part of mine. Now, the only way Pitt is going to find out about our little private conversation with Larry Spiegel is if he tells her. Do you think that's going to happen? I don't because if he does, he will absolutely lose any chance he still has to get those listings. As long as he has hope for getting those, he's going to keep quiet and pray for a miracle. And, if he does tell her, so what? She'd be a fool to try to use his testimony."

"Damn, that's diabolical," observed Manny.

"Oh, ouch—how about creative or brilliant?"

"Call 'em like I see 'em," said Manny. "But I want you for my attorney if I ever need one."

"Thanks, Manny. So, you're OK having the Devil represent you? By the way, you did a great job on this."

October 1989

On October 2, Ernest returned from a long lunch with a client and was handed a message by Tracey. "Your favorite opposing counsel called while you were out. Phone was ringing when I returned from lunch. I just caught it before it went to the answering machine."

"Pitt?"

"Good guess. May be my imagination, but she seemed relieved when I told her you weren't available."

"Can't be because she's afraid of me. She doesn't impress me as the type that scares easily. I'll call her and try not to toss my lunch."

"Good luck with that."

Ernest always preferred to get the most difficult and detestable tasks out of the way first, so he dialed Sandra Pitt's number as soon as he reached his desk. When the receptionist answered, she put him on hold for several minutes before returning to tell him that Pitt was unavailable for the rest of the day. *Fine with me—I'll be able to keep my salmon salad down.*

On Tuesday, October 10, the day after Columbus Day, Tracey handed Ernest his mail. It included an envelope from Sandy Pitt. As she handed over the envelope, Tracey said, "It has Pitt postage," which had become their euphemism for postage due.

"That was cute a couple of times, but it's become pathetically predictable. She needs to show a little more creativity in her boorish pranks." If Ernest had opened the envelope before speaking, he would not have made that comment. Its contents were quite creative. There was a notice of deposition, a copy of a subpoena and an acceptance of service. The subpoena was directed to a woman whose name he had seen in Pitt's disclosure statement—Elva Delgado—and the acceptance of service was signed by her. According to the notice, the deposition was set to begin at nine on October 16 in Pitt's offices—the first day of Ernest's trial in Aspen. The notice also stated that Pitt had cleared the date with Ernest on October 2—the day that Pitt's receptionist had said Sandy Pitt was unavailable to talk to him.

Ernest picked up his phone and dialed Sandy Pitt's number. After keeping him on hold for several minutes, the apparently very busy Sandra Pitt answered.

"This is Sandra Pitt."

"And, this is Ernest Schreiber. I just received your notice to take the deposition of Elva Delgado. Do you have a postage scale that works in your office?"

"What is that supposed to mean?"

"Most of your envelopes to me come with postage due, and I've had to pay it in order to see what delights await me inside. I want you to know, I've had to dip into my children's college fund in order to pay for those."

"Is that why you called—to make stupid wisecracks?"

"Oh, if only it were true. No, I called because your plan to take Elva Delgado's deposition comes on the same day as the first day of my Aspen trial, but you already knew that because I told you."

"It was the only time available for Ms. Delgado—sorry."

"No, you're not. And, it's not the deponent's schedule that matters here. It's mine."

"You approved the date."

"The hell I did. When did I do that? Yeah, I know the notice says I did agree to the date on October 2. We never even talked on that date."

"I left a very detailed and clear message with your secretary— Tracey Trent—that I intended to take the deposition at nine on the sixteenth in my offices. And, I instructed her to tell you that if you had any objection you should contact me to tell me so. You never got in contact with me. So, I rightly assumed that you were OK with the date and time."

"You are as full of it as a Christmas goose. It's amazing how you do that. Do you practice lying in the mirror in order to do it so convincingly and self-assuredly?" Accidentally, Ernest had hit on one of Sandy Pitt's exercises before entering court.

"Do you practice insulting people? Ask your secretary if you don't believe me."

"I don't have to, and I won't insult her by doing that. Here's another problem with your deposition—it comes after the cutoff date for discovery under the civil procedure rules."

"Not for special circumstances. Ms. Delgado's mother, who lives in Peru, has become ill and needs her daughter to come and care for her—and she has to leave right away and will be in Peru during the week of the trial."

"So, you intend to use Delgado's deposition at the trial in the place of her testimony in person?"

"Yes, I have no choice."

"I see. I get it now. That not only denies me an effective cross-examination, but it denies the judge the opportunity to observe Ms. Delgado's demeanor under my cross-examination. Your reason for conducting this deposition is not supported by the law. I know that the rules provide that a deposition can be used in place of live testimony because of illness, but it's referring to the illness of the witness, not a family member—not even their mother. And, the rules also provide that as long as the person can be subpoenaed, she has to appear. In order to do what you want, you have to provide a strong reason to the court and get the judge's approval. You haven't even attempted that. You must be very concerned that Ms. Delgado's testimony won't hold up under scrutiny."

"You can have some other attorney substitute for you at the deposition, but it's happening when I have scheduled it—with you or without you."

"Ms. Draper is entitled to an attorney of her choice, and that's me."

"Are you through? I need to do something productive."

"Oh, we're through."

After hanging up, Sandy reached for her stash box to do some productive coke snorting.

On October 16, Ernest waited outside the door until 8:58 a.m. Then, he went in and said to the woman sitting behind the receptionist's desk, "Good morning. My name is Ernest Schreiber. I'm here for the Delgado deposition." *Huh, you look shocked. Not expecting me maybe?*

The woman recovered her composure quickly. Then instead of taking Ernest to the room where the deposition would be conducted or calling her boss on the intercom, she got up and went down the hall leading out of the waiting room. Ernest heard a door open and close and then open again. Soon, both the receptionist and Sandy Pitt appeared from the hallway.

"What are you doing here?" asked Sandy.

"I'm here for a deposition—remember?"

"I thought you had a trial this week in Aspen," said Sandy.

"So did I, until last Friday. The judge in my case collapsed in the courtroom and was taken to the hospital. There was no substitute judge available on such short notice, so here I am. Lucky me, huh?"

"The deposition was cancelled."

"Really? Why didn't you tell me, or did you leave one of your imaginary messages with my secretary?"

Sandy's face briefly pinched with anger. "I didn't think it was necessary, since you said you wouldn't be coming anyway."

"Well, a simple courtesy call would have been appreciated. Good day, Ms. Pitt."

Ernest left to do more productive things.

Within fifteen minutes after Ernest had left, Pitt's court reporter came out of the elevator into the foyer of the office building where Sandy Pitt's office was located. After another twenty, Elva Delgado emerged from the same elevator.

As she headed to the front door to leave, someone behind her said, "Is that you, Ms. Delgado?"

She turned to see a tall man in a dark-blue suit with a bowtie. "Ms. Delgado, my name is Ernest Schreiber. Do you have a couple of minutes to talk?"

Elva's eyes widened, and without a word she turned and scurried out of the building.

I guess not, thought Ernest. *I don't think I'll be seeing you again.*

After he had returned to his office on October 16, Ernest decided to use his newly freed-up time to refine his case for Rita Draper, so he called her to schedule an appointment with her and Blair. On October 18, only Rita showed up, even though Ernest had wanted both of them. He had intended to interview them separately but have them both available so that he could go back and forth between them to see how their independent stories lined up. He'd have to do that some other time. Rita explained that Blair wasn't feeling well—again. Ernest questioned if that were going to be a problem when it came time for the trial, but Rita assured him it would not. He never bothered to ask what Blair's illness was. It would have been wise to do so, but Ernest was so focused on preparing for the trial and with Rita's assurance, it did not seem important.

Rita was dressed in a short, tight-fitting black skirt and an even tighter, low-cut cream sweater. Her figure-reveling outfit seemed rather out-of-place for the occasion, but it wasn't his place to be her sartorial advisor, at least not before the trial. They met in the conference room where Ernest had laid out the evidence for the case on the conference table. Their meeting was intense with minimal breaks and extended through the lunch that Ernest had brought in by Tracey. Sometimes Ernest would role play, asking questions as if they were in the courtroom with him playing the part of himself at times and that of Pitt at others. At one point, Rita came over to sit next to him to review exhibits that Ernest intended to use at the trial. More than once either her arm, leg or her breast would brush against him, and he would immediately pull away in response. Occasionally, Rita would place her hand on his arm and a couple of times on his leg. Ernest was not comfortable with the physical contact, but chose to ignore it and move on. His interest was concentrated upon honing their case into a smooth-flowing story for the courtroom, while knowing full well that regardless of the extent of his preparation, his well-oiled presentation would get gummed up along the way. It usually did, and with an opponent like Sandra Pitt it was an absolute guarantee. However, Ernest found that the process of repeatedly going over and adjusting his questions and the order and manner of presentation of evidence not only allowed him to make his story easier to understand, but it gave him insights into what the opposition would do to challenge him and this evidence. Toward the end of the afternoon, Ernest was pleased with the day's work. It had been a productive work session, but there was one problematic issue he needed to cover with Rita.

He rolled his chair back from the conference table to distance himself from Rita and then swiveled to face her. "Rita, this has been a very productive day. I can use what we did today to refine our case and then meet with you again before trial to go over all of it again and do some final brush up. Before you go however, we need to discuss my outstanding fees. Currently, they're sitting around thirty thousand dollars, and they're going to be close to fifty thousand after the trial. You've paid less than a thousand. We've spent your original retainer, so I'm paying for all the costs out of my own pocket. Rita, I'd like to have some payment. Do you think my fees are unreasonable?"

While Ernest was speaking, Rita had slowly bent forward to slip on her shoes which she had removed earlier in the day. Her movement and position gave Ernest a very clear view beyond the décolleté of her sweater. When she raised up and crossed her legs one at a time to slip on her shoes, the clear view shifted to one up her skirt. When Ernest had finished, Rita said, "Not at all. You've put a lot of work into my case and have made fantastic strides with it. I just don't have the money right now." Then she gave him a coquettish look and said, "Maybe I can pay you some other way— with something in kind?" As she said that she gave Ernest another flash up her skirt as she adjusted a shoe.

So that's what the vampish look and all the "accidental" touching was about. Ernest had had women try to entice him into cheating on his wife before, but never a client. In the past, he had always played dumb and ignored the perpetrators of impropriety, and it had worked. So, he tried the same device with Rita. Ernest gave Rita his best attempt at a look of perplexity. "Well, your photos are lovely, Rita, but I really would prefer to be paid in money."

It was Rita's turn to look perplexed. "Photos? Well, yeah, I suppose, but there are other things I could offer."

"Rita, look, I really want to be paid with legal tender."

"I'm just not flush with cash right now." She gave it one last shot. She crossed her other leg and adjusted her shoe. "Until I can get some income from photo assignments all I can offer is something else. If you think of something, let me know—anytime, anywhere."

It was time to break this conversation off. He was getting nowhere. It was clear that he wasn't going to get paid. "I'll call you when I'm ready to go over the case again. It'll be the week before trial. Also, tell Blair *(you know, the guy you're engaged to)* I'll be in touch to set up an appointment with him. Good night, Rita."

Rita rarely (never that she could remember) failed at seduction. They had always been easy to bed. She was angry, but she didn't know if she was more upset with the rejection or Ernest's dumb-ruse in rejecting her. "Good night, Ernest."

That night after Danielle and Chris had gone to bed, Ernest related Rita's attempted seduction to Claire. After he finished his telling of the event, Ernest said, "This puts a real strain on my representation of her."

"No kidding. It's so close to the trial too," observed Claire. "If you pull out now, that leaves Draper hanging without an attorney and you without getting paid. And, you've put so much time and effort into this case. If you stay in, you have the pall of her offer of sex—and your rejection—hanging over the two of you. She's probably not feeling very happy towards you right now—a woman scorned, you know. Not an enviable position to be in."

"So—you want me to take her up on her offer? Is that what you're saying?"

Claire punched him in the arm.

"Ow—so, now you don't want me to have sex with her."

"Keep it up, buddy, and I'll punch you again." They both laughed.

"This has actually been helpful, Claire. I know what I have to do."

"And, what's that?"

"I have to stay in the case. If I'm going to get paid, I have to win that case. Then I'll be able to get paid. Rita Draper won't be able to stop it."

"How so?"

"I'll file an attorney's lien—technically a charging lien— against the judgment, and I'll get paid first. And, she wins too."

"And, if you lose?" asked Claire.

Ernest let out a big sigh. "Well, I don't get paid for one thing, but if she's really pissed with me, she might file a malpractice suit. I don't know. It's not something I want to think about. I just have to win."

"With Gentilini as the judge? You told me about her reputation for hating men."

"Hate men? I don't know if that's true. She's definitely a lot tougher on them than she is on women. Hey, I have a good case— good facts, good law. I should be able to win."

"Then, there's that lovely Sandra Pitt."

"Geez, whose side are you on here? Throw me a bone. Give me some hope, Claire."

"Do you think you and Rita Draper can sit next to each other through a four-day trial and stay civil to each other?"

"Yes, absolutely, I know I can, and I'll give her stern instructions on how to behave—and dress—no more distracting skirts and blouses."

"So, you admit you were distracted by her—ahem, revelations."

Ernest raised an eyebrow and said, "Well…"

"Come here, you. I'll give you something to distract you."

CHAPTER 12

Unappealing Trial

November–December 1989

November 13, 1989

Ernest had been wondering how Gentilini's prejudice against men would play out at the trial. The last time he had appeared before her in person was at the temporary restraining order hearing back on September 1, 1988. Every dealing he had with her since then had been through written documents or her clerk. At the TRO hearing, both attorneys were male, and Gentilini had shown equal contempt for each of them. Now, Petroni was represented by a woman. It was a smart strategic move on Petroni's part, but would it give him the competitive advantage he was hoping for? Maybe not by itself, but the woman he had selected was no ordinary one—she was a cunning, treacherous liar who could spellbind with intoxicatingly convincing deceits. Ernest was worried.

He didn't have long to find out whether his concerns were misplaced. Today was the first day of the trial. He and Rita were sitting together at the plaintiff's table and to his right at the defendant's table were Sandra Pitt and Leonard Petroni. Between Pitt and Ernest was the podium from which the two attorneys would deliver the majority of their questions and arguments, and in Pitt's case—her lies.

Shortly before 9:00 a.m., the court reporter entered and got seated by her steno machine. She was soon followed by Beatrice, Gentilini's clerk, who called all to rise— "all" being the two attorneys, their clients and Blair Barker. After ordering everyone to be seated, Gentilini read the name of the case, its case number and the fact that they were all gathered together for the actual trial. Ernest was relieved that Pitt's actions would now be under the watchful eye of the judge. Maybe Pitt would be a little less uninhibited in her prevarications. His relief was quelled by the chill that ran over him when Gentilini looked up and gave a warm smile to Sandra Pitt and then an angry scowl to him. *Guess I don't have to wonder anymore how I'll be treated. This is going to be a long trial.*

"Counsel for the plaintiff, enter your appearance," ordered Gentilini with a fixed glare at Ernest.

Ernest sprang out of his chair and answered, "Ernest Schreiber, registration number five two two five appearing on behalf of the plaintiff, Rita Draper."

Then, with a softer tonality in her voice and smile on her lips, Gentilini said, "Ms. Pitt, would you enter your appearance?"

Ernest didn't even hear what Pitt said while he thought, *Ms. Pitt? She's Ms. Pitt, and I'm just some nameless supplicant to be ordered about? Oh, man, lady, what is your problem?*

"Counsel…" When Ernest failed to snap to fast enough to her liking, Gentilini shouted, "Counsel for the plaintiff."

"Yes, Your Honor."

"Could you grace us with your opening statement?"

I was verbally abused by a domineering older sister my whole childhood, and I was in the Army. There's nothing you can hand out that I can't take.

Ernest smiled a disarming smile at the judge and said, "Thank you, Your Honor. I'd be delighted to give an opening statement."

Ernest got well into his narrative about the case and what he would prove before Sandy Pitt interrupted him.

"Your Honor, I really hesitate to interrupt counsel while he's making his opening statement, but before he gets too far into it, there's a matter that should be addressed as early in the case as possible," beseeched The Pitt Viper.

"Your Honor, it's highly irregular to interrupt an attorney during his opening statement, especially for something that could have been raised earlier. May I continue, please?" said Ernest.

"No—what is it, Ms. Pitt?"

"I'd like to request the exclusion of witnesses from the courtroom with them to be allowed in only upon being called to testify."

Oh, for crying out loud, thought Ernest. "Your Honor, I'm giving an opening statement, not testimony. Rule 615 of the Rules of Evidence speaks to excluding witnesses so that they can't hear the testimony of other witnesses. Besides, right now, there's only one witness in the courtroom, Blair Barker, and he and the plaintiff are engaged to be married. He's not going to hear anything right now he hasn't already."

"I'm granting Ms. Pitt's request to sequester witnesses until they're called."

That's it? You're not going to order that they can't talk to other witnesses? OK, I can live with that, thought Ernest.

Ernest turned and gave Blair a nod to leave. Blair was noticeably unhappy with his ostracism, but he left without verbal protest.

"Your Honor, may I continue?"

"Get on with it, counsel," instructed Gentilini.

After twenty-five minutes Ernest concluded with a statement that his client also was requesting an award of her attorney's fees as provided for in the contract to the prevailing party in a lawsuit on the contract. Although he was concerned whether Gentilini had paid attention, he was even more concerned that he had made a clear statement for the record in case there was need for an appeal. He was getting a bad feeling there would be.

When Ernest sat down, Gentilini looked over and smiled at Pitt and requested her to give her opening statement. Sandy Pitt got up and started a rambling rant of lies that crossed the boundary of opening statement and into closing argument more than once. Halfway through, Ernest could take it no longer and knew he had to object, if just to make a record for appeal.

"Your Honor, counsel is giving an argument and not an opening statement. I must object."

Gentilini glared at Ernest and sneered, "Overruled, and don't you interrupt Ms. Pitt's opening statement again."

Once he had suffered through Pitt's opening statement, Ernest called Rita to the stand. During the morning session, Ernest walked Rita through her professional background as a photographer. It was a laborious process made even more so by repeated interruptions from Sandy Pitt for erroneous objections that were sustained by Gentilini, which were soon followed by interruptions by Gentilini ordering Ernest to move his case along. He felt like he was getting worked over by a team of fighters in a team-boxing match where he had no partner. At noon, he was just getting into Rita's years of travels collecting photos of endangered animals, when Gentilini called the lunch recess. Though he had been whipsawed between Pitt's delays and Gentilini's orders to speed it up, he was high on adrenaline and accomplishment. He had made an excellent record and even better foundation for his case against Petroni.

At Sandy Pitt's request, Gentilini bestowed upon them an hour and a half for lunch. Pitt had reasoned that all restaurants were downtown, walking was the best mode of travel to them, and ten minutes was the minimum time to walk to the closest one, making for a twenty-minute round trip. Sandy Pitt's real reason for asking for an hour and a half for lunch was to have time to powder her nose with coke and to smoke a Marlboro or four.

Ernest and Rita exited the courtroom and grabbed Blair to head to lunch. Blair wanted to go to the Buffalo Rose Saloon, so naturally, they went to the Buffalo Rose. It was fifteen minutes away, making for a thirty-minute round trip—not a problem for Blair. It just sliced into Ernest's preparation time for the afternoon's festivities. As they walked along Clear Creek to the bridge at Washington Avenue, Blair barraged Rita and Ernest with questions about the morning hearing. Ernest answered a couple, but tired quickly of Blair's prattle. He really wanted to focus on what was coming up in the afternoon session, and he needed to go over some questions with Rita and identify facts they needed to get into evidence. In order to think clearly, Ernest fell back a couple of steps from the other two, while hoping that Rita would answer all of Blair's pressing questions by the time they sat down for lunch. It turned out to be a false hope.

The Buffalo Rose was promoted as the oldest, continuously operating saloon in Colorado, tracing its origin to 1859. It even stayed open during Prohibition when soft drinks were served in place of alcohol. The second floor of the building in which it was located served as a meeting place for the territorial council from 1862–1866 when Colorado was still a territory and Golden was its capital. In addition to hosting a few shootouts, it was visited by

Generals Ulysses S. Grant, William Tecumseh Sherman and Philip Henry Sheridan. As Ernest entered the old saloon, he half-expected to see one of them sitting in a dark corner in the back of the room. The place was rich in history and poor in acoustics. It was a lousy place to conduct business, made worse by Blair's mouth diarrhea, which had morphed from questions to suggestions. Ernest smiled, nodded his head occasionally and heard nothing after realizing Blair's comments were ridiculous ramblings.

When the waitress came over and told them that the wait for lunch would be thirty minutes, Ernest protested and pointed out that they had to be back in court by one thirty. She replied with a non-tip-warranting inflection that they could sit at the bar if they wanted to and then left them for more important customers. Ernest ushered Rita and Blair to the bar rather than leave on a quest for another eatery with probably just as much of a wait, or more. They found only three barstools that were vacant, but one was separated from the other two by a large man in cowboy garb whose butt engulfed the stool he was on. When Ernest asked if he would mind moving over one, the fat guy gave him a look like he was weighing the advantages and disadvantages of punching Ernest against hoisting his hump to another stool. From the looks of him, either one involved more exercise than he had gotten in a month. As Ernest locked eyes with the brute, he thought, *Looks like you might need a surgeon to get that stool removed.* Deciding that moving would conserve more energy, the cow-man moved after a display of annoyed exasperation. Ernest thanked him for being so gracious, and immediately guided Rita to the center stool to use as a buffer from Blair. As he did, he realized he might have been smarter to have left the big guy where he was. It was a lost opportunity. But he did manage to get Blair seated next to the behemoth.

The bartender came and took their orders, and when he left, Ernest was finally able to get Rita's attention drawn away from Blair. Blair looked pouty until his half-pound cheese-and-bacon burger with a mound of greasy fries was set down in front of him.

He lit up and tucked in while Rita and Ernest conducted business over their salads. When he finished his burger, there was evidence of Blair's enthusiasm for his lunch on the corners of his mouth and shirt. Both Rita and Ernest noticed, but only Rita helped him wipe it off. On the way back to court, Blair was less talkative than he had been on the way to the Buffalo Rose. That was quite a relief to Ernest, as was Rita's maintenance of a professional façade even though he could sense tension between the two of them still lingering from Rita's inappropriate advances on October 18.

They arrived at the courtroom doors at 1:25 p.m., barely before the beginning of the afternoon contretemps. As he opened the doors, Ernest saw that Leonard Petroni and Sandy Pitt were already in their seats. He vowed not to allow Blair to pick the restaurant tomorrow. As they walked to the front of the court, passing through the gate in the bar and into the well of the courtroom, Ernest instructed Rita to retake her seat on the witness stand. He then retrieved his notes from his locked briefcase (a precaution against the prying eyes of the untrustworthy Pitt) and stood at the podium, as he had just before lunch. Hardly had he taken his position when the court reporter entered, followed by the clerk and an "all rise." Gentilini glided in and took her throne above them all. Since her feet were not visible under her long black robe, Gentilini gave Ernest the impression of a black-clad specter of doom—hovering, rather than walking, over the floor.

With Gentilini's announcement that they were back on the record for the afternoon session and a cold stare in his direction, Ernest had his cue to begin and picked up his questioning of Rita from where he had left off before lunch. Having been given a lot of encouragement by Gentilini during the morning session, The Pitt Viper felt a special privilege to continue her obstruction of Ernest's progress toward justice with a tad more gusto. Most of her objections were for relevance, materiality and lack of foundation. These are typical, lackluster objections often thrown out by attorneys, when they don't have something more concrete to offer, in the hope of netting a "sustained" from a judge.

Sometimes, they are rewarded for their lack of creativity or finesse. It's what keeps them doing it. Sandy Pitt was getting more than her fair share of judicial encouragement for her bad behavior. Ernest was not to be deterred—only annoyed. Pitt's objections and Gentilini's sustaineds did nothing more than add time to Ernest's examination of Rita. He always was able to get the facts he wanted into the record, and always by using the same method— asking more background questions to establish relevance, materiality and foundation. It was a tedious process that a different judge would have cut short. Instead, Gentilini sustained the time-wasting objections and then blamed Ernest for the slowdown. At long last, by 4:12 p.m. Ernest was finished with his direct examination of Rita. He had gotten evidence in on her photojournalistic expertise; world travels in pursuit of photos for her book; events leading up to the contract with Petroni; Petroni's revelation that he didn't own the property; Rita's insistence on adding language to fill the space for a closing date that was left blank by Petroni; her giving Petroni her address and phone number in California before she left in November 1987; the discovery of Petroni's betrayal in August 1988; and an excellent list with values of her damages. He even was able to get Rita's testimony about the payments she made to Blair for the construction he did and her valuation of her damaged and destroyed photos. Rita had performed beautifully, answering questions with the right amount of certainty and emotion, something that welled up in a combination of deep sadness and incredulity seasoned with the appropriate amount of anger whenever the topic of her damaged and destroyed photos came up. Now, the true test of her will, stamina and credibility would come with The Pitt Viper's cross-examination. It was something that Ernest and Rita had spent long hours together training for.

Upon Gentilini's cordial invitation, Sandy Pitt lubricated the back of her left hand against her nose, rose to the podium and with an intended-to-be-disarming smile began her questioning. Rita did not relax her vigilance just because Pitt smiled pleasantly at her.

Ernest had covered that probability during their meetings. Neither did she show tension in her voice or posture. She sat comfortably erect and looked directly into Pitt's eyes with a soft but assertive physiognomy that conveyed confidence and that she had practiced at length with Ernest. After a half hour of questioning by Pitt, Ernest was quite proud of his student, even though he was wary of her and her honesty with him. Pitt was getting visibly frustrated with Rita's composure and iron-willed certainty about her previous testimony. Ernest was enjoying the show, and unlike Pitt who tried to disrupt his examination of Rita, he made no objections; however, every once in a while, he stirred in his chair as if to get up to make one. That was more unnerving to Sandy Pitt than if Ernest had constantly interrupted her. At least that would give her a chance to show off her skills at vacuous legal babble while denigrating Ernest. The first time he moved, Pitt turned to him and waited for his objection. Ernest pretended that he didn't notice and just looked up pleasantly at Judge Gentilini. When she realized that no objection was forthcoming, Pitt turned back to Rita with a slight huff under her breath. Throughout her cross-examination, Pitt expected Ernest to object with some nonsensical objection like she had. Ernest, on the other hand, knew that his silence was more unsettling to Pitt than Pitt's previous interruptions of him for reasons that never would be sufficient to overturn a case on appeal. If anything, Pitt's objections would look bad for her on the record if there were an appeal, while Ernest's silence would appear as if Pitt had free rein with his client. Ernest was relying upon his pretrial prep of Rita to protect her, rather than any prowess at disruption. And, he was training Pitt. Since he was not giving her a biscuit each time he adjusted his position, it wasn't exactly respondent conditioning, like Pavlov did with his dogs, but when he thought about it, that might be a good way to break her of her disgusting nose wiping.

At 5:30 p.m. Gentilini stopped Pitt and called a recess until the next morning at 9:00 a.m. In response to Ernest's question, Gentilini assured him that the courtroom would be locked once all parties and their counsel had left, so they could leave any evidence or other materials they didn't want to carry with them. Rita came out of the witness box and over to Ernest and kept quiet as he had previously instructed her—no talking around the opposition. Once he was packed up, Ernest waited until Pitt and Petroni made a move to leave. Pitt was dragging her feet, so Ernest sat back down with Rita and waited. After a slow show of methodically packing up, Pitt decided that Ernest wasn't going anywhere until she did, so she quickly finished and motioned for Leo Petroni to head toward the door. Ernest and Rita got up to follow them out.

As soon as they were outside the courtroom doors, Blair jumped to his feet off the bench he had been warming and peppered them with questions. Ernest asked him to save them until they were out of earshot of the enemy. Ernest led them to an unoccupied jury room. As soon as they entered the room, Blair started in with the questions again. Ernest let Rita give him a few answers before interrupting. Blair looked rejected, dejected—and annoyed with Ernest.

"I thought you did very well, Rita. How did you feel?" asked Ernest.

"I was a little nervous when Pitt first started, but, really, for the circumstances, there wasn't anything I wasn't prepared for. All the questioning you did with me when we practiced made it pretty easy."

"Well, you looked great. There was no sign of nervousness. You looked confident and showed just the right emotions at the right times. I'm really happy with the way you never got angry at Pitt's badgering questions. Tomorrow, do the same, and not only will you frustrate the hell out of Pitt, but you'll have your story before the judge and in the record."

"How much longer do you think I'll be on the stand?"

"I think we should be done with Pitt's cross-examination and my rebuttal by noon." Ernest then looked at Blair and said, "Blair,

I'll call you after Rita is done. Then I plan on calling Molly Richards, and then I'll conclude our case with Andrew Edison. He should be pretty impressive with the credentials he has. Blair, I want you to testify just like we practiced—don't get creative. Look Pitt in the eye and answer the question that is being asked. Don't glance over at me or Rita when Pitt asks a question. She'll make that look like evasion of the truth or fabrication of a lie. And, don't try to anticipate the next question or answer one that you'd like to. That may work for politicians, but it doesn't play well on the witness stand. Sit erect and comfortably and don't answer until you're sure you know what the question is. If you don't understand the question, ask for clarification. And, above all, tell the truth. Blair, are you ready for tomorrow?"

"Oh yeah, I've been practicing in the mirror and going over my notes. I'll do a great job. You'll see. You'll see."

You worry me. What is it about you that seems—different? Maybe I should just wing it with Rita's testimony about the construction costs. "I'm going to keep your testimony brief. I'll focus on the costs of your labor and the construction materials. That's the main thing I want in the evidence, but I'll also ask you about the meetings you had with Petroni, both when Rita was present and when she wasn't. That's it."

"Don't worry. I was thinking that maybe I should wear some glasses."

Where did this come from? "Glasses? Do you wear glasses sometimes?"

"No, but people look smarter and more trustworthy when they wear glasses. I think it would make me look more credible."

Ernest's eyes flicked over to Rita to see her reaction. She looked away. "If you don't generally wear glasses, don't start tomorrow."

"I thought I'd wear an ascot—or maybe a bowtie like you."

Good heavens, were you just beamed down from the mother ship? And, I'm the only guy who gets to wear a bowtie on this team. "No ascot, no bowtie—no tie or neck decoration of any kind, Blair. Oh, and especially, no gold chains—nothing. Dress business casual—nice pair of clean, pressed slacks; clean, ironed dress shirt; shined shoes; maybe a sweater vest. We went over this before—remember? Do you want to go over some questions now that Pitt will ask?"

"No, no, we've been over that plenty. I'm good. I'm good. I'll be great. Don't worry."

Say 'don't worry' again and I'll have to see a shrink for panic disorder. "All right, I'll see you both tomorrow—here, no later than eight thirty, preferably around eight fifteen. Have a good night."

Only Rita said good night. When they were down the hall a ways, Blair started chattering to Rita—about what Ernest could only guess.

As usual, after Danielle and Chris were in bed for the night, Ernest and Claire debriefed and decompressed from their days— hers from teaching a room full of first graders and his from trying to teach a belligerent judge. Ernest asked Claire to go first. Like all great teachers, Claire took pride in her job and worked hard at it because she loved informing, inspiring and empowering young children. She was most pleased with the improvement in reading levels of her students because reading well was crucial to learning, critical thought and success later.

After she finished relating stories from her day, Ernest said, "It seems so unfair that you work so hard and get so little pay for doing it. Maybe you should have been a football player or Hollywood actor. What is it about this country? The people who contribute the least to society get paid too much and the people who contribute the most get paid too little."

"We've had this conversation before, sweetie. It's the compensation-to-contribution inversion principle. Anybody can be a teacher, and they get the whole summer off to prepare for the next year of under appreciation and inadequate pay. I'm surprised that people, especially men, aren't clamoring for this do-nothing job. So, shhh, don't let the word out. Now, how was your day? How was that maybe-man-hating judge?"

"You know, she was downright awful. If she doesn't hate men, she sure does a good imitation of it. She's married too—to a divorce lawyer. Don't even want to think about what goes on in their bedroom. But, Rita Draper did a superb job. In spite of constant interruptions by Pitt making dumb objections, I was able to get all the evidence in that I had wanted, more, actually, with her testimony about the costs of the construction she paid her boyfriend. And, she held up great under cross-examination by Pitt, at least for the little bit she did today. Tomorrow she goes under The Pitt Viper's knife again, but I'm confident that Draper will do all right. However, I am pretty worried about her boyfriend. He seems...I don't know...erratic, I guess, is a good way to say it, maybe unstable. And, I put him on after Draper. Honestly, though, Claire, this is not one of my fun cases. I'm not sure I like anyone in that courtroom—anyone I know, that is. I don't know the court reporter and clerk."

"How about you? You're in that courtroom. I like you, so you should too."

"Oh, you're such a teacher. I love you."

November 14, 1989

Ernest was back in his seat with Rita at his side at 8:46 a.m. Sandy Pitt arrived with Leo Petroni at 8:52. Before she sat down, Sandy looked over at the plaintiff's table and thought, *Asshole.*

When he was sure that Pitt had seen him, Ernest put his crayons back in their box, closed his Dr. Seuss coloring book and put them all into his briefcase while removing four highlighters—yellow, pink, orange and green. They each had a corner of their sticky adhesive labels pulled down. He lined them up neatly on the desk in front of him for easy viewing from the podium next to him. Shortly, the processional of justice began—court reporter, clerk, "all rise" and judge. After announcing the case and its second day of trial, Gentilini ordered Rita back into the witness stand. As Pitt took her place at the podium, she saw the lineup of highlighters. Ernest tapped them with his right hand and looked up at Pitt with a wisp of a smile. Ernest noticed that Pitt seemed jumpier than she normally was and bit more leaky under the nose. *Asshole,* thought Sandy again.

Ernest never peeled the labels, nor did he intend to. What he did was tap them and move slightly in his seat at certain questions that if he were the questioner, Pitt would have objected for one of her favorite reasons—relevance, materiality and foundation. On the fourth tap and move, Ernest did object. Sandy ignored him on that one and kept talking. Ernest had to make the objection again before she stopped. Pitt had asked the same question four times in four different ways and gotten the same answer from Rita each time. It was about why Rita had not called Petroni from California to find out the status of his quest for title to the property. Rita had explained that she had tried that while she lived in the house and had been told by Petroni that she didn't need to keep doing it because he would let her know when he did have title. Also, Petroni made that same promise when she gave him her contact information before leaving for California in November 1987. Rita explained that she still trusted him to do what he promised—he is Leo Petroni after all. It was a great answer—one that Sandy Pitt should never have asked for in the first place and certainly should have backed away from after the first answer. Evidently, Gentilini was just as tired of hearing the repetition as Ernest and sustained his objection. It was as much a surprise to Sandy Pitt as it was to

Ernest, and that and the extra snort of coke she had before arriving at the courthouse was enough to throw her off her game. Ernest noticed and tried something just to see how it would be received.

"Your Honor, I've been very patient with defense counsel's line of questioning, but much of what she is asking is nothing more than a fishing expedition that could have been avoided by her taking the deposition of Ms. Draper, but that was never done. Ms. Pitt elected not to take her deposition. Maybe we can shorten this trial by stipulating to some of the points that the defense is struggling to squeeze from Ms. Draper."

Neither Pitt nor Gentilini liked the way he had phrased that.

Pitt objected angrily, "Your Honor, I am entitled to conduct my pretrial preparation and my cross-examination of Ms. Draper as I see fit. Stopping this trial to allow the two attorneys, who have never seen eye-to-eye on anything in this case so far, to waste time trying to identify facts to stipulate to would be a waste of time."

Ernest for once agreed with Sandy Pitt, and so did Gentilini, "I agree. Continue Ms. Pitt, and you, counsel, please sit down."

Whoa, what? Did you just say 'please' to me? You do remember who I am, right?

Pitt was slightly flummoxed and lost her place. In a slightly elevated volume she ordered, "Answer the question."

Rita gave a quizzical look and for a brief moment forgot Ernest's instructions and glanced over at him.

"Look at me when you answer. Your attorney can't help you now."

Rita looked back at Pitt and said, "What question?"

"The last question I asked, Ms. Draper."

Rita looked at her with a perplexed look and said, "You didn't ask a question."

With an exasperated sigh, Sandy Pitt looked at the court reporter and said, "Please read back my last question to Ms. Draper."

The court reporter picked up the stream of steno tape flowing out of her machine, read it, and announced, "There was no question."

Ernest tapped his lineup of highlighters. Pitt noticed with her peripheral vision, then continued her cross-examination of Rita trying to escape her embarrassment. After another half hour, she gave up and turned Rita over to Ernest for rebuttal. Pitt had failed to shake Rita, but she had accomplished one thing. She solidified Rita's prior testimony under direct.

Ernest got up behind the podium, gestured with his right hand at Sandy Pitt and said to Rita, "During cross, Ms. Pitt questioned you at length about there being no actual date specified in the contract or by Mr. Petroni ever for the closing of your purchase of the property in question, and you admitted that no specific date was mentioned. Is that correct?"

"Yes."

"What did you mean by that answer?"

"Just what it sounds like—there was no specific date with a month and a day of the month, or year, for that matter, set for the closing."

"Why was that?"

"Leo didn't have title so he didn't know when the date would be and couldn't tell us when it would be."

"Did you ever think that there would not be a closing date?"

"Absolutely not. Leo was very certain that he could get title and that we would close after that."

"And, when would that happen?"

"Objection—calls for speculation," cried out Sandy with a note of triumph in her voice.

"No, it doesn't, Your Honor. I'm merely asking the witness to give us her understanding of when the closing would occur after Mr. Petroni obtained legal title. That could mean a date, a number of days or could be some way of determining an actual date, but whatever it is, it is the witness's understanding." *And, thank you, Ms. Pitt, for giving me the opportunity to signal to Rita the answer I'm looking for.*

"Overruled," said Gentilini.

Well, look at that—that's two objections ruled in my favor. "Go ahead and answer the question, Ms. Draper."

"I thought the closing would be as soon as Leo and I could reasonably get all of the paperwork done to close. It wasn't some specific date, at least not until we knew when all that could be done. We'd figure that out later after Leo got title."

Perfect, thought Ernest. "Now, I want to direct your attention to the handwritten language on page three of the contract for sale that says, 'Buyer shall pay when due all costs associated with the property, including, but not limited to, taxes, HOA dues and insurance premiums.' On cross, Ms. Pitt asked whether you were certain that language was not on the contract you signed before Mr. Petroni left with the contract to make a copy in his home office. Later, you refined that answer to saying that you were reasonably certain."

"Objection to Mr. Schreiber's characterization of the testimony as being 'refined.'"

"Your Honor, I think you're perfectly capable of interpreting the testimony independently of my 'characterization' or that of Ms. Pitt."

"Overruled."

Hot damn—that's three for me. "When you said you were 'reasonably certain' did you mean that you had some doubts about your previous testimony?"

"Not at all," said Rita.

"What did you mean?"

"I meant that I was dealing with Leonard Petroni, who has a reputation as a powerful, influential and, as far as I had heard, honest man. It's hard to think that he would do something as dishonest—and petty—as insert language in a contract after it had been signed by him—and me. That just goes against logic, so when I first saw the new language in his handwriting, I was confused by the new words. I mean, how could he do that? What makes a big powerful man like him cheat on a real estate contract?"

"Objection," said Sandy who was almost apoplectic over Rita's testimony and wanted to stop it, but had no reason to give for her objection.

"Your Honor, defense counsel is the one who opened this door."

"Overruled."

"Please continue, Ms. Draper," said Ernest.

"Well, when I used the word reasonably, I just meant that I believed that Leo would honor the contract—and his word—and, well, I wanted to believe him. I guess part of me still does, but everything he has done shows I can't."

Ernest and Rita had gone over this particular issue at length. When Ernest first asked Rita whether Leo had written that language in the contract after she had signed it and before he had made a copy, she was uncertain. He then delved into the reason for her uncertainty. He discovered that her uncertainty was due to what she had just testified to. He probed further to see if she had another logical explanation for the appearance of those words in the contract. There was none. The words weren't there when she signed the contract; she had not reviewed the copy when Petroni handed it to her; they were in the contract two months later when she looked at it for the first time after the copy was made; and, sure as heck, neither she nor Blair inserted the words. Ultimately, she could find no explanation other than that Petroni had inserted the words just before he made the copy.

"Thank you, Ms. Draper. Your Honor, I have nothing further for this witness."

"It's almost eleven thirty. We'll be in recess for lunch until one this afternoon," pronounced Gentilini.

When Ernest and Rita exited the courtroom doors, Blair was waiting for them. Ernest was pleased to see that he was not wearing any ties, ascots or gold chains. Blair had driven himself this day because he did not want to be stranded on the bench in the hall like he had on the first day. Ernest noticed that Blair was quite nervous and twitchy—more so than he sometimes was. *You and Pitt—maybe it's the phase of the moon.* When Blair said he wanted to return to the Buffalo Rose for lunch, Ernest vetoed the choice and said that The Gold Den was much closer and had a better selection of menu choices. Blair did his little sulky face, but it didn't stop him from his running line of questions, interspersed with his self-perceived sage counsel.

Since it was still a little before noon, they got a table reasonably fast. It was in the center of the restaurant, but that was acceptable to Ernest. He wouldn't be sitting on a stool at a bar with loud distractions all around him, and there was a real tablecloth and cloth napkins on the table. This promised to be a much better work environment than yesterday, even though he would need to sit between Blair and Rita, so that he could debrief with Rita and do some last-minute prep work with Blair.

Blair went quiet when he was given a menu by the waitperson. Food and ordering it were two of the best ways to temporarily silence him. Once they ordered, however, Blair set to again.

"Here's what we should do this afternoon. I have a list of questions you should ask me," began Blair.

Ernest looked at him with incredulity. "Blair, we went over your testimony for today—at length. Are you not comfortable with it?"

"I was thinking about it, and I can improve upon your approach. I want you to start with me finding the property with Rita and then go into how I negotiated the contract."

"But that's not relevant to your testimony. I already have that in the record through Rita, and she's made a strong record." *Besides, I'm afraid you'd screw up her testimony.* "I want to focus on the work you did on the house and how you billed for it." Ernest turned to Rita to plead for her assistance when—BAM! Ernest jumped, along with the silverware on the table. All heads in the restaurant turned in their direction.

After slamming both fists on the table, Blair jumped out of his chair, tipping it over, and started screaming, "You never listen to my advice. You think you're such a hotshot, but you're not. You're going to lose this case if you don't listen to me. You're a stupid, arrogant bastard. Fuck you and your Ivy League law degree." And with that, Blair ran out of the restaurant leaving Ernest and Rita withering with embarrassment under the shocked stares of the other patrons.

When he regained his voice, Ernest said, "What was that all about?"

Rita said, "Don't follow him out there right now. He's very dangerous when he gets like that."

"Oh, don't worry about that. I had no intention of following him."

"I'll be right back. Stay here," said Rita as she got up to follow in Blair's wake.

"Like I said, I'm sticking right here."

The other customers turned their heads, but not their attention, away from Ernest. *So, this is what eternity feels like. Well, folks, have you heard the one about the lawyer who was told to get fucked in a restaurant full of people? Oh, you have? Maybe you can tell me how it ends. Please hurry back, Rita.*

Eternity finally passed, and Rita returned to her seat and said nothing.

"Are you going to tell me what just happened or not?"

Rita let out a sigh and said, "I talked to him before he left—"

"Left? He left? He's my next witness. He can't just leave."

"Well, he did," replied Rita.

"Why did he leave?"

"He can't testify this afternoon. He wanted to do this without taking his medications. I told him not to, but he wanted to see if he could do it without them."

"Medications? What medications? For what?" asked Ernest.

"He takes lithium and some other meds for his bipolar disorder."

Oh my gosh, so that's it. That's what I've been noticing all this time. Of course—dammit, why didn't I see that? "Why didn't you tell me this before now—when it's a crisis?"

"It didn't seem important. He's generally OK when he takes his meds," pleaded Rita.

"And, so, today—of all days—Blair decides that he wants to go off his meds to see if he can testify without them in a case that is highly important to you. That is just mindboggling. Where is he going? Maybe I can get my private investigator to catch him."

"I don't know where he is, or where he's going. He just screamed at me that he wasn't going to work with you. That it was all your fault."

"Yeah, right, nice try," said Ernest.

Their lunches were delivered by an apprehensive waiter.

"Would you box these for us, please, and give us the check? We have an emergency to attend to," said Ernest.

"This one too?" asked the waiter, pointing to Blair' abandoned lunch.

"Sure—if I'm paying for it," answered Ernest. Then he turned to Rita and said, "I want you to call Molly Richards and ask her if she can come right in. She was going to be my next witness after Blair. I had asked her to come in at two thirty, but obviously, I need her now. Then call Andrew Edison and explain my predicament and ask him to come in too. While you're doing that, I'll change my exhibits around and get ready for the new lineup. If I have to, I'll stall the judge with—hell, I don't know—something."

They got their boxed lunches, Ernest paid their bill and then they left with a mental sigh of relief. *Shows over, folks. Nothin' to see here,* thought Ernest as he tried not to run to the exit.

Rita split off from Ernest to a bank of telephones in the main hall of the courthouse while Ernest continued up to the courtroom. When he arrived, he changed his mind and decided that honesty was always the best policy, so he headed to the judge's chambers. Screwing up his courage, he went in and found Beatrice at her desk.

She looked up at him and said, "Why are you here?"

Hi, I like you too, and that judge of yours—she's a peach. "To tell you that I have a problem. My next witness for this afternoon has fallen ill and won't be able to testify. So, I'm making arrangements for the next two to come in earlier than I had originally told them."

"So, how is that my problem?"

Well, aren't you sweet? "I just wanted to save the judge the trouble of coming into the courtroom before there was anything to hear and having to wait around for my next witness."

"The judge doesn't wait for anyone. It's the attorneys' responsibility to make sure their witnesses are here when the judge is present, not the other way around."

Oh, you are a delight. I like you just as much as I like your judge. "And here I thought you both were public servants, serving at the will of the people to dispense justice and not just expediency." *Oh, damn, did I just say that out loud?*

Beatrice looked like she had been slapped in the face with a wet mackerel. Rarely, like never, had she had anyone stand up to her like that. But rather than getting angry, she got up and went into the judge's chambers. Ernest's words were the truth, and she couldn't deny it.

When Beatrice returned, she said, "The judge said you have twenty extra minutes. Let me know as soon as your witness arrives."

Ernest said in his most humble voice, "Thank you. I will."

As Ernest headed back to the courtroom to prepare for the rearranged afternoon session of his case, Blair Barker was at Stapleton International Airport buying an airline ticket to Honolulu. When Sandy Pitt got the word that there was a delay because one of Ernest's witnesses was ill, she leered at him with an air of delight.

Molly Richards showed up with five minutes to spare on the extra twenty granted by Gentilini. Ernest rushed back to Beatrice to tell her, and within another two they were all back in the courtroom and on the record. His direct examination of Richards went fairly smoothly, considering the opposing counsel and judge he had to contend with. Molly Richards' main function was to add weight and validity to Rita's testimony that she really was an author of a book-to-be about endangered animals and how they got that way. Even Pitt's cross-examination was light.

At two thirty, he was ready for his star witness on damages— Andrew Edison. The man presented himself well and professionally—for about five minutes. Then, he started to look at Rita every once in a while with what looked to Ernest like a flirtatious smile. *What the hell are you doing, Andy?* When he got a chance, Ernest stole a look at Rita to see what she was doing, and to his horror, she was reciprocating with her own amorous antics. It was something that he had not warned them against because— why would he have to? He could only hope that Sandy Pitt, or at least the judge, were not picking up on this—but they were. He could see the sparkle of delight in Pitt's otherwise cold dark eyes. He also saw Gentilini looking first to Edison and then to Rita. All he could do was to soldier on with the facts and hope that the reasoning behind Andrew's estimates of between $1,000 and $1,500 per photo would outshine the sexual tension being evidenced. At long last, at four thirty, he was done, and glad of it. Pitt was happy and confident with what she could do with Andrew's demeanor so she waived cross-examination. That was it for Ernest's case, so he told the court that the plaintiff rested, and Gentilini sent them all home with instructions to return at nine tomorrow when Sandy Pitt would step up to the batter's box.

Ernest was so upset, all he could do was give a short courteous thank you to Andrew and say good night to the two of them, while thinking that they probably couldn't get to bed soon enough.

That night during debriefing time at the Schreiber home Claire asked for an account of his day. After he told her the whole story, she asked, "What are you going to do now?"

"Remember that old, non-PC, joke about Irish foreplay?"

"Brace yourself, Bridget?"

"That's it. All I can do is watch the show tomorrow and ask some good questions on cross. At least I had fun coloring in my Dr. Seuss coloring book this morning."

"You're a dope," said Claire appreciatively.

November 15, 1989

While Rita and Ernest were sitting in court in Golden, Colorado, Blair was lying in a hospital bed a thousand miles away. He never made it to Honolulu the night before. Although he had been stable enough to get on his flight in Denver, he had not been able to hold it together during the relatively short flight between Denver and San Francisco. The passengers on his connecting flight to Honolulu would never know how lucky they were that Blair had his meltdown before he could join them for six hours in their claustrophobic, winged tube to Paradise. Blair too was lucky since there had been a doctor on board his flight and no federal air marshal with a gun to shoot him. Just a little over half way to their destination, Blair had started crying loudly in remorse over his failed attempt to operate normally without medication. He soon switched to anger and a running tirade directed mostly at Ernest.

The passengers sitting next to him were terrified—and trapped, since Blair was in the aisle seat. To their great relief, Blair got up and started pacing the aisle, muttering and yelling in concert with the voices in his head. When a flight attendant started toward him from the rear galley, Blair at first turned to head away, but a larger male flight attendant was coming at him from that direction. Failing to register that he was on a plane thirty-five thousand feet above the ground with no escape that involved his survival, he rushed the female attendant. Although there were no good choices for him, that was worse than the one he had just tried to avoid. A large, muscular man popped out of his aisle seat and blocked Blair's path before hitting him in the chest sending him flat on his backside. The large man was a member of the defensive line for the Denver Broncos headed to Hawaii with his family. His quick action got him and his family first-class seats on their next flight to Honolulu. While the big guy pinned Blair, a doctor had come over, made a quick appraisal of the situation, and administered a sedative that sent Blair to a safer place for him and, most importantly, his fellow passengers. In the ambulance on the way from the airport to the hospital, Blair had been lucid enough to give the ambulance attendants his name and health problem and Rita's contact information. When a doctor at the hospital called in the middle of the night to tell her what had happened, Rita was in bed with Andrew Edison. She told the doctor that she did not want to speak to Blair because she knew that if she did, he would beg her to come to his aid, and that was something she did not have the luxury of doing. Also, she was having a lot of fun with Andrew. Now, Blair was strapped to a bed and heavily sedated instead of helping Rita with her case against Leo Petroni or sitting on the beach in Waikiki.

Back in the Golden courtroom, Sandy Pitt was questioning her primary witness, Leonard Petroni. During the previous two days of the trial, Leo had dressed in expensive power suits, and today, he had on one of his most powerful, a dark-blue pinstripe number, along with a dark-maroon paisley tie and matching pocket square.

It conveyed wealth, power and integrity with only two of those being correct. Ernest had to admit that the guy looked dignified and believable. He also spoke that way. Leo did a fine job of lying. He testified that Rita never tried to talk to him, much less did she actually do so, before she left for California in November 1987. He didn't even know she had left until a couple of months later. The poor man had no way of knowing where she had gone or why. Rita never gave him any of her contact information, so how was he supposed to know where she went? And he was left with a mess to clean up in his house with special emphasis being given repeatedly during his testimony to the maggots that had taken up residence in spoiling food in the refrigerator and stove. He was a victim, not a perpetrator, of abuse. He had entered into a contract with Rita Draper, and she had breached it, not him. Also, the language requiring Rita to pay all the costs of the property was a statement of what she was required to pay instead of rent since she otherwise was living in the house free of charge. Pitt wrapped up her questioning with a focus on Leo's alleged damages for Rita's construction he had to have removed and devaluation of his house by her work. It all was a bold distortion of the truth that was told with such unabashed temerity that the natural reaction was to believe it because the mind rebelled against believing anyone could be so mendacious. Once Sandy had concluded her questioning, the hour was close to noon, so Gentilini called the lunch recess and ordered everyone to be fully prepared to begin at one thirty.

Since Blair had tarnished their character by association with him at The Gold Den, Ernest had no intention of returning there for lunch today. However, since Golden was a small town, there was a good chance that regardless of where they went for lunch, they would cross paths with some of the same people who had witnessed Blair's blare, and anyone who had was sure to remember. Yesterday, Ernest ended up taking his lunch home and not eating it before the afternoon session. It would take more than embarrassment for him to do that two days in a row. They went to a place called Hanna's House. The people at The Gold Den who had witnessed the floorshow by Blair all had blurred faces as far as Ernest could remember. He could never pick any of them out of a lineup even if his life depended on it—if only that were true for the individuals who had witnessed yesterday's spectacle. Judging by some of the looks of surprised concern he and Rita got as they entered Hanna's, he had a strong feeling that these folks knew exactly who he was, if not by name, by celebrity. Rather than look away, Ernest met the stares straight on by nodding and smiling as he passed the gawkers. They in turn wanted no part of a social interaction with him and quickly averted their eyes. Lunch with Rita was, if not unfriendly, on the frosty side of courtesy. Ernest was not happy with her lovefest with Andrew Edison while he was testifying the day before, but knew of no way of discussing it without blowing the lid off the powder keg they had between them. Besides, what good would it do? Rita did tell him about Blair's overnight adventure to San Francisco—but left out the parts Ernest would have found most fun, like the football player who knocked Blair on his padded rump. When she finished with her telling of Blair's sad story, Ernest's only comment was, "Guess he's not coming back to testify then." After they finished their lunch of hot soup and chilled conversation, they headed back to court and Ernest's cross of Leo Petroni.

Sometimes, building up from lesser important questions that progress from little furballs, then to pinpricks and ultimately to the spearhead that harpoons an opponent is a good tactic. When he was back behind the podium in the afternoon, Ernest decided to go straight for the harpoons.

"Mr. Petroni, you testified that the contract wasn't enforceable because it had no closing date. You also have impressed upon us that you are a very prominent attorney, who owns several parcels of commercial real estate, and that you have more than just a passing knowledge of real estate law—in fact, you're an expert in real estate law. Why would you, an expert in real estate law, draft a real estate contract that wasn't enforceable, knowing that if it weren't, you could keep the property after Ms. Draper had improved it—like by putting a new roof on it?

"Objection, Your Honor," spit out Pitt.

"Objection? That's a perfectly valid question based upon Mr. Petroni's testimony under direct, Your Honor. And, if you're like me, you've been wondering about the answer to that throughout this trial."

"It calls for speculation and—" stuttered Pitt.

Ernest cut her off. In fact, he preferred that Petroni did not answer the question. His answer would just be a puffed-up lie anyway. Ernest had already planted the seed of suspicion in Gentilini's mind, and the way he put it to her as something she should have already been wondering about would encourage her to give it some serious thought—if she was as smart as her reputation would indicate. "Your Honor, I withdraw the question." But, of course, it really wasn't withdrawn from anyone's mind—only the answer was. And, an unanswered question was better than an answered one in this case, because Ernest could build upon the suspicion he had created and provide his own logical answer during closing argument.

"Mr. Petroni, you testified under questioning by your attorney that you didn't know that Ms. Draper and her fiancé, Blair Barker, had left, as you put it 'abandoned', the property until a couple of months after November 1987. That would be January 1988 when you discovered they had gone. Is that correct?"

"Yeah, I guess."

"You guess? You testified a couple of months and that would be January 1988 wouldn't it?"

Pitt was up again, and said, "Your Honor, we'll stipulate that a couple of months after November 1987 would be January 1988."

Hmm, you seem nervous, Viper. "Your Honor, may I continue? I'm not asking for Ms. Pitt to stipulate or to testify in place of her client. I'm entitled to hear the answer from Mr. Petroni, if nothing more than for the record."

"Go ahead, but get to your point, counsel," ordered Gentilini.

"Thank you. Mr. Petroni, your answer, please."

"Yes, that would be January 1988," said Leo in an exasperated tone of voice.

Ernest picked up a document, took it to the court reporter and had her mark it with an exhibit number. Then he headed to the witness stand and handed the document to Petroni.

"Mr. Petroni, I've just handed you a document that's been marked as Plaintiff's Exhibit 58. Would you identify that, please?"

"It's a quiet title complaint."

"It's also file stamped by the court. Please continue to read that file stamp and whose name is mentioned as the plaintiff."

"It's file stamped February 4, 1988, and I'm the plaintiff."

"Is that the complaint for the quiet title action by which you were awarded title to the property at issue in this case—a little over five months later on July 29, 1988?"

Pitt didn't know how to stop this line of questioning, so she decided to not attract a lot of attention to it by ignoring it now and dealing with it later—somehow. She tried to look unconcerned.

"Mr. Petroni, I asked a question. I'd like an answer."

"Yes, that's my quiet title complaint."

"Why did you wait to file that complaint until a few days after you knew Ms. Draper and Mr. Baker had, as you put it, 'abandoned' the property?"

"It was the first time my attorney, Michael Wesley, could get it started. It was his decision—his schedule that dictated when to start the quiet title," lied Petroni.

"When did you instruct him to begin the action?" asked Ernest.

"Objection," shouted Pitt. "Attorney-client privilege."

"Not so, Your Honor," fired back Ernest. "I'm not asking what he and his attorney talked about. I'm asking when the witness instructed his attorney to do something, not what he may have said in doing it."

"Overruled," said Gentilini.

Good for you, judge. "An answer, please, Mr. Petroni."

"I don't remember," lied Petroni again. Leo was starting to think that entrapping young women to rape was a lot easier than being interrogated by Ernest.

"Well, let me help you with that, Mr. Petroni. Was it near the time that you signed the contract to sell the property to Ms. Draper?"

"I don't know—maybe."

"Did you ever ask your attorney to speed it up and get the process going so that you could transfer the title to Ms. Draper?"

Leo decided that not knowing was the safest answer for everything coming his way from Ernest. "I don't know—I could have."

"Guess it wasn't important enough to you to remember," interjected Ernest.

"Objection," fired off Pitt.

"Withdrawn, Your Honor," but, everyone knew it wasn't.

Ernest decided to end his cross-examination there. He had enough to argue his case right now—well, except for the damage done to his claim for damages by Barker, Edison and Draper.

There was little that Pitt could do to repair the injury inflicted by Ernest to Petroni's testimony and credibility, so she decided to deal with it in her closing and not by an attempt at rebuttal. She called her last witness, the real estate broker who had given a fake value to fake damages. By the time Ernest had finished with him, the poor guy was wishing he'd never heard of Sandy Pitt or Leonard Petroni. At one point during Ernest's questioning about the background support for his valuation, the expert flipped his hands up and said, "I don't know."

That was Sandy Pitt's last witness, because early that morning Larry Spiegel had called her and said, "I can't testify today."

Pitt snapped back, "What do you mean you can't? You're under subpoena. I'll send a cop to drag your ass to court."

"If you do, you won't like what I have to say. I'm not going to lie for him."

"We had a deal."

"Not one worth losing my real estate license over."

"You won't get any commercial real estate listings from Leo."

"Like I said, call me and you get the truth."

"You cowardly sonofabitch."

Larry hung up and decided to show up at court since he was under subpoena. When Pitt saw him, she asked if he had changed his mind. When he said that he had not and that he would tell the whole truth if she called him, she told him to get the hell out of her sight. Ernest had defanged two lying witnesses—Larry Spiegel and Elva Delgado—without having to throw a punch in court.

At 5:05 p.m. Sandy Pitt rested her case. Ernest told Gentilini that he had nothing for rebuttal, so closing arguments were scheduled for nine thirty the next morning.

————————

That night at the Schreiber home the big news was Blair Barker's mental breakdown during his attempted escape to Hawaii and hospitalization in San Francisco. At the end of the bizarre tale, Claire said, "It's so weird. And, you said you're sure that Draper and Edison are having an affair. How does Barker not know that? And, an even bigger question is, why are he and Draper together in the first place?"

Paraphrasing Dr. Leonard McCoy on Star Trek, Ernest said, "Dammit, Claire, I'm a lawyer, not a psychiatrist."

————————

November 16, 1989

The hearing started with the usual morning cortège. The gliding specter robed in black had a particularly tetchy look on her face that she favored Ernest with as she landed on her elevated roost. Ernest wondered if her peevishness was because of him or an unpleasant beginning to her day at home. Regardless, the impact would be equally unpleasant—with him as the target.

All that was left of the trial for the attorneys was their closing arguments. Ernest was first with an opportunity for rebuttal after Pitt—if he saved time. They each had forty minutes, an arbitrary allotment selected by Gentilini. Once all were ordered to be seated after paying homage to the judge, Gentilini gave Ernest a penetrating stare and ordered him to begin.

Not wishing to waste a second of his precious forty minutes, Ernest rose quickly with his legal pad of notes and took up his, by now familiar, position behind the podium under the intense glare of Gentilini. He began by reminding the judge of what he had said he would prove during his opening statement and then ticked off the evidence during the trial that showed he had. Gentilini listened intently and watched his every move. Ernest actually appreciated that. Some judges he had appeared in front of failed to extend that courtesy—instead, being distracted by other cases and even obviously working on them while they were supposed to be focused on the here and now. Ernest called it JADD—judicial attention deficit disorder. When he came to a summary of the damages, Ernest concentrated on the hard, cold evidence that had been introduced, hoping that Gentilini would do the same, especially with the testimony of his expert, Andrew Edison, who wasn't quite the star Ernest had originally thought he would be. He built up Edison's credentials as a photojournalist with personal experience in creating, publishing and selling narrative photography books like the one Rita Draper was close to completing until Leonard Petroni unlawfully and arrogantly destroyed the photos she had labored so very hard in collecting. He emphasized both the monetary loss and the immense emotional toll that took on her. His hope was to divert Gentilini's attention away from the romantic emotions evidenced in court between Draper and Edison and onto the devastating emptiness of loss felt by Draper that resulted from Petroni's thoughtless, if not vindictive, act. Finally, at the end of his argument, he asked for an award of Draper's attorney's fees as provided in the contract for sale of the property.

Hardly had he finished that request, when Gentilini's eyes flickered with anger and she said, "You're not entitled to attorney's fees."

Are you kidding? The contract provides for it. Trying not to heat her anger more, Ernest meekly said, "But, we are, Your Honor. The contract provides for the award of attorney's fees if the contract is breached."

"You never indicated in your pretrial disclosure statement that you intended to ask for fees."

"But, I did, Your Honor—take a look." Ernest grabbed his pleading packet and thumbed to his indexed disclosure statement. "Here, I have it right here."

Gentilini had no interest in looking. Instead she said at a slightly higher octave, "You never indicated that you were going to ask for fees during your opening statement."

"But, I did. I'm sure the court reporter's transcript will bear me out."

"Dammit, counsel, you never offered any proof of the amount of fees during presentation of your case. How the hell am I supposed to award fees if I don't have any proof showing how much you're claiming?" Then she leaned back and sneered.

"Your Honor, fees were being incurred throughout the trial, and are right now. I can't know what the fees will be until the trial is concluded. I can't prove something that hasn't happened." As he said that, he thought, *Like Ms. Pitt seems to be able to do.* "Your Honor, the law in Colorado allows for the proof of fees at the conclusion of the trial by separate hearing." Ernest was ready for this, because he had previously intended to incorporate his legal authority into the motion he would file for fees. "Here, I have copies of cases to support me—Ball v. Weller; Roa v. Miller; Bakehouse and Associates v. Wilkins; and —"

Gentilini had no interest in Ernest's cases. She yelled, "What makes you think you're entitled to fees in this case?"

Frustrated, Ernest just blurted out without thought, "Well, if you won't accept the law or the facts, I guess all I have to rely on is my thirteen years of experience in the courtroom."

Gentilini's eyes grew even wider than they had been and her face became almost purple as she launched out of her seat and leaned over the bench pointing down at Ernest and screaming, "God dammit, Schreiber, don't be impertinent with me and don't forget who I am. You will not talk to me in that tone of voice in my courtroom. Do you hear me?"

Ernest could not believe what was happening. As Gentilini yelled and shook her finger, all he could think was, *I'm going to jail. She's going to hold me in contempt. I can feel it, and I didn't even bring my toothbrush.*

Then, satisfied that she had established her dominance over Ernest, the fire left Gentilini's eyes and face as quickly as it had come. When it was obvious that he was not going to jail, Ernest realized something—*that's the first time she called me by my name.* During the whole time of their exchange, Sandy Pitt could hardly contain her delight.

With ten minutes of his original forty left, Ernest decided to break it off. "Your Honor, I'd like to reserve my remaining time for rebuttal."

"You have eight minutes remaining," pronounced Gentilini.

Going to short change me on time too?

Sandy Pitt got up and, while she moved over to the podium, looked down her leaking nose at Ernest with triumph in her eyes. She then launched into her litany of lies. Every once in a while, she would slip in references to Leonard Petroni's prominence in politics and the law in order to give the lies a false luster of veracity. She even asked, "Why would a man of such position and power waste his time and jeopardize his impeccable reputation on such an insignificant matter as this dispute with someone like Rita Draper?"—inferring that Rita was a lesser human being. It was completely inappropriate to a closing argument, but Sandy Pitt felt empowered to go the extra mile after witnessing Ernest's dressing-down by the judge. For his part, Ernest knew that to object would only result in another verbal lashing with no positive return—The Pitt Viper's venom had already been injected. He sat and took his beating with at least the appearance of dignity. Although she was obviously enjoying her closing attack, her greatest glee came when she came to the topic of Ernest's claim for damages.

"I don't know if you noticed, but did you see the interaction between Rita Draper and Andrew Edison when he was on the stand?"

Here it comes, thought Ernest. *Brace for impact.* He refused to look at Rita or anything other than Gentilini. *Yeah, she noticed. I can tell by the look on her face.*

"Those two have a very special relationship. Throughout Mr. Edison's testimony he would look at Ms. Draper ardently, and she would bat her eyes back in amorous reply. This was in a court of law. They couldn't even hide their emotions for the brief time that he was on the stand. It was as if he were saying to her, 'I'd do anything for you—even lie while under oath. Just watch.' Mr. Edison's testimony should be ignored in its entirety, Your Honor. It has no credibility."

That was a good place to leave her argument, so Sandy Pitt did. It was probably the strongest part of her case. And, it was valid—as to the exchange of emotions between Draper and Edison, but not as to the validity of his opinion about the value of Rita's damaged photos. That opinion was honest, valid and supported by Edison's experience and extensive factual testimony. It also was tainted by the emotional factor, and there is no emotion that people love to sit in judgment of others more about than that of sex. It is a characteristic of human nature to condemn the sexual behavior of others that is exposed for its hypocrisy by the overpopulation of the Earth. By leaving off with her prurient argument, Pitt, not only besmirched Andrew Edison's expert opinion, but she provided an element of veracity to the rest of her fabrications. It was the last thing that the judge heard, so it would naturally be the most prominent in her mind.

It was Ernest's turn at the podium again. He attacked the last first. He condemned Pitt for her lurid portrayal of a fabricated love affair between Rita and Mr. Edison and then swept it aside as being irrelevant to his excellent credentials and to his detailed opinion. Then he attacked Pitt's legal argument that the contract between Rita and Petroni was unenforceable because it had no closing date. He pointed out that her argument might have had some scintilla of validity if the place in the contract for the closing date had been left blank, as Petroni originally had left it, but not after Petroni added the words, "once Seller gets legal title." While those words did not provide a firm actual date, they did provide a way of calculating a closing date. He told Gentilini that the law favors enforceable contracts and will interpret contracts in a way, if at all possible, to enforce them. In this case, the law would require the closing to occur within a reasonable time after Petroni obtained legal title. Then, Ernest moved to what he thought was the weakest of Pitt's claims—that Rita had abandoned the property. He pointed out that whether the court believed that she had left her California contact information with Petroni or not when she left in November 1987, it was undeniable that she left behind a wealth of personal property, including perhaps her most cherished treasure—her photos. He argued that no one would do that who was abandoning the property. He didn't even give an honorable mention to Petroni's counterclaims of breach of contract, slander of title and outrageous conduct or to his claim that there was spoiled, maggot-infested food. Those would all fall under the weight of the same facts and arguments that would win his case. With an internal sigh of relief, he sat down.

Gentilini ordered them all back next week at nine on Tuesday, November 21, for her ruling from the bench. Ernest had little confidence that he would prevail, even though he was pleased with the case he had presented in spite of the barriers thrown up by Blair, Rita and Andrew Edison. He told Rita he'd see her the following Tuesday and got away from her as fast as he could. He had no desire to dissect the trial with her.

When Claire asked for his report of his morning in court and heard about Gentilini's blowup, she was sympathetic and incredulous. "What brought that on?" she asked.

"I have no idea," answered Ernest. "It was very strange. I think she was trying to establish her dominance over me. I can't find any other explanation. She's totally wrong too. I've gotten attorney's fees awarded in several other cases the same way I tried to today."

"It sounds like it may have some sexual undercurrent to me," said Claire.

"She did seem to enjoy it—a lot."

"Maybe she was mentally or physically abused as a child by an overbearing father, and this is her way of getting back at men," offered Claire.

"Like I told you before, I'm a lawyer, not a psychiatrist," said Ernest.

"So, you going to take your toothbrush and a pair of clean underwear to court from now on?"

"I wasn't that scared."

November 21, 1989

Ernest and Rita Draper were seated, stomachs aflutter, awaiting judgment day when Sandy Pitt strutted in with Leo Petroni. She was high on confidence and coke. Sandy knew she had this judgment in the bag. So did Ernest. There was no doubt in his mind, especially after the browbeating he got last Thursday. Sandy gave Ernest a smug triumphant look as she sat down. He refused to give her the pleasure of her gloat by looking at Rita. Petroni stared ahead regally with his nose in the air. Ernest Schreiber wasn't worth his recognition. He was an insignificant pest soon to be squashed and forgotten. Leo was anxious to get the nonsense of this trial over and prepare for his next quest for young women.

The tension and anticipation were palpable as the entourage of two entered soon followed by Judge Gentilini. When ordered to take their seats, Ernest picked up his pen to take notes of the ruling to come. Since the winning side would be required to put into writing what was said from the bench, it was more an exercise to quell his nerves than an indication of any confidence in a positive outcome.

Gentilini immediately started reading from her notes. She started by stating, "The court finds that the parties entered into a contract for the plaintiff to buy and the defendant to sell the property at 10209 Wild Rose Circle in Wheat Ridge, Colorado on the specific terms set forth in the contract."

So far so good, and big deal. No big revelation there, thought Ernest.

"The contract had no specific closing date, and the defense argued that the lack of a specific closing date made the contract unenforceable."

Oh boy, here it comes.

Gentilini then said, "The court finds the defendant's argument to be without merit."

Wait, did she say 'without' merit? Now, don't get my hopes up just to dash them to smithereens.

"At the plaintiff's request, the defendant inserted the words 'once Seller gets legal title' in the blank in the standard form contract for the closing date. The court finds that the parties intended to close the sale from defendant to plaintiff at some time after defendant cleared title in his name. It was defendant's responsibility to obtain title, but he delayed in doing so. Under such circumstances, the law will provide a date that is reasonable after the date that defendant quieted title in his name. Title was cleared in his name on July 29, 1988. A reasonable date for closing would be within sixty days after that date. The defendant has alleged that the plaintiff had abandoned the property without providing him with her contact information in California. The court finds defendant's allegation also to be without merit. The plaintiff left valuable property in the home, including photographs of endangered animals that she was assembling into a book she was close to publishing. That is not the action of someone who is abandoning a property, but clearly establishes an intent to return. The court also finds that defendant's testimony contradicting plaintiff's that she gave him her contact information is not credible. The defendant breached the contract, wrongfully evicted plaintiff and illegally converted plaintiff's property to his own use and purpose."

As Gentilini kept reading, Ernest scribbled faster on his legal pad, being buoyed higher like a drowning man being rescued after days without hope at sea. He had no time to look over at Pitt and Petroni to see how this victory for plaintiff was being received. However, if he had, he would have seen one face in shocked disbelief and another imprinted with rage.

At the end of her ruling, Gentilini entered an order for specific performance against Petroni requiring him to transfer title to the property to Rita on the terms of the contract and to close the sale within sixty days. Of course, Rita would be obliged to pay the promissory note of $195,000 as consideration, but after Gentilini's award of damages that would be a near wash. Gentilini awarded Rita the full value for her damaged property with two notable exceptions. She even gave Rita credit against the promissory note for the HOA dues, real estate taxes and insurance premiums she had paid in response to Petroni's deceptive insertion of that language just before he made a copy of the contract. Then, Gentilini poured some salt into Petroni's wound by granting Ernest's request for prejudgment interest compounded annually from September 27, 1988, sixty days after he got his quiet title judgment. However, Gentilini refused to accept Andrew Edison's valuation of Rita's photos, and while she did not state her reason, everyone who had seen the embarrassing romantic display between Draper and Edison knew exactly why. Since Blair had fled before testifying, none of those damages were, or could be, awarded. And, then there was the issue of attorney's fees. Gentilini dug her heels in on those and refused to award them. Still, it was a tremendous victory for Ernest, and one that would be reported in future legal journals.

After Gentilini was finished, she ordered Ernest to prepare the written judgment for her signature before leaving for her chambers. Ernest looked over just in time to see Petroni storm out of the courtroom leaving Pitt to slink away on her own. His look was one of curiosity and not of gloating. It wasn't part of his nature to gloat. Gloating served no purpose as far Ernest could fathom other than to inflate a false sense of superiority—gloat one day and be a goat the next.

When they were alone in the courtroom, Ernest turned to Rita and said, "Congratulations. That's about as close as one gets to a one-hundred-percent victory."

Rita was overjoyed and effusive, "I really thought we were going to lose when I came in here this morning. You're incredible. What a fantastic job you did. Buddy Dunce was right about you. So, what happens now?"

"Let's go find an empty jury room and discuss that," replied Ernest.

Ernest knew the statistics for client appreciation of attorney performance in a situation like this. It went from gushing praise and adoration to a crashing nosedive through ingratitude, criticism, annoyance and sometimes anger directed at the attorney— generally, all of it traceable back to a reluctance to pay for services rendered. Since Rita had already failed to pay his fees as billed, the risk of complete evaporation of her gratitude was high. Ernest wanted to confront the elephant in the room quickly.

When they found an open jury room, they took seats at the conference table, and Ernest began, "As I said, Gentilini just awarded you a big win. One that I worked very hard in getting for you, and on which, I spent a sizeable sum from my own pocket for your costs. According to our fee agreement, my representation of you is finished. I agreed to represent you through the trial, and, Rita, you agreed to pay me—as we headed to and through trial. That's something you have not done. Now, that I won your case, I would like to get paid."

Rita looked shocked at Ernest's audacity at asking to be paid. Before she spoke, her look changed to one of anger, "You didn't get fees awarded by Gentilini."

"I never said I would. I never guaranteed any results. In fact, I promised to do my best on your behalf, and I have done that. You promised to pay me. You have not."

"I don't have the money."

"I think you do. Do you deny having had several well-paying photo assignments since I began my representation of you?"

She gave him a surprised look, followed by realization. "You had me investigated by your private investigator, that Dickerson, didn't you?" Then with an air of indignation and self-righteousness, she said, "How dare you have me investigated?"

Actually, Ernest had not had her investigated, by Manny or anyone. He was merely playing a hunch. "You're trying to deflect from the real topic of conversation. Are you going to pay my fees or not?"

Rita felt cornered. She was hoping to string Ernest along and get a little more work out of him, and then either stiff him, or at least negotiate his fees down substantially. "Not unless you get my fees awarded against Petroni by an appeal. That was my understanding of our deal."

"No, it wasn't. My fee agreement that you signed is quite clear about your obligations. I'm glad we're having this conversation. It gives me a clear path forward. Here's what I'm going to do. I'm going to file several documents in the next few days, besides the judgment that Gentilini just requested. One is going to be a detailed motion for those fees you want. I will lay out the facts and the law, and I think you should win on an appeal because the law is on your side. Along with that I'm going to file my own claim for fees and a lien against the judgment I just got you. It's called a charging lien, and it will require that I get paid out of your judgment before you do. You look surprised. Get used to it. And, the last document will be my withdrawal as your attorney. Rita, you need to start looking for a new attorney right away. Good luck with that, and congratulations on my win."

Ernest got up and left Rita in a fume of bewilderment and anger.

November 29, 1989

On November 28, Ernest mailed to the court and to Rita Draper all the documents he promised he would when he last talked to Rita on November16. While he was having dinner with his family on the twenty-ninth, the phone rang. Claire answered and told him that Rita Draper was on the line.

"Really? At dinnertime?"

"I'm sure she wouldn't do that to intentionally disrupt your family time," said Claire sarcastically.

"I'll take it in the other room. No sense ruining everybody's meal."

After Ernest picked up the phone in the bedroom and heard the other receiver click, he said, "Ernest Schreiber."

"I just got your bullshit documents in the mail. What do you mean by this?" yelled Rita.

"Yeah, what do you mean?" chimed in Blair who apparently was well enough to be his normal level of annoying.

"Glad you got them. Those are the documents that I told you I was going to file when we talked last, Rita. Those are my last official act on your part. The only relationship we have now is creditor and debtor. You're the debtor by the way."

"You can't withdraw," piped in Blair. "Remember when Pitt tried to withdraw and you said she couldn't. It's the same thing."

"You're wrong, Blair," said Ernest while thinking, *as usual.* "The difference is there are no pending matters remaining in this case, and my contractual obligations to Rita have been fully performed."

"There's still the appeal," countered Blair.

"First off, an appeal is a matter of discretion. There's no requirement that you file an appeal. However, I do want to point out that the motion and brief I filed requesting attorney's fees sets Rita up for filing an appeal. In fact, I've laid out the whole argument in my brief. You're welcome. Second, I have no obligation to be your attorney in an appeal, if that is your decision."

"You don't' have the balls to do the appeal," yelled Rita.

"Are you forgetting whom you're talking to? By 'balls', I take it you mean courage. I think I've pretty well established my level of courage for you throughout this case. And, if that's your idea of a good negotiating tactic to get me to represent you, you need to take some classes in negotiation skills," replied Ernest.

"You handled this whole case wrong," blustered Blair. "You never listened to my advice—treated me like I had nothing important to say. I had some great ideas and you just acted so high and mighty. You just—"

"Blair, you do realize that I won the case, don't you? You can't argue with success. The only things that I lost on were the damages that you weren't around to testify to because you decided to go without your medications on the one day taking them counted most—and the damages for the photos. That one was lost because Rita and Andrew Edison were acting like two oversexed teenagers in front of the judge."

That was met with silence. *Well, now I know how to shut you two up.* "Did either of you want to say anything, other than yelling at me for winning the case? Good, then good night, and don't ever contact me again unless it's to pay my bill."

December 4, 1989

At 9:46 a.m. Tracey buzzed Ernest's intercom. There's an Anthony James on the phone for you, Ernest. Says he represents Rita Draper."

"What's his last name?"

"Do you want it or not, funny man?"

"Yes, put him through, T."

"Hello, Mr. Schreiber. My name is Anthony James, and I represent Rita Draper."

"Yes, I got that from my secretary. I'm pleased to hear that she has new counsel."

"Yes, well, I'll be handling the appeal on her claim to attorney's fees in the Petroni action. She also has asked me to resolve your claim for attorney's fees."

"I hope that means she's going to pay them," said Ernest.

"I have advised her that settling with you is the best course of action for her."

"That's wise counsel, counsel."

James laughed, "Thanks. You probably realize that money you receive today is worth more than money you have to fight for into the future—"

"Mr. James, I apologize for interrupting, but we both know where you're going with this, and I would like to cut to the chase. I've got a busy day, and, yet, I would like to be rid of Rita Draper, but not at any price. Right now, my fees are sitting at forty-eight thousand dollars and some change. If she settles with me and pays me—that last part is absolutely nonnegotiable—by the end of next week, I'll settle for a flat figure of forty-three thousand. Otherwise, I'm prepared to enforce my lien, and I'm happy to wait until the appeal is over. I'm very confident that you can win that appeal with what I have already put in place. I've given you all the law and facts in my motion, brief and my personal affidavit. It's as close to a slam-dunk as you can get in this business. So, I'm comfortable in waiting and letting the interest pile up. Rita knows me well enough by now to know that I'm not bluffing."

Mr. James was silent for a while, decided against bluster, and prudently said, "Well, let me discuss that with my client and get back to you."

"Thank you, I appreciate the fact that you didn't try to huff-and-puff me into a lower number."

"You didn't sound like you were the kind of guy who would respond to that. I'll advise Rita to take your offer and get back to you."

"Mr. James?"

"Yes."

"You seem like a reasonable person, so let me just warn you to be careful with Ms. Draper. Don't become her next victim."

On Wednesday of the following week Ernest signed a settlement agreement with Rita Draper and was handed a cashier's check for $43,000 by Anthony James. At last, Ernest could forget about Rita Draper, Blair Barker, Sandra Pitt, Leonard Petroni and Judge Saralee Gentilini.

CHAPTER 13

Forced Retirement

After Rita settled with Ernest over his fees, she and Blair decided to leave for California again—this time until the appeal was done. There was no reason to stick around. Anthony James could handle the appeal of her attorney's fees claim without her, and since Leo Petroni was going to file a cross-appeal, closing on the transfer of title was stayed until the appeal was finished. This time, however, Rita and Blair would have someone looking after the property—an older gentleman who had knocked on their door several months before and had given them his card. He said that they should call him if they ever needed someone to look after the house. He had a background in law enforcement and private investigation and now took care of a few homes for people when they were absent in order to subsidize his pension and Social Security payments. Mostly, he enjoyed the work and wanted something to do instead of sitting on his porch yelling at the neighborhood whippersnappers. He also was a lot less expensive than other security services.

Leo fired Sandy Pitt the day after Gentilini read her ruling from the bench. He had no use for losers. His new attorney was from the large Denver law firm of Cheater, Stutter and Dodge.

Leo no longer cared about the cost. This case had started as one about his financial gain. It now was about his damaged pride. When he heard that Ernest Schreiber no longer represented Rita Draper, he was both relieved and upset that he wouldn't be able to deliver the courtroom butt-kicking Schreiber deserved. There still was Draper, and he desperately wanted to humiliate her.

In addition to being fired by Leonard Petroni, Sandra Pitt was the recipient of more fallout from the Draper-Petroni case. On December 23, she received a notice from the Grievance Committee of the Colorado Supreme Court that a complaint had been made against her for subornation of perjury. It was a complaint that Ernest had filed the day after he settled his fee claim with Rita Draper. His complaint included a copy of Larry Spiegel's deposition and Manfred Dickerson's investigative report on Spiegel. Although Ernest had told Spiegel that he would not file a complaint against him with the Colorado Real Estate Commission, he had no control over what the Grievance Committee would do. After Pitt filed her response to the accusations against her, the investigating officer for the Grievance Committee sent information regarding Spiegel's participation in the aborted perjury to the Colorado Real Estate Commission. Spiegel was quick to flip on Pitt in exchange for a reprimand by the Real Estate Commission, thus averting a more serious penalty in exchange for a slap on the wrist. It was a wrist-slap that stung enough to make Spiegel realize that he had narrowly escaped a more serious punishment and that he never wanted to get that close again. With Spiegel testifying against her, Sandra concluded it would be best for her to capitulate by showing some remorse and negotiating a lighter punishment too. By March 30, 1990, she was able to smarm her way into a six-month suspension from practicing law. The Grievance Committee reasoned that this was her first offense and they really did not have the resources or inclination to take her case all the way before the Colorado Supreme Court. They had bigger fish to fry—repeat offenders who had stolen funds from their clients. Sandy closed her law office and took a short vacation from the practice of law, intending to sit out her suspension in a blizzard of cocaine, a bottle of bourbon and a cloud of Marlboros.

Fate stepped in to disrupt Sandy's plan when Stanley Turner got reeled into custody in a big drug bust in Boulder. He was kicking himself for venturing out of familiar territory, but the score was so big in the deal he got suckered into that his weak willpower was trampled by his rampaging greed. In the past, Stanley had never needed an attorney in Boulder. Sandy Pitt had served him well, and she was close to his home turf. She also accepted payment in blow. Since Sandy was under a six-month suspension, Stanley needed a replacement. Since he was in Boulder, he decided that a Boulder attorney would have more credibility, if not influence, with Boulder judges and prosecutors. A name he had heard in his circle of underworld friends was Carl Manthey. Carl had worked as an assistant district attorney in Boulder and had the respect of the law enforcement community and judges. Carl was a wise choice. Stanley made a call to Carl from jail.

When Carl received the call from one of the defendants busted in the high-profile arrest, Carl first got details of the charges and Stanley's rap sheet from the district attorney's office and then rushed over to the Boulder County Jail to meet his new client. After hearing his new client's account of his arrest, Carl told Stanley that with his criminal record and the size of the current bust, Stanley was going away for several years—unless he could offer the DA something or someone in exchange for a lighter sentence. With little hesitation, Stanley offered several someones—many were upper middle-class professionals. One in particular stood out to Carl—Sandra Pitt.

Carl was able to negotiate bail for Stanley and a lighter sentence, provided that he cooperated with law enforcement. Part of the deal required Stanley to contact his former higher-profile clients and tell them about his situation, except the being a snitch part, and to refer them to a trusted friend of his, who could still provide them with white product. It was a welcome conversation for Sandy because she was running low on snow and didn't trust any of her other drug-dealing clients like she did Stanley. When Officer Sanchez, Stanley's trusted undercover cop, received the call from Sandy Pitt about purchasing some of his high-grade goods, he was quick to set up a meeting to exchange Sandy's money for handcuffs. The whole sale was captured on the wire Sanchez wore and on film by another officer hidden from view in a building across the street from the hotel where they met. Sandy did not go quietly. After the initial shock of being caught red-handed, she rushed to the hotel room door only to be confronted by two burly policemen when she opened it. Then she punched one in the face and kicked and screamed until they were able to subdue her. Sandy was headed to a long time behind bars and a permanent time barred from the Bar.

July 30, 1990

Clara was gone again. She hardly spent time at home with Leo anymore, and when she did, the house was large enough so that she could avoid him a lot of the time. She spent more time with her two daughters and their families than she did with her irritable husband. He had become more so after losing the Draper lawsuit. This time Clara was in Pittsburgh with her daughter, Sophia. Leo was just as happy without her as she was without him. It was 8:45 p.m., still twilight, on a pleasantly warm summer's evening. Leo was headed upstairs to get ready for bed when the front doorbell rang. *What the hell? Who could be rude enough to ring the bell at this hour?*

Leo stomped down the five steps to the upstairs he had just ascended and went to the door and opened it. The .38 caliber pistol stuck in his face looked like a cannon. It was all his mind could register at first. He was forcefully shoved inside with the free hand of the man with the gun. Then the door slammed shut.

Trying to bolster his courage with false bravado, Leo said, "Who the fuck are you? You here to rob me? Is that it?"

"I'm a friend of a friend, and I'm not here to rob you. I'm here to dispense some justice."

"I don't have any friends who'd shove a gun in my face in my own home. So, I doubt you're a friend of any of my friends."

"Clyde Smaldone—you remember him. He used to be your friend. He helped you get to where you are today—didn't he, Professor? Some gratitude you've shown him—never go to see him."

"You still didn't say who you are."

"The name's Terrence Murphy. Don't worry about the name. After tonight, you won't remember it—or anything, from what I've been told."

"Murphy? I don't know any Murphy."

"I used to be a detective with the Denver police. Later, I became a private investigator. Back when I was a detective, I used to hound Clyde, trying to catch him committing some crime, and I did a few times. The funny thing is—the things that Clyde used to do are hardly crimes anymore. Liquor is legal and gambling looks like it will be soon—and payday lenders charge just as much and more than the Smaldone boys did in their loansharking racket. Of course, there were a few murders that always benefited him, but we could never pin any on him. Clyde denies having anything to do with them to this day. But, then again, the murders that we never were able to solve were always of lowlife scum, so it was no loss to society. Clyde and I are friends now. We get together every week. I've learned a lot about you from him."

"This is about that Joe Roma, isn't it?"

"Roma? What about Joe Roma?" said Murphy, not understanding why Leo mentioned the cold case of Joe Roma's shooting so long ago. Then, a light of understanding lit his eyes. "That was you—wasn't it? You put those bullets into Roma. I'll be damned."

Leo realized he had said too much.

"What other crimes were you involved in with Checkers? How about that mystery man who was with Checkers when he blew up Leo Barnes' car in—December of 1936?" Murphy, still an astute observer of human behavior, watched for a hint of a reaction. "Right again—I can see it in your eyes. Well, we're going to take care of a lot of sins tonight, Leo." Murphy pulled out Leo's atomizer from his jacket.

"What the hell—"

"I took the liberty of borrowing this from your greenhouse special-storage cabinet. Before we get started, I want to explain a few things. It's mostly for my benefit because I want to see the look on your face. Back in the thirties you raped a young lady who worked in the police department—where I was a detective. You didn't rape her just once—you did it several times over several months. Ring any bells, yet? You called it a 'date', and you used to threaten to kill her and dismember her body with maybe the second one coming first, if she ever told anybody. She lived in absolute terror of you and your phone calls. She was a sweet, smart, young girl who had dreams of becoming a doctor—until you got a hold on her." Terrence could hardly control his anger as he told the story. "She was working in the police department in order to get enough money to go to school. I got her that job, you filthy pig. Her name was Margaret—Margaret Kilroy—her mother's married name. Her mother's maiden name was Murphy—my deceased sister. Margaret was my only niece. You ruined her life. I could never figure it out. She went from this wonderful, open, young woman with hopes for the future to a withdrawn, sullen shell of herself. She went for years without saying a word. She didn't trust men because of you." Leo looked like he was going to say something and Terrence shoved the barrel of his pistol in Leo's mouth and said, "Go ahead—try to say something. I'll blow your fuckin' brains out right now. You're going to listen to me. Margaret later, when she was in her late thirties, met a really wonderful man. It took a while, but he gained her trust and her hand in marriage. After several years of marriage and a relaxing weekend in Aspen, she opened up and told him the whole horrible story. She said she couldn't carry that around inside her any more. Her husband convinced her to tell her uncle, me, so they both did. I actually had introduced the two of them to each other. I had worked with her husband on some cases at the end of my career. He's a forensic toxicologist, and she became one too. They now have a lab in Durango—far away from Denver, and you. You may wonder why I'm telling you that. Well, we knew that if we took her story to the police, nothing would happen since you're such a powerful man. Who would believe such a story from a woman about the great Leonard Petroni? You became my hobby—then my obsession. I had a suspicion that you had raped more young women, but could never get any proof. So, I broke into your precious greenhouse to see if there might be something there that I could use against you. A couple of years ago—April of '88—I found some vials of white powder—"

"That was you. I knew I wasn't losing my mind. I knew some was miss—"

Terrence hit Leo in the stomach, and Leo bent over gasping in pain. "Told you to shut up. So, I thought it was cocaine. It looked like cocaine. It wasn't proof of other rapes, but it still was a crime. I took some samples and brought them to my niece for analysis. If it had been cocaine, I would've tipped off the police. Well, you know what we found out, don't you? It took us a while but we eventually figured out what you were doing with this scopolamine. I even followed you on a couple of your trips, but you were good at covering your tracks. But in Miami, I got lucky. You made the mistake of raping a young hooker—someone I could track down easy. I did lose you when you and the girl separated at the hotel, so I missed out in saving her from your attack. I'm really sorry about that. At first, I followed you, but, as I said, you were good, and I lost you. I thought I'd try to find out from the girl what you said to her, so I doubled back to the hotel—but by the time I got back to the hotel, she was gone. However, I got her name from the bartender and later tracked her down. She couldn't even remember meeting you. All she could remember was waking up bruised and raped with a horrible drug hangover. This stuff is quite the rape drug. A lot better than alcohol. Right, asshole? Now, Leonard Petroni, it's time for atonement in a way that the law never could."

"If you're going to kill me, get it over with."

Terrence laughed. "You're not getting off that easy."

"What are you going to do?" asked Leo. Leo was trembling with fear.

"This is all I'm going to do." Terrence hit Leo in the solar plexus again and as Leo gasped for air gave him several squirts from the atomizer. "You're going to do the rest."

July 31, 1990

Leo opened his eyes to a sharp glare. His head was pounding with a fierce headache and everything around him was spinning. He tried to make the spinning stop by shutting his eyes again, but it persisted even with them closed. After several moments, he opened them again to find out where he was. He started to move his right arm, but it caught on something. When he looked at it, he saw a tube leading out of it to a drip bag above him. Raising his head, he saw more tubes running out of the sheets around his waist. It seemed like there were monitors and tubes everywhere he could see. A nurse was looking at one of the monitors. She turned and saw that he was awake, but she neither smiled nor said anything.

He struggled to talk, and finally got out, "Whe...re...am...I?"

The nurse didn't answer. She looked at him like he was some kind of disgusting lab experiment and continued about her business.

Leo drifted off again. When he opened his eyes again, the nurse was standing over him, as if she knew he would be coming to. She used one hand to lift each of his eyelids open while shining a harsh light in them with the other. After she was satisfied with what she saw, she left the room. After minutes, hours, days, years—Leo couldn't tell—another woman came in with the nurse who had been there before.

The new woman looked at a chart at the foot of his bed, surveyed the monitors and tubes and then came over to the side of the bed next to Leo's head. "I'm Doctor Turner, Mr. Petroni."

Leo didn't even protest having a woman doctor, he just wanted to know, "Where am I?"

"You're in Lutheran Medical Center in Wheat Ridge—in intensive care. You suffered a severe trauma."

Leo looked bewildered. "Trauma? Intensive care? For what?"

"Do you remember anything from last night? Last night— July 30. It's now close to seven fifteen in the evening on July 31, Mr. Petroni. Do you remember last night?"

He could not—not one thing. Leo became frightened, shook his head and said, "No."

Dr. Turner glanced at the nurse who in response moved her hand to the drip bag. "Mr. Petroni, you came in last night to emergency care. You called for emergency care. You had a self-inflicted trauma, Mr. Petroni." Dr. Turner took in a breath before continuing. "You cut your penis and scrotum off—with a garden shears."

At first, Leo couldn't believe what he had heard. When he realized the truth, he screamed and started to tug at the tube in his arm. Dr. Turner nodded to the nurse who adjusted the drip, and Leo quickly passed out.

August 6, 1990

After Dr. Turner's announcement on July 31, Leo slipped into a deep depression that was treated with sedatives and visits by a psychiatrist—something he didn't get from his family. Today, he was being transferred out of intensive care and into a private room. When he was rolled into his new room, there were two somber-looking people in suits waiting for him—a man and a woman. They both were African American.

When Leo was settled in and the hospital staff left, the two came over to him. The woman spoke, "Mr. Petroni, I'm Special Agent Shantya Burton and this is Special Agent Steven Knowland. We're from the Federal Bureau of Investigation. We'd like to ask you some questions."

Leo would have wet his pants if he had pants or equipment with which to wet them. Instead, his urostomy bag just continued to get its usual trickle. He said nothing in reply.

Agent Burton continued by handing a document to Leo and saying, "Mr. Petroni, this is a copy of a document that we found in your greenhouse, where you damaged yourself. Is that your handwriting?"

Leo said nothing.

"Well, our lab has analyzed it along with some white powder we found, and they concluded that it is your handwriting." Agent Burton waited for a response or reaction.

Leo said nothing.

"This is quite a confession you made. It's incredible how many rapes you admit to in it—some with actual dates and names of your victims, but most without. There were so many according to your confession that you couldn't remember them all. If these prove to be true, I'd have to agree with your assessment of yourself as being 'a vile monster who deserves public censure and the worst punishment that can be imposed by the courts.' We're seeing what we can do about that, Mr. Petroni. We came by today to find out if you wanted to reaffirm your confession, or maybe add to it, but it doesn't look like you do. I guess you're having a change of heart. Oh—we're also working with the Colombian authorities on that murder you confessed to down there."

Leo said nothing.

"Come on, Steve, we'll come back when we have more information for Mr. Petroni. Here are our cards in case you want to aid our investigations. And, Mr. Petroni?"

Leo looked up at her, but said nothing.

"Don't try to go anywhere."

"Fuck you, bitch."

"Well, look at that, Steve. It does talk."

March 10, 1991

The Schreiber family was getting ready to go out to the Orchid Pavilion, their favorite Chinese restaurant, to celebrate Claire's forty-fourth birthday. Outside of San Francisco, the Orchid Pavilion was the best Chinese restaurant west of the Mississippi, and the owner, David Ko, was a personal friend.

As they were getting dressed, Ernest said, "I ran into Anthony James today at a CLE program on adverse possession."

"Is that supposed to mean something to me?" asked Claire.

"Probably not, but the fact that he was the attorney who replaced me as Rita Draper's attorney should."

"Oh sure, I remember you telling me about him. You thought he was a pretty good attorney."

"Well, I thought he was a nice guy and reasonable. Turns out he is a good attorney. So, after exchanging some comments about the spectacular downfall of Leonard Petroni—by the way, the criminal charges just keep piling up for him—anyway, he told me that I was right about two things."

"Is that all?"

Ernest laughed before continuing. "Yeah, right—one was the appeal. He won on the claim for attorney's fees on the arguments I had made to Gentilini. I'm sure that won't sit well with her."

"Maybe you'd better avoid going to Jefferson County in the future."

"I already made that promise to myself. He also said that Petroni lost on all of his appeal claims, which means he piled up a bunch of fees by some high-priced lawyers all for nothing—for all the good a win would've done him with all the jail time he's facing. He also said that there are a bunch of civil lawsuits starting to form against Petroni by some of the women who are now learning the identity of their rapist, as well as the few who already knew, but were too afraid to come forward. We figured that since Draper won the right to title to the property before these new lawsuits against Petroni, she should still be able to get title to the house in Wheat Ridge, but the process will be slowed down. However, Petroni's attorneys might not get paid. We shed some crocodile tears over that. He also had some choice things to say about the lovely and talented Sandra Pitt. No one's going to miss her—except her shady clients."

"So, what was the second thing you were right about?"

"Rita Draper—I had warned him not to become her next victim. She stiffed him too. I told him I was sorry to hear that."

"What's he going to do?"

"He's already done it—same thing I did—file a charging lien against the judgment. He'll get paid eventually. She's a piece of work."

"And, what about the odd couple—Draper and Barker?'

"Well, I guess they have each other, which is punishment enough for their bad behavior. And, I have you—and Danielle and Chris."

"At least you didn't say 'they have each other like we do.'"

They laughed and Ernest said, "Now, let's go celebrate the birth of your parents' gift to our family."

******

ABOUT THE AUTHOR

The author is a retired attorney who lives with his wife, Cheryl, in Boulder, Colorado.

Other Frohlich novels in the Schreiber Series are:

-Tender Years Presumption

-Abuse of Confidence

Made in the USA
Middletown, DE
17 April 2019